IN THE
NAME OF
HONOUR

RICHARD NORTH
PATTERSON

PAN BOOKS

First published 2010 by Henry Holt and Company, New York

First published in Great Britain 2010 by Macmillan

This edition published 2011 by Pan Books
an imprint of Pan Macmillan, a division of Macmillan Publishers Limited
Pan Macmillan, 20 New Wharf Road, London N1 9RR
Basingstoke and Oxford
Associated companies throughout the world
www.panmacmillan.com

ISBN 978-0-330-45651-7

1 3 5 7 9 8 6 4 2

A CIP catalogue record for this book is available from
the British Library.

Typeset by Ellipsis Books Limited, Glasgow
Printed in the UK by CPI Mackays, Chatham ME5 8TD

IN THE NAME OF HONOUR

RICHARD NORTH PATTERSON is the bestselling author of *The Spire*, *Eclipse*, *Exile*, *The Race* and fourteen other critically acclaimed novels. Formerly a trial lawyer, he was the SEC liaison to the Watergate special prosecutor and has served on the boards of several Washington advocacy groups. He lives in San Francisco and on Martha's Vineyard with his wife, Dr Nancy Clair.

Praise for Richard North Patterson's fiction

'An astonishing book, a hugely entertaining human drama'
Bill Clinton

'Easily the most compelling novel about US politics since *Primary Colors*'
Spectator

'A grippingly believable portrayal of the nitty-gritty of American politics'
Sunday Times

'Every now and then – but a lot more rarely than that implies – you come across a thriller so important that it absolutely demands to be read. This is one'
The Times

'Richard North Patterson has combined the legal and political
ical
graph

ALSO BY RICHARD NORTH PATTERSON

The Spire
Eclipse
The Race
Exile
Conviction
Balance of Power
Protect and Defend
Dark Lady
No Safe Place
Silent Witness
The Final Judgment
Eyes of a Child
Degree of Guilt
Private Screening
Escape the Night
The Outside Man
The Lasko Tangent

For Bill and Janet Cohen, Bob Tyrer,
and all my friends at the Cohen Group
without whom this book—and parts of many others—
would not have been possible

PART ONE

THE KILLING

JUNE 2005

1

THE PHONE CALL awakened Paul Terry from the dream of his father.

Disoriented, he sat up in bed, staring at the wall of the hotel room. In the dream, he was thirteen, the age at which the image had first come to him. His father had just died; reappearing in Paul's sleep, Frank Terry assured his son that he was fine, just living in a different place. Relieved, Paul would awaken, and then feel more abandoned and alone. Even now, at thirty-one, the dream left tears in Terry's eyes.

His cell phone rasped again. Beside him, Jenny stirred. Groping, he found the phone on a nightstand and flipped it open.

"Captain Terry," he said in a sleep-stunned voice.

"Paul. It's Colonel Dawes."

"Morning, sir." Glancing at the drawn curtains, he detected no light. "Is it morning?"

"Six A.M. Where are you?"

"D.C. I'm spending the weekend here."

"Not anymore, I'm afraid." Dawes's southern-tinged voice was soft. "I guess you haven't seen the papers. There's been a shooting on the post. A captain's dead."

Terry tried to process this. "Are they preferring charges?"

"Not yet." The colonel's voice lowered. "The shooter is Lieutenant Brian McCarran."

Terry was instantly alert. "The general's son?"

"Yes. He's in need of a lawyer, Paul. Hopefully not for long."

At once Terry understood his superior's undertone of caution and regret. "I'll be there in an hour and a half," he promised.

When he turned the phone off, Jenny was awake, blond hair falling across her forehead. "I'm sorry, Jen. There's been a shooting at Fort Bolton—one officer killed another. I have to go."

Jenny switched on the bedside lamp. The disappointment he read in her pretty, intelligent face was mingled with resistance. "Don't they have other attorneys? Why you, Paul?"

"The colonel didn't explain himself. Just sounded worried."

She shook her head. "I thought you were leaving the service. I mean, isn't a Wall Street firm about to pay you a ton of money?"

Terry paused to assess her mood. Six years after a law school romance had revealed them to be unsuited as life partners, they had become lovers of convenience, who connected only at the end of her sporadic business trips to Washington. For the odd forty-eight hours, they would always rediscover their shared sense of fun, their enjoyment of verbal combat, the luxury of sex without anxiety or inhibition. It was too bad, Terry often thought, that their differences prevented more. Now Terry grasped that their scattered weekends meant more to Jenny Haskell than she let on.

"They are," he told her. "But for another month I can't debate an order." He gave her a lingering kiss, then added gently, "However much I'd like to."

He sensed her regret becoming withdrawal. "I think I'll stay here for a while," she said in a subdued tone. "Order room service, read the paper. Maybe I'll call friends in Bethesda."

Terry felt his own regret, both at leaving and, as with other women, that leaving did not matter more. He kissed her again, this time on the forehead, then reluctantly headed for the shower.

SHORTLY BEFORE SEVEN-THIRTY, dressed in the uniform of a JAG Corps captain, Paul Terry passed through the main gate at Fort Bolton, headquarters of the Seventh Infantry and, for one more month, Terry's home.

Over twenty miles square, Fort Bolton was sequestered amid a wooded area of northern Virginia, an enclave sufficient to itself: shopping centers, athletic facilities, offices, a hospital, apartments, town houses, and, for senior officers, commodious colonial-style houses dating back to the fort's establishment eighty years before. Turning down its principal thoroughfare, McCarran Drive, Terry was reminded of the three generations that preceded Brian McCarran. That Brian had killed a fellow officer, whatever the circumstances, would reverberate all the way to the Pentagon, where the family's most revered member, Anthony McCarran, served as the chief of staff of the army. Parking at the headquarters of the regional defense counsel, Terry felt edgy.

The aftershock of the dream still muddied his thoughts. But by this time, at least, he resembled the officer Lieutenant Colonel Dawes expected to brief. He had taken a large black coffee for the road, and the mild hangover he had earned through a bibulous dinner with Jen was fading. Fortunately for Terry, his life circumstances had lent him an air of near-perpetual alertness, accenting the swift intelligence reflected in his penetrant blue eyes. Jen sometimes teased him that he looked like an officer whether he meant to or not: tall and fit, he had jet black hair and strong but regular features accented by a ridged nose, which, broken during a high school basketball career based largely on determination, added a hint of ruggedness. That Terry had never fired a shot in anger did not detract from the success he'd had in the courtroom.

Taking a last swallow of lukewarm coffee, Terry went to meet Harry Dawes.

COLONEL DAWES SAT BEHIND a desk so orderly that, Terry often thought, even the piles of papers appeared to be standing in formation. For Terry, this thought was a fond one: a soft-spoken Virginian, the colonel treated Terry with an avuncular regard enhanced by the military courtesy that governed their relationship. As Terry entered, a brief smile crossed Dawes's ruddy face. "Sit down, Paul. Sorry to get you out of whatever bed you happened to be in."

The remark was delivered with quiet humor; a committed Christian and devoted husband of twenty-five years, Dawes never concealed his belief that Terry's rotating cast of female friends suggested an attenuated adolescence that could only be cured by marriage. "A warm one," Terry responded. "But even in my sleep, I grasped that this case is special."

Without asking if Terry wanted coffee, Dawes poured him a cup and handed a Washington Redskins mug across the desk. "It is that," Dawes concurred soberly. "In the last twenty-four hours, the media's been all over this. You must have been living in a cave."

"When I take time off, sir, I commit myself. Please catch me up."

Pensive, Dawes ran a hand through his dwindling gray-brown hair. "To say the least, the relationships surrounding this shooting are complicated. For one thing, the victim,

Captain Joe D'Abruzzo, was married to General McCarran's goddaughter, Kate Gallagher—"

"Hang on, sir," Terry interjected. "The general's *son* killed his goddaughter's *husband*?"

"Yes," Dawes answered unhappily. "It seems that her father was General McCarran's classmate at the Point. After he died in Vietnam, the families remained close. So Kate's relationship with Brian McCarran predated her marriage to D'Abruzzo by many years. To top it off, D'Abruzzo was Brian's company commander in Iraq. Whatever *their* relationship, this tragedy leaves two kids—an eight-year-old boy and six-year-old girl—without a father."

Terry found himself squinting; the summer sunlight, brightening, hit his face through Dawes's window. For a painful moment he imagined the children's shock at learning their father was dead. "Tell me about the shooting, sir."

Even in difficult circumstances, Dawes was the most considerate of men; noting Terry's squint, he stood to lower the blinds. "It happened in McCarran's apartment," he began, "between seven and eight on Friday evening. Sometime before eight, Lieutenant McCarran called the MPs and calmly advised them that he'd shot Captain D'Abruzzo. The MPs and paramedics found D'Abruzzo on the floor of the lieutenant's apartment. There were four wounds, including one in the dead man's back. Despite this, when two men from the Criminal Investigation Division questioned him, McCarran claimed self-defense."

Terry put down his mug. "He gave a statement to CID?"

"A fairly comprehensive one, I'm told. It also seems that McCarran's the only witness."

"What do you know about the gun?"

"It was a semiautomatic—a nine-millimeter Luger. What's odd is that it's D'Abruzzo's gun."

"So he brought it to McCarran's apartment?"

Dawes grimaced. "Apparently not. According to both Brian McCarran and D'Abruzzo's wife, Brian took it from D'Abruzzo's home after he threatened her with it. Brian's story is that D'Abruzzo came looking for the gun. The shooting followed."

Terry took a sip of coffee. "Do we know anything more about the relationship between Lieutenant McCarran and the widow D'Abruzzo?"

"Just that they still had one. At the least, it's clear that their families have been intertwined over many years."

As Terry took out a pen, Dawes handed him a legal pad across the desk. "What else do we know about Brian McCarran?" Terry asked.

"Only good things. He was third in his class at West Point, a leader among his classmates, and a first-class soccer player. He graduated in 2003 and turned down a Rhodes scholarship in favor of serving in Iraq. By early 2004, Brian was a platoon leader in Sadr City, one of the most dangerous assignments in the war. He's got a scar on his neck—three months after his arrival an RPG came within inches of removing his head. But he served out his year there without missing any time. By all accounts, he was an outstanding combat officer." Dawes's tone was respectful. "He certainly isn't cruising on his father's reputation. Even in a family of decorated soldiers, Brian has more than held his own."

Terry nodded. "What's he doing now?"

"He's the executive officer of Charlie Company, his outfit in Iraq. Once again, his fitness reports are excellent."

"And D'Abruzzo?"

"Not as stellar, clearly. He didn't go to the Point, and his early record lacks McCarran's glitter. But he comes across as capable—he's been serving as a battalion operations officer, in line for promotion to major. There's nothing on the surface that suggests any real problems."

"Including domestic violence? That's starting to show up among Iraq War vets, and it certainly fits with the story about the gun."

"All I can tell you," Dawes responded cautiously, "is that there were no reported incidents. At least before he died."

Terry scribbled a note: "Check out DV." Looking up, he said, "What's happened since McCarran reported the shooting?"

Dawes gazed at the desk, organizing his thoughts. "The MPs taped the call, of course. The paramedics were there in minutes, at which point D'Abruzzo was pronounced dead. The CID man secured the apartment, called in the crime lab team, and requested that the county medical examiner come out. Then CID started questioning McCarran."

"What do we know about that?"

"Other than what I've told you, very little. Nor do we know anything more about what Kate D'Abruzzo told them."

"So where does this stand?"

Dawes's forehead creased with worry, no doubt reflecting the level of scrutiny each step in the case would receive. "As you can imagine, it's being handled by the book. On the recommendation of the staff judge advocate, General Heston has ordered a formal inquiry, to be carried out by CID and the office of the chief trial counsel, Colonel Hecht. In turn, Hecht has designated Major Mike Flynn to monitor the investigation and, if necessary, prosecute the case as trial counsel."

"No surprise," Terry remarked. "By reputation, Flynn's the best. Where are they keeping McCarran?"

"Not in the brig. On the recommendation of General Heston's chief of staff, Brian is living at the bachelor officers' quarters. On Monday he'll continue his normal duties." Dawes grimaced. "Outsiders may feel he's getting special treatment. But this is an officer with an unblemished record who claims self-defense. Your job will be to help him."

"I gather that, sir. But this assignment raises a number of questions."

Dawes's eyebrows shot up, a sign of irritation that betrayed the pressure he felt. "Such as?"

Unfazed, Terry responded, "Why me? For openers, the McCarrans can have anyone they want, including the top defense lawyers in America—"

"Few of whom understand the military, and none as well as we do. The McCarran family knows that. And if this one comes to a court-martial, the court would have no doubt about the integrity of military defense counsel. That is *not* an assumption granted to civilian lawyers."

Fair or not, Terry knew that this was true. With the smallest of smiles, he responded, "It's true that our integrity is unique, sir. But not unique to me."

Dawes was unamused. "There are other considerations—beginning with my own. Lieutenant McCarran has requested a lawyer. As regional defense counsel, it falls to me to detail one. Given that he's from a notable military tradition, and that his father is odds-on to be the next chairman of the Joint Chiefs, everything we do must be beyond reproach."

The same skeptical smile played on Terry's lips. "At least for the next month. As you'll recall, sir, there's a law firm in New York expecting me to show up."

Caught, Dawes allowed himself a rueful smile. "To my

regret. But Anthony McCarran seems to prefer you, nonetheless."

Terry laughed in astonishment. "Me? I've never met the man. How does he even know I exist?"

Dawes steepled his fingers. "The general has been very decorous—as chief of staff, he has to be. But there was nothing to keep him from visiting his neighbor in the Pentagon, the judge advocate general. General McCarran made it clear that he didn't wish to exercise undue influence. He merely expressed the hope that his son would have the help of an able lawyer. Meaning, General Jasper assumed, the best defense counsel at Fort Bolton."

"In all modesty, sir—"

"Naturally," Dawes continued, "General Jasper responded that *all* our lawyers are highly qualified. It was then that General McCarran said that he had heard that a certain Captain Terry was particularly able.

"The judge advocate general did not inquire as to where he had gotten this information. He merely assured the general that his son would be well represented, and then made his own inquiry of me." Dawes's voice became softer. "What I told him, Paul, is that you were the best young lawyer I've ever seen. And that if Brian McCarran were my own son, I'd want you to defend him."

Though touched, Terry smiled yet again. "You're a devious man, sir."

"There's no wind so ill," his mentor answered blandly, "that it can't serve someone's purpose. In this case, mine. I assured General Jasper that, as a short-timer, you wouldn't mind breaking a little china if it served young McCarran's interests. And if it came to a trial, God forbid, I hoped you might be willing to extend your tour in the army. I generously promised not to stand in your way."

As Terry framed a droll reply, the seriousness in Dawes's

face stopped him. "You know I'd like you to stay, Paul. But if this goes to trial, it could be the high-profile case of a lifetime, with all the human challenges and opportunities that involves. No matter what awaits you in your Wall Street firm, you'll likely be a better lawyer, maybe even a better man. That's part of what I'm trying to do."

Absorbing this, Terry nodded. "Thank you, sir. Unfortunately, the firm has already assigned me an investment banker to defend, with more to follow. Whatever Brian McCarran's problems, I don't think the firm will wait. But I'll go to see him, of course."

Briefly, Dawes frowned. "There's someone else you should meet first. Brian McCarran's sister."

Terry gave Dawes a puzzled look. "No doubt she's concerned," he answered. "But I should meet my client first."

"Meg McCarran's more than a concerned sister. She's a lawyer, and she came here from California to help her brother. She's also quite insistent on 'helping' you."

Terry felt himself bristle: he did not want to deal with an anxious relative standing between him and his client—or serving as a conduit to her father, the general. "Is there anything I can do about this?"

"Meet her and see." Smiling faintly, Dawes glanced at his watch. "It's eight-forty. I told her to be in our reception area at nine o'clock. If she's as businesslike as she sounds, she's already here."

As Dawes had predicted, Meg McCarran was waiting outside his office.

She stood, briskly shaking hands with Terry as the colonel introduced them. Her looks surprised him. Encountering her at random, Terry might have seen an Irish beauty, a fantasy from his Catholic youth: glossy auburn hair, large blue eyes, softly glowing skin, a button nose, and a wide, generous mouth, which, parting for a perfunctory smile, exposed perfect white teeth. But her suit was the pin-striped carapace of the courtroom, and the skin beneath her eyes was bruised with sleeplessness. The effect was somewhere between trial lawyer and the vigilant older sister of a juvenile facing trouble, and her swift appraisal of Terry combined a palpable wariness with an air of command worthy of her father.

Standing to one side, Dawes offered them the use of an empty office. "Mind talking outside?" Terry asked her. "I could use some fresh air, and there's a park across the street where we can sit."

Meg gave a fractional shrug. Opening the door, Dawes reminded Terry of an anxious parent watching two recalcitrant teens embark on a blind date. Instinctively, Terry wished that the occasion were as trivial as a high school dance, and would be over with as quickly.

THEY SETTLED ON A bench beneath a cluster of oak trees, set back some distance from McCarran Drive. Terry reminded himself that less than two days ago, this woman's brother had called her to report killing a man she must have known well. "I understand how worried you must be," he ventured.

"Clear-eyed," she amended. "I know the army. Because of our father, they'll bend over backward not to show Brian any favoritism. So whoever we engage to help him, I need to be here."

Briefly, Terry weighed his response. "No matter whose son Brian is, there's an orderly process. CID will investigate; Major Flynn will make recommendations; ultimately General Heston will determine whether to refer charges for trial. What Brian needs right now is an advocate."

Meg faced him. "What Brian needs," she said with quiet

urgency, "is for the army to comprehend what it's done to him. I'm absolutely certain that Brian acted in self-defense. But the man who shot Joe D'Abruzzo is different from the man they sent to Iraq." Her voice slowed, admitting a first note of entreaty. "Sadly, Captain Terry, Brian's not very trusting anymore. He's not likely to trust you or any lawyer but me. That's another reason I'm here. Of all the people in Brian's life, I'm the one who knows him best."

Terry contemplated the grass at their feet, dappled with light and shade. "How long do you plan to stay?"

"Until Brian's out of trouble. Whether that's days or weeks or months."

"What about your job?"

"I'm a domestic violence prosecutor in the San Francisco DA's office." She bit her lip. "I love my work, Captain Terry. But the DA can't have a prosecutor from his office acting as a defense counsel. If Brian's charged with Joe's death, I'll have to resign."

Even under the circumstances, the depth of her resolve struck him. "We're not there yet," he reminded her. "Even if we were, I'm not sure Brian will need that kind of sacrifice."

Meg shook her head. "He's my brother. I won't let anything happen to him."

Something in her fierce insistence suggested the conscientious child she might have been, charged with protecting a younger brother. "Are there just the two of you?" he asked.

"And my father," she said. "My mother's dead."

The flatness of her tone deflected further questions, let alone any rote expression of sympathy. After ten minutes of acquaintance, it was hard for Terry to imagine Meg McCarran seeking sympathy from anyone. She had a quality of independence as striking as her beauty, suggesting both intelligence and a considerable force of will. But Terry also intuited a trait he understood all too well— the instinct for self-protection. Facing him on the bench, Meg said in a neutral manner, "I know my father made inquiries. But I don't know anything about you, or much about the JAG Corps."

"It's pretty straightforward. Every major installation has JAG offices, including a legal adviser to the commanding officer, judges, prosecutors, and defense lawyers. The Trial Defense Service, my unit, has its own chain of command. The purpose is to ensure that our superiors don't punish us for winning—"

"That's reassuring," Meg interjected tartly. "How, specifically, was Brian assigned to you?"

Terry was determined to maintain his equilibrium. "In any case occurring at Bolton, Colonel Dawes details a defense counsel. As you suggested, your father also made inquiries. I'm the result."

Meg regarded him closely. "No offense, Captain Terry, but you're obviously young. Don't you think Brian might do better with an experienced civilian lawyer?"

Briefly, Terry had the thought that if he were to be relieved of this case, and this woman, his departure from the army would be far simpler. "It's not my call," he answered. "I can tell you the pros and cons. A JAG lawyer knows the military justice system and the psychology of the potential jurors. Most people don't trust defense lawyers; military people trust them less. If you asked the average army officer, odds are he'd say that many civilian lawyers are ethically challenged or just in it for the money.

"A defense lawyer in uniform avoids that bias. On the other hand, a civilian lawyer is less inclined to be deferential, and the talent pool is larger." Terry paused. "Military or civilian, what a court-martial comes down to is how good the lawyer is. Hopefully, you won't need one. Right now the idea is to persuade the army not to prosecute."

A light breeze stirred Meg's hair. She pushed her bangs back from her forehead, her intense blue-eyed gaze still focused on Terry. "Why did you choose the JAG Corps?" she asked.

Terry decided to be direct. "First, my family had no money, so a ROTC scholarship to college helped get me where I am. Second, I don't like taking orders.

"That may sound strange coming from a JAG officer. But a number of my law school friends wound up as gofers in big corporate firms, shuffling papers miles from the courtroom. To have the career I wanted, I needed to try cases—hard ones, and a lot of them."

"Have you?"

"Over a hundred twenty in the last six years, the first ninety as a prosecutor. I didn't always get the sentence I wanted, but I never lost a case."

"'Never'?" Meg repeated skeptically.

In the face of Meg's challenge, Terry stopped resisting the sin of pride. "Means never. When the Trial Defense Service got sick of losing to me, they asked me to switch sides."

A first sardonic smile appeared at the corner of her mouth. "At which point you started losing, too."

"Rarely."

This stopped her for a moment. "What about homicides?"

"I've defended five. Three acquittals; one conviction on a reduced charge; another on second-degree murder. In that case, the victim was a six-year-old boy, my client's prints were on the knife, and he confessed to CID *and* the victim's mother. Clarence Darrow couldn't have saved him." Terry's speech became matter-of-fact. "I'm getting out next month, so I hope to wrap this up by then. But I chose defense work on principle—too many prosecutors lack a sense of justice. Temperamentally and professionally, I'm more than capable of helping your brother."

She gave him a considering look. "Why do you think you've been so successful?"

"Simple. I hate losing." Terry paused, then decided to finish. "Since the age of thirteen, no one has given me anything. I got here by sheer hard work, the only asset I had. Lose a case, and I'm haunted by what I might have done better.

"There may be smarter lawyers. But no one hates losing more than I do, or works harder for their clients. I've defended thirty cases; I've lost four. I still can't shake them."

Meg sat back, her eyes meeting his in silence. "I think I understand," she said at length. "At least for now, I'd like you to represent my brother."

For some reasons he could identify, and others that eluded him, Terry felt both satisfaction and a deep ambivalence. "Then let's go see him," he answered simply.

2

BRIAN MCCARRAN, his sister explained, had disliked enclosed spaces since returning from Iraq. Now the quarters into which the army had moved him, both alien and confining, evoked the cramped living room in which he had killed Captain Joe D'Abruzzo. They would meet on Brian's sailboat in the Fort Bolton marina.

It was a little before ten o'clock, and the morning sun caused the aqua surface of the Potomac River to glisten. Weekend skippers in sail- or powerboats slid across the water, and a young water-skier left a spume of white. Meg led Terry along a catwalk to a trim sixteen-footer where a lone man in a polo shirt and khakis sat in the stern, preternaturally still, watching the river with the keen gaze of a sentinel.

Terry's first sight of his client surprised him. General Anthony McCarran was famously tall and lean and sharp of eye and feature, an eagle in uniform. Facing his sister and Terry, Brian McCarran was as striking as his father without in any way resembling him. He was surprisingly blond, with long eyelashes, light blue-gray eyes, and features that, though chiseled, had a refinement about them, almost a delicacy, causing Terry to wonder about how his mother might have looked. Shorter than his father, he had a fine-drawn fitness; if martial analogies applied, Brian McCarran was a rapier. Terry had heard him called a golden boy, but his appearance lent the term new meaning; hair glinting in the sun, Brian had the look of a warrior-poet, his perfection marred only by the puckered red welt at his throat. As Meg introduced them, the gaze he fixed on Terry was oddly impersonal, as though he were gauging the level of threat.

"Good morning, sir," Brian said in a cool, clear voice. "If you can call it that. Can I get you some coffee?"

"Sure. Thanks."

Terry and Meg sat next to Brian on a padded seat. Reaching for a thermos, Brian poured coffee into a mug. For an instant Terry thought he saw a tremor in Brian's hand; then Brian seemed to stare at it, willing his hand to be still, before he finished pouring with exactness. Terry noticed that the boat was spotless.

Handing him the mug, Brian again regarded Terry, his expression neutral save for his eyes, as sharp yet guarded as his sister's. Quiet, Meg watched them closely.

"So," Brian said, "Meg says you're my lawyer."

"Only for the next month," Terry answered. "But you're right to seek legal representation. If you want that from me, anything you say here will be privileged." Glancing at Meg, Terry added, "Assuming that your sister is also acting as your lawyer. Is she?"

Brian tilted his head toward Meg, a first hint of amusement in his gaze. "What about it, sis? Are you?"

Rather than smiling, Meg looked briefly sad. "Yes. I am."

Brian nodded, facing Terry again. "Meg's always represented me, Captain Terry. Years before she went to law school."

The dry remark made Terry wonder when their mother had died; with their father consumed by his duties, the two of them might have formed a family unto themselves. Whatever Terry was sensing, he felt like an outsider.

"One preliminary question," Terry said to Brian. "Under the Uniform Code of Military Justice, if CID suspects you of a crime, they have to tell you that. Did they?"

"Yes, sir. The sergeant said that it was routine."

Terry did not comment. "Then let's start with the basics. Where's your apartment?"

Brian gave him the location and address. At once Terry recognized the building: its standard unit—a living room, bedroom, and eat-in kitchen—was identical to Terry's own. And, as with Terry's, its second-floor location would offer its occupant little chance to escape from an intruder. "Where did you keep the gun?" Terry asked.

Brian hesitated. "Nowhere in particular. The gun was Joe's."

Meg leaned forward. "You have to understand the relationships," she told Terry. "As Colonel Dawes may have mentioned, Joe was married to Kate Gallagher, the daughter of our father's closest friend at the academy—Dad was best man when Jack married Kate's mother, Rose. But Jack was killed in Vietnam before Kate was even born. Dad helped Rose cope. So our families were always together." She glanced at Brian. "Our mother died when I was twelve, and Brian nine. Dad and Rose tried to keep things stable. When Dad was overseas, or somewhere he couldn't take us, Brian and I lived with the Gallaghers."

"So they became your family?"

Meg seemed to hesitate. "As best she could, Rose replaced our mother. Kate is six years older than me, and nine years older than Brian. So she helped look after Brian, too." She turned to Brian again, as though explaining their own past. "She and Brian have always had a special bond. And when Joe and Kate were married, all of us were there. At the wedding, my father gave the bride away—"

Interrupting, Terry asked Brian, "What was your relationship to Joe?"

Brian's gaze became opaque. Softly, he answered, "The shooting was about Kate."

As Terry registered the evasion, Meg placed a hand on Brian's arm. "Tell him how you got Joe's gun."

Prompted, Brian briefly closed his eyes. Gazing past Terry at the water, he began in a toneless voice, as though reciting a scene by rote. But the detail and precision with which he spoke summoned, for Terry, a vivid picture that Brian portrayed as truth.

WHEN KATE CALLED HIM, it was evening, and Brian was alone. "It's Kate," she said in a tight voice. "I need help."

Brian tensed. "What's wrong?"

"Just come—before Joe gets back. I'm afraid of him."

In the twilight, Brian drove the ten minutes in his convertible, a tension in his gut. Kate opened the door of the town house before he could knock.

Dark and pretty and refined, Kate was the youthful replica of her mother, Rose, and the young boy Brian's first image of feminine beauty. Kate was usually the picture of self-possession; tonight, her face seemed frozen, her eyes stunned.

Pushing past her, Brian looked swiftly from side to side. "Where is he?"

"At the Officers' Club," Kate said quickly. "He's already been drinking."

Crossing the living room, Brian searched the hallway. "And the kids?"

"With my mom." Her tone became wan. "Joe and I were supposed to go out for dinner."

He joined her in the living room, his tone softer but still urgent. "What happened?"

She sat on the couch, awkwardly and abruptly, as though the adrenaline that propelled her had evanesced. "Joe hits me," she said. "Ever since he came back from Iraq."

Brian felt a jolt of anger and surprise. "He hit you tonight?"

"No." Her voice became brittle. "He threatened me with a gun. I can't go on like this."

Brian sat down beside her, covering Kate's hand with his. "You should go to his battalion commander. He'll put a stop to this."

Kate slowly shook her head, a gesture of despair. "That would end Joe's career and destroy our marriage. The kids—"

"What if he kills you? Where would the kids be then?" Brian made himself speak slowly and firmly. "Get help, Kate. Or I'll get it for you."

Tears misted her eyes. "Please, Brian—"

He put his arms around her, Kate's hair brushing his face. "If Joe won't stop," he said softly, "we don't have a choice."

She leaned her face against his shoulder, saying in a muffled voice, "I can't yet."

"Then I'll talk to him myself." He paused, then asked in the same insistent tone, "Where's the gun?"

He felt her swallow. With seeming effort, Kate stood, then walked toward their bedroom like an automaton.

Following, Brian saw Kate's nightgown thrown over a chair, the black dress she'd meant to wear lying on the bed. She opened the drawer of the nightstand, drawing back from what she saw.

Taking her place, Brian withdrew the gun. Black and freshly oiled, it was a nine-millimeter Luger semiautomatic, perfectly balanced in his hand. He checked the safety, then snapped it open to scrutinize the magazine. "This is loaded, Kate."

Pale, she sat on the edge of the bed. "Does he have more bullets?" Brian asked.

"In the closet, I think."

Brian found the box of cartridges on the top shelf, next to the cap of Joe's dress uniform. He stuffed the box in his pocket and the gun in his waistband. "What are you doing?" Kate asked.

"Taking it away. If Joe wants his gun back, he'll have to talk to me." Brian felt his anger stir again. "Don't worry, Kate. I won't forget to call him 'sir.' "

Kate gave her head a vehement shake. "Please, Brian— you have no idea how he'll react. If he loses control, he could kill you. Even without a gun."

"Because he's the Karate Kid? So he's told me."

Gripping his wrists, Kate looked up at him, fright filling her eyes again. Brian kissed her forehead. "Get help," he repeated softly. "Before this spins out of control."

He left with Joe D'Abruzzo's gun.

MEG, TERRY NOTED, HAD listened with taut alertness, as if hearing Brian's account for the first time. "Between that night and the shooting," he asked Brian, "how many days passed?"

"Three."

"Did you talk with D'Abruzzo?"

"No."

"Did you know he was coming to your apartment?"

Once again, Brian glanced at Meg. "Kate called to warn me."

"Tell me about that."

With the same detachment, Brian recited his version of events.

WHEN HIS LANDLINE RANG, Brian was emerging from the shower. The ringing stopped before he could pick up his bedroom telephone. He dried himself, dressed, then listened to the message.

"He's coming over." Kate's recorded voice was high-pitched with anxiety. "If you're there, don't let him in."

Brian's cell phone was on the nightstand, the D'Abruzzos' number on speed dial. Within seconds Kate answered. "He knows about the gun," she blurted out at once. "He was hitting me, and I had to tell him—"

Jittery, Brian interjected, "It's okay, Kate—"

"He's drunk and crazy. Please get out of there."

"This has to end." Brian drew a breath, calming himself. "I need to tell him that."

Kate's voice rose. "You can't reason with him, Brian. He wants his gun back."

"He can't have it," Brian answered, then heard the shrill bleat from the building's outside door, the signal to admit a caller. Steadying his voice, he said, "He's here, Kate. I can handle it."

Hanging up, Brian removed the handgun from his dresser drawer, then walked to the living room. The buzzer sounded again. Quickly, he concealed the gun beneath the pillow on his overstuffed chair. After a moment's hesitation, he buzzed Joe in.

It would take less than half a minute, Brian calculated, for Joe to climb the stairs to the second floor. Opening his door, he backed into the room, standing beside the chair.

Thudding footsteps echoed in the stairwell. In Brian's hallway, they slowed, and then Joe D'Abruzzo filled the door frame.

Dressed in a sweatshirt and jeans, Joe looked like a day

laborer emerging from a bar. His face was flushed, his forehead shiny with sweat, his eyes—the mirror of Joe's vitality—darting and unfocused. The living room felt claustrophobic. At once Brian was viscerally aware that Kate's husband was four inches taller, heavier by thirty pounds, and trained to kill or disable an opponent. *This is like Iraq*, Brian told himself. *Think and feel nothing.*

Joe entered the room, hand outstretched, eyes focusing on Brian. In the tone of a commanding officer, though thickened by drink, Joe said, "You have my gun, Lieutenant."

To Brian's ear, his own reply sounded faint. "You threatened Kate with it."

Joe moved the curled fingers of his outstretched hand, signaling that Brian should fill it with the Luger. "She's none of your business."

Brian shook his head. "This is about family. In all but name, Kate's a McCarran."

Joe gave him a sudden sarcastic smile. "And I'm an outsider—I've always known that. But I'm her husband."

"You don't have the right to beat her." Brian inhaled, fighting to slow the racing of his pulse. "I can ruin your career—"

"You little shit." Joe's broad face was a mask of anger, his dark eyes wild with unreason. "If I want to, I can shatter your windpipe. Or gouge your fucking eyes out."

He took another step forward, closing the distance to perhaps three feet. Stepping back, Brian hit the chair, briefly stumbling before he righted himself. D'Abruzzo emitted a bark of laughter. Brian felt the room closing around them, his enemy's distorted face filling his line of vision. Without thinking he reached for the gun.

It was aimed at Joe before Brian knew it. Joe flinched, eyes widening with surprise as he took one step back. "Get help," Brian said quickly. "Or I'll protect her any way I can."

D'Abruzzo tensed. In a tone of forced bravado, he said, "Going to shoot me, McCarran?"

"Get out—"

In a split second, Joe spun sideways, hands raised to attack. Brian's finger twitched, the gun jumping in his hand. Joe's outcry of surprise and pain mingled with the popping sound Brian knew too well.

HE STOPPED ABRUPTLY, STARING past Terry as though at something on the river. "What happened next?" Terry asked.

At first he thought Brian had not heard. Seconds passed, and then Brian answered in a voice so distant it struck Terry as dissociated. "I don't know, sir."

The military formality made the words sound even stranger. Terry saw Meg's lips part, but she made no sound. "Did you fire more than once?" Terry prodded.

"Yes."

"How do you know that?"

Still Brian did not face him. "I could tell from the body."

Terry thought swiftly. "Where was it?"

"By the wall."

"Which wall?"

"Near the door."

Meg leaned forward to intervene. "He was in shock," she told Terry.

"You weren't there," Terry reminded her softly. As Meg's eyes widened at the tacit rebuke, he asked Brian in the same quiet voice, "How many feet was his body from your chair?"

The CID, Terry knew, would have measured this. Vaguely, Brian said, "Ten feet, maybe twelve."

"How did he get there?"

When Meg tried to speak again, Terry held up his hand, his gaze fixed on Brian's profile. Brian closed his eyes. His tone was less resentful than perplexed. "I can't bring it back. The whole time before seeing his body—it's just gone . . ."

His voice trailed off. With the same dispassion, Terry asked, "What position was the body in?"

Brian's gaze seemed more focused on a powerboat scudding across the water, the rhythmic thud of its motor punctuating the silence. At length Brian said, "He was lying on his side."

"Facing you or the wall?"

Meg, Terry saw, had clasped her hands, her interlaced fingers tightening. "The wall," Brian answered.

"Was he dead?"

Brian swallowed, rippling the puckered welt on his neck. "He didn't move."

"After you saw him on the floor, what did you do next?"

Brian did not answer. "Look at me," Terry ordered quietly.

Silently, Brian turned to face him. "Did you call the MPs?" Terry asked.

Brian blinked. "He called *me*," Meg admitted in a low, flat voice.

Surprised, Terry remained focused on Brian. "Is that right?"

Slowly, Brian nodded. "What did you tell her?" Terry asked.

More silence. At length, Brian said, "That I'd shot Joe D'Abruzzo."

"That's all?"

"Yes."

"How did Meg respond?"

Now Brian sounded weary. "She said to call the MPs."

"How long did you talk to her?"

Brian shrugged, a gesture of helplessness. "I don't know. I wasn't keeping time."

Abruptly, Terry turned to Meg. "Where were you?"

Meg met his gaze. "My office. It was before five o'clock in San Francisco."

"There'll be a record of the call," Terry said. "How long was it?"

"Maybe five, six minutes."

"Of silence?"

"Brian was disoriented," Meg answered for him. "It took time for me to get a fix on this. I also told him not to talk to CID, and to ask for a lawyer right away." Her fingertips resting on Brian's shoulder, she added with resignation, "Obviously, he didn't hear me. When you're in shock, conditioning takes over. Brian is conditioned to tell the truth."

For Brian's sake, Terry nodded his understanding. "How long, Brian, until you called the MPs?"

"I don't know that either."

"When they arrived, did someone pronounce D'Abruzzo dead?"

"I don't remember—one guy took me to the bedroom, and we waited for the CID." Brian's puzzled voice suggested the strangeness of the memory. "I told them everything I could remember, just like I told you. But a piece was missing."

"What else did they ask you?"

"Random stuff. Who my friends were. What hours I work. What I'd done that day. If I was dating anyone—"

"Are you?"

"No."

"Did they ask if you were dating Kate D'Abruzzo?"

Brian seemed to stiffen. "Yes."

"What did you say?"

"That it was a bullshit question." Brian shifted his weight, his thumb and forefinger rubbing together. "I love Kate like a sister. Her kids call me Uncle Brian."

"Before Kate asked for help," Terry asked, "how was your relationship with D'Abruzzo?"

Brian sat straighter. "He was Kate's husband. Sometimes he talked about himself too much. But he was the guy she chose." Pausing, he seemed to search for an easy summary. "When all of us were together, we got along fine. Mostly I felt neutral."

"Including when you both served in Iraq?"

Brian shrugged again. "Joe gave orders. I followed them."

Terry wondered whether he heard, or imagined, a note of buried contempt. "Was he a good company commander?"

Suddenly Brian seemed to withdraw; he was as still as, the moment before, he had started to seem restless. Leaning forward, Terry asked, "Did something come to you, Lieutenant?"

Brian's eyelids flickered. "Iraq's got nothing to do with this. Joe beat Kate; I took his gun; he came for it; I shot him before he attacked me. Now he's dead."

Meg squeezed his shoulder in support, watching Terry closely as she did this. Quietly, Terry asked, "Why didn't you unload the gun?"

Brian eyed him with renewed calm. "The guy was beating Kate—I didn't know what he might do. But I knew that he could kill an unarmed man. Once she called, I figured I might need it to protect myself. That's what I told CID."

For the moment, Terry thought, he had pushed this man far enough. "About CID," Terry said, "from now on, you should discuss this only with me. If CID contacts you, give them my number. Otherwise, as hard as this situation is, do your job. If there was ever a time to be an exemplary officer, it's now."

Brian considered him. With such mildness that it could have been sarcasm, he responded, "I always try, sir. It's genetic."

Terry smiled a little. "Have you spoken to your father, by the way?"

"Not yet," Meg put in. "I told Dad to give Brian a couple of days."

"When you do," Terry told Brian, "remember that heart-to-hearts between father and son aren't privileged. Familial concern doesn't buy you confidentiality."

Brian gave him a quizzical look. With the same soft voice he said, "Don't worry, sir."

Standing to leave, Terry said easily, "Try to call me Paul. At least in private, we can bag the military courtesies."

This induced the trace of a smile. "Habits are hard to break, sir. Even when I should."

Terry headed for the catwalk. Only when he reached it did he realize that Meg had lingered with Brian, talking softly before she kissed his cheek. A fair distance away, he stopped to wait in the hot noonday sun.

As she came toward him, Terry was struck again by her distinctive presence, self-possession mixed with an aura of solitude. At length she joined him, walking in contemplative silence. "Is he always like that?" Terry asked. "Or is it that he just killed the father of two kids who call him 'Uncle Brian'?"

She gave him a cool sideways glance. "Joe D'Abruzzo isn't the first man Brian has killed, Captain Terry. As I said, Iraq changed him."

"We should explore that. But next to Brian, the most important witness is Kate. I need to see her."

"When?"

"Now, if she can handle it."

They stopped at the end of the catwalk. "I'll have to feel her out," Meg replied. "If she's able to talk, I'll call you in an hour or so."

It was not a suggestion, but a statement. Meg, Terry thought, was cementing her role as go-between. But he needed Kate D'Abruzzo, and only Meg knew her. So here he was, stuck with the most attractive and intelligent woman he had ever wanted to be rid of.

"Fine," he said. "I appreciate your help."

3

WITHIN THE HOUR, to Terry's surprise, Meg called to say that Kate D'Abruzzo would see him.

He found the town house easily, in a pseudocolonial development offering two stories and three bedrooms to the families of Fort Bolton. When he rapped the door knocker, Kate D'Abruzzo let him in.

She was dark, slender, and superficially composed, with aquiline features, wounded blue eyes offset by pale skin, and a bearing that, despite a T-shirt and blue jeans, retained a natural elegance. Whereas Meg McCarran was a classic Irish beauty, Kate, much taller, had the aristocratic aura that, in their very different ways, also adhered to Meg's father and brother. But, like Meg, Kate appeared drained by sleeplessness and trauma.

Greeting Terry, she made no effort at animation. Meg was already there: when Kate sat beside her on the couch, across from Terry, he sensed two female allies confronting a stranger, except that these women did not seem to look at each other.

Kate and Joe D'Abruzzo's son and daughter, Meg had informed him, were with Kate's mother, Rose Gallagher; the adults could speak freely. The only sign of what had been a family was a side table with framed photographs of a black-haired boy, Mathew; his brunette younger sister, Kristen; and, more unsettling, of a smiling Kate and her late husband. A quick appraisal of Joe's photograph modified Terry's image—though the black crew-cut hair, broad peasant face, and prow of a nose suggested the intimidating man described by Brian McCarran, Joe's dark brown eyes sparkled with vitality, and the crooked smile that split his face lent his rugged features a look of warmth. From this picture, Terry might have cast D'Abruzzo as the captain of his football team: ferocious on the field, a loyal and fun-loving friend once the game was over. But Terry's job now was to reconstruct who D'Abruzzo had become in the months before his death.

Observing his inspection of the photographs, Kate spoke to no one in particular. "Last night I still couldn't sleep. I drank two glasses of wine, and found the courage to look at our wedding album. In the middle was a picture of Joe and Brian, two men I love, grinning at each other. I had to close the album." She stared past Terry at the wall. "What do you do with memories, I wonder, when something terrible turns them from joyous to unbearable."

This stark recitation, Terry found, evoked his own childhood, even as it deepened his sense of tragedy overtaking two families—both adults and children. "How *are* your kids?" he asked.

The question focused her attention back to Terry. "Mathew hardly says a word," she answered. "He's trying to be so stoic, like his dad would have been, that it makes me ache for him. Kristen cries. Right now they're all that's keeping me from wishing I were dead." She paused, giving a quick shake of the head, as though correcting herself. "No, that's not true. There's Brian. Because of me his whole life may be ruined. That's why I'm talking to you."

Terry nodded. "Can we talk about your husband, Mrs. D'Abruzzo?"

Kate folded her hands. "Yes. It's not like I haven't spent hours and days thinking about who he came to be."

Meg, Terry observed, watched Kate with deep attentiveness, but without the look of pained sympathy she had
accorded to Brian. "How did Joe change?" Terry asked.

Kate contemplated her husband's photograph, perhaps
to reacquaint herself with a person who, even before his
death, had vanished. "There was always more than one
Joe," she said at length. "Ebullient, active, insecure, fun-
loving, quick to feel hurt or slighted—in a day, he might
be several of these men. But with the kids, he was always
the same guy, at least when he had time: fiercely protective, and very attentive. If he did right by them, he told
me once, they would always know they were loved, and
never, ever, feel inadequate in any way." Her voice softened. "Joe was a blue-collar guy. You wouldn't call him
introspective. But he understood his own wounds, and he
didn't want to pass them to his kids. I loved him for that,
and I counted on his decisiveness and strength. Despite
his moods, he always tried to show how much he valued
me."

"And that changed?"

"I suppose we both changed," Kate responded at length.
"Before Joe went to Iraq, I found myself picking fights with
him. I realize now that I felt he was deserting me, like my
father did by dying in Vietnam.

"That wasn't fair—Joe was a soldier, and I chose to marry
him. Still, once he was there, I worried obsessively about
him dying—as if, like my mother, two men in uniform
would show up at the door and tell me I was a widow. But
Joe didn't die." She cocked her head, reflecting. "Actually,
he started dying in slow motion. His letters got shorter
and more phlegmatic, his phone calls less frequent and
more distant. His world seemed to close during some calls,
he barely asked about the kids. I could feel him slipping
away."

Kate, Terry sensed, was struggling to understand how her life had come to this. His own presence was less the cause than an occasion to reflect aloud. "Did he ever mention Brian?" Terry asked.

Kate regarded him with sudden curiosity. "I didn't think much about that then," she said. "But it changed. At first he'd mention Brian and say he was fine or doing a good job. Then that stopped. Even when I asked about Brian, Joe hardly answered. Brian vanished from his letters."

"How was Joe when he came back?"

Kate gazed at the coffee table in front of her, searching for words. "It was like some part of him *had* died inside, seeping poison into his soul. I know Brian seems haunted. But when he forces himself to focus, like he can with me, he's still completely present. Joe wasn't.

"Sober, he was quiet and faraway. Drinking induced a deeper silence—then suddenly he'd break into a rage so consuming his body trembled." A look of remembered anguish contorted Kate's face, and she turned to Meg as though seeking expiation. "He scared me—so much that I think he scared himself. I didn't know where to turn."

In response, Meg stared silently at the carpet. Hurt surfaced in Kate's eyes; Terry wondered whether they were ever as close as Meg's description of familial entwinement might suggest, or whether the distance he perceived was that Meg held Kate responsible for Brian's plight. Gently, Terry asked Kate, "Tell me more about how Joe changed."

"He couldn't sleep. He barely noticed Mattie and Kristen, except when they made him edgy—often just by wanting him to be the dad he'd been before. He'd react like he was being badgered by kids he didn't know." She paused abruptly, her voice lowering. "He started keeping a loaded gun in the nightstand by our bed. Sometimes he'd wake up with a start and reach for it—like he was afraid it wasn't there. Then, one night, he found it missing."

With the last phrase, Kate seemed to blanch. When Terry glanced at Meg, her lips were compressed, her posture tight. To Kate, he said, "What about Joe's drinking?"

Kate composed herself again. "Joe had a pattern. He could maintain at work. Then he'd get home, pour himself a tumbler of whiskey, and begin compulsively drinking and pacing like he needed to calm himself. But sometimes the lid came off and he'd get angry over nothing. You never knew what would light the match.

"One night, Joe stumbled over one of Kristen's dolls. He just blew up, shouting at me that the living room was like a garbage dump. In desperation, I grabbed him by the shirt, pleading with him to get help. That was when, for the first time, he slapped me." Her tone held muted wonder. "It *hurt*—I remember feeling faint, my legs wobbling. But what hurt even more was the shock of it. When my vision focused, I saw he couldn't believe it either. His eyes were glassy, like he'd gone into shock. I watched him slowly absorbing what he'd done. Then he left the house without a word."

"Did you talk about it later?"

Kate shook her head. "When he came back from the Officers' Club, he begged me to leave him alone. In the morning he went back to work with his battalion, like nothing had ever happened."

"When was this?" Terry asked.

"Four months ago."

"And he kept on hitting you?"

A flush colored Kate's pale cheeks. "Yes."

"How many times?"

"Nine," she answered softly. "I counted them. Always across the face with an open palm."

Terry hesitated. In a mild tone, he asked, "Was there sexual abuse?"

Eyes keen, Meg turned to Kate. But Kate stared straight ahead. "No," she said flatly. "We had no sex at all. Not since Joe came back."

"Did he ever talk about Iraq?"

"He wouldn't. Or couldn't." Her shoulders hunched. "Once when he was drunk, Joe mumbled something about Brian chickening out, that he didn't have the guts to do the job. When I asked what he meant, he went completely silent. But I *knew* Joe—something had happened in Iraq, involving Brian, that made Joe feel either angry or guilty. Maybe both. But I don't know what it was."

Terry glanced at Meg. "Do you?"

"No," Meg answered with a trace of sadness. "For me, my brother's service in Iraq is terra incognita. I only know from my father that the fighting Brian went through was particularly bad."

It was the first time, Terry realized, that either woman had mentioned Anthony McCarran, the head of their quasi-family. Looking at Kate, Terry asked, "Before Iraq, how did Joe get along with the male McCarrans?"

Eyes narrowing, Kate seemed to turn away from Meg. "With General McCarran," she said carefully, "Joe entered our family feeling this deep respect. Not only was Tony already a general with a superb reputation, but Joe knew that Tony had stood in for my father. On both counts, Joe saw him as an authority figure, a statue on a pedestal."

Listening, Meg's face seemed to close. When Kate added nothing, he asked, "And Joe's feelings about Brian?"

Kate's brow knit. "They were always pretty different. Brian was a McCarran, high up in his class at West Point, and Joe imagined him as predestined for success. West Point rejected Joe. He'd gone to the Citadel as a fallback, killed himself to succeed. As personalities, Joe was pretty straight-ahead, Brian more internal and reflective." Kate glanced at Meg, as though acutely conscious of her presence. "Until Iraq, they always seemed to do all right. But when they came back, Joe avoided seeing Brian off-duty, even though we live less than ten minutes apart. Except for that one comment, he refused to acknowledge that Brian McCarran existed."

"What did Brian say about Joe?"

Kate was very still. Softly, she answered, "Until recently, nothing."

"What was *your* relationship to Brian?"

Kate mustered a smile that did not quite take. "I met Brian when I was nine, the day after he was born. He was where I learned to change diapers. Fortunately, things improved. Brian was always bright and perceptive—by the time he was sixteen, we could talk to each other about anything. He even became Mathew's babysitter, the one I relied on most." She paused, speaking with more emphasis. "I love Brian, and I trust him. He's a wonderful person. Whatever happened with Joe, I know Brian didn't mean to kill him."

If it came to choosing a character witness, Terry thought, the victim's articulate wife would be hard for a prosecutor to tarnish. "You mentioned that Brian seems haunted. Did he talk about that?"

"No. Like Joe, he just wouldn't."

"After Brian came back, how often did you see him?"

Kate hesitated. "Maybe once a week. He'd come over for lunch, or we'd go for a walk."

"Always without Joe?"

"Yes." Kate paused again, then added in a defensive tone, "That wasn't just about Brian. Joe began to isolate us, so we saw friends less and less. Because of his drinking,

I was afraid to be alone with him or go out with other couples. Brian was a refuge."

Terry sat back, watching her closely. "Who knew that Joe was hitting you?"

Kate crossed her arms, looking away. "Only Brian."

"Not even your mother or a girlfriend?"

Kate shook her head. "They couldn't help me, and I knew they'd say to turn Joe in. I couldn't." Her eyes met Terry's. "If I'd reported Joe, his commanding officer would have had him investigated by the military police. It might have ended the career he worked so hard for. I don't think he could ever forgive me." She froze suddenly, as if seized by the irony in her use of the present tense: instead of his career, Joe had lost his life. Softly, she finished, "We're Catholic, Captain Terry. All of us—the McCarrans, Gallaghers, and D'Abruzzos. Divorce would have been hard for me, and I know the damage it does to children. So I prayed for us both, until Joe put the gun to my head."

"Tell me about that," Terry requested.

As Meg turned to her, Kate seemed to steel herself. Haltingly but clearly, she began to paint a portrait of a tragedy unfolding.

THEY WERE GOING TO dinner, like a normal couple. Kate dropped the kids with her mother; alone in the car, she could almost imagine that their life was as before.

Joe had come home from work. She found him in the living room, restless and impatient, though their reservations allowed her an hour to get ready. Trying to ignore his mood, she went to take a shower. Finished, she put on a robe and, before drying her hair, decided to ask how his day had been.

He was drinking from a large tumbler of whiskey. She hesitated, then spoke in a voice she hoped was not reproving. "Could you wait until we're at the club? I'd like us to have cocktails together."

Joe looked nettled and defensive, the warning signs of anger. "I'm fine," he snapped, and took another swallow.

Kate drew a breath, then sat beside him on the couch. Softly, she said, "You're not fine, Joe."

She left it there, awaiting his reaction. When he turned to her, his expression was calm, even attentive. "What are you trying to say, Kate?"

Beneath the emotionless tone, she sensed Joe warning her to be cautious. But she pressed ahead, hoping that he was sober enough to hear her. "I've already said it," she responded gently. "Many times. Now the kids are telling both of us."

With a barely discernible edge, he inquired, "What about the kids?"

"Mattie gets angry at nothing, Kristen's becoming weepy and withdrawn. Both of their teachers have noticed." She paused, choosing her words with care. "I can't be so intent on keeping the peace that I ignore our own children. If you won't get help to face whatever has happened to you, you're in danger of losing everything."

" 'Everything'?" he echoed quietly.

She hesitated, finding his calm unnerving. "Everything you care about—your career, the kids, the friends who notice how much you've changed. And me." Seeing his eyes harden, she touched his arm. "You can't manage this anymore, and it's harming Mattie and Kristen."

He turned from her, drink clasped in both hands, staring into some middle distance. Kate felt torn between her hope that he was weighing her plea and her fear of breaking the silence. Fingertips resting on his shoulder, she said in a mollifying tone, "We can talk about this at dinner. Please, just don't have another drink."

He did not speak or look at her. Quietly, Kate returned to the bathroom.

She dried her hair in front of the mirror, trying to imagine the confusion of his thoughts. Perhaps, this time, he had heard her. The whine of the hair dryer erased all other sounds.

His face appeared in the mirror.

Kate started, but did not turn. Standing behind her, Joe said with ominous quiet. "Turn off the hair dryer."

Kate complied, frozen where she stood. He placed the tumbler on the sink, then roughly grabbed her shoulders to spin her around. In a low, tight voice, he demanded, "Who knows, Katie?"

Bracing herself, she felt her bottled fear and anger become defiance. "Everyone. Don't you know how different you are? Are you so far gone you've stopped seeing yourself? If you don't believe me, look in the mirror. Look at *us*."

Joe's eyes flickered toward his reflection. As if they had a will of their own, his hands fell to his sides.

More evenly, Kate urged, "It's not too late, Joe. Together, we can face this."

Joe stared at her. She could not tell whether his mind had accepted or distorted her plea. Without speaking, he turned and left.

Shaken, Kate reached for the hair dryer. Then Joe reappeared in the mirror. She saw, then felt the gun he held to her temple.

In a taut voice, he asked, "Have you told Colonel Parrish?"

Kate's stomach felt hollow. *"No."*

Numbly, she wondered if this stranger, her husband, would put a bullet through her brain. Silently their images in the mirror watched each other. Kate saw his eyes shut, then his hand move, relieving the metallic pressure on her temple. He turned, closing the door behind him with exaggerated care.

The click of the door latch broke her spell. Tears running down her face, Kate knelt beside the toilet and vomited.

FACING TERRY, KATE LOOKED and sounded tired. "I don't know how long I stayed there. Finally, I cracked the door open. The bedroom was empty. The gun was in the drawer, but Joe was gone. That was when I called Brian."

Meg seemed to tense, as if experiencing the moment. "How did he react?" Terry asked.

Kate told him, speaking without emotion, as though her narrative had happened to someone else. Except for a few details, insignificant in themselves, her account mirrored Brian McCarran's. Listening, Meg closed her eyes.

"What led to the shooting?" Terry asked.

THE IRONY, KATE TOLD him, was that Joe had suggested going on their previously aborted dinner. As before, the children were gone, and Joe had started drinking.

For once, it did not appear to taint his thoughts. Still dressed in street clothes, he sat on the edge of their bed, watching Kate put her earrings on. "Just the two of us," he said. "Remember when we used to do this?"

The tenor of his remark, spoken as though until now they had simply been too busy, filled her with unspeakable sadness. "Yes," she answered in a shaky voice. "I do."

Something in her tone seemed to jar him from his reverie. His face changed, as though a veil had fallen, leaving his eyes distant and bleak. Then he stood and—for reasons Kate would never fathom—slid open the drawer of the nightstand.

She watched him stare at the empty drawer. Quietly, he asked, "Where is it?"

She should have prepared an answer, Kate knew. "What are you talking about?"

He turned slowly, heavily, as though processing her feeble evasion. The rage in Joe's eyes made her shrink from him.

With swift catlike movements, Joe threw her on the bed, her arms and legs flailing like a rag doll's. Panicked, she felt his hands around her throat, both thumbs pressing her Adam's apple. She began to gag, her windpipe narrowing. His face was inches from hers. "Where?" he inquired with lethal softness.

He would kill her, Kate thought, before he grasped what he had done. With the last reserves of air, she croaked, "Brian."

The stench of liquor filled her nostrils. "McCarran took it?" Joe demanded.

All she could do was nod, until he lessened the pressure. "I gave it to him," she managed to say. "It's not Brian's fault—"

"Nothing," he interrupted harshly, "is ever Brian's fault. It's always mine."

Suddenly he stood. Lying on the bed, Kate felt violated. Her throat was raw and tender.

Turning, Joe headed for the door. Afraid, she asked, "Where are you going?"

"To get back what's mine. It's time that little faggot remembers his rank."

Joe stalked from the room. Helpless, Kate heard the front door close behind him.

She made herself stand. Dazed, she could not remember Brian's phone number. Then she started dialing, the numbers coming back to her.

His phone kept ringing, and then she heard a click. In the hollow tone of a recording, he answered, "This is Brian McCarran . . ."

LISTENING, MEG INHALED VISIBLY. "So you left a message," Terry prodded.

"Yes."

Led by Terry, Kate recited her version of the message, then the hasty conversation when Brian called back, cut short when Joe pressed the buzzer. Almost word for word, her account of both squared with Brian's.

"When did you hear about Joe?" Terry asked.

"Hours later," Kate answered wanly. "From the CID man. It was what I'd always feared—a uniformed stranger at my door. Except this man didn't tell me Joe was dead."

"What *did* he say?"

"That there'd been an incident involving Joe and Brian. He asked if I could tell him what I knew."

"Did you?"

Perched at the end of the couch, Meg watched Kate closely. "Yes," Kate answered. "Everything—the missing gun, Joe leaving, the two phone calls. Exactly like I just told you. But I was too afraid to ask what had happened. Instead they started asking about Joe and me."

"What, exactly?"

"His job at the battalion; mine teaching at the school. Who we socialized with. How often we went out. Who babysat our kids." She paused. "Then it got more personal. I remember him asking if I ever spent a night away without the kids or Joe."

"What did you say?"

"Never."

Terry glanced at Meg. Softly, he inquired, "Did they ask if you were sleeping with Brian?"

Answering, Kate looked straight at Terry. "I said that we were lifelong friends, and that his question was insulting. That's when he told me Brian had killed Joe."

Turning away, Meg's expression was opaque, as though she was absorbed in her own thoughts. "Since then," Terry asked, "who have you seen or spoken to?"

Kate stared at him. "Other than telling our kids that their father was dead?"

Unruffled, Terry answered, "Yes."

The emotion drained from her face and voice. "So many people left messages. Even Brian—saying he was sorry, wondering if I was okay, asking how the kids were. I couldn't bring myself to call him back."

"Just as well," Terry said. "Who have you spoken with?"

"My mother, of course. Meg. My friend Christy Winslow." She hesitated. "Also, Tony."

"General McCarran?"

"Yes. He called to ask what he could do." Her tone grew testy. "He's the nearest to a father I've ever had."

Terry wondered if the defensiveness he heard was directed at Meg and, if so, for what reason. Meg's expression told him nothing. "With any of these people," Terry asked, "did you discuss what had happened before the shooting?"

"Just the man from CID. And now the two of you."

From her manner, Terry judged that Kate's reserves were close to spent. "For Brian's sake," he requested, "from now on please talk only to us. We don't want CID picking out petty inconsistencies in what you say to someone else, or wondering if you and Brian are ginning up a story. The one you've already told is good for Brian. You can help us keep it that way."

Kate stood, signaling that they were done. "The funeral is tomorrow," she answered tiredly. "I only wish I could bury this with Joe."

4

TERRY AND MEG STOOD on the sidewalk outside the D'Abruzzos' town house. She looked tired and preoccupied, parsing in silence what they had heard from Kate and Brian. Checking his watch, Terry saw that it was past four o'clock—hours had vanished without a trace. "Do you have time to sort this out?" he asked.

She turned to him, her eyes grave and filled with questions. "Of course."

"Then let's go to my place. As near as I can make out, the floor plan is identical to Brian's."

They got in his car and headed for Terry's apartment complex. Glancing at Meg, he asked, "What did you make of Kate? You seemed a little remote from her."

"I'm exhausted, that's all. My brother has killed a man. I don't have much energy left for Kate." She slumped back in the car seat. "To tell the truth, I'm angry at her. Maybe that's not fair. But if she'd reported Joe to his CO, she'd still have a husband. Instead, my brother's in terrible trouble, and I don't know what will happen to him."

"One way or the other," Terry answered mildly, "half of my cases are about family—sometimes the way one member acts upon another, causing a chain reaction no one really means to happen. I don't know your family and don't presume to judge it. But it seems that the change in

Joe D'Abruzzo intersected with pretty complex dynamics—including Kate and Brian's—which predated his appearance in your lives. Kate couldn't have foreseen them all."

"Maybe not," Meg responded in a tone of resignation. "Nonetheless, she lit the match. The only question now is what happened in Brian's apartment."

Terry pulled up at his building. "It's *one* question," he amended. "If we can keep the answer simple, that's best for Brian, and perhaps for everyone else. The deeper reasons are likely beyond the reckoning of lawyers."

The two of them got out. As Terry opened the front door of the building, he noted Meg checking her watch, no doubt timing how long it took for Joe to climb the stairs to Brian's apartment. Their arbitrary partnership was of one day's duration, and Terry had the impression of a linear mind intently focused on fact. When he opened his apartment door, she stepped inside, methodically inspecting the living room. "The furniture's different," she said. "But the layout and dimensions are the same."

To have her inside his apartment felt strange to Terry. The only women who had come here—none of them as striking or electric as Meg—had not come to work. Silent, he imagined how the room must look to her. It had been furnished on the cheap by a young officer who sent money to a mother with little of her own; its best feature was a partial view of a few recently planted saplings that aspired to be trees. "The living room is fifteen by twenty," Terry said at length. "On the right is the kitchen; the door to the bedroom is to the left. Neither room has an exit."

Glancing at him, Meg took out a legal pad. "So the only escape would have been blocked by Joe."

"According to Brian's account. Fortunately, he's the only witness."

Meg turned to him, edgy. "That's a cynical remark."

"Practical," Terry answered calmly. "Claiming self-defense is easier when the other guy is dead. We control the narrative of events—"

"We also have two men in a confined space. One was drunk, angry, considerably bigger, and skilled in martial arts."

"Assuming we can prove all that." Terry remained standing, his hands in the pockets of his uniform. "What's less fortunate is that Brian shared his lapse of memory with the CID. He's given back some of his advantage."

Meg shook her head, resistant. "We can point out how cooperative he was."

Terry shrugged. "People who plan a murder are often very cooperative—they've worked out their lies in advance. The problem now is that Brian can't easily revive his memory to explain away unhelpful facts."

"That came after the first shot," Meg argued. "If he was afraid for his life at the moment he fired, isn't that self-defense?"

Despite her efforts, anxiety kept creeping into Meg's face and voice. "We still have to sort out the physical evidence," Terry said evenly. "For example, how far from Brian's door was the chair where he hid the gun?"

Her brow furrowed. "Ten feet, maybe fifteen."

"CID may wonder how D'Abruzzo ended up lying with his face to the wall a fair distance from the chair. Right now we don't know where his wounds were, how many shots Brian fired, or whether D'Abruzzo was close enough that Brian's shots left gunpowder on his body. We're also assuming that Major Flynn can't conjure a motive beyond the one Brian gave—defending himself against the abusive husband of a quasi-sister."

"What other motive would he have?"

"I don't know enough to guess. But Flynn will turn over

every rock—especially if the physical evidence is subject to multiple interpretations." Terry made his tone more reassuring. "*His* threshold problem is that a claim of self-defense reverses the burden of proof. Under the law, Flynn would have to prove that Brian *wasn't* forced to shoot D'Abruzzo. Without a witness of his own, that's tough to do."

Meg exhaled. "So you think Brian will be okay."

"Given what I know," Terry temporized, "I'd rather be Brian's lawyer than the prosecutor. But Flynn will slice and dice what Brian and Kate told CID. Then he and CID will ask anyone he can find about Kate's relationship to Joe, Kate's to Brian, and Joe's to Brian—"

"Ask what, exactly?"

"Had Joe really changed? Did anyone suspect Joe was abusing Kate? Are there other reasons why Joe hated Brian or Brian hated Joe? Did something happen between them in Iraq that may bear on this shooting? And even if Joe was abusing Kate—which CID won't accept at face value— Flynn could see that as a motive for Brian to kill Joe, whether or not he needed to." Terry paused, letting her absorb this. "Then there's the unexpected. The guy next door is a freak for John Wayne movies, and these walls are paper-thin; every other night, the Duke shoots me in my sleep. There's a fair chance one of Brian's neighbors heard voices or gunshots. If so, CID will find him."

Meg scribbled furiously, her sharp slanted handwriting attacking the page. In a subdued tone, she said, "You've prosecuted these cases. What else will they be after?"

"Flynn won't like Brian's delay in calling the MPs, or that he called you first. He'll want to know from the medical examiner if D'Abruzzo died at once, which wound killed him, and whether any of the wounds suggest that D'Abruzzo was trying to defend himself rather than attack.

He'll also ponder whether the number of wounds suggests that this was overkill—"

"Joe invaded Brian's apartment, for godsakes—"

"Not precisely—Brian let him in." Terry paused, then continued firmly: "You also need to consider whether being both Brian's sister and his lawyer is more than any human being can do. As Brian's lawyers, we have to think like Flynn. You can't fall in love with the client's story because you love the client."

Meg gazed at him. "I try domestic violence cases," she answered quietly. "They're all about 'clients' I care about— the women I protect from abusive husbands. Unlike Kate, they went to the police, often at great risk. They need me to do my job.

"I learned early to separate myself from fear or anger. I've never done a homicide case, but I can learn. Brian's too important for me to let my emotions interfere."

This had the ring of truth: even after these few hours, Terry guessed that Meg was skilled at cauterizing painful feelings. "Then remember I'm not your adversary," Terry answered. "I'm trying to anticipate Flynn and CID. That's *my* job."

"And mine," Meg responded with a hint of sarcasm. "I'll do my best to keep up with you."

Despite himself, Terry smiled briefly. "Then let's suppose the physical evidence somehow contradicts Brian's story. Self-defense requires that Brian shot Joe in the reasonable belief he was in grave danger. The fallback position is that while a reasonable person wouldn't believe that D'Abruzzo was a threat to life, Brian genuinely did. That's *imperfect* self-defense, reducing murder to manslaughter. One potential basis is PTSD—a reflexive response to a perceived threat, conditioned by combat experiences, which manifests itself in different ways—"

"Like Brian's nightmares."

"Yes. I'd like you to write down everything you noticed about his behavior since Iraq—vigilance, jumpiness, sleeplessness, detachment, outbursts. If necessary, we'll bring in an expert in PTSD." Terry softened his tone. "I hope we'll never need one. But on the evidence of two-plus hours, Brian's walking a very thin line between self-control and dissociation. That could help explain his loss of memory. In the right case, I'd argue that—of all courts—a court-martial should recognize the damage this miserable war is doing to our soldiers." Terry smiled a little. "Respectfully, of course."

Meg made a note. Dryly, she said, "I'd certainly be interested in hearing you explain that to my father."

"I plan to. So please tell General McCarran I need to see him. Also Kate's mother. Both of them without you."

Abruptly, Meg looked up. "For what reason?"

"Because your presence will affect how they react. Today you helped me deal with two traumatized people you've known your entire life. But I'd like to form my own relationships with Brian's father and Kate's mother, as I would in any other case." Terry paused. "Ditto Mike Flynn. By reputation, Flynn wouldn't trust the shooter's sister any more than he'd trust bin Laden to babysit his kid. Your position here is anomalous—you might even end up as a witness. For Brian's sake, let me judge when that requires special handling."

Meg's face took on a stubborn cast. "Just as long as we discuss it," she said at last. "I don't want to learn about something after you've done it."

"Fair enough."

The alacrity of his response produced a look of veiled doubt. Whatever else, Terry thought, Meg McCarran was no fool. Pointedly, she asked, "Is there anything else you need to tell me?"

"Yes. I can't suggest this, but I don't want your father or Rose Gallagher talking to the CID. Do you think Rose will avoid that?"

Meg considered this. "I think so. For Kate's sake, and to spare her grandchildren more pain. She's been protecting children since Kate was born. Including me and Brian."

Terry nodded. "That's it, then. Let me drop you at your car."

He did that, Meg remaining silent until they arrived. Then she turned, extending her hand with the trace of a smile. "Thank you, Captain. I know this wasn't what you were expecting on your Sunday off. Let alone the bonus of a co-counsel."

Her hand was cool, her touch light. "You didn't pick the circumstances," Terry said. "And I don't mind the company. Let's hope that Brian doesn't need either of us for long."

Nodding, Meg got out, giving him a quick backward glance before getting in her car.

When Terry was back in his apartment, he made himself a drink, sorting through all he had heard and observed. Despite his sympathy for Brian and his sister, Terry grappled with a deep unease he could not define. But the draw of the case, and the people in it, was undeniable.

He poured himself another scotch. Twelve hours before, heedless of the McCarran family, he had been sleeping beside Jenny Haskell. It felt like a year.

5

ON MONDAY MORNING, Terry met with Major Michael Flynn, the trial counsel directing the inquiry into Joe D'Abruzzo's death.

The prosecutor waved Terry to a chair. By reputation fiercely disciplined and intense, in person Mike Flynn had the whippet thinness of a fitness fanatic, and the skin on his sculpted face looked close to the bone, as though God—in whom, Terry had heard, Flynn believed with unnerving zeal—had stinted on raw materials. From the reddish-brown crew cut to his probing green eyes, Flynn radiated alertness, intelligence, wariness, and a focus that rivaled Terry's own. His preparation for trial was storied.

But that, Terry knew, was not the only reason the regional trial counsel had assigned this matter to Flynn. The flip side of his disinterest in matters outside his faith and the army was a devotion to military justice that permeated his life, a deep resolve to protect its institutions from taint. Because of Flynn's own high standards, Colonel Dawes had opined, he would strive to be both rigorous and ethical. The main problem for Terry was Flynn's lack of self-doubt. Unlike Terry, Flynn was a prosecutor to his core.

Without preface, Flynn said, "What can I do for you, Captain Terry?"

Terry was prepared for brusqueness. "Work with me," Terry answered. "If we're candid with each other, we can avoid a mistake that could damage both Lieutenant Mc-Carran and the army."

Flynn's laser stare radiated disapproval. "What you're suggesting is that your client's surname creates a leverage all its own. There's another officer involved here: a captain without connections who gave the army and his country everything he had, and whose death left two kids without a father. He was every bit as valuable as your client, and is equally entitled to justice."

Flynn, Terry saw at once, drew purpose from victims, in this case perhaps strengthened by a subliminal identification with D'Abruzzo. "I agree," Terry answered. "But Brian can't help being named McCarran, and how we define justice in this case will reflect on the army in a very particular way. Nothing I've heard suggests this wasn't self-defense."

Flynn gave him a thin smile that was no smile at all. "And you'd like me to tell you what I know."

"My client's entitled to that, Major Flynn. For us to play cat and mouse increases the chance of a serious mistake."

For a moment Flynn scrutinized him in silence, signaling his unwillingness to be prodded. "It's my practice to be candid, Captain Terry. Within the limits of your obligations to McCarran, I expect the same from you. If you can persuade me that there's no probable cause to charge McCarran, so be it. But you won't accomplish that today."

This last statement put Terry on edge; Flynn's tone suggested something deeper than punctiliousness or caution. "I didn't expect to," Terry answered. "I'm focused on what you've learned so far, and how you see it."

Flynn picked up a pen, clasping it with the fingertips of both hands. "You know the rudiments. McCarran called the MPs to report he'd shot D'Abruzzo. From the tone of his voice on the tape, McCarran could have been calling his pharmacy for a refill. He sounded dispassionate, to say the least."

"Brian was a combat officer," Terry objected. "Calm is a requirement of survival. Though what you heard may have been the shock of killing the husband of a woman Brian thought of as a sister."

"Perhaps," Flynn said in a neutral tone. "Certainly, their stories mesh seamlessly—domestic violence, McCarran taking the victim's gun, D'Abruzzo coming to get it."

Terry nodded. "True. To me, their accounts make sense."

Flynn shrugged, a dismissive twitch of the shoulders. "Assuming their accounts are truthful. According to your client and Mrs. D'Abruzzo, she called to warn him that her husband was coming for his gun. But McCarran says he erased the message; the phone company doesn't maintain records of local calls on landlines. There's no evidence that the call ever happened."

With mounting disquiet, Terry began to perceive the pattern Flynn was constructing. "That would also be true," he rejoined, "if Mrs. D'Abruzzo had called you in this office and you'd deleted her message after listening to it. But you would know, as Brian did, that she'd called. That's why he called her back."

Flynn smiled faintly. "Or called Captain D'Abruzzo."

Terry feigned incredulity. "To invite him to a shooting? Talk about a crime without a future—what officer in his right mind would plan to kill his fellow officer in his own home?"

Flynn had assumed the clinical manner of a scientist testing a hypothesis. "If murderers had less self-confidence, Captain, there'd be a lot less murder. Let me pose a question of my own: If McCarran feared this man's supposed propensity for violence, why did he let D'Abruzzo in? Of course, that's where your assumptions may betray you. As

I noted, there's no evidence that D'Abruzzo was violent at all."

"That would make Kate a liar," Terry said flatly.

"All I know," Flynn countered with the same relentless dispassion, "is that she never reported her husband for striking her. Even though—like McCarran—she claims to have been terrified of him. Once again, there's no evidence to corroborate a critical aspect of the story."

"What about at the crime scene?"

"That's problematic, too. The gun was on McCarran's chair—the location from which he claims to have shot D'Abruzzo. But the four cartridges on the floor were in different locations, all closer to the door, which may indicate that McCarran was moving—"

"Brian doesn't remember," Terry interposed.

"So he claims. But there were four bullets in the corpse, suggesting that McCarran may have had more in mind than discouraging an unarmed man."

"Where were the wounds?"

"Arm, chest, palm of the hand." Flynn skipped a beat. "And back."

Though the position of the body troubled him, this revelation jarred Terry far more. "In a deadly confrontation, things happen quickly. People move."

"They can," Flynn allowed. "But we think the bullet in D'Abruzzo's back was the last shot McCarran fired. Of course, he 'doesn't remember,' so he can't help us. But one interpretation is that D'Abruzzo was trying to escape and McCarran executed him."

Terry restrained himself from objecting. "Do you know which wound caused D'Abruzzo's death?"

"The chest wound." Flynn's tone held a trace of anger. "Or maybe he died from neglect. Some of us wish that McCarran hadn't paused to call his sister."

With unsettling clarity, Terry grasped another source of Flynn's disdain. "You're assuming a lot," Terry argued. "Did the ME have the body tested for blood alcohol content?"

Flynn nodded. "D'Abruzzo was intoxicated. But query whether a man who was drunk could be as lethal as McCarran asserts. Or whether D'Abruzzo was impaired enough to be an easy victim."

Terry shook his head. "That's where your thesis breaks down. Brian didn't get D'Abruzzo drunk, and couldn't have predicted it—"

"Unless Mrs. D'Abruzzo called to tell him." Flynn twisted the pen in his fingertips. "If she *did* call McCarran, maybe she told him that her husband was drunk, susceptible to goading. After all, she knew McCarran had her husband's gun."

"That would make them co-conspirators in murder," Terry countered in a clipped voice, "and turn Joe D'Abruzzo's widow into Lady Macbeth. That's a far bigger stretch than to believe that they're telling the truth."

"Only if you *do* believe them. So let's go on. McCarran claims to have fired the first shot because D'Abruzzo was attacking him. But there was no residue of gunpowder on D'Abruzzo's clothing."

"Beyond three feet," Terry pointed out, "there might not be. There's nothing to say that D'Abruzzo wasn't four feet away, and moving forward."

"Or fifteen feet away and moving backward." Flynn's voice was cold. "There's also nothing to say what caused your client to fire. Nothing and no one—except McCarran, the only witness. Who, as we discussed, has conveniently 'forgotten' the somewhat crucial details of how he killed D'Abruzzo. You can pick at each piece of evidence, Captain Terry. That's your obligation. But together the pieces start to form a very troubling mosaic."

"Mosaics can be arranged," Terry rejoined, "or re-arranged. Right now, you and I can change the pattern at will."

"But only to a point. Here's another piece. From Brian McCarran's phone records, he called the D'Abruzzo home at seven-fifteen, supposedly returning Kate's call. The call lasted one minute, at which point—or so McCarran says— D'Abruzzo arrived." With deliberate effort, Flynn slowed the tempo of his words, speaking softly but emphatically. "McCarran's next-door neighbor, a major, heard what sounded to her like firecrackers. She remembers the time because she'd been watching *Jeopardy* and had just turned off the TV. We called the local station: *Jeopardy* ended at seven twenty-nine. Which suggests that McCarran and D'Abruzzo chatted for ten minutes."

Terry thought swiftly. "We don't know *when* D'Abruzzo arrived. But a leisurely chat discredits your suggestion that Brian invited D'Abruzzo over to—as you put it—execute him."

To Terry's utter surprise, Flynn flashed a sardonic grin. "It also discredits the idea of D'Abruzzo in a frenzy. But if what McCarran's neighbor heard were gunshots, the suggestion of an execution stands." His look of amusement vanished. "McCarran didn't report the shooting until seven forty-one. All that time, D'Abruzzo was alive."

"If Brian was in shock," Terry answered, "he wasn't considering time. And if he was as clever as you say, he wouldn't have forgotten the shooting itself. As the only witness, he'd have concocted a convenient story."

Flynn slowly shook his head. "If McCarran was *really* clever, he'd know better than to concoct a story on the fly that a medical examiner or ballistics expert could refute— far better to say nothing until the facts emerge. And he certainly grasps that he's innocent unless the army can prove him guilty beyond a reasonable doubt. Not to mention that, as you intimate, no one would lightly prosecute Anthony McCarran's son."

Terry let a moment pass in silence. "I have one question, Major. Why?"

Flynn cocked his head. "Motive, you mean?"

"Among other things. Why would Kate D'Abruzzo lie about almost everything: that her husband beat her; why Brian took the gun; the nature of her phone call the night D'Abruzzo died. And how did both Kate and Brian, questioned separately, synchronize their lies so well?" Terry's tone was etched with disbelief. "To pull that off would have required more rehearsals than a Broadway play, with risks far worse than bad reviews. What would make them chance a life in prison?"

"And yet," Flynn countered, "they claim that this tragedy occurred because D'Abruzzo beat his wife. But Kate never asked for help from anyone. That troubles me, Captain Terry."

At that moment, Terry absorbed Flynn's certainty that some concealed truth awaited his discovery. "So there we are," Terry said.

"There we are." Flynn paused a moment. "At least for now."

The clear intimation was that the case would not end easily, if at all. For the first time, Terry imagined Brian McCarran facing a court-martial, his sister—now separated from her life and career—at his side. Standing, Terry said, "Thank you for your candor, sir. I'll be in touch."

"Do that, Captain." From behind his desk, Flynn regarded Terry with the cool eyes of a recording angel. "Once I find the motive, I'll call you."

6

TERRY SPENT SEVERAL HOURS reviewing the bare bones of Brian's service record, then arranged to see General Anthony McCarran the next morning. At seven-thirty, he met Meg for dinner at a French restaurant in Old Town Alexandria.

The room was quiet and intimate, white tablecloths and candlelight adding to its serenity. Terry hoped that the change of scene would help—he had much to learn about Brian, and troubling news to convey. When the waiter inquired, Terry ordered Irish whiskey; Meg, a glass of red wine. For a time, Terry tried to learn a bit about the life she had led before Brian had interrupted it.

She had attended law school at the University of Virginia, she told him, then had moved to San Francisco without the prospect of a job. This seemed so unlike Terry's conception of her that he bluntly asked why.

She gave him a look of surprising candor. "I wanted to own my life," she said simply. "The McCarrans are from Virginia; I was born at Fort Bolton. I'd begun to feel claustrophobic. Moving to San Francisco was like opening a window."

Her response, Terry noted, mentioned places but not people. Lightly, he asked, "You never thought of entering the army?"

The small smile at one corner of her mouth seemed to

reflect some unexpressed thought. "I'd already served," she answered.

"What about Brian? Is this the career he wanted?"

Her blue eyes grew somber. "Brian is a male McCarran, our father's son. 'Want' implies choice. I don't think my brother knew he had one." She paused a moment, studying Terry's face. "You chose to volunteer, even if your reasons involved financial hardship. Brian was born into the army. So now we're here."

The last phrase, tinged with resignation, implied that she and Brian were bound by ties more profound than her wish for independence. "I met with Flynn today," Terry said. "It was grimmer than I'd hoped. One scenario he's considering is that Brian's loss of memory is a sham, and that he and Kate have constructed an edifice of lies."

Meg cradled the wineglass in her hands, never taking her eyes off Terry. "Why would they do that?"

"Flynn hasn't figured that out."

Meg shook her head. "You met them both," she said after a time. "What do you think?"

Terry considered his answer. "I'm inclined to believe the essence of their story, especially because of Kate. She paints a compelling picture. But Flynn's a prosecutor, and not easily impressed. I'd be willing to bet that some of the wife beaters you prosecute are gifted liars and loaded with charm."

Her eyes froze in an expression of challenge. "Are you saying that's my brother?"

"Sometimes the charm is missing." Terry softened his tone. "Yesterday I asked about all the ways that Brian had changed. Are you ready to get into that?"

The combativeness in her eyes receded. "Yes. I spent the morning making notes."

She took a brief sip of wine, reflective gaze refocused on the yellow-orange flame of the candle. "My first intimation," she began, "was a phone call two months or so after he arrived in Sadr City. His voice was flatter, and he refused to talk about the fighting, or even what his days were like. Instead, he kept trying to deflect the conversation back to my life in San Francisco. Even then, it worried me a lot. Now it reminds me of how Kate describes Joe's phone calls from Iraq."

Terry nodded. "I thought that, too. From the records, Brian's platoon took heavy casualties. Did he tell you about being wounded?"

"No. But for the rest of his tour he was like a robot—flat, uncommunicative, asking rote questions." Her voice lowered. "I didn't even know about the wound until after he got back, when I came out here to stay with him. When I asked about it, he was curt to the point of rudeness. 'I'm still alive,' he told me, as though he felt less relief than contempt—for the wound, or for himself."

"Do you think that was 'survivor's guilt'?"

Meg moved her shoulders. "I don't know. He'd just come from visiting the wife of a man in his platoon—the soldier had died just before their child was born. All Brian said about it was 'She named the kid Brian. Funny, huh?'"

Sadness softened her face, Terry noticed, hinting at a vulnerability beneath her willful impassivity. "Did he say who this man was, or how he was killed?"

"No. The way Brian was acting, I was afraid to ask."

"How do you mean?"

Meg stared at the wineglass, as though searching for her reflection. At length, she said, "It happened the first night I was here."

MEG HAD TAKEN HIM to dinner outside the post, hoping that he would open up. But Brian refused to talk about the war, even how it felt to be back in the States. Nor did the other difference she noted—that Brian, who drank sparingly, had consumed most of a bottle of wine—make him any more voluble.

Reaching across the table, she touched his arm. "I feel like I'm losing you," she said. "It's as if we're still talking on the telephone, and you're ten thousand miles away."

Brian's lips formed the briefest of smiles. "Fifteen thousand," he corrected her. "But thanks for coming, sis."

His attempt at lightness renewed her hope. It did not last the night.

His couch was Meg's bed. She lay awake in the darkened living room, unable to put aside her worries. The sudden sound she heard was so unlike him that at first she thought it was someone else's television. Then she remembered Brian's nightmares after their mother's death.

She sprang up, wholly alert, hurrying to his door. She knocked twice, then cracked it open to softly call, "Brian?"

In the darkness, Meg could not see him. She crept softly to the bed and sat at its edge, one hand reaching out to find him. Her heart was still pounding.

She heard a startled cry of fear or anger; suddenly vise-like fingers grasped her neck. He began to strangle her, pressing her windpipe with frenzied strength. "No—" she cried out.

As Meg began to gag, her brother's hands loosened. "It's Meg," she croaked.

Still she could not see his face. "Meg," he answered in a strange voice.

Meg breathed deeply. She tasted bile in her mouth, and swallowing felt painful. "I'll turn on the light," she managed to say, much as she had when Brian was nine and, still feeling their mother's haunting presence, he had slept on her bedroom floor. Fumbling for the wall switch, Meg felt suspended between past and present.

The ceiling light made Brian start. He sat up, his bare torso rigid, his forehead glistening. His tangled sheets were soaked with sweat.

Shaken, Meg asked foolishly, "Are you all right?"

Brian nodded, unable to speak. Meg waited for the film of unreason to vanish from his eyes.

Quietly, she said, "You had a nightmare, Brian."

He got up and walked slowly to the living room. Following, she saw him investigating objects: a table, a framed picture of both of them from Meg's college graduation. "Look at us," he murmured. From his tone and manner, he did not remember strangling her.

Meg drew a breath, absorbing that this was her brother's new reality. "Sit with me on the couch," she requested.

With affecting docility, he did that, still studying their picture. "Nights are the worst part," he murmured.

Lightly, she touched his bare shoulder. "Do you talk to anyone? Friends, or maybe a girlfriend?"

Brian laughed softly. "Girlfriend?" he repeated. "I have to change my sheets every morning. It would be like sleeping with a bed wetter."

"You need help, Brian."

"It'll pass," he insisted. "Just don't talk about this, especially to Dad. Meanwhile, just try not to startle me, okay?"

Without another word, Brian got up and returned to his bedroom, closing the door behind him. Alone in the living room, Meg could not sleep.

THEIR WAITER RETURNED. ORDERING, Meg sounded as though food held no appeal. "Maybe dinner out was a bad idea," Terry ventured.

Meg shook her head. "At least it's a distraction. And we have to talk about this, don't we?"

Terry nodded. "*Did* you talk with General McCarran?" he asked.

"In a way," she answered. "The next night we met Dad for dinner in D.C. Brian drove us in. He'd always been a very good driver—calm and competent, which was Brian's way. Now he drove too fast, switching lanes and constantly looking from side to side. But the worst part was when we got stuck in traffic.

"'Move, you fuckers,' he kept shouting through the windshield." Meg glanced around at the other diners—a young couple, two business types with synthetic smiles—then continued in a softer tone. "A motorcycle began trying to edge between the cars. Its motor backfired. Suddenly Brian pushed me down by the back of the neck as though we were being shot at.

"I cried out for him to stop. Right away, he snapped out of it, though for an instant his hands seemed to tremble on the wheel. Within seconds he was utterly calm."

"Did he say anything?" Terry asked.

"A single word: 'Reflexes.' Like what had happened was normal."

"How was he at dinner with your father?"

Pondering the question, Meg seemed to struggle for an answer. Softly, she said, "I wish you could have been there."

At DINNER, THOUGH PRETENDING not to, Meg watched her brother closely.

Their father sat between them; Meg faced Brian. The first thing she noticed was that her brother had maneuvered to sit so that he could scan the restaurant, as if preparing for the unexpected. The second troubling oddity was that neither Brian nor their father spoke about his time in Iraq.

Instead, the conversation meandered from Meg's job, to Brian's new responsibilities as executive officer of Charlie Company, to their father's long days as chief of staff and his worries about the problems of an evolving army faced with a two-front war. These exchanges disheartened Meg. They seemed like a tour of life's surfaces, meant to consume an hour and a half, while Brian silently suffered from something he chose to conceal. It was, she thought sadly, the McCarran way.

Her father was unreadable. Though Meg loved him, he was often like this. She had given up on trying to penetrate the qualities so many admired—intelligence, ambition, courage, faith, a certain sweetness, a stoic dignity under pressure. She did not know what her father thought or felt; perhaps he did not know himself. Anthony McCarran was a soldier.

Throughout dinner, their father was soft-spoken and attentive—perhaps, Meg thought, he was more interested in her work than he had managed to convey across the miles. He asked good questions, his incisive mind cutting to the core of a matter. Though Brian watched him with a clinical eye, like an anthropologist observing the representative of a unique people, Meg began to sense that her brother felt a terrible anger.

All this beneath the surface.

As dessert arrived, they heard a sudden crash of shattering dishes. Brian flinched, ducking in his chair. At once he caught himself, giving their father a surreptitious glance. Unruffled, Anthony McCarran watched a mortified Hispanic busboy kneeling over the ceramic wreckage. "Poor guy," he remarked. "These days, jobs are hard to come by."

Brian excused himself, heading for the bathroom.

Watching him, Meg perceived how her brother was getting by. Few people saw him outside work: as best Brian could, he limited his environment, avoiding surprises, while maintaining an apparent self-control at great internal cost. No one but Meg had seen him late at night.

Quietly, she told her father, "He's not right."

"I know."

His tone was at once sad and certain, as though Anthony McCarran had known how Brian would be before he returned from Iraq. Or perhaps before he went.

Absorbing this, Meg felt more desperate for her brother. "What should we do?" she asked.

For a moment her father's eyes were bleak. "Nothing. With enough time and space from us, he'll get through it. Good officers do. They better understand what happened to them."

His calm acceptance upset her. "I've been staying with him, Dad. I'm not sure that's true."

He gazed at the table. "After Vietnam," he said at length, "I wasn't always present. That was hard, particularly on your mother. Yet there was no way out but forward. After a while, the past recedes."

Meg was surprised; for her father to mention Mary McCarran was even rarer than his allusions to Vietnam. Glancing up, she saw that Brian was returning. "Respect his privacy," her father admonished gently, "and don't mother him. Let Brian be strong on his own. There are things about this you don't understand."

And you do? she wanted to ask. But she was the McCarran who had never seen war.

BRIAN'S SILENCE ON THE drive back to Fort Bolton prompted her decision.

They sat together in his apartment, drinking decaffeinated coffee. "You need to talk about this," she told him. "If not to me, with a professional, or maybe a support group."

She could read resistance in his expression, as remote as their father's had been. "I'll deal with this alone," he said. "Sometimes I can't even remember."

"Can't?" she challenged him. "Or don't want to?"

He stared straight ahead. "It's not a choice. Over there, you live in the present, blanking out whatever happened the day before. Or else you don't survive."

Though his voice was even, his tone bespoke something implacable—perhaps fear. "You're not there anymore, Brian. You're home. There's no such thing as a perfect soldier—not even our father." She softened her tone. "Everyone has a breaking point. If you talked with other vets, you'd see that."

Brian shook his head. After a time, he said, "All I feel is numb, Meg. Have you ever felt that way?"

Yes, Meg wanted to say. *When I was twelve.* But she had never spoken of her mother's death to anyone, and could not now.

"HE WON'T TALK ABOUT Iraq," Meg told Terry. "Maybe he can't."

Terry finished his last bite of duck. "Do you know why he's afraid?"

Meg paused, dabbing her lips with a cloth napkin. "Brian's more sensitive than most men. Maybe he's afraid of cracking up." She looked across the table. "In Brian's mind, our father has no problems. Neither did *his* father or his grandfather, the black-and-white photographs we grew up with. Of course, dead soldiers have no problems. Only medals."

This was the most, Terry realized, she had said about her family. "And Brian internalized that?"

Meg rearranged her utensils around a half-eaten dinner. "Brian's code—the McCarran code—is to exemplify leadership and self-possession. That's part of why he doesn't reach out to fellow veterans: if you *appear* in control, then you *are*. I'm sure that Brian's current company commander would have given him the highest marks. But the tension between how he tries to appear, and what he's suffered, is chewing him up inside. Even before this, I was afraid of what might happen to him. But it feels like I'm the only one who sees it."

Except for the last phrase, Terry wondered if she was describing herself. Brian's isolation, he sensed, deepened her own feeling of solitude and responsibility. "Not Kate?"

"Kate needed him," Meg answered. "Brian responds to need."

Her clipped tone made Terry wonder again about her relationship with Kate. Quietly, he said, "So you feel alone in this."

She gave him a look of deep regret. "Not 'feel.' Am. Before this, we were always close. Now it seems that I'm his closest friend, maybe his only friend. That's why he called me after he shot Joe." She paused, then added with quiet determination, "When someone's hurting or in trouble, a single person can save them. For my brother, I'm that person. I'm going to get him through this no matter what."

For a moment Terry was quiet, parsing the implications of this for Meg and his client. "Does Brian want to stay in the army?"

"After this?" Meg considered the question. "He says that some of his classmates from the Point are already talking about leaving. But none of them is General McCarran's son."

Always that, Terry thought. He wondered who he himself might be had he grown up with a living father whose positive example was so strong that it inspired—if not demanded—emulation rather than fear. "Whatever else," Terry observed, "this incident could be Brian's chance to bail."

Meg shook her head. "You don't understand. To cut and run in the face of hardship—whether PTSD or suspicion of murder—would be to betray the family. McCarrans suck it up."

Though ironic, her tone conveyed a simple fact. But Terry could feel the weight of it on Lieutenant Brian McCarran. "This may sound odd, Meg. But I've been thinking about something Kate D'Abruzzo said. Is there any chance that Brian is gay?"

She contemplated the question without visible offense. "I guess you think that might help explain some things."

"Yes. Actually, it might help explain *him*."

Meg placed her napkin on the table. "The woman thing has been sporadic," she said after a time. "That's not surprising, given the Point and his assignment to Iraq. And there's been no sign that he isn't straight. But the truth is that I don't know. Maybe Brian doesn't either." Her voice softened. "I'm not sure it's time to get into that. It will be hard enough piercing his defenses about the war. I pray to God we don't have to."

"So do I," Terry answered. "That would mean that Flynn has found whatever he's looking for."

They both fell quiet, aware of each other, yet mulling their own separate thoughts. Toward the end of the evening, he realized that Meg was studying him again. "What is it?" he asked.

She looked oddly disconcerted, as if he had caught her at something. Then she covered this with a smile. "I was thinking about you and my father, trying to imagine you both in the same room. I'm sorry to be missing that."

7

THE NEXT MORNING at seven a.m., Captain Paul Terry arrived at the Pentagon to meet with the chief of staff of the army, General Anthony McCarran.

Terry was escorted by Colonel Jed Marsh, McCarran's executive officer, down a long corridor flanked by oil paintings of former chiefs of staff of the army reaching back before Terry's birth. Along the way, he reviewed all he knew about General McCarran—much the stuff of army lore, the rest gleaned from Meg or the public record.

He had graduated from West Point in 1969, fourth in his class, a leader among cadets. Within six months he was a platoon leader in Vietnam, ensnared in heavy fighting near the Cambodian border. His best friend from the Point, Jack Gallagher, was killed two months after arriving in Vietnam. McCarran was himself wounded while trying to save three wounded men, the citation later said, "without regard to his own life." For this he received a Purple Heart and a Bronze Star with "V" device for heroism in combat. As a junior officer he had passed a crucial test: under fire, some young lieutenants lose their men; others lose their judgment. Anthony McCarran had excelled and, unlike his father and grandfather, lived.

This experience exemplified the hallmarks of McCarran's rise—a willingness to risk his life, and the mettle to lead in battle. Until the invasion of Iraq, he had fought whenever the army went to war, distinguishing himself as a commander in the Gulf War, when his battalion decimated its enemies in the Euphrates River valley. But McCarran's gifts transcended combat. He had a versatile intelligence that, combined with a subtle grasp of strategy and diplomacy, won the respect of influentials within Congress, the State Department, the media, and foreign governments. Known for his judgment, he opposed the reflexive use of force, and it was rumored that he had questioned the recent invasion of Iraq. That no one could trace this rumor was testament to his discretion.

This aura of intellect and courage was complemented by charisma. Instead of the theatrical pretensions of a MacArthur, McCarran had an unwavering self-possession enhanced by the ability to speak with a persuasiveness and clarity suitable to the occasion, whether addressing the Senate Armed Services Committee or inspiring enlisted men to face combat in harsh conditions. And his competence seemed unfailing: a brilliant administrator, as chief of staff he effectively ran the United States Army, overseeing the budget, training, and governance of the largest military force on earth.

But Brian's father was more than the sum of these considerable gifts. To the men he served with, Tony McCarran embodied honor. He never lied or dissembled, whether as superior or subordinate. No one ever doubted that, in any circumstance, McCarran would do right as a good man saw it. Long a widower, he was noted for self-discipline, self-denial, and a Catholic faith that was deep and abiding. More than one observer had called him a priest in uniform, and now he seemed about to become the pope—chairman of the Joint Chiefs of Staff, the apex of the American military.

All of which, Terry thought as he approached McCarran's office, would make him a hard father for a young lieutenant. Terry, who had spent much of his youth envying sons with living fathers, did not envy Brian McCarran. Nor, despite his own resolve, could he quite repress his sense of awe at meeting Anthony McCarran.

Colonel Marsh led Terry to a corner office, where Anthony McCarran rose to meet them. "Sir," Marsh said, "this is Captain Terry."

Marsh's quiet gravity bespoke the tragedy that had enveloped McCarran's son. "Thank you, Jed," McCarran answered simply, and Marsh left the room, closing the door behind him.

McCarran stood a shade over six feet two. His frame was lean and erect, his features aquiline, his eyes gray-blue, his short, curly hair completely silver. This air of command was leavened by a surprisingly gentle voice. "I appreciate your coming, Captain Terry. Please have a seat."

Everything about him was economical—his words, his movements, the absence of fat on his body. His eyes, unmoving, appraised the lawyer in front of him. From the evidence of his photographs, they could maintain a flinty stare or, in better humor, glint with a bright, surprising smile that transformed his face. But for now, McCarran used them to invoke his psychic force field, taking stock while taking his time.

Terry was prepared for this. By reputation McCarran knew the uses of silence. Speaking too much or too quickly can lead to mistakes; quiet induces others to blurt things out. But Terry, too, had mastered the human need to fill a void with words. With considerable effort, he pretended to pass the time perusing the bookshelf behind McCarran's desk, spotting tomes on geopolitics, history, and Catholic philosophy as well as a leather-bound copy of *For Whom the Bell Tolls*. At length, McCarran said, "I hear you're one of our best."

Terry managed to smile. "If not, sir, I keep trying."

"And winning, it seems. Even on the defense side. I'm told you're very inventive, with a keen grasp of the psychology of a military jury." McCarran's voice softened. "How do you assess my son's situation?"

Terry hesitated, measuring his words. "With the greatest respect, sir, we should review the ground rules for this conversation."

All expression vanished from the general's face. "Please do, Captain."

"I understand your concern for Lieutenant McCarran. But I literally don't work for you. My conversations with Brian are privileged; ours are not. So I can't tell you everything I know, or even what I'm thinking. Protecting my client has to be all that matters to me."

McCarran absorbed this in silence; in an institution grounded in hierarchy, his relationship to Brian's lawyer was a novelty. "I accept that, Captain Terry. At the risk of mouthing pieties, the army relies on the integrity of its institutions—including the military justice system." He sat back, eyeing Terry across his polished desk. "I'm curious, though, as to what made you choose the JAG Corps."

Meg's report, Terry gathered, had been thorough. "ROTC helped pay for college," he answered. "I don't like owing people. But I *do* like trying cases, and JAG is the place for that." Terry paused, then decided to say the rest. "I'm no combat hero, sir. But I've got no time for cocktail-party patriots—the ones who talk about 'supporting the troops' they've never met in a war their kids will never see. Compared to that, at least, I like to think I *am* supporting our troops." Terry paused, measuring his words. "When it comes to Brian, I deeply respect his service. I don't want to see him shafted by a self-righteous prosecutor who's far too certain he not only represents the army but God."

McCarran's eyes became more probing. "I also understand, Captain, that you don't like this particular war."

There was no point in mincing words. "No, sir. Even less because of what it's doing to our soldiers."

"Including Brian?"

"Perhaps. That's part of what I wanted to ask you."

For a moment, McCarran's gaze turned inward. "Brian faced unique pressures," he said quietly. "Because of me, it was inevitable that people would look out for him. The flip side was that everyone would be watching his performance. Brian's only recourse was to excel." His voice hinted at pride and regret. "Brian sought out combat. From what I understand, his baptism was harsher than my own."

"What do you know about that, General?"

McCarran paused to organize his response, then recounted the facts in a dispassionate tone. "Seven months after his graduation, Brian arrived in Iraq. He was posted to Sadr City, where Muqtada al-Sadr, the Shiite cleric, had just sanctioned his Mahdi Army to kill Americans and murder Sunni civilians at random. His tactic was to create such chaos that Iraqis would blame us for the misery he inflicted.

"Brian's company was assigned to fight the Mahdi Army, and to help pacify Sadr City. From the reports I received, he insisted on sharing whatever risks he asked his men to take. Judging by the dead and wounded, they were considerable."

This laconic account suggested undescribed horrors. "Has Brian ever talked about that with you?" Terry asked.

McCarran grimaced. "His own experience? No. But he's quite vehement about the impact on his men."

"In what respect, sir?"

McCarran looked off into the distance. "He spoke of one sergeant in particular. The man's closest friend had been blown apart by a rocket-propelled grenade, within feet of where this sergeant was walking. The man insisted on bagging the remains, piece by mutilated piece, and taking them to a storage site to be returned for proper burial." McCarran's tone was weary but factual. "As Brian described it, the sergeant receded within himself. His marriage was already troubled; shortly after he returned, his wife asked for a divorce.

"The man began talking about suicide. My son sent him to the VA for a mental health evaluation. Instead, they put him on a six-month waiting list. Three weeks later, the man hung himself in his wife's garage. I'd never seen Brian so filled with rage." McCarran shook his head. "In great part I agree with him. 'Supporting our troops' includes caring for them after they return. But Brian seemed to lump me with those who had failed his men."

Terry waited a moment. "Was he critical of D'Abruzzo?"

McCarran looked somber. "After Iraq," he replied slowly, "I don't think my son mentioned Joe at all. He became part of Brian's silence."

"But you also had your own relationship with D'Abruzzo."

For the first time, McCarran looked down, his head slightly bowed. "Yes."

"Did you see him after he returned?"

McCarran hesitated. "Only once."

"What were the circumstances?"

"It was about Kate," the general finally answered. "She came to me, saying there was trouble in their marriage."

Terry heard a tangible reluctance. "This could be very helpful, sir. How did she describe their problems?"

"Joe had become mercurial and withdrawn, she told me, including with the children. She wanted him to get psychiatric help. I tried to urge that on Joe, less as a general than an older member of the family who cared about them both." McCarran's tone was flecked with regret. "Obviously, I did no one any good."

"How did D'Abruzzo seem to you?"

"Defensive. Kate had told me to expect that. Joe had never felt he quite belonged, but he was even touchier than before."

"Did she mention physical abuse?"

McCarran looked up. "She was frightened, Captain. That was clear."

It was equally clear that McCarran found the subject painful—he had failed his surrogate daughter, his manner suggested, and in doing so had ensnared his own son. Quietly, Terry asked, "How would you assess Brian's relationship with Kate?"

McCarran gave him a cool, level glance. "They've always been very close. Is that what you're asking?"

"The question was open-ended, sir."

McCarran held his gaze. "If I'm to free-associate, the first phrase that comes to mind is 'younger brother.' Except that it seems Brian wound up looking out for her." Abruptly, the intentness vanished from McCarran's eyes. "When they were young, I could never have imagined all this. Let alone when I stood in for her father at Kate's wedding."

Terry nodded his sympathy. "He was your closest friend, I gather."

"And always will be." McCarran paused, then asked with surprising reticence, "How did Kate seem to you? There's so much we can't talk about, it seems, until this thing is over."

"I'd say she's coping, General. She seems pretty strong. Having two kids may help to keep her that way."

McCarran nodded. "She also has Rose, her mother.

You've not met her, I believe. But she's a remarkable woman."

The words held something close to reverence. "I mean to see her," Terry said, "if only to help me delve into Brian's life. Who would you say knows him well?"

"Well?" McCarran's voice became rueful. "Perhaps the men he served with. Certainly the women in our family—Meg, Kate, and Rose. I'm not so sure that I do anymore."

"You agree that Brian's changed, then?"

"Yes." McCarran searched for words. "He's jumpy or distracted, and then a veil falls across his eyes. Suddenly he'll watch you like he's examining a slide beneath a microscope. It feels like staring into the eyes of a bird."

The quiet with which he said this suggested that McCarran rarely discussed such feelings, and never with a man he did not know. This violation of self, Terry sensed, was an offering to his son.

He decided to extend the moment. "From all that I know, General, *your* first combat experience was hard. How did you get through it?"

Briefly, McCarran closed his eyes. When they opened, his expression was distant. "My father and grandfather died in combat. Before my first battle, I told myself I was already dead. That way I could dull extraneous emotions, like fear or horror or even misplaced compassion. All that's left is for you to carry out the mission and save what men you can. If you're already dead, your own fate doesn't matter."

That this remarkable statement was delivered without discernible feeling gave Terry a chill. "Did you say this to Brian?" Terry asked.

"No. Because he was my son."

But perhaps a piece of Brian McCarran, Terry thought, was already dead. He did not say this. Instead, Terry thanked Anthony McCarran for his time, and left.

8

On his way to meet Meg at Dr. Blake Carson's office in Bethesda, Terry reviewed his encounter with Brian's father. Anthony McCarran impressed him as both steely and complex, with a layered persona that concealed from others—and perhaps sometimes from himself—the thoughts and feelings at his core. Unlike many parents he had seen, the general had not protested his son's innocence. General McCarran, Terry judged, knew that hardships do not yield to outrage or dismay.

He found Meg in Carson's waiting room. Swiftly, Terry summarized what he knew of the psychiatrist: an expert in the treatment of PTSD, Carson had left the Veterans Administration because, as he'd put it to Terry on the phone, "we were fucking over the guys Iraq fucked up." Carson had sounded young—hip, slangy, and funny—and his résumé suggested that he was under forty. But Terry was unprepared for the boy-faced man who came through his office door, with the blond mane and bright, adventurous blue eyes of a surfer, his jeans and work shirt faded. Reading Terry's expression, he told him with a grin, "I don't look much older in court. But I get myself a haircut and a suit."

He ushered Meg and Terry into his office, a bare-bones room with a chair, a couch, and a poster of the Grateful Dead. Taking the chair, he abruptly told Meg, "I don't know your brother from Adam. But Paul mentioned that

Brian hates the VA. No surprise—the VA is paranoid and secretive in direct proportion to its incompetence. They're lousy at screening soldiers for PTSD, and when they get one right it's like 'take a number.' They're looking at a mental health tsunami, and they haven't got a clue."

"Then it's really as bad as Brian says."

"Worse. The stats on suicide among Iraqi vets are so shocking that the VA tries to hide them. By the time this stupid war is over, we'll have hundreds of thousands of guys semi-incapacitated by trauma, and the VA will have denied treatment to far more of them than they've helped. It's criminal."

Terry caught Meg's look of worry. With renewed force, he saw that—given Brian's self-destructive quality—she lived in constant fear that he might take his own life. But Terry also wondered how Carson would fare as an expert witness; beneath the man's laid-back facade was an angry energy. In part to test this, Terry asked, "Is Iraq worse for soldiers than any other war?"

Carson's eyes darted from Meg to Terry, as though seeking to engage them both. "Different," he answered. "At least in Vietnam you had cities like Saigon, where you could get drunk and laid without risking death. In Iraq there's nowhere to hide, and no safe place to blow off steam." He paused, as though perceiving Meg's need to understand the change in Brian. "Sadr City was particularly brutal—it was hostile, and densely populated by civilians you couldn't tell from members of the Mahdi Army. And the mission was schizoid: playing with Iraqi kids by day, storming their parents' homes at night, looking for militiamen or weapons. Not to mention RPGs and IEDs—"

"You're talking about homemade bombs?" Meg interrupted.

"We call them improvised explosive devices. The bad guys plant them where our guys will be, hidden in ditches by the road or under a pile of garbage. RPGs are rocket-propelled grenades. Either can blow you to pieces, like whatever nearly took your brother's head off. What do you know about that?"

"Zero," Meg said slowly. "As though it never happened."

A somber look crossed Carson's face. "God knows *what* your brother experienced in a year. In Sadr City, our soldiers couldn't control their environment and couldn't escape it. On the worst days there was carnage all around you—not just dead but dead friends in pieces. And you never knew if the can of Pepsi that cute Iraqi kid was holding was a soft drink or an IED. Or whether the Iraqi woman you shot for driving through a checkpoint was pregnant and desperate to get to a hospital. Or maybe you were trapped for days in a building surrounded by Iraqi militia, and your dead had started decomposing. I've heard all those stories, and more. And now we're sending the guys who told them back for a second tour."

"Among other things," Terry said, "Brian can't handle being stuck in traffic. How does that fit?"

"In the greater sense, being trapped and unable to escape is a metaphor for everything I'm telling you. But for our purposes, I'd have to know the specifics of what happened to Brian McCarran." Turning back to Meg, Carson inquired, "Does he tell you anything at all?"

Meg shook her head. "Brian won't talk about Iraq. To anyone."

"Typical. From what Paul told me on the phone, he's also hypervigilant and easily startled, treats driving like combat, doesn't sleep well, and suffers from recurring nightmares. Right so far?"

"Yes. He also tunes people out, like his soul has suddenly left his body."

"Dissociation," Carson said crisply. "Another symptom. So are depression, substance abuse, spousal abuse, alienation from family, sudden rage, unpredictable violence, and suicide." He paused for an instant, seeing Meg wince. In a softer tone, he added, "Some of these guys have a kind of death wish, a gravitational pull toward reckless behavior. Like letting a guy in your apartment who may want to kill you."

"Or going there," Terry countered, "when you know the other guy has your gun."

"That, too." Carson angled his head toward Meg. "What do you know about D'Abruzzo's combat experience?"

"Also nothing. And now he can't tell us."

As though absorbing the death of another husband and father, Carson was quiet for a moment. "That's a problem," he said at last. "I can tick off symptoms in the abstract. As to your brother, I can even guess that he feels a deep responsibility for whatever befell his men. But I can't interpret Brian's behavior—let alone this shooting—unless I know what happened to him."

"Our father never spoke of his own experiences in Vietnam," Meg said. "Much less expressed any feelings about it, even though his closest friend died there." She paused, her tone becoming both melancholy and ironic. "That's how we grew up. It seems that Brian has become a true McCarran."

"This may involve more than your family," Carson told her. "However enlightened the army may try to become about PTSD, there's a warrior ethic which holds that combat stress is a form of weakness. A lot of guys like Brian worry that seeking help may be a career killer. So they try to hide it. Which brings me to an important question:

Is there anyone but you who can testify to how much Brian has changed?"

Meg flicked back her auburn bangs, her thoughtful expression darkening. "Maybe our dad, to a limited degree. But outside the predictable office environment Brian has clung to since Iraq, he's tried to isolate himself. And as far as I can tell, I'm the only person who's seen him late at night."

Carson frowned. "Too bad. The cause of PTSD is a scarifying experience of combat that the soldier keeps reliving. But that damage is intensified by the failure to seek help, or even to acknowledge there's a problem. Instead, these guys will try to build a wall around the traumatic event. When they sleep, the wall breaks down. But we don't know what Brian's nightmares are about."

The reference seemed to deepen Meg's sadness. "Flynn," Terry told the psychiatrist, "suggests that Brian's claimed loss of memory about the shooting is a ploy. Is there a more appealing way to explain that?"

Carson shook his head. "Not unless I learn more about his experience in Iraq. I can rationalize Brian's lack of emotion after the shooting, and even his delay in calling the MPs. But if you're using PTSD to knock murder down to manslaughter or seek a lesser sentence, I'll need a helluva lot more material than you've got." He angled his head toward Meg. "Maybe you or your father can describe the symptoms. But only Brian can say what caused them."

Terry, too, faced Meg. "That brings up another issue," he told her. "If this comes to a trial where we rely on PTSD in any way, I think you'll have to testify."

Meg gave him a look of puzzlement. "As defense counsel, I can't."

"Someone else can defend a homicide, Meg. You're far

more valuable as a witness than as an active participant at trial, and Brian will need all the testimony he can get."

Meg was briefly silent. "Isn't there a problem with raising PTSD at all? On the one hand, we'd be claiming classic self-defense—that Brian acted reasonably. In contrast, the idea of relying on PTSD is to argue that killing D'Abruzzo was reasonable only in Brian's mind, but reduces his culpability. It seems like one theory undermines the other. Brian's defense could look desperate and confusing, especially to a jury inclined to think the PTSD defense is sophistry."

Meg might not try homicide cases, Terry thought, but she had the practicality of a good trial lawyer. "Maybe so," he conceded. "Brian's lawyer would have to be careful. But I'd feel better about relying on straight-out self-defense if the physical evidence weren't ambiguous and Brian had a better story about the shooting. Which brings us back to the real problem: Brian.

"In theory he's his own best witness. But he claims not to remember firing the last three shots, and he won't say a word about Iraq. That makes him iffy on self-defense, and completely useless on PTSD."

"Which means that I can't help you," Carson put in. "You want me to interview him, and I will. But to testify in court, I'd need to relate the events of the shooting to a combat event so horrendous, yet so similar, that I can ask a military jury to believe that Brian killed D'Abruzzo not knowing if he was in Virginia or Iraq. And at least for the moment, he can't tell us what happened in *either* place."

Meg, Terry saw, looked deflated. "Flynn still doesn't have a motive for murder," she finally said. "Unless he finds one, Brian may not have to tell us anything. Right now that's my hope."

9

Terry and Meg stood outside the building, each absorbing what Carson had told them. It was June, and summer heat made the humid air feel as searing as a sauna. "Can you get Brian in to see him?" Terry asked.

The look Meg gave him was troubled and uncertain. "You think Brian's facing charges, don't you?"

Quiet, Terry tried to sort through his confusion to give Meg the answer she deserved. "It's more a feeling of disquiet. Flynn believes there's a missing piece that can explain why Joe D'Abruzzo died. All *I'm* sure of is there's too much I don't know—"

"Brian's not a murderer," Meg insisted.

"But he is an enigma, you'll admit. So are the circumstances of the shooting." Terry put on his hat. "It's human nature to want certainty. Flynn won't rest until he makes the pieces fit or believes he never can. The time that takes won't matter."

Terry watched Meg contemplate the prospect of being trapped at Fort Bolton, and perhaps in her own past, without a certain future waiting on the other side. "It does for you," she answered. "In a few short weeks we won't be your problem anymore."

Terry did not answer. When his cell phone rang, it took him a few seconds to respond.

"Captain Terry?" The woman's voice was tentative. "My husband got your name from Colonel Dawes."

"Who is this?" he asked.

"Lauren Scott." Her speech was rapid yet tentative. "You don't know me, but I'm a friend of Kate D'Abruzzo's. CID's been talking to other friends of Kate's, and I'm worried they've got my name."

Terry glanced at Meg. "Does that concern you?" he asked.

The woman was momentarily silent, then responded in a hesitant voice, "I think there's something you should know."

There were moments when instinct told Terry that his conception of a case, and perhaps the people enmeshed in it, was about to be upended. From her expression, Meg read this on his face. "I'd like to meet with you," he told Scott.

THEY FOUND HER IN a grassy park near Fort Bolton Elementary, watching her three-year-old daughter and a playmate scamper from slide to swings to sandbox. Lauren Scott was blond and plump and harried-looking; in the heat, damp tendrils of hair stuck to her forehead, and the cooler beside her on the wooden bench was filled with ice and bottled water. "I try to keep them hydrated," she explained.

Terry and Meg sat on either side of her. Meg's impassivity barely disguised her concern; when she had asked Kate to list her women friends, Meg had told Terry, Lauren Scott was not among them. In a conversational tone, Terry asked her, "How do you know Kate?"

"The usual way of moms—our kids." Delivered in a nasal voice, the phlegmatic answer bespoke a life in harness. "My son Jason has learning issues and Kate teaches him remedial reading. I'm new at Bolton, like her, and pretty much home all day. So now and then we'd have coffee or watch each other's kids."

"Did you ever see each other socially?"

"As couples?" A small frown appeared. "I kind of thought we might. But Kate never seemed that interested. When I talked about Tom, she barely mentioned Joe at all."

"Did you think there was trouble in her marriage?" Meg put in.

Scott folded her hands, watching the two girls skitter down a miniature slide. At length, she answered, "That's what I called to tell you."

KATE AND LAUREN SAT on the same bench in the same park. But that late-spring morning was mild and pleasant, and Lauren had brought a thermos of coffee. As always, they chatted about their kids, the army, movies old and new, and the various activities Bolton afforded families; as always, Lauren wondered why Kate D'Abruzzo, so smart and poised and self-contained, had turned to her for company. She had begun to wonder if Kate's silence about her marriage reflected a solitude deeper than Lauren knew.

This morning Kate seemed unusually preoccupied, glancing at her watch as though afraid of missing an appointment. Lauren was edging toward another inquiry about her new friend's husband when Kate's cell phone rang. With a jumpiness that seemed unlike her, Kate snatched it from her purse. She listened with what Lauren thought of as a mother's alertness, brow furrowing, and then her slender body seemed to slump. "I'll come get her," she said tiredly. "It'll just be a few minutes."

Shutting off the cell phone, Kate put it back in her purse, more slowly than she had retrieved it. She looked so distressed that Lauren, certain that the call concerned Kate's daughter, worried that Kristen D'Abruzzo had some serious health problem. "Is everything okay?" Lauren asked.

This commonplace inquiry seemed to startle Kate. "You mean Kristen? It's just a stomachache—she's been having them lately, for whatever reason. She seems to be going through a phase."

Her tone was odd; though Kate impressed Lauren as a caring mother, she could have been discussing someone else's child. It struck her that Kristen's stomachache might reflect some emotional difficulty that Kate D'Abruzzo was reluctant to acknowledge. Abruptly, Kate turned to her. "I need a favor, Lauren. Could you watch Kristen today? I wouldn't ask, but I've got an appointment."

Combined with Kate's distractedness, the urgency of this vague request piqued Lauren's curiosity. Perhaps Kate and her husband had sought out marriage counseling. "When would you need me?" Lauren inquired.

Kate still looked flustered. "The middle of the day. From eleven-thirty to maybe a little after three."

This was not an appointment, Lauren realized. Nor was it an extended shopping trip—improbable, given the stores that Bolton offered on site—anything a mother would not postpone. Watching Kate's expression, Lauren said slowly, "I'd like to help. But Annie and I are meeting Tom for lunch at the Officers' Club. It's such a treat for her."

Kate glanced at Annie and her little friend, as though rediscovering their presence. With a somewhat desperate air, she said, "Would it be possible to take Kristen to lunch with you? I promise to make it up to you."

To Lauren, the request revealed a surprising obliviousness—to the Scotts, whose family time would be disrupted; to Kristen, six years older than Annie, who would bring a stomachache to lunch with three near strangers. More sharply than she intended, Lauren asked, "What's wrong, Kate?"

Kate's face, usually so lovely yet so unrevealing, seemed frozen with mortification. "I'm meeting someone, off the post," she said in a parched voice. "All I can tell you is that I need to do this."

Her meaning seemed as unmistakable as it was shocking: Kate D'Abruzzo was having an affair, and felt so alone that she was begging for help from Lauren, a Mormon, knowing that it violated her moral code. Silent, Lauren searched her conscience. But all she felt was a swift dart of empathy she did not fully understand, followed by pleasure that Kate D'Abruzzo—who had so much Lauren lacked—needed Lauren's indulgence for her sin. In a grudging tone, Lauren answered, "I guess we can take Kristen with us. If she's too sick, Tom can take Annie alone."

Kate gave her a quick, silent hug, and rushed off to get Kristen.

MEG STUDIED LAUREN SCOTT closely. "Did Kate *say* she was having an affair?"

The edge in her voice seemed to rattle this woman. "Not in so many words," she answered in a defensive tone. "But it was obvious."

"Not to me," Meg said.

Terry touched Meg's arm. "Did you and Kate ever talk about this again?" he asked.

Scott gave a quick shake of the head. "Never. I think it embarrassed us both."

"So you have no idea who she was meeting."

"No." Scott sounded ashamed of her own thoughts. "But Tom and I talked about it. We figured it must be a military guy."

Terry caught Meg's look of dismay—Scott's suspicions, once expressed, might have spread beyond her husband. "Why did you think that?" he asked.

"It's obvious," Scott said with a hint of impatience. "Where else do any of us meet men? Bolton's like our own city—some of us don't leave for weeks. What came as a surprise is that Kate would meet a guy so soon after coming here."

At least, Terry thought, Scott did not assume that it was Brian. "So you haven't talked to CID."

Scott looked away, then glanced at her daughter and her playmate. "No. And I'm not eager for that to happen."

Meg's expression remained cool. "Have you told *anyone* else about this?"

"No." Scott turned to Terry. "Tom's a captain in the Signal Corps. He didn't know Kate's husband, and we don't really know their friends. It's not the kind of thing we share outside the family."

Terry chose his words with care. "That's a kindness, Lauren. Meg's right—in itself, this incident means nothing. But talking about it could only hurt Kate and her children, and maybe other innocent people as well."

Scott regarded him with caution. "I understand. But if the CID asks me a question, I can't lie to them." Her voice lowered. "I've prayed on this, Captain Terry. That's why I had to call you."

Meg stared at the ground. "I appreciate your coming to us," Terry said. "If CID contacts you, please just let us know."

AT THE EDGE OF the park, Meg turned to face him. "Whatever else that means, it wasn't Brian."

"Are you still so sure?" Terry asked. "This woman's right—it would be easier for Kate to start an affair with a man she already knew. And who else but someone who cared for her would take that chance? In the army, adultery can end a career."

Meg's eyes clouded. "I know my brother, that's all."

"Then tell me this: Kate says she never spoke about Joe hitting her to anyone but Brian. But you'll never convince me she wouldn't tell whoever she was sleeping with. If it isn't Brian, then she lied to us. And if it is, she lied about that." Terry thought swiftly. "Whoever it was, they had to meet off the base, just as Kate told Lauren Scott. Sooner or later Flynn will find out where."

"If it ever happened," Meg objected.

"If it happened," Terry retorted, "it's time for Kate to tell us. I need to see her right away."

Meg considered him for a moment, her blue eyes conveying an emotion—regret or perhaps confusion—he could not quite label. Then her expression changed utterly. "You're right," she conceded. "Please, let me talk to Kate first. If there's something about our family, I'm the one she'll tell."

TERRY WAS IN HIS office when Meg called. In a tired voice, she reported, "Kate won't talk about this. Except to say that it didn't concern Brian."

Terry felt his own frustration. "Does she acknowledge the conversation?"

"Only to say that Lauren misunderstood it. She sees the devil under every bed, Kate told me."

"Then why were they friends?"

Meg was silent for a moment. "I talked to Brian," she said. "He denies it, too." Her voice softened. "We should leave this be, Paul. If we go around looking for Kate's phantom lover, we'll only stir things up."

This had a certain logic, Terry thought. Then it struck

him that Meg had never before used his given name. "Okay," he allowed. "For now."

He got off the phone, then called Kate D'Abruzzo's mother.

10

ON MEETING ROSE GALLAGHER, Terry's first thought was that Kate D'Abruzzo resembled her mother so completely that Kate's father had left no trace. His second was that Rose was the image of a general's wife: dignified in carriage and manner, she was quite tall, with a handsome face, perceptive brown eyes, and dark hair streaked with white. In a dry voice with faintly patrician East Coast tones, she said, "You must be Captain Terry."

Standing at the threshold of her town house, he responded, with a slight smile, "And you're certainly Kate's mother."

"I am that. Please come in."

Her living room was furnished in traditional style and, like her daughter's, filled with family photographs, including several of her grandchildren and a formal wedding picture in which a proud-looking Rose and Anthony McCarran were flanked by Joe D'Abruzzo and a radiant Kate; Meg, wearing a somewhat forced smile; and Brian at about sixteen. A stranger would have taken them for a single family, celebrating a milestone of their years together. But another photograph showed a young army lieutenant with a bright smile, clear blue eyes, and the can-do look of an American ready for a challenge. Following Terry's gaze, Rose said, "That's Jack. The one who grows no older."

Her tone, mixing sadness with acceptance, suggested a

penchant for facing life as it was. Turning to her, Terry said, "I'm sorry for all that's happened."

"Thank you." She waved him to a seat, then said in a softer voice, "I spoke to Joe's mother, not an hour ago. It's hard to imagine the devastation they must feel. They never had much—in many ways Joe was their reason for living, the culmination of so many hopes. They revered Tony, and loved all the McCarrans. Now, of course, any fault was Brian's, not Joe's. Placing blame is all they have left."

"How do *you* feel?"

She gave him a look of striking directness. "Unspeakably sad. For my daughter, of course, and my grandchildren even more. Kate will survive, as I did. But the death of a parent leaves scars in a child that linger, and a violent death all the more so. Then there's Tony and Meg—and most of all, Brian, facing charges for killing Kate's husband. For me, there's no one person to blame, and too many people who are suffering."

Terry placed his hat on the coffee table, signaling his hope of staying awhile. "I'm all the more grateful for your time, Mrs. Gallagher."

"And I'm more than willing to give it. If Brian is charged with murder, that will only deepen the tragedy, perhaps in ways that none of us can imagine. Better that we bury this with Joe."

She spoke in the measured tones of a woman accustomed to loss and what loss leaves behind. "Part of my job," Terry told her, "involves understanding Brian and how this might have happened. I take it that your family and the McCarrans are very close."

"More than close," she corrected. "Intertwined. Tony and Jack were best friends at the academy—the first time I met Mary was on a double date with Tony and Jack. Tony was best man at our wedding, and Jack was Tony's." She paused a moment. "When they went to Vietnam together, as infantry platoon leaders, Mary and I saw them off. As you know, Jack died there."

Even when sitting, Terry noticed, her posture was erect. "That must have been hard," he ventured.

"It was," Rose answered simply. "I was eight months pregnant when two men in uniform came to my door. I knew at once that my life had been divided in two—before Jack died, and after. I remember feeling sympathy for the terrible role they had. But I really can't remember anything I said."

For an instant, Terry flashed on Brian's loss of memory. "I gather General McCarran helped you."

Rose smiled a little. " 'General McCarran,' " she repeated softly. "He was 'Tony' then, a twenty-three-year-old junior officer. When he came back from Vietnam, Tony did everything he could for me—helping get all my benefits, finding a job teaching on the base." She paused, reflective. "On the phone, when you asked how the war affected Joe and Brian, I thought at once of Tony. Jack came back from Vietnam in a coffin; a piece of Tony never came back at all."

"How do you mean?"

Rose seemed to parse her thoughts. "He was quieter, more distant. He'd suddenly lapse into silence, like Brian does now. When Joe stopped playing with his children, I remembered something odd—that Tony, who had no children then, lost interest in the hunting dog he'd always adored. All three of them were somewhere else." She paused, as though hearing a question Terry had not asked. "They were volunteers, I know. But I think we have no idea what we ask of them in war, and they only know once it happens. If they ever really allow themselves to know."

Terry considered his next question. "I'm interested in

General McCarran," he said at length. "I think he's central to understanding Brian and how he might have reacted to what he experienced in Iraq. As I told Meg, this feels like a family story."

Rose gave him an enigmatic smile. "How did she respond to that?"

"Sometimes I'm underwhelmed by her enthusiasm. Because of Brian, and perhaps for reasons of her own, I think she finds the subject of family painful. That's part of why I need your help."

Rose nodded her understanding. "Meg can be a hard one. Though, for reasons I doubt she's shared with you, she comes by that honestly. But you were asking about Tony after Vietnam."

"Yes. Among other things, I'm curious about whether *he* appreciates what happened to him there."

"In other words," Rose inquired pointedly, "does he also grasp what may have happened to Brian? To a degree, 'yes' to both. Tony never talks about Vietnam. But after Brian returned from Iraq, Tony admitted to me that his experiences affected him for a time. What he may not perceive is that the change was permanent. Even now, sometimes Tony just shuts down. That's when I know to give him solitude, and silence."

She sounded like a wife, Terry realized. "How did that affect his marriage?"

The keen look she gave him suggested that she had followed his thoughts. "You *are* curious, aren't you? I suspect that extends to Meg as well."

It was time, Terry realized. Instead of answering, he tried his most disarming smile. "I'm knee-deep in McCarrans," he said. "There's a lot to unravel—including why Brian's first call after the shooting was to Meg."

Rose studied him for a moment. "Perhaps we share a

common sensibility, Captain Terry. Sometime after Mary died, I began working toward my master's degree in child psychology. What got me started in that direction was Kate, Meg, and Brian.

"But you were asking about Tony and his marriage to Mary. After Vietnam, Tony wanted peace. Mary had none to give. She had always been histrionic and somewhat needy—what she needed was a husband who expressed his feelings openly and made her the center of his life." Rose shook her head. "From the beginning, the expectations she had of Tony were impossible. In the end, the gap between her fantasies and the reality of her marriage nearly destroyed them both."

Rose Gallagher, Tony judged, was not prone to melodrama. "General McCarran," he observed, "doesn't strike me as easily derailed."

"He's not. But Mary was a force all her own." Rose's tone became ironic. "You've heard all the clichés about army wives, I'm sure. Many are true. My father was a two-star general, and my mother helped make him one. When you marry an officer with ambitions, she told me more than once, you find that he's really married to the army and that you're the other woman. You get the time that's left after he's met his spousal obligations.

"I was prepared for that. To succeed, you enjoy the time your husband can give and fill the void with family and whatever activities the army offers wives." She angled her head, attuned to Terry's thoughts. "That sounds antiquated, I know. But back then most officers' wives didn't dream of working. Your job was to help your husband rise as far and as fast as he could. For Tony, nothing less than the top would do. That was another way in which Vietnam defined him."

"How so?"

Her gaze became distant, pensive. "I don't believe Tony thought he'd survive the war. Instead, Jack was the one who died. After that, I think Tony felt impelled to fulfill the potential that his father and grandfather *and* Jack, by dying, never could. When you're from a line of heroes, that means achieving nothing less than the highest rank the army has to offer." She shook her head in wonder. "Whatever it took, Tony did—not just combat but eighteen-hour days, six to seven days a week. Success was non-negotiable. And now he's very close to achieving all his dreams—head of the Joint Chiefs of Staff, apex of our military. Unless this tragedy takes it from him."

"It shouldn't," Terry responded. "Viewed rationally, Brian killing your son-in-law has nothing to do with that."

"I hope you're right. Tony has wanted this so badly for so long, and at several points Mary nearly lost it for him." She paused, studying his face. "How old are you, Captain Terry?"

"Thirty-one."

"Then you may not know that once it was common practice to include positive comments on spouses in an officer's fitness report. If there was nothing good to say, nothing was said—which screamed that the wife was a real problem. Everyone knew of cases where a superbly qualified officer lost a command to a man not quite as good, when the only apparent reason was a woman who had come unglued. A few men tried to keep their wives hidden from view, like Mrs. Rochester in *Jane Eyre*. It never worked."

"That sounds like a lot of pressure on everyone."

"It was. But some women stepped up to the challenge. They could function as a single parent—disciplinarian, leader, shopper, and car pool driver—while their husbands were at war or on an assignment somewhere else. They could bond with other wives to find common values or sort out common problems. They could deal with dislocation, the uprooting of an entire household." Rose looked at Terry intently. "For someone like Tony McCarran, there's no such thing as maintaining a balance between career and family. For the right couple, the rewards can be great. But the demands can be hard on new marriages, and young families. There's a high divorce rate, a fair amount of infidelity, and more depressed or damaged children than anyone cares to admit. Some women fall apart."

"Like Mary McCarran."

Rose nodded slowly. "She was a striking blonde, used to attention, who resembled Brian much more than Meg. She was also very high-strung. Three early miscarriages made that worse—even though I was a widow, it was plain she envied me for having Kate so easily. All too often the sight of a pregnant woman would upset her to the point of spite. Empathy was not her strongest quality."

Nor, it seemed clear, had Rose Gallagher much liked her. "How was she as a mother?" Terry asked.

Rose gave him a sour smile. "Empathy," she responded, "would have been particularly helpful there. But Mary believed that having Meg would make her feel whole. It didn't. That was when she began to drink in earnest—in private and, later, in public. One never knew where or when her inner Zelda Fitzgerald would emerge." Rose's tone became quieter and sadder. "Tony tried to be patient. He's a devout Catholic, as am I—leaving the marriage was out of the question for him. But I knew how angry he was beneath his surface calm, and knew that she'd get no better.

"She never did. As a mother she was volatile and erratic—losing her temper for no reason, forgetting birthday parties or play dates, passing out when she was supposed to pick her children up at school. The impact was worse on Meg—in fact, I believe it shaped her. She was the oldest, the one who learned to call me if Mary didn't show up, the one who started remembering things so Mary wouldn't forget, the one who watched out for Brian when Mary failed. Mary McCarran turned her sweet-natured baby daughter into a small adult."

"Did the general understand that?"

"As best he could. Tony's a kind man, at times a very sweet one—though I suppose few people really see that. He was always solicitous of Kate and tried to serve as a substitute father." Her voice softened. "I'm sure fatherhood was strange for him. He was the first McCarran in three generations to actually *be* a father, as opposed to a myth who'd impregnated his wife before dying."

Listening, Terry thought of Rose's own husband, even as he absorbed that, for her, Tony deserved more compassion than did his wife. "Tony," Rose continued, "experienced his father only in terms of abstract values—courage, honor, fidelity to God and his country. He tried to pass those on to his children. But, as individual people, I think they often mystified him—Meg most of all. Tony had imagined creating a model military family, not the family he had."

"Which also made things harder for Mary, I assume."

"Oh," Rose said dryly, "I'm not unsympathetic. But where I found community among the wives, she saw gossip and negativity, even when it wasn't there. Most of us tried to support her: no one wanted to see Tony McCarran's wife stumble and fall. But the monthly luncheons, the scholarship fund-raisers, the holiday crafts fairs—it all drove her insane.

"At bottom Mary, like Tony, was deeply lonely. But Tony had his work. Unhappy wives drink or turn to other men. The whole truth about Mary didn't emerge until the end. But it was clear to everyone that she'd turned away from Tony and her children." Rose's tone took on the weight of memory. "Over time, Meg came to be much as she is now—serious, determined, self-reliant. Brian was more obviously vulnerable. I remember him as a solitary little boy who looked up to his father but kept his thoughts to himself. He learned at a pretty young age to rely more on Meg than on either of his parents."

"What role did you and Kate fulfill?"

A mirthless smile played on Rose's lips. "A highly relevant inquiry, if I follow your train of thought. But Kate's role in their lives was far less complex than mine. Especially before Kate went to college, she'd watch them quite a lot, or drive them somewhere when I couldn't—Brian more than Meg. She had a gift for listening to him, and Brian talked to her more openly than he did to adults. Later on, I suppose he might have had an adolescent crush on Kate." Her voice flattened. "But nothing more. Long before she married Joe, Brian had come to see her as an older sister."

For the first time, Terry noted, Rose looked vaguely uncomfortable. "My role," she added slowly, "was more ambiguous. As time went on, Tony asked me to keep an eye on Mary and the children. No one spoke of it; everyone knew. Mary despised me for it. But I hadn't supplanted her in Tony's bed. If there was a problem, and Tony was gone, most people knew to call me."

"What kind of problem?" Terry asked.

Rose was quiet for a moment. "They usually involved alcohol," she answered. "The worst of them was the last."

IT BEGAN WITH A late-night call from Betty Kramer, the wife of the commanding general's chief of staff. Mary McCarran had nearly crashed into the guardhouse at the main gate; too drunk to drive, she was also too belligerent to accept that. "She's creating a scene," Betty said in apology. "Tony's in Germany, I guess you know. We were hoping you could take her home and look in on the children."

Rose felt torn between her loathing for Mary's selfishness and pity for Meg and Brian—reserving, she silently acknowledged, a little for herself. "Of course," she said. "I'll call if I need help."

Throwing on slacks and a sweater, she ran a comb through her hair, jumped in the car, and took the highway to the main gate. Caught in the pitiless light surrounding the guardhouse, Mary McCarran leaned against her station wagon for balance with a soldier hovering over her, looking like a refugee trapped at a border crossing.

Rose parked a few yards back. For a moment, Mary did not see her, and then humiliation filled her eyes. The overhead light made her thin face look haggard, accenting the unhealthy pallor beneath a little too much rouge. With a jolt, Rose felt that she was looking at an X-ray of the future, a woman becoming old before her time. The soldier beside her, out of his depth, gave Rose an imploring look before backing away.

Softly, Rose said, "I've come to drive you home, Mary. We can get the car tomorrow."

Angrily, Mary swiped at a strand of hair that had fallen across her face, as though to restore her own composure. "Who called you?" she demanded in a surprisingly lucid voice.

"Don't humiliate yourself in public," Rose said evenly. "Too many people depend on you—"

"Tony?" Mary burst out. "Tony just wants a broodmare. *You* could do that for him."

Rose wanted to slap her. More softly yet, she said, "No doubt Meg's waiting up for you. Try to give her some semblance of a mother, instead of a narcissistic bitch."

The unaccustomed harshness seemed to startle Mary as much as it did Rose. The wildness in her eyes dulled. "So you're not a plaster saint."

Rose glanced toward the guard, standing like a statue fifteen feet away. "Not at all," she said quite calmly. "Personally, I no longer care whether you live or die. Your family may. Too bad they get so little from you."

Perhaps it was her own self-control, Rose thought, that prompted Mary to draw herself up, as though to match her in dignity and height. "I'll let you play your role," she said. "Your little, pitiful role—Tony's shadow spouse. Drive me home."

Rose did not trust herself to speak. Instead, she angled her head toward the car. As though to assert her freedom of will, Mary walked ahead of her, tripping as she reached the car. Opening the door, she tumbled into the passenger seat.

Rose slid behind the wheel. Inside the car, Mary smelled of whiskey and tobacco—when drunk, she became a chain-smoker, snatching cigarettes from whoever had them. "God," she said in a long exhalation of breath. "What's happened to us."

The change of mood unsettled Rose. "I don't know."

Mary stared out the windshield as Rose drove, the grounds of Fort Bolton, dark and silent, enveloping them. "The army," she announced with the sententiousness of drink. "Vietnam. Our husbands died in Vietnam."

"No," Rose snapped. "Jack did. Seventeen years ago, you got back a man who is still worth loving."

Mary turned to her. "And who does Tony love? Besides the army?"

Rose was afraid to answer. "Well," Mary said in a bitter voice. "No matter, anymore. Tonight I was with a man who gives me what I want."

Rose parked in front of the Irish Georgian house with the nameplate "Colonel Anthony McCarran." There was a light on in the living room. Turning to Mary, Rose said, "No one can, Mary. You're a black hole of need, and you're sucking your family in with you. You might consider giving them a break."

Lips parted, Mary gave her a long stare in which pain and anger were so commingled that Rose wanted to turn away. Without speaking, Mary left the car.

Rose watched her tread the brick walk to the house, a solitary figure on unsteady feet. As she neared the door, it opened. Meg had waited up for her.

Rose could not see the girl's face. But by now she knew Meg's expression by heart, the sad mixture of uncertainty and hope with which she so often greeted her mother. Rose's heart filled with pity for this lonely girl. Who, she wondered, would Mary McCarran destroy first—her husband or her daughter?

SITTING ACROSS FROM TERRY, Rose Gallagher briefly closed her eyes.

"It never came to that," she told him in a parched voice. "Two weeks later, when the children were in school, Mary took a kitchen knife and slashed her wrist to the bone. When Meg found her, she was dead." Seeing Terry wince, she added, "I suppose you didn't know."

Mute, Terry shook his head, a current of horror and pity running through him. He found himself imagining the moment of discovery, yet shrinking from its details. In that instant, he began to understand Meg on a visceral level, changing how he saw her. "I've thought about that awful time so often," Rose said quietly. "Our last conversation; Mary's suicide. Its impact on the children—especially Meg. She'll never forget that moment for the rest of her life." She settled back in her chair, as though to reclaim a certain neutrality of feeling. "It changed her. After that I saw a fear of becoming like her mother, a deep ambivalence about the military, and an aversion to depending on anyone. And, beneath the surface, a feeling of responsibility for Mary's suicide. Meg takes responsibility for anything McCarran."

"So do you, it seems."

Rose smiled, a brief movement of lips. "True. But I didn't build a fortress around myself. Meg became afraid to trust—except for Brian and, to some extent, Tony. At some level, I think she's angry at both her father and her mother, and her defensive feelings about Brian are also a surrogate for that anger. But don't expect Meg to tell you that."

"I won't," Terry answered. "With Meg, I sometimes feel like I'm walking through a minefield, and don't know where the trip wires are. Including her relationship to all the rest of you."

"It's complicated," Rose concurred with a trace of sadness. "But don't misunderstand me. Meg also loves her father immeasurably, and still craves his approval. That's part of Mary's legacy, as well. From the day Meg found her body, she tried to be the best girl in the world."

"What about General McCarran?"

Rose's eyelids lowered, lending her a thoughtful air. "Tony had his faith to fall back on. Add to that the experience of combat: part of Tony's job in Vietnam was to kill Vietnamese. And he did.

"I counsel children, not soldiers. But combat involves coping with hard things by repressing them. I know that Tony felt a terrible guilt about Mary's suicide, complicated by an anger just as strong." She hesitated. "Perhaps I shouldn't tell you this. But one night shortly after Mary's death, when the children were in bed, he got truly drunk for the only time I ever saw. He sat beside me, staring into the fireplace, and said that he'd wished her dead for years. Men like Tony don't take those feelings to a psychiatrist. They kill them."

She said this with such finality that Terry felt shaken. "How did that affect the family?" he asked.

"In some ways, it made them closer—the McCarrans closed around their own hurt. And beneath Tony's iron discipline is a reservoir of sweetness." Pausing, Rose studied the wedding picture that captured Meg's artificial smile. "I think Meg felt that. But she kept looking for more than Tony could give her—in part because of what his life had made him, in part because he was so often unavailable. So her love of Tony is marbled with resentment over Mary's death, and the death of her own childhood."

"And Brian?"

"Received most of the attention Tony could bestow. Brian alone could redeem the failure of Tony's marriage by carrying on the McCarran tradition. At least that's how I saw it."

"High expectations."

Rose's smile suggested irony rather than amusement. "Perhaps placed on the wrong child. Meg was the resilient one, with an extroversion and assertiveness that concealed her scars, perhaps even from herself. Brian's good looks and quiet manner always drew others to him. Still, Brian was lonely and—unlike Meg—he knew it. But he would never buck his father, any more than he was capable of truly knowing him.

"It really struck me on the Christmas before Brian applied to the academy. I helped host a party for Tony, and one of his oldest friends from Vietnam took a shine to Brian. He sat there, drink in hand, regaling Brian with stories of all that Tony had done, especially in times of war. It was a Scheherazade's bounty of wonders Brian had never dreamed of, related by a man whom Brian had not known existed yet whose relationship to Tony seemed closer than Brian's own. It was as if, to Brian, his father had become as much a myth as the dead McCarrans who had preceded him." Rose shook her head. "I recall Kate listening, too. But she didn't expect to have known these things—hearing them only increased her adoration for Tony, a substitute father figure for a girl who craved one. For Brian, they increased the burden of being Tony's son."

"Yet Brian and Kate were close."

"Always." Briefly, Rose smiled in recollection. "When Brian was commissioned, Kate said she could look right through Brian's uniform and see the boy she used to read aloud to. Brian draws adoration without trying. It's his gift—or was."

Terry watched her face. "And Kate and Meg?"

"Were different. No doubt there was real affection. But I think Meg saw Kate as competition for what little Tony had to give. Both of them wanted a father."

"Is that why Kate was drawn to Joe?"

A veil of caution fell across Rose's eyes. "One can surmise all sorts of things," she said, "but you don't challenge a daughter's pride by asking. At least not Kate's."

This suggestion of a certain distance between mother and daughter, Terry thought, might conceal a reticence of Rose's own. "You must have an impression," he replied.

"An indirect one—it all happened rather quickly." Rose folded her hands. "They met at the Christmas party I just mentioned. Kate was visiting home from New York City; Joe was a newly commissioned second lieutenant, a friend of someone's friend. He went for Kate like a laser—whatever Joe lacked in subtlety, he made up for in resolve. I was never certain he was a match for her, and Tony wondered, too. But Kate seemed overcome, as though Joe's drive and determination lent him a certain authority.

"As so often, the army played a role. It doesn't recognize girlfriends or even fiancées. The only woman who can follow an officer is his wife. Kate became that in six months."

Terry waited for a moment. "What did Brian think of Kate's marriage?"

Rose hesitated. "Perhaps he told Kate," she finally answered. "But I can only guess. Joe was combative and competitive, a blunt instrument who tended to bark out words without reflection. Everything Brian was not. But I never sensed any jealousy or friction."

Terry sat back. "I'd like to ask you about Kate's marriage," he told her. "That may be sensitive, I know. But it's at the heart of what Brian and Kate told the CID and what they're investigating now. I need to understand that."

Rose gave him a long, considering look. "What does Kate say?"

"Among other things, that Joe struck her on the face repeatedly and once held a gun to her temple. And that she didn't tell anyone for fear of ending his career."

For an instant Rose appeared shaken. "When Joe came back from Iraq," she said at length, "he was palpably different—silent and volatile by turns. That much I knew. But if I'd known what you just told me, all of this never would have happened. I care more about my daughter and grandchildren than any officer's career. Look at what's come of *that*.

"Missing parents are a theme here, Captain Terry. For Tony and Kate, a father; for Brian and Meg, a mother. Now there's Mathew and Kristen. For children, that's not the way it's meant to be."

Terry paused again, parsing his emotions. "Brian *did*

know," he said. "As they both tell it, that's what precipitated his confrontation with Joe."

"I see." Her lips parted again, as though to add something. She did not.

"For the CID," Terry went on, "that raises other questions. After Joe and Brian returned from Iraq, do you think Brian's relationship with Kate changed?"

Rose met his eyes. "How do you mean, Captain?"

"Whatever you think. Anytime I raise that question within the family, the person I'm asking becomes edgy."

"Perhaps because you're so obviously implying an affair. I simply can't imagine that."

"For Kate and Brian, Mrs. Gallagher? Or just for Brian?"

"For both of them," she answered tartly. "Which is all that matters here."

"Not to me, I'm afraid. Was Kate involved with someone else?"

Rose stared at him. "Why do you assume that my daughter would have told me?"

"Did she?"

Rose steepled her fingers. "Kate told me once that I was always perfect. It was not a compliment. One doesn't share their imperfections with the perfect."

"That's not quite an answer, Mrs. Gallagher."

"It *is* an answer—mine." Rose spoke more softly. "You seem like an empathetic man, Captain Terry. Perhaps even a good one. But you'll be leaving us soon. And what good would it do you or anyone to know more than you do now? I don't want my grandchildren hurt any further; I don't want this family hurt any further. By which I mean the McCarrans, the Gallaghers, *and* the D'Abruzzos. I hope you can respect that."

Terry stood. "Let's say I understand it. And I certainly respect you. Thank you for your time."

Rose extended a cool, dry hand. "I do want to help Brian, in whatever way I can. It's best for everyone that this end soon."

"Including for me," Terry answered. "I don't like unfinished business."

PART TWO

THE REFERRAL

JULY 2005

1

ON THE FOLLOWING MONDAY, at Major Flynn's request, Paul Terry went to the trial counsel's office. From the outset, Terry sensed that Flynn was toying with him.

Passing him a steaming cup of coffee, Flynn said, "You should take another run at Brian McCarran."

"On what subject?"

With his harshly angled face and bleak, watchful eyes, Flynn had the accusing aspect of a bitter saint. "Among other things, the murder weapon. We've found your client's fingerprints on the magazine."

This was not what Flynn had called him for, Terry knew at once. He said nothing.

"No reaction?" Flynn asked.

"None. After D'Abruzzo threatened his wife, Brian checked the magazine to see if it was loaded. Both he and Kate said as much to the CID."

Flynn shook his head briskly, an expression of impatience. "That assumes they're credible. Another interpretation is that he took the Luger and the bullets from D'Abruzzo's town house, then loaded the gun himself, preparing to shoot D'Abruzzo in a premeditated ambush."

Shrugging, Terry asked, "Are Brian's fingerprints on the bullets?"

The glint that surfaced in Flynn's green eyes converted the ascetic to a tactician. "They're hard to lift. We found partial prints; they could have been McCarran's or D'Abruzzo's."

"Then your theory's stillborn, Major."

He would not ask, Terry decided, if Flynn had anything more. After a moment, Flynn said, "I understand you spoke to Lauren Scott."

Steeling himself, Terry simply nodded.

"Then you know that Mrs. D'Abruzzo was having an affair."

"I know she needed a babysitter."

Flynn leaned forward, elbows resting on his desk. "She took a room at the Marriott about five miles from here. She gave them cash, of course, so her husband wouldn't see it on her credit card. But since 9/11 you have to show ID. So the room was registered to Katherine D'Abruzzo."

A kaleidoscope of thoughts flashed through Terry's mind. "I assume you questioned people at the hotel."

Flynn nodded, closely watching Terry's expression. "And showed them photographs. They identified Kate D'Abruzzo."

Terry cocked his head. "But not Brian McCarran."

"No," Flynn conceded in a matter-of-fact tone. "But they recognized Joe D'Abruzzo."

The sheer surprise of this threw Terry off balance. Casually, he said, "Maybe they were escaping the kids."

"*She* was. But her husband surprised her. A bellhop saw him waiting in the lobby. When Mrs. D'Abruzzo got off the elevator, he confronted her. A quarrel ensued, and then the two of them left separately." Flynn's tone became cool and prosecutorial. "She'd checked in there several times before. She was having an affair, and her husband knew it. This puts a very different complexion on the family dynamic. As well as on all the events she and Lieutenant McCarran described—her quarrels with D'Abruzzo, Brian taking the murder weapon, the critical phone calls, her husband's fatal visit to your client's apartment. Not to mention McCarran's credibility."

Terry feigned indifference. "At most," he countered, "it suggests that D'Abruzzo may have had other grounds for holding a gun to Kate's head. But nothing tells me that Brian was the reason."

Flynn stared at him, then stood, a gesture of dismissal. "Ask him again, Captain. Once a lie is embedded in a defendant's story, it begins to fester. Eventually it putrefies."

Terry could imagine the vultures circling. "I'll hold the thought," he answered. "But so far I can't smell a thing."

But he could. At least one person had lied to him. Perhaps more.

"I EXPECT TO BE lied to," he told Meg harshly. "But I can't accept knowing less than Flynn does. Not that this is personal. It's your brother who'll get fucked."

She stared at him, lips parting, her eyes reflecting alternating currents of anger and uncertainty. The confines of his office felt hot and close.

"Tell me what I'm missing," he demanded. "You know these people. That's what you're supposed to be good for."

"This is about Kate, not Brian." The tremor in her voice betrayed her struggle for self-control. "What makes you think I know?"

Terry forced himself to play this out. "Don't spit back my bullshit to Flynn," he snapped. "If Kate was screwing someone, Brian knew it. The only question is whether she had to tell him anything."

Meg was silent for an instant. Softly, she answered. "Spare me the fake outrage, Paul. Before you start accusing anyone, let's go to the Marriott. Until we do, you still don't know as much as Flynn."

Terry's instinct was to confront his client at once. But perhaps she was right—details could be telling. "Then let's go," he said.

Meg stood, squaring her shoulders, walking ahead of him to the door with a swift, determined stride. For a moment, as Rose Gallagher had said, she looked like the best girl in the world and, perhaps, the most lonely.

THE DESK MAN AT the Marriott, a friendly sort who knew this must be trouble, identified Kate from a snapshot in Meg's wallet. But he recognized neither of the men who flanked her—Joe D'Abruzzo and Brian McCarran. Pointing to a slight Hispanic man in a bellhop's uniform, he said, "Ask José. He's the one who knows about this."

Stationed by the door, the bellboy was watching their conversation. As they approached, his doelike eyes regarded them with distinct unhappiness. He did not like trouble either or, perhaps, authority figures in uniforms. Terry wondered if he had his green card.

Up close, he seemed very young, with a downy mustache that underscored his lineless face. Quietly, Terry introduced himself and Meg. Then he steered José Calvo to a corner sitting area with a table and three chairs. Sitting between them, Calvo hunched forward, quiet and attentive. Terry slid Meg's snapshot across the table. "Do you recognize any of these people?" he asked.

Gazing at the photograph, Calvo slowly nodded, placing a fingertip on Kate's face, then her husband's. "The lady. And him."

"Not the blond man?"

"No. That's what I told the others."

"What else did you tell them?" Meg asked.

Calvo seemed to squirm, becoming slighter. Finally, he said, "I don't like seeing people fight."

Meg, Tony noticed, knew to remain silent until Calvo explained himself. "Too much like my parents," he murmured.

As ALWAYS, JOSÉ WAITED near the door, looking toward the entrance or the elevators for anyone needing help with luggage. When the elevator door opened, he felt immediate disappointment. She was certainly a pretty woman. But he had seen her here in the afternoon, several times before. Always she carried only a purse—no business for José; only monkey business for the lady. He was about to turn away when she froze near the elevator, staring at something that seemed to rob her of speech or movement. The stricken look on her face stirred a sorrow in José's soul.

The man was a soldier, standing with his arms crossed, his expression of confusion and fury too much like José's father's. But his movements when he went for her, heavy-muscled yet catlike, had a quality José had never seen.

At the corner of his vision, an elevator door slid open. An old woman with two heavy suitcases looked about for assistance. José hesitated, then went to help. He passed the man and woman, a few feet from him. Her face was pale, his contorted; both were heedless of José. In a low, savage voice, the man told her, "I saw him, you cunt."

Too much like his parents. Smiling nervously at the old lady, José hoped she had not heard.

EVEN THE MEMORY MADE Calvo seem miserable. Studying Kate's picture, he said, "I wanted to help this lady. But I couldn't. Maybe the man had a right to his anger."

Meg, too, looked miserable. "Had you seen him before?" she asked.

Calvo shook his head, still looking at the photograph. "We see soldiers all the time here," he said slowly. "They sort of look alike to me. But this one I'd remember. He scared me just by how he walked."

On the drive back to Bolton, Meg seemed to concentrate so deeply that she receded within herself. Her head was bowed, and her thoughts opaque save for the worry written on her face. Terry's own concern was simple: If not Brian, who? But the problem hardly ended there.

WHEN BRIAN CAME THROUGH the door of his quarters, returning from his first interview with Dr. Blake Carson, Meg and Terry had been waiting in his living room for over an hour. Looking from one to the other, Brian said to Meg, "It's a good thing you called me, sis. Otherwise I'd have shot you. Sadr City, you know."

Though he tossed off this mordant remark casually enough, Brian's handsome face looked weary. Gently, Meg asked, "How was it with Dr. Carson?"

Brian sat across from them. "Not going *there*," he said softly. Terry could not tell if "there" meant Iraq or his meeting with Carson. It was not even clear that he was addressing Meg.

Abruptly, Terry asked, "Who was Kate's lover?"

At once Brian was alert, looking directly at Terry. In an even voice, he said, "Meg already asked me."

"Now *I* am. And don't even dream of telling me you don't know. In the McCarran-Gallagher family, your filial bond is the stuff of storybooks. It's all I ever hear."

Brian glanced at Meg. Then, to Terry's complete surprise, he flashed a smile no less captivating for its irony. "Families love their stories, don't they? Sometimes they're even true, though not as often as you'd like. That's why Norman Rockwell is the great American artist."

"Not in my family," Terry retorted. "All I want from you is the truth."

Brian regarded him in silence. Slowly and succinctly, he said, "It wasn't me, Captain Terry."

"Then who?"

"That's Kate's business, isn't it?"

"Not anymore. Now it's Flynn's—and mine. If Kate had a lover—no matter who it was—you knew that when you took D'Abruzzo's gun."

Brian held Terry's gaze. Calmly, he asked, "Why is that?"

"You'd known her your entire life. In the last few months, you saw each other once a week. She told you about Joe hitting her. She turned to you when she needed protection. And yet Kate didn't tell you she had a lover or that Joe knew that?" Lowering his voice, Terry demanded, "Tell me what you're hiding, Brian."

Brian's face became stone. After a moment, he said, "Were you ever ashamed of anything, sir?"

Terry hesitated. "Now and then."

"Then maybe, at least once, you were too ashamed to talk about it. Even—or especially—to the people who think they know you best."

Behind the mask, Brian's blue eyes held a seriousness so profound that Terry wondered if he was speaking about Kate or about himself. "A man's dead," Terry retorted. "What you're talking about is a luxury."

Terry felt Meg watching them, as still as a caught breath. Then Brian broke the silence. "Not to me," he answered simply. "I didn't plan to kill Joe D'Abruzzo. That's the only truth that matters to me. Or should matter to you."

Terry stared at him. At length, he said, "Maybe you'll tell the next guy, Brian. Hopefully before it's too late."

Without looking at Meg, or awaiting an answer, Terry walked out the door. He stood on the sidewalk in the soft light of early evening, watching officers and soldiers drive home from work. He felt Meg behind him, just before she touched his arm.

"I'm sorry I can't help you," she said quietly. "But Brian's an honest person. I know that he has reasons for whatever he chooses not to say."

Though surprised at Meg's touch, Terry shook his head. "This is suicide in slow motion, Meg. I hope you can change his mind."

Meg's fingers slipped away. Their drive back to her hotel was silent, Terry struggling to sort out his thoughts and feelings. Once or twice Meg glanced at him but said nothing.

2

THE NEXT MORNING, Terry got up at five a.m. and drove in darkness to the Fort Bolton Athletic Center.

Almost no one was there. He took the basketball out of his locker and went to one of several courts, the thud of his sneakers echoing in the barnlike structure. His sleep had been broken by the dream of his father; now, trying to sort out his troubled thoughts, he played the solitary game his father had devised for him.

It was before their family had lost everything. Paul was ten, intent on sharpening his shooting eye. So Frank Terry had bolted a hoop to the garage and marked ten spots along the driveway, creating an oval from one side of the basket to the other—which Paul followed from one spot to the next, taking a shot from each. His goal, all the more special because it was so seldom reached, was to sink ten shots without missing. Paul would try every morning before school when the weather was good; on most mornings his father would drink coffee and watch him from the porch. On Paul's first morning of perfection, his father, proud and not entirely teasing, had suggested he might go to Notre Dame on a basketball scholarship. Even then Paul sensed that finances were tight; within three years, his father was dead, and the bitter truths that emerged opened the fault line in his life. Walled off from him by her own evasions, his forlorn mother had turned to God. Paul had turned inward.

Now, as he remembered Frank Terry, his thoughts of his father's death merged with his reflections about Meg McCarran. Since his conversation with Rose Gallagher, Terry realized, he understood Meg far better than he had allowed her to know. But the shock of recognition, uncomfortable in its resonance for Terry, did not make decoding the McCarrans any simpler.

His first shot clanged against the iron rim. "There's something I'm not getting here," he had told Colonel Dawes the day before. "Not just whatever Brian isn't saying. There's a missing piece, one that has to do with family. And I can't grasp what it is."

Sitting with Paul at the Officers' Club, Dawes had sampled his bourbon, tasting the first sip with obvious relish. "Your instincts are pretty good, Paul. You've always been more than a by-the-numbers lawyer—you have a deeper sense of people. Trust that." At that moment Terry had realized how deeply he would miss Harry Dawes.

His second shot fell through the net without touching metal.

Brian was lying to him—or, at the least, concealing something painful. Perhaps others were, as well. What Terry did not know was whether this had anything to do with Joe D'Abruzzo's death.

Were you ever ashamed of anything? Brian had asked him. But Terry could not decipher what—or even who—had surfaced this elliptical reference.

He missed the next shot, a metaphor.

TWO HOURS LATER, PAUL Terry and Meg McCarran sat with Dr. Blake Carson in the corner of a Starbucks in Bethesda. Looking at Meg, Carson said, "What I have to tell you isn't news—your brother is in tough shape. To say the least, his psychic defenses are elaborate. But he's also quite self-aware: when I went through the behaviors you described—the twitchiness, the spacing out, the sudden spurts of anger—he pretty much copped to all of them. A couple of times he displayed a certain gallows humor and a keen sense of irony. I very much wish I'd known him before Iraq."

Meg was silent. "What about his nightmare?" Terry asked.

Carson put a curled finger to his lips. "When I asked him, all he said was that it's about Sadr City, that it makes no sense, that he really can't remember much. I pressed him for details, and finally he said something about a young Iraqi boy. In the dream, Brian reaches out to him, even though he knows the kid is dead."

Meg's eyes clouded. "Did you ask him what it meant, or whether it related to some actual experience?"

"Sure." Carson gave a brief shake of the head. "It was the damnedest thing—for a moment he closed his eyes, and the blood drained from his face. All he gave me was a riddle wrapped in a monotone, 'Dead kids can't explain themselves.'"

Terry felt a brief frisson. "That was all?"

"Yup. After that, he completely shut down. It was painful to watch." He turned to Meg. "Your brother has a core of toughness—he can still put one foot in front of the other. But he's haunted by something he won't—or can't—reveal. And as near as I can tell, he has almost no vision of the future. When I asked him how he saw his life in five years, he said, 'The same as it is now, except maybe in a military prison. Assuming the best.'"

Meg touched her eyes. "What did he tell you about combat?"

"Not much." Carson ran his fingers through his thick mane of hair, his expression puzzled and a little frustrated.

"When I asked about his worst experiences, he said, 'People dying. Gives me a lot to choose from.' But he wouldn't offer names or details."

"What about the scar on his neck?"

Carson puffed his cheeks. "That *was* weird. He sat back in the chair and gave me that incredible smile of his, like we were two pals sharing a joke. 'RPG damn near took my head off,' he told me. 'Another few inches, and I'd have joined the McCarran Hall of Fame. I just can't catch a break.' "

Meg turned away, gazing out at the street so that neither man could see her face. When she turned back to them, Terry saw a film in her eyes. "My impression," Carson told her gently, "is of a sensitive man who's in a great deal of pain. Unlike so many other vets, he doesn't drink in an effort to dull it. Your brother's still on the cross, Meg. Maybe that's what Brian thinks he deserves."

Meg gazed at her coffee. "You call Brian 'sensitive,' " Terry said to Carson. "Are some people predisposed to PTSD?"

"There's a lot of debate. Some analysts think that childhood experiences likely create a heightened vulnerability. Others believe that prewar variables can help account for some, but not most, of the occurrences of PTSD." He glanced at Meg. "Of course, your mother's problems with alcohol, and her ultimate suicide, must have been traumatic for him. Brian was nine, right?"

Meg glanced at Terry, her gaze suggesting discomfort that he knew about the manner of Mary McCarran's death. Then she slowly nodded. "Yes," she told Carson, "Brian was nine."

Carson pretended not to notice her reaction. "We talked a little about his childhood," he told her. "He said you were the best sister on the planet, and that Rose and Kate helped look after you both, especially when your dad was gone. All three of you are very important to him."

Meg looked too shaken to respond. For her sake, Terry pretended to watch the customers drifting in and out, the usual mix of business types, mothers who had just dropped off their kids, and students with part-time jobs. "What about the general?" he asked.

Carson wagged his head, eyes narrowing in thought. "In certain ways I think Brian feels like an orphan. I didn't know Mom, but to me she sounds depressed, maybe even paranoid, and not able to give her kids much emotional support. In contrast, Dad personifies dignity, strength, and honor. But he wasn't around that much.

"It's clear that Brian tried to identify with his father. What choice did he have? He was a male, and his mother had killed herself. But, because of that, Brian may also have felt that his father failed Mary the way he failed Brian himself. That sets up a fairly ambivalent relationship between Brian and General McCarran—Brian had no one else to emulate, yet your father set expectations without providing the warmth Brian craved. Which is more or less, I'd guess, what the general must have felt about his own father. Except that *his* absence was sanctified by death."

Terry saw Meg grimace. "You disagree?" he asked.

"I just don't think about it much." Turning to Carson, she said, "In your business, don't they call wallowing in the past 'counteradaptive'?"

Carson smiled a little. "So is ignoring it. In my book, people who wall off their past too often sleepwalk through their future. But we were talking about Brian."

After a moment, Meg nodded. "I understand," she said. "Given where Brian is now, this stuff matters."

"It surely does." Carson turned to Terry. "Take how pissed off Brian is at those dolts at the VA. That's genuine—

Brian clearly cares about his guys, and understands how war has hurt them. But his anger is also symbolic of his feelings toward the general. As with the general, he thinks the army expects these kids to perform wonders in Iraq but provides no support when they come back fucked up as a result."

Terry felt himself trying to imagine Brian's inner landscape. "So how does Brian see himself?"

Carson considered the question. "He didn't say much about Iraq. But my guess is that—as bad as it clearly was—Brian found an identity different from his father's. General McCarran succeeded by always completing the mission; quite consciously, Brian seems to have cared less about the mission than about his men."

"On what do you base that?"

"A couple of things," Carson answered in a contemplative tone. "Including what little he was willing to say about D'Abruzzo."

"Such as?"

"That Joe was 'leadership material,' for whom 'no sacrifice of others' was too great. Stated with less sarcasm, that encapsulates one of the classic problems of command. Great generals can't be impeded by sentiment."

Meg's clear blue eyes were fixed on Carson. "Joe," she said, "would have killed to be like my father."

Carson nodded. "Precisely my point. I may be out on a limb here. But if Brian resented your father, I think he saw D'Abruzzo as an ersatz General McCarran, a man with the general's willingness to sacrifice his soldiers but without the general's character or talent. That reduces D'Abruzzo to a mindless butcher, doubling down on Brian's resentment."

Terry stared at the psychiatrist. "That's not a suggestion I'd care to hear in public, Blake. Butchers deserve to die;

one could even see it as a mercy to others. I'd prefer that Brian took D'Abruzzo's gun out of deep concern for Kate. That squares with his concern for the defenseless."

Carson smiled. "You can relax, Paul. I'm free-associating here—I wouldn't stake my professional reputation on very much of what I've told you. Brian hasn't given me near enough to go on.

"The one thing I'm certain of is that Brian—like his father, I'd imagine—is exceptionally intelligent. But I don't see him as naturally aggressive, or even assertive, unless life presents him with a reason. Without the McCarran tradition, I doubt that he'd have considered entering the military."

Meg looked down. Quietly, she said, "I used to wonder if I could have stopped him. Now I wish that all the time."

"You're not responsible," Carson told her firmly. "Maybe a strong mother could have redirected him. But you weren't much older than Brian when she died. From then on, Brian had only one parent to define what kind of man he should be." He softened his voice. "I think Brian has struggled with the question of identity for most of his life. And PTSD is a profound blow to a soldier's sense of self—to his value system, and to his belief that he can control his life.

"I see these guys all the time. I keep encountering the same two questions: 'After what I did in war, do I deserve to be happy?' And 'After what I saw in war, can I believe in a world that makes moral sense?' It all comes down to 'Who am I now, and how can I live?' Brian has no answer."

Meg briefly shook her head, a twitch that suggested her distress. "What about D'Abruzzo?" she managed to ask. "Everything we know suggests that Brian *should* have been afraid that night."

Carson frowned. "As Paul points out, 'everything we

know' comes from Kate or Brian. There weren't any witnesses to their fights, and no one but Kate to say that D'Abruzzo hit her at all. In his case, I'm not diagnosing a living man, but someone else's version of a dead one."

Meg gave Terry a quick glance, as if to learn whether he had told Carson about the apparent fact of Kate's affair. Then she asked, "Aren't there other sources?"

"Who?" the psychologist inquired gently. "Joe's kids? His parents? Maybe you can find someone. But on the surface, his service record was problem-free."

"Still," Terry interjected, "combat stress from Iraq could explain the changes in behavior Kate describes: volatility, self-medication, withdrawal from his kids, and outbursts of anger that end in spousal abuse. As well as his withdrawal from sex."

Carson hunched forward, coffee cradled between his hands. "In the abstract, all of those could be symptoms, as could a profound emotional numbness. Time and again, I encounter feelings of hopelessness and an inability to express difficult thoughts or feelings—which could become our biggest problem when it comes to helping Brian."

"Brian doesn't fly into rages," Meg put in.

"Not that you've seen." Carson sat back, addressing both Terry and Meg. "But in combat veterans, exposure to unceasing violence can cause the circuitry of the brain to change. The result is a lack of inhibition of anger and blindness to the behavior that results. Take Joe as Kate describes him. Maybe he couldn't communicate with her because he had no gift for it or because what he felt was too wrenching to express. So Kate's demands for intimacy—physical *or* emotional—could have triggered explosions of anger aimed at making her stop. Assuming, again, that Kate's account is truthful."

Terry feigned a pensive look, as though something had

just occurred to him. "Suppose that D'Abruzzo felt threatened by his wife's relationship to Brian. How might he have reacted once Brian had, in the literal sense, 'disarmed him'?"

Carson's smile came with a raised eyebrow. "How phallic are we getting here? Are you positing an affair?"

Ignoring Meg, Terry responded blandly, "I'm wondering about anything that could have made D'Abruzzo resent the relationship. In Joe's headspace, a lifetime of closeness between his wife and another man could have felt threatening in itself."

Carson's amiable WASP features, concentrated in thought, gave him the earnest look of an altar boy confronting the possibility of sin. "If he literally thought his wife was betraying him, the impact could have been combustible. Again, if you believe Kate, consider the ingredients: anger; shame; rage; betrayal. And, quite possibly, sexual impotence. Now another man has taken his gun. If that's all mixed up with adultery—" The shrug with which Carson cut himself off suggested that the rest was obvious.

"Adultery aside," Terry answered, "the rest squares with Brian's story of events leading up to the shooting. D'Abruzzo was bigger, trained in martial arts, outraged to begin with, and disinhibited by alcohol. Brian says that Joe started a karate move that could have been instinctive. Brian had no time to think and only one means of protection: D'Abruzzo's gun. Which supports a claim of self-defense."

"Sure," Carson concurred. "But it *is* based on Brian's version of events—or his *perception* of events. My opinion is only as good as Brian's credibility. For example, I keep wondering why he let D'Abruzzo in, which perplexes me almost as much as Brian's lack of memory. I keep hitting the wall between supposition and everything I don't know, beginning with what happened to Brian in Iraq and how—in terms of specific parallels—it might relate to D'Abruzzo's death. If at all." Elbows resting on the table, Carson opened his palms. "And then," he said more slowly, "there *is* the whole question of anger. Brian's, that is."

"Meaning?" Meg asked.

"Self-defense is based on an objectively reasonable fear. An insanity defense, as Paul imagines it, rests on an unreasonable but genuine fear. Either way, fear is the basis. But you don't get to shoot somebody just because you're angry at him. A belief that D'Abruzzo was beating Kate didn't license your brother to kill him."

"Not even if he was afraid for her?" Meg protested. "Joe held a gun to her head."

Terry shook his head. "Flynn would say, 'That's why you call the MPs.' Or report D'Abruzzo for domestic violence, and ask the army to counsel him. Brian can't shoot him as a substitute. And, as Blake keeps pointing out, there's no evidence but Kate's word that D'Abruzzo ever hit her."

"What if Brian believed her, whether or not it was true?"

What struck Terry about the question was its tacit supposition that Brian could have been Kate's dupe, perhaps acting as a stand-in—or even a scapegoat—for an unknown lover. Then Terry remembered that José Calvo had overheard the dead man saying, *I saw him, you cunt.* "Same difference," Terry said at length. "Starting with the physical evidence, we're mired in ambiguity. Okay, there's a good chance D'Abruzzo was a tinderbox. We also think Brian suffers from PTSD, and you tell us he was strung out from lack of sleep. So both of them could have had trouble controlling anger, an oversensitivity to threat, and reflexes conditioned by combat under extreme conditions. Brian had a weapon; D'Abruzzo *was* one. It's hard to sort out fear from anger, or whose fear or anger it was."

Abruptly, Meg turned from him to Carson. "I hope we never see a court-martial," she said bluntly. "But if we do, and you're a witness, somebody's going to ask you whether Joe's death stems from something far more culpable than spontaneous combustion. Specifically whether—despite how damaged Brian is—he could be using PTSD to cover up his role as triggerman in a premeditated murder."

Carson threw up his hands, an exaggerated gesture meant to express his own frustration. "You might as well ask me how D'Abruzzo ended up facing the wall with a bullet in his back. Only Brian can answer that, and he says he can't remember. Which, by the way, I'm by no means ruling out." He softened his voice again. "Brian is literally a trained killer. But I don't easily leap to the conclusion that he's a cold-blooded one. Still, one huge X-factor here is his relationship with Kate, whatever it was, and whether that changed in the last six months.

"Was he afraid for her? Did he feel gratitude to her from childhood and protective of her now? Or had he come to feel something more passionate and possessive?"

"D'Abruzzo had lost interest in sex," Meg responded. "So now, despite whatever anyone says, you're wondering if my brother and Kate became lovers. Even though Brian told me he wouldn't date for fear of freaking out at night."

Carson was unfazed. "Ask a question, and I'll give you my best answer. I don't know shit about your brother's relationship to women, or even about his sexuality before *or* after Iraq. But it's Psych 101 to imagine that, in adolescence, he had sexualized feelings about Kate. Or even about you and Mrs. Gallagher—subconscious incest is the game the whole family gets to play. Of *those* feelings, the one most likely to survive would focus on the woman who isn't his sister, and is reasonably age-appropriate.

"On multiple occasions I've seen protectiveness ripen into sex, sometimes unleashing repressed desires strong enough to shatter the strongest barriers. That Brian and Kate are part of a quasi-family might not be enough to stop them, *or* that adultery is a sin in the army and your church. Your brother is a textbook case of repression: as a soldier, as a man, and as a member of the McCarran family, he's treated his own feelings as the enemy. But sometimes the defenses shatter, too."

Meg stared at him. "Brian's also a study in depression," Terry pointed out.

"True," Carson allowed. "And depressives usually don't make terrific lovers. I'm just looking at all the psychic angles." He turned to Meg. "I'm flying blind here. If what I'm up against with Brian is a matter of trust, not calculation, maybe we can make some headway in figuring out what happened—not only in Iraq, but that night in his apartment. Then we can go after why it happened. I'd like that, if for no other reason than that Brian's still alive. I don't want him to live in a prison, literally or emotionally."

To Terry's surprise, tears sprung to Meg's eyes. "All I want," she said, "is for Brian to be free." The weight she placed on "free" suggested more than a fear of prison.

AT TEN O'CLOCK THAT night, Terry put two cold bottles of Sam Adams in a bag, left his apartment, walked to the shadowy park across the street, and sat against the trunk of the thickest tree. Sipping from the first cold bottle, he felt the humid air on his skin and listened to the chirp of the crickets in darkness.

No one knew he did this. It was not the conduct of a military officer, but of a man conditioned by the feeling of loneliness and confinement that pervaded the tiny bungalow he and his mother had tried to keep after his father's death. It was the escape of a sixteen-year-old who would return from a date with girls who could never truly know him and, aware that his mother was sleeping, take a beer into their fenced backyard and numb himself in a reverie of cricket sounds and leaf-shrouded moonlight.

So much comes from family, he knew. His family had numbered only three; the two who remained were scarred in different ways. His mother relived the past; Paul burned with the fierce ambition to control his future beyond anyone's ability to take it from him. Law became his grail. Now, at last, he was skilled enough to go to New York and obliterate his past, paycheck by paycheck and trial by trial, using his firm's signing bonus to buy his mother a modest home and pay the last of his student loans. Three weeks left, all bound up with someone else's family.

He took a deep swallow of beer.

Neither Paul Terry nor his mother were hard to understand. Their trauma had been simple—the rest of their story was written by it. The McCarrans were different. Especially since meeting Rose, Terry saw them as locked in a complex web that, as one family member acted on another, enveloped them further. Meg, their protector, was at its center. In many ways, she was the most elusive of them all—by turns tough and vulnerable, bound to Brian by love and responsibility, yet deeply alone. Sometimes Terry sensed her wanting to reach out to him, then pulling back. He wondered if he imagined this.

Three more weeks. He would work this to the end; his creed was never to let up. That meant learning about the McCarrans, not just from what one or the other might say but from interpreting what he heard and sensed. He had learned from his father's death, and his mother's lies, how mutable truth could be.

He would find a way to use what Meg knew, and not just as a lawyer.

3

FOR THE FIRST FEW HOURS of the following day, Terry reviewed the history of Brian's battalion in Iraq. Around noon, he reflected for a moment, then telephoned Meg McCarran. "Can I take you to dinner?" he asked. "I keep thinking I should have asked you yesterday."

The allusion to her tears was unmistakable. In a tone that mingled embarrassment and reserve, she answered, "I'm okay. Really."

"Even better then. I've got a place picked out, and I'm sick of my own cooking."

A moment of silence followed. "All right," she answered more lightly. "Maybe Brian could use a break from me."

Imagining her dislocation from her home and career, Terry wondered how it felt to be entangled with her family, once again, after making her own life. "Pick you up at six," he said, and got off before she could change her mind.

VIDALIA WAS A BRIGHT restaurant with crisp white table-cloths and enough space between tables to encourage private conversation. Across the table Meg, though still lovely, looked like someone who'd had too little sleep and too much time with painful thoughts. That she found her emotions so difficult to acknowledge deepened Terry's sense of her aloneness. *Who takes care of you?* he wondered. But the answer seemed clear enough: no one.

Watching Terry observe her, she asked, "Why did you invite me to dinner?"

The mildness of her voice did not diminish the directness of the question or the caution behind it. "I owed myself," Terry said easily. "I canceled a reservation here when Colonel Dawes called me about Brian. You're the incidental beneficiary."

"What about your date?"

"She's back in Chicago. She was just here for the weekend."

Given all that Brian faced, Terry doubted that an aborted dinner would strike Meg as a tragedy. In a voice so dry it contained a trace of humor, she said, "Sorry about that."

"Don't worry too much," Terry answered philanthropically. "She and I are evolving into friends."

With a twitch at the corner of her mouth, she said, "Define 'evolving.'"

"It's complicated."

Her smile lingered. "Somehow I could have guessed that about you."

Their waiter arrived, soliciting drink orders. To Terry's surprise, Meg ordered a vodka martini, a trial lawyer's drink. When each had taken a first sip, Terry said, "The truth, okay? This has been awkward for both of us. You're scared for Brian; I'm used to being in charge. But I understand your feelings, at least as well as I can."

The guarded look in her eyes receded. "It has been hard," she allowed. "Most of it's fear for Brian. Some of it's just how I am, I'm afraid."

Terry nodded in recognition. "Most cases like this are hard for me to turn off—I'm too afraid that someone else will pay for what I missed. My mind keeps working until I wish I could escape myself."

Meg shook her head, as though answering the question Terry had not asked. "I've got no choice, Paul."

For a moment Terry imagined the twelve-year-old girl Rose Gallagher had described, made too serious too soon. "I know that."

The quiet that followed suggested a certain peace. After a time, Terry asked, "Mind if we talk about your family a little?"

Meg's eyes became hooded. "I thought you'd covered that with Rose."

In Meg's eyes, Terry knew, Rose had crossed an unspoken boundary, becoming his collaborator in something akin to betrayal. "Your family is distinctive," he answered. "As is its role in making Brian who he is. I can't worry about anyone else's sensitivities." He softened his tone. "Your domestic violence cases are family stories, Meg. To help the battered women you're protecting, you need to understand how they got there. No doubt the reasons are painful for them to share. But that can't stop you from asking."

Meg stared at the table, then briefly nodded, a silent concession. "We're a military family," she said at length. "No disparagement intended, but the army is like a cult—you're separated from the rest of the world. And the McCarrans are a kind of cult, as well." She looked up, meeting Terry's eyes. "Our cult has its own values—familial, martial, and religious. And our head's a living legend descended from dead heroes.

"In our own small way, we're like the Kennedys or the Bushes. I don't know what your dad was like, Paul. Somehow I don't imagine him saying at the dinner table, 'Terrys do this' or 'Terrys never do this.' But that's part of how Dad raised us."

"My dad never tried that," Terry responded simply. "It would have had no meaning."

Meg smiled a little. "After Brian was born, when Dad and I picked up Mom and the baby at the hospital, he took us home on McCarran Drive. I always knew the McCarrans were special, and that Dad had to live up to that—or die trying. Brian was right: by dying as heroes, Dad's father and grandfather hit the jackpot." Her voice became musing. "No one ever knew those men. They had no personalities, or frailties—just a legacy of courage and sacrifice, like the words of my great-grandfather's Medal of Honor citation. My father said that God had granted them the honor of dying for their country. It sounded strange until I realized that was all he had."

Beneath her veneer of self-reliance, Terry realized, Meg had contemplated her family far more than he had guessed. "How did that affect him growing up?"

"I wasn't there, of course. I do know that his father's friends encouraged him to enter the academy. But I don't think he ever doubted that the army was his destiny. Fortunately, God granted him the privilege of living. *And* the burden—to cope with, and pass on." Meg cut herself off, saying, "This must sound utterly demented to you. Not to mention completely self-absorbed."

"Not at all," Terry said. "My dad was an accountant, and I can still recite the words of his CPA certificate."

Meg surprised him by grinning. "Exactly my point. You've already decided that we're all completely nuts. That doesn't exactly promote self-revelation."

Terry smiled at this. "Every family," he assured her, "is nuts in its own way. Yours is just more interesting.

"Mine, like yours, was Catholic. God was a source of comfort and consolation, and He still pervades my mother's thoughts to a degree that resembles magical thinking. But *our* God never drafted us to be heroes. He had other things in mind."

Meg sipped her martini. After a time, she said, "I think we all imagine the God who meets our needs. Other than the photographs, my dad's most tangible legacy was the prayer book his father read from as a child. Dad uses it now. He still won't start his day without reciting the Daily Office, the Hail Mary, and the Glory Be.

"You could say he's just devout. But it's more than that. My grandmother told me that he began reciting those same prayers when he was six, the morning after learning of his own dad's death. These days I almost never hear him; he closes his bedroom door. But I know he's keeping a compact with his father."

Despite his skeptical feelings about religion, Terry found this story touching. "Too much certainty scares me," he told her. "I've always found the legend of your father's piety a little off-putting. This makes him far more human."

"Dad's very human," Meg said softly. "He's learned to hide that. But what causes the most harm is when he hides it from himself."

The enigmatic remark, Terry felt certain, did not allow for questions. Instead he asked, "How religious *is* your dad?"

"Very. In Dad's sensibility, religion and the military reinforce each other. Both venerate self-sacrifice and a sense of duty; both require obedience to higher authority." Meg's voice was soft and almost valedictory, as though the man she described no longer lived. "But there was nothing blind or mindless in what he felt. My father believed that only a clear-eyed adherence to rules could free us from selfishness and random impulse, allowing us to be better than our fallible nature might allow. Impulse led to misery."

"And so abortion—"

"Is the taking of a life created by God, which is not our

right as humans. Except, of course, for war in defense of freedom." She gazed at the table, frowning. "I learned early that abortion was a sin. So were adultery and divorce. A husband's or wife's duties included loyalty to their family, which depended on order to survive. To betray the family was to betray God."

Terry detected in her tone the faint discordance of bitterness and belief. "So if one of you committed adultery," Terry ventured, "or were gay, that would betray your father?"

Meg looked up at him. "We're talking about Brian, I assume. My father didn't say these things harshly; he's not a harsh man. It's simply what he believed to the depth of his soul. So rather than rebelling, we grew up wanting never to disappoint him. As his son, Brian felt this most of all." Meg's tone remained even. "I've got no evidence that Brian's gay. But I'm very sure he never slept with Kate. All I'm saying is that it was always hard for him to disappoint my father.

"I'm not sure you can ever understand what that feels like. Two things Dad said are with us still. The first is 'Character is who you are in the dark.' But the second was that we should always behave as though someone else was watching us. Dad meant God. But when we were young, we thought of Dad instead."

Terry tried to imagine feeling this about his father. Perhaps he could have, before his father's death. Now it was painful to remember his own innocence, and far easier to indulge his curiosity about Meg's family, and Meg herself. Cautiously, Terry asked, "How did your mother take that?"

The faint smile Meg gave him was no smile at all. "Rose already told you, Paul. Our mother resigned."

"I meant before that."

Meg studied him. "If you really want the flavor of things, I remember her saying, 'You're so impressive, Tony, when you chisel your marble tablets.' I'm sure she wanted to diminish him in our eyes. But she was way too drunk and fragile to resemble Dorothy Parker. Her most successful impression evoked Sylvia Plath."

Terry winced inside. "I'm sorry, Meg."

"For asking, or for what she did?"

"Both."

Meg drew a breath. "Outside the family," she said at length, "we never talked about it. We still don't. So this is hard for me."

This was ventured less as a rebuff, Terry sensed, than as a request for understanding that would also close the subject. For the rest of dinner, neither spoke of Mary McCarran.

WHEN TERRY SUGGESTED A nightcap, Meg hesitated, and then, to his surprise, accepted.

They sat in a shadowy corner of Vidalia's bar, swirling brandy in snifters. At the first harsh sip of amber liquid, Meg seemed to shiver. She put it down, staring past Terry, absorbed in unspoken thoughts. Suddenly, she asked, "Why are you so curious about me?"

"Am I?"

"Yes. I can read it in your face. Is that only about Brian?"

Terry paused, and then saw the truth before he spoke it. "No," he acknowledged. "Especially since I met with Rose."

She angled her head, giving him a quiet, probing look. "Did she tell you that I found her?"

"Yes." Terry hesitated. "I've been imagining how that felt."

"How can you, Paul?"

"Maybe I can't. But I was pretty young when my father died. That gives me a place to start."

Meg gazed into her brandy, as though watching her own memories resurface. With a detachment so complete that it seemed an act of will, she said, "It was different than you might think. Finding her was the beginning, not the end."

As often happened when her mother did not appear, Meg called Aunt Rose to take them home from school.

Brian sat in back, Meg next to Rose. It was a beautiful spring day and, except for worry about her mother, Meg felt happy. For the first time in sixth grade, her report card showed straight A's. She almost told Aunt Rose, except that she wanted to save it for her mother. If it was not too late, they could call her father in Germany.

Their house was unlocked. Brian went to his bedroom to dress for soccer practice. Meg hurried to her mother's bedroom, filled with excitement and trepidation. She hoped that her mother had not passed out.

The room was empty. Her clothes were strewn across the double bed; Meg barely noticed the envelope on her father's pillow. Knowing her mother's pleasure in warm baths, Meg slowly approached the bathroom door.

"Mom?" she called.

No answer. But she could see that the light was on through the crack beneath the door. Hesitant, she knocked, worried that her mom had fallen asleep in the bathtub.

Still no one answered.

The doorknob turned in her hand. For reasons she did not comprehend, Meg feared to step inside. She tried imagining that her mother was in her robe, perhaps drinking in silence at their kitchen table. But surely she would have called to them when she and Brian entered.

Slowly, Meg cracked open the door.

The first thing she saw was her mother's face, still and pale. Her long blond hair lay in glistening strands against the white of the bathtub. Only then did Meg grasp that the water was dark red.

Stomach knotting, Meg struggled to take in what she was seeing. Then she spotted the knife on the bath mat, its sharp edge tinged with blood. When Meg dared look at it again, the mask that was her mother's face said that her soul had left her body.

Reeling forward, Meg fell to her knees. She fought to stand again. On wobbly legs, she staggered from the bathroom without looking at her mother. Remembering Brian, she softly closed the door behind her.

She had to keep her brother from seeing this.

Frozen in the bedroom, she tried to narrow her thoughts to an image of Brian's face, still innocent beneath his tousled blond hair. Then she saw the vanilla square against her father's pillow. Edging toward the bed, she saw "Tony" on the envelope, written in her mother's perfect script.

Without quite knowing why, Meg put the letter in her backpack. She drew herself up and went to her brother's room.

He sat on the edge of his bed, his soccer uniform on, staring into space. Brian was a daydreamer; while dressing for school, he sometimes drove their father crazy by drifting so deeply into thought that he lost all track of time. She sat on the bed beside him.

"Mom's not feeling good," she told him. "We need to call Aunt Rose."

Her voice sounded synthetic, as though she were a recorded message. In profile, Brian's eyes clouded. But he was used to this; when they found their mother comatose,

Rose stepped in to help them. They never questioned why—Rose's compassion was a given, one thing they could rely on. If there was a problem, their dad had told Meg, Aunt Rose is there for you.

Briefly touching Brian's shoulder, Meg went to the kitchen and dialed Rose for the second time in an hour.

As always when Meg called, Aunt Rose sounded calm. "Is your mom not well?" she asked.

On any other day, Meg would have appreciated Rose's matter-of-factness, her willingness to spare Meg humiliation by acting as if her mother had the flu. Now she could not seem to deviate from the script. "Yes," Meg answered. "Brian has soccer practice."

"I'll come get him. Just make sure that Mr. Dreamy is ready."

When Meg hung up, she heard voices in the living room, then realized that Brian had turned on the TV. Going there, she asked him, "Hungry?"

Without turning from the screen, Brian shook his head. "Aunt Rose is coming," she told him. "She'll get you to practice."

Brian simply nodded. When Rose came to get him, Meg asked if she could come back to the house.

For an instant, Rose stopped to look at her. "Of course," she said. With her usual efficiency, she roused Brian from his torpor and steered him to her car.

The time until Rose returned seemed endless. Too stunned to cry, too sickened to move, Meg stayed on the couch.

When Rose came through the door, Meg flinched. Entering the living room Rose asked, "Can I make you a peanut butter sandwich?"

Meg gazed up at her. In a toneless voice, she said, "Mom's dead."

Rose stared at her, lips parting. "She's dead," Meg repeated. "I found her in the bathtub, all filled with blood. I didn't want Brian to see."

Rose's eyes closed. Almost seeming to collapse, she sat beside Meg, pulling her close as though to give, but also receive, comfort. For a moment, she stroked Meg's hair. "Wait here," Rose murmured.

She walked toward Mary's bedroom. Minutes later she emerged, quite pale, and went quickly to the kitchen. Meg heard her calling someone. When Rose returned, she said, "The military police are coming. We're going to my house. Kate will stay with you while I go get Brian. He'll never see your mother."

"What about Dad?"

"I'll call him. I'll tell Brian, too." Rose took her hands, adding softly, "No sister or daughter could do any more. It's my turn now."

Meg gave herself to Rose.

THAT NIGHT SHE SHARED a room with Brian. He cried himself to sleep. Tearless still, Meg kept thinking about the note.

She touched Brian's shoulder to herself make sure that he was asleep. Then she got up, turning on the lamp, and found her backpack on the dresser.

Meg withdrew the envelope.

She paused, fixated on her father's name. Then, with stiff, fumbling fingers, she opened it. There was only one sentence.

Now you can marry Rose.

Moments passed before Meg felt the tears running down her face. Mechanically, she opened her backpack, concealing the note that Brian could never see.

*   *   *

THE NEXT EVENING HER father returned from Germany.

He, too, stayed at Rose's town house near Fort Bolton. He looked older than Meg had remembered him. But he was unfailingly gentle. For once, he let Brian sleep with him.

Before that, he sat beside Meg on her bed, his gray-blue eyes regarding her with sadness. "I know how terrible that must have been," he said quietly.

Remembering her mother's waxen face, Meg could only nod.

Her father hesitated. "Your mother was very sick and very confused. It's no one's fault. But I know she loved you very much. Try to forgive her for what happened."

Meg swallowed. "Will you stay here to take care of us?"

Her father clasped her shoulders. "For two weeks, yes. Then Rose will look after you until I get back. She also loves you, Meg—very much."

Tears came to Meg's eyes. Touching her face, her father asked, "What is it, sweetheart?"

Mute, Meg went to her backpack. When she reached inside, she felt a tremor go through her, and hesitated. "What is it?" her father repeated.

She could not answer. All she knew was that she could no longer bear this alone. With relief and dread, she gave him her mother's note.

Reading it, her father blinked, and then his eyes became fixed. He was so quiet for so long that he seemed to have forgotten her. Then, in an instant, he became himself again. "Where did you find this?"

Despite the compassion in his voice, something in its quality implied that he was speaking to an adult. Perhaps it was this that made her response so level. "On your pillow," she said. "No one else has seen it."

Her father absorbed this. "She was sick," he told Meg.

"Maybe it was the alcohol. Her brain stopped working the way it should."

She waited for something more—an explanation or a denial. "You did right," her father continued. "This would only hurt your brother, and other people as well. No one else should know about this except for you and me. Can you do that for our family?"

Yes, Meg promised. She could.

As Meg finished, her face showed so little that Terry marveled at her gifts of repression, even as he fought to contain his muted horror. "Does Brian know about the note?" he asked.

"No."

Terry hesitated. "And Rose?"

"I don't know. We've never spoken of it."

Terry shook his head. "That's a lot to carry around, Meg. And a lot to place on a twelve-year-old."

"It wasn't his fault. *She* did that—I'm sure that having me find that note was part of Mother's exit strategy. My dad was nowhere around." Her voice was flat and weary, hinting at what the memory still cost her. "My age didn't matter to her, so it couldn't matter to me. I could fall apart, or I could help my dad and Brian. That's what I chose to do. If you want to see some cosmic significance in that, I can't stop you."

The look in her eyes, searching Terry's, was far more vulnerable than the words implied. "I was wondering," Terry said, "how that affected your feelings about Rose."

Meg looked away. "I could never sort them out," she answered. "I think part of me wanted them to marry. But the note took Rose's kindness to us and turned it into treachery. No doubt our mother knew that."

"Do you think she was right?"

Meg's brow furrowed. "I've never known. I could only read the tea leaves, imagining portents in what little I saw."

FOR YEARS THE IMAGE had stayed with her.

It was Christmas that same year. Their father was home; they were back in the house where their mother had died. Brian was not yet ten. Before his bedtime, Meg played Monopoly with him, then headed toward the kitchen for a Coke.

She paused in the hallway. Her father and Rose were in the living room. They had turned out all the lights, save for the multicolored bulbs on the fir tree all of them had decorated. The two of them stood together, gazing at the tree, and then Rose took her father's hand.

Neither of them spoke, or even glanced at the other. For a moment, Rose leaned her head against his shoulder. Then she released his hand.

Meg went to her room. When she came out again, Rose Gallagher was gone.

"THEY WERE ALWAYS FRIENDS," Meg said. "Rose kept on looking after us. She tried to do as much for me as any mother could."

Terry sipped his brandy. "And you looked after Brian. And, to some extent, your father."

"Mostly Brian. I didn't want him hurt. Now he *has* been, terribly, and I don't want him hurt anymore." She searched his face for understanding. "Among all of us, he's the special one. Or was."

"And you think he entered the military to please your father."

"It's more than that. Brian wanted to *become* my father.

If he could manage that, maybe he wouldn't feel pain anymore." The sadness in her voice was marbled with regret. "Someone should have stopped him. Instead of replicating my father, he couldn't escape him. Brian became an infantry officer, just like Dad and the dead McCarrans who preceded him. So the army gave Brian a lot, but expected more. I always thought he'd have been better in a place like USAID, trying to help people without dragging around a rifle and my father's reputation. Instead he ended up in Sadr City."

Terry wondered whether Rose, had she married Anthony McCarran, would have functioned as a counterweight. Perhaps Meg wondered, as well.

"And now Brian resents him for it," Terry said.

"That's complicated, too. No one had to give me permission not to be my father—I *couldn't* be. But Brian was a McCarran male." Meg took a deep swallow of brandy. "Look at how he reacts to PTSD. He's livid that the VA is screwing his guys. But our dad never complained about combat stress in Vietnam. So for Brian to be a basket case is as unthinkable as being gay. Now I'm scared that he'll kill himself, like our mother did."

With that admission, Meg lapsed into silence. Though she finished her brandy, for a time she barely looked at him. It was as though she had said too much and now feared what she had done.

TERRY DROVE THEM BACK from the restaurant. On the way, Meg asked about his plans once he left the army.

"A month in Europe," he answered. "I could never afford to go. After that I'll be doing defense work for a Wall Street firm, with most of my clients investment bankers in trouble."

She turned to him, the lights of an oncoming car illuminating a face that, when curious, became even more appealing. "Is that your dream job?"

"It's the means to my end. My dream has been to own my life and never worry about money again. But the money you make is never free—you pay for it with your time. At least my experience in the army will buy me a good quality of work." Glancing at Meg, he added, "I'm not just a trial jock, Meg. I want to leave Brian in the best shape I can. At least with respect to the law."

She gave him a wispy smile. "I'm actually beginning to believe that."

Reaching the hotel parking lot, Terry glided to a stop near the entrance. "I've enjoyed our dinner," he told her. "And you helped me quite a lot. Brian, too, I hope."

Meg gazed at him. Then, as though on impulse, she leaned across the console and gave him a swift but incisive kiss, its warmth lingering on his lips.

Skin tingling, he laughed. "*That* was a surprise."

Meg's grin turned oddly bashful. "Oh, I'm full of them. Sometimes I even shock myself. But don't worry, Paul. I'll still respect you in the morning."

Before he could answer, she opened the door and was gone.

FOR SEVERAL HOURS, UNABLE to sleep, Terry thought of Meg. His thoughts were a jumble. She was attractive in far more than appearance; at times, he felt the shock of recognition—that she was his equal not just in capacity but in experiences few others shared. But she remained an enigma, as did her family. Thinking of her, he could not shake the sense that there were things she withheld, and might always withhold. And she was, in the end, his co-counsel.

At last he drifted off. In early morning, he awoke from his nightmare, sweating.

The images had changed. Now his father's voice, reassuring Paul, came through a bathroom door in someone else's house. Terry was afraid to open it.

4

THE NEXT MORNING, Terry glanced at his desk calendar and realized that he would leave the army in a little over two weeks. His thoughts had drifted back to Meg when the telephone rang.

The caller was Captain Nathaniel Pace, a company commander in the battalion Joe D'Abruzzo had served as operations officer. More to the point, Pace explained, he'd been a classmate of D'Abruzzo's at the Citadel, and had encountered him at the Officers' Club less than a week before he died. "In all fairness," Pace told him, "there's something you should know."

His tone and phrasing suggested nothing good. Terry proposed that they meet as soon as possible.

A LITTLE AFTER SEVEN, Terry found Pace sitting at the bar of the O Club—a black officer with an air of intelligence and self-containment, taking in the first inning of the Mets-Giants game. "I'm from San Francisco," Pace explained. "Huge Barry Bonds fan, even if steroids give him a head like a medicine ball."

"Yeah," Terry said. "I never knew that lifting weights would make your hat too small. Buy you a drink?"

Pace glanced around the bar. "Let's get a table, so we can talk."

They ordered two mineral waters and took them to a table beside the window. Terry had always liked this bar, with its dark-stained wood, leather chairs, and panoramic views of the Potomac. The club itself was a magnet for couples and families, with a dance band on Wednesdays, a seafood buffet on Friday nights, and banquet rooms for weddings or major celebrations. It was also, according to Kate, where her husband had gone after threatening her with his gun. By Terry's calculation, this could have been when he had encountered Nate Pace.

"So," Terry said, "Joe D'Abruzzo. Pretty sad, for everyone."

Pace nodded, his smooth face troubled. "Yeah. Pretty sad."

Terry sipped his drink, waiting. Pace ran his fingers through the close-cropped bristle of hair. "Funny. Hadn't been for Barry Bonds, Joe might not have noticed me. Would have been just fine by me."

"Tell me about it," Terry said.

SINCE HIS WIFE HAD left him, Nate Pace's new quarters made him feel like an exile from the only life he had ever wanted. He started to put off going home by pausing at the O Club for a drink—there were people around, even if Nate wasn't talking much, and the bartender knew to troll the TV baseball package in search of a Giants game.

That night the Giants were playing in Philadelphia. Bonds had just hit one out; perched at the bar, Nate silently hoisted his CC and Coke, saluting his bloated hero as he ambled around the bases. "Cheater," someone said from behind him in a thick, heavy voice. "I can't stand cheaters. *Or* phonies."

Turning slowly, Nate saw Joe D'Abruzzo staring at the screen, and realized that Joe was offering random commentary that, however hostile, was not directed at Nate himself. It seemed like D'Abruzzo had been drinking for a while; his face was flushed, his eyes a little unfocused. Nate did not like drunks. He was about to turn away when D'Abruzzo spotted him. "Hey, Nate. How you been?"

"So-so."

Joe nodded solemnly. "Yeah. I heard."

Nate figured everyone had, which didn't mean that he cared to talk about it. "How about you?" he asked.

Joe shook his head, the inebriate's expression of sadness and commiseration. "Buy you a drink, Nate. We should catch up."

Beneath this suggestion of more camaraderie than Nate thought was warranted, Joe's tone sounded half peremptory, half beseeching. At the Citadel the man had always been a little touchy. Weighing whether accepting or refusing would cause more grief, Nate resigned himself to abandoning the Giants. "One round," he said. "Then I need to go."

They had sat at the table he and Terry occupied now. Moodily, Joe stared at the river in the gathering dusk, the darkening outline of woods on the other side. "So," he persisted, "Janie bailed on you."

Jesus, Nate thought in exasperation, answering in the most grudging voice he could summon without rudeness. "That's done."

"Too bad." Joe scowled at his scotch, turning something over in his head. "Was there another guy?"

Sometimes Nate wondered about this, but never in public. Stifling his annoyance, he said tersely, "Not that I know about. Seems like I'm a self-made man." Out of curiosity and to divert the conversation, Nate asked, "*Are* you all right?"

Joe stared at his glass. "No," he said under his breath. "I'm not all right."

Nate waited for more. To his astonishment, tears surfaced in Joe's eyes. Instead of trying to wipe them away, the big man shook his head. "You ever think you could actually kill a woman?"

The bizarre question carried an undertone of anguish and confusion. Carefully, Nate said, "We talking about Iraq, Joe? Sometimes things happened there that no one meant to happen."

Joe looked up at him. "I was talking about wives."

Nate summoned a halfhearted laugh, then saw that Joe was serious. "Kill Janie?" he repeated. "No. Maybe once or twice I wanted to send her to time-out and not cut her loose until she told me she was sorry. But that's all."

Joe shut his eyes. His soft voice was laced with misery. "For years she was this prize I couldn't believe I'd won. Tonight, I wanted to put a gun to her head and pull the fucking trigger."

Nate took this in, reprising his role as the officer people said was so good at counseling others. "If you really feel that way, Joe, you need help. They've got all sorts of good people here at Bolton."

"Too late." The smile that flickered across Joe's face was both melancholy and derisive. "No help for this one. Kate's been fucking McCarran."

The shock Nate felt was physical. Though he had spoken to Brian McCarran only on occasion, his presence at Bolton was known to all—a striking blond man as handsome as a film star. Although Joe usually did not cotton to such types, Lieutenant McCarran seemed self-effacing and capable, a good guy trying to do his job without a lot of fuss. But adultery in the army was a crime: for any officer, but especially this kid, Joe's assertion could be incendiary. Quietly, he responded, "That's a heavy thing to say. You sure it's so?"

Joe bristled visibly. "You think I'd make up shit like

this? Go around Bolton bragging that McCarran put the horns on me, like it's a fucking badge of honor 'cause it's him? I *caught* them."

This was bad, Nate knew, perhaps explosive. "If that's true, it's not just your marriage that's in trouble. It's this guy's whole career."

"It's my whole fucking life," Joe burst out. "You don't get it, Nate. I feel like my skull's exploding." His voice softened abruptly. "Kate loves him, always has. She said they're family—that they didn't mean for this to happen. But there's more between them than Kate and I will ever have. Bring him down for this, and I blow up my marriage and lose my kids."

The waters were getting deeper. Every instinct Nate possessed told him to hear no more. "Get help," he repeated. "This starts with you and her."

"You still don't get it," Joe said in a defeated voice. "It'll destroy me." Taking a deep swallow of whiskey, he said, "Don't tell anyone about this. I mean it."

Sensing that the revelations were over, Nate felt relieved. "It's not my story to tell, Joe."

Nodding curtly, Joe gulped the last of his drink and slapped a twenty on the table. Standing, he rested a hand on Nate's shoulder, then walked away without saying another word.

Nate turned to watch him leave. Except maybe for himself, he had never seen a man who looked more lonely.

SITTING ACROSS FROM Nathaniel Pace, Terry imagined a new, more human Joe D'Abruzzo, overcome by emotions he could not endure. Then he tried to absorb that Brian might have deceived him. Stifling his dismay, Terry asked, "How drunk was D'Abruzzo?"

"Pretty drunk." Pace paused, considering the question

further. "He wasn't out of it, though. Toward the end, talking about his marriage, he seemed to focus on what was happening to the family, and the consequences of whatever he might do. This was a guy in real pain."

Terry nodded. "Did he give you any details about this so-called affair?"

"None. Of course, I knew who Brian was. I didn't want to hear about it."

"So Joe said nothing about how he 'caught' them?"

"No." Pace pressed his lips together. "Here's the thing, though. After the shooting, I brooded on this for a while. But this is about military honor, I decided—not saying what I knew would be like covering up for someone who could be cheating on his finals. Except this could involve something a helluva lot more serious." He hesitated. "In the end, I had to call Major Flynn."

It was, as Pace suggested, a question of military honor. "I understand," Terry assured him. "That's why Brian has a lawyer."

But at that moment, Terry realized, he was also thinking of Meg.

FLYNN WAS WORKING LATE. As he waved his adversary to a seat, Terry detected a glint of competitive pleasure; he was learning that Flynn could keep his face so immobile that the only clue to the prosecutor's thoughts was in his eyes. Briskly, he asked, "What's up, Captain?"

"Nate Pace. I thought we should meet before this festered too long."

"I already know the argument," Flynn responded in clipped tones. "As a matter of law, D'Abruzzo's statement to Captain Pace is hearsay, inadmissible in a court-martial."

"For openers. It's also vapor—without substance or detail. As to D'Abruzzo saying that he 'caught them'—

whatever *that's* supposed to mean—it sounds like detritus from the alcohol-fueled imaginings of a guy already screwed up by combat. If you want to start beating your wife, it's good to have such a sympathetic reason. There's no basis for anyone to verify these ramblings."

Though Terry was far from certain of that, Flynn was briefly silent. "That's true," he conceded. "But tomorrow it may not be. I'm recommending that the commander prefer charges against Lieutenant McCarran and convene a pretrial investigation under Article 32."

Though startled, Terry saw at once where this was going. Feigning controlled outrage, he retorted, "On what ground, Major? The physical evidence is inconclusive. Pace's story is inadmissible. There's still no case."

A faint smile played on Mike Flynn's lips, a deliberate goad. "Don't play coy, Captain. Adultery provides a motive for murder, and lying about it suggests a consciousness of guilt." He sat back, his voice cool and sure. "At the Article 32 hearing, I can try to call Kate D'Abruzzo as a witness. As to your client, he's the only witness to the killing. Does he really want to invoke the Fifth Amendment? I needn't insult your intelligence by walking you through Kate and Brian's stations of the cross."

"No. You don't."

"Nonetheless, I'm willing to do you a favor. Before I go to the staff judge advocate, I'll give you time to talk to McCarran. *And* Mrs. D'Abruzzo, if she hasn't already hired a lawyer of her own. She's not subject to military law. But conspiracy to murder is still a crime in the Commonwealth of Virginia."

There was nothing else to say; Terry could see his hope of a safe exit for Brian slipping away and, with it, Meg's chance of returning to the life she had created for herself. "I'll do that," he told Flynn.

5

WHEN MEG APPEARED at Terry's door, she said without preface, "What is it, Paul?"

"I think you'd better sit down."

She perched on the edge of her chair, hands clasped and elbows on knees, as though hunched to receive a blow. At this moment, Terry felt so deeply sorry for her that he almost reached for her hand.

"Flynn has a witness from D'Abruzzo's battalion," he told her. "The short of it is that D'Abruzzo showed up drunk at the Officers' Club, apparently on the night Kate says he threatened her. He told this man she was 'fucking McCarran.'"

Meg bowed her head a little more, a tightly balled fist held to her lips. "What else did he say?"

"That's all," Terry answered. "But Flynn thinks it's enough to prefer charges against Brian under Article 32."

She looked up at him, eyes widening. It was almost as if, Terry thought, she could not comprehend what he was saying. "Against Brian," she repeated, "for murdering Joe D'Abruzzo. Because of a single phrase mumbled by a drunk."

"Yes."

She shook her head, as though to clear it. "It's not evidence, Paul."

"I know. But Flynn believes it's true. He means to use an Article 32 hearing to corner Kate and nail Brian."

She ran a fingertip across her eyes. Beneath this distracted gesture, Terry imagined her trying to discipline her thoughts. "How would that work?" she asked.

"It's like a pretrial hearing. In a case of this magnitude, it's likely that the hearing will be presided over by a military judge who serves as investigating officer for the 'convening authority'—General Heston, the commander of Fort Bolton. If there's sufficient evidence to establish probable cause, the investigating officer will recommend that Heston convene a general court-martial."

"Do we have the right of cross-examination?"

"Yes. We could also call our own witnesses and put on a defense, though I probably wouldn't recommend that. Why tip your hand if there's a good chance you'll face a court-martial?" Terry's voice softened. "The real problem is that Flynn won't just charge Brian with murder, but with adultery."

"Based on hearsay." Meg objected. "Talk about overprosecuting. What if Brian *wasn't* Kate's lover?"

"He'd have to say that on the stand, or risk conviction. If that's a lie, he'd be risking perjury charges. Or he can take the Fifth."

Terry stopped there, waiting for Meg's normally quick mind to catch up with him. "Kate's a civilian," she said. "The army's got no jurisdiction to try her for Joe's murder— or for adultery. Can they force her to testify at a preliminary hearing?"

"No. And I damned well hope she doesn't volunteer." Terry leaned forward. "Flynn would make her choose between telling the truth about her and Brian—whatever that is—or risk federal prosecution for perjury. Not an attractive option for a widowed mother of two young kids.

"It's certainly hardball—prosecutions for adultery are pretty rare. But Flynn thinks that Brian is a murderer and that an affair with Kate spells motive. It would also mean that both of them lied to the CID. Which is not a helpful fact when you're trying to refute a murder charge."

"Only if they did lie. I still don't believe it, and Flynn can't prove it." Meg's voice lowered. "As you once pointed out, his only witness is dead."

"That's not quite true," Terry countered. "José Calvo heard Joe D'Abruzzo say to Kate, 'I saw him.' Flynn means to keep digging until he finds out who Joe meant. If it turns out to be Brian, I can work with that. But I'd rather know right now than have your brother crucified at a court-martial."

Chin resting against a cupped hand, Meg suddenly looked wistful and too young for this ordeal. "You were right," she said softly. "This is about our family."

"Meaning?"

Meg gazed at him directly. "Give me time to talk to Brian. Together, we can figure out what's right for him to do."

"I'd rather surprise him. I don't want to give Brian time to think before he talks to me."

Vehemently, Meg shook her head, "You've *seen* how Brian is. Please, let me do this. Brian may be your client, but he's *my* brother. When you're in Europe or New York, I'll still be trying to help him deal with everything that's happened."

Perhaps it was a pleading note that he had never heard from her—for herself and for the brother who, in some recess of her mind, must still be the boy she had protected on the day she found her mother dead. Knowing that Meg would bear this burden without him, Terry could not insist on his prerogatives as a lawyer.

"All right," he said. "I can stall Flynn for a day."

At once Meg stood. She stopped beside him, touching

his wrist without looking into his face. Then she squared her shoulders and left.

That night he barely slept. As hours passed, he tried to imagine the dynamics between brother and sister.

It was noon before she called him, and she sounded unspeakably tired. "I talked to Brian." She hesitated. "Then I talked to Kate."

Terry was surprised at this. "And?"

"I'd like to bring Kate to your apartment. I think it's better that you hear this from her first."

TERRY HAD NOT SEEN Kate D'Abruzzo in nearly two weeks. His first thought was how startlingly she resembled her mother. His second was to consider how desirable she might appear to a man made heartsick by war, yet who could trust her as he did few others. An affair with Brian had more logic the more one knew about the McCarrans and the Gallaghers.

Though Kate sat beside Meg, he sensed the same coolness between them. Kate met his gaze, her expression desolate. But her voice was emotionless and stilted. "You should know that I'm not a murderer, Captain Terry. Neither is Brian. But as you already assumed, I am an adulterer."

Silent, Terry waited for her lover's name. When Kate said nothing, he asked softly, "Who did your husband see with you?"

Pale and still, Meg watched Kate closely. At length Kate said, "Brian and I both lied to you. That day at the hotel, Joe found out what was going on."

Though Terry was prepared for this, her admission colored everything that she and Brian had asked him to believe. "How long was your affair?" he asked.

"Three months."

Quite deliberately, Terry remained as emotionless as she. "Walk me through this from the beginning."

Kate sat straighter, as though fighting off her own humiliation. "Everything I said about my marriage was true—Joe's withdrawal, the verbal and physical abuse, the total absence of affection. I was so miserable that I went to his apartment and poured my heart out to him." She gazed past Terry, her voice quieter. "I started crying, so he held me. Suddenly I could feel our bodies discovering what we wanted."

Meg, Terry thought, looked as mortified as Kate. She turned away, as though wishing not to look at the woman beside her. "And after that?" Terry asked.

"We saw each other every week. I couldn't risk going to his apartment. So I always went to the hotel and waited for him in the room." Her throat twitched. "It lasted until Joe followed me."

"How did he know?" Terry asked. "Phone records?"

"He wouldn't tell me. But it couldn't have been that. I was careful not to use any phone where Joe saw records of who I called." A trace of shame surfaced in her voice. "We had a regular day and time—Wednesday at noon. It made things simpler. We only needed to talk if someone had to cancel."

Terry thought of Lauren Scott describing Kate's desperation at her daughter's sudden illness. "So when Brian took the gun," he said, "Joe already knew."

"Yes."

"Then let's go over that again, Kate. This time include the context."

"You mean my affair," Kate retorted in a brittle voice. "Otherwise, I told you the truth. Except that my complaints about his drinking and ignoring the kids also served as my excuse."

"You also said Joe held a gun to your head because he thought you were telling people about him. That's not quite true, is it?"

Kate closed her eyes. "Not that part, no. He was afraid that other people might know about *me*."

"Tell me about it. Everything."

As Kate began, Terry envisioned the new version, searching for inconsistencies, comparing its details with what she had said before.

SHE WAS DRYING HER hair in front of the mirror when his face appeared behind her. With ominous quiet, he said, "Turn off the hair dryer."

Kate complied, frozen where she stood. He placed the tumbler of whiskey on the sink, roughly grabbing her shoulders to spin her around. In a low, tight voice, he demanded, "Who knows about you and McCarran?"

Bracing herself, she felt her bottled shame and anger become defiance. "No one. But everyone knows about you. Don't you know how different you are? Are you so far gone you've stopped seeing yourself? If you don't believe me, look in the mirror. Look at *us*."

Joe's eyes flickered toward his reflection. More evenly, Kate said, "I'm ashamed of what I've done, Joe. But together we can face this."

Without speaking, he turned and left.

Shaken, Kate reached for the hair dryer. Then Joe reappeared in the mirror. She saw, then felt the gun he held to her temple.

In a taut voice, he said, "It's not our marriage you care about. You're trying to protect him."

Kate's stomach felt hollow. *"No."*

Numbly, she wondered if this stranger, her husband, would put a bullet through her brain. Silently, their images in the mirror watched each other. Kate saw his hand move, relieving the metallic pressure on her temple. He turned, closing the door behind him with exaggerated care.

The click of the door latch broke her spell. Tears running down her face, Kate knelt beside the toilet and vomited.

"That was when I called Brian," she told Terry. "He took the gun out of fear that Joe would kill me."

"And the night of the shooting?"

Kate hesitated. "We were going to dinner," she said softly. "Just as I told you before."

Once again, Terry listened, imaging the scene as she described it, even as he wondered at its truth.

AS BEFORE, THE CHILDREN were gone, and Joe had started drinking.

For once, her affair did not appear to taint his thoughts. He sat on the edge of their bed, watching Kate put her earrings on. "Just the two of us," he said. "Remember how we were before?"

The reference to her transgression, once unthinkable to her, filled Kate with unspeakable sadness. "Yes," she answered. "I remember how safe I felt."

Something in her tone seemed to transform his thoughts. His face changed, as though a veil had fallen, leaving his eyes distant and suspicious. Then he stood, sliding open the drawer of the nightstand.

She watched him stare at the empty drawer. Quietly, he asked, "Where is it?"

She should have prepared an answer, Kate knew. "It's gone, Joe."

He turned slowly, heavily. The rage in Joe's eyes made her shrink from him.

With swift catlike movements, he threw her on the bed. Panicked, she felt his hands around her throat, both thumbs pressing her Adam's apple. She began to gag, her windpipe narrowing. His face was inches from hers. "Where?" he inquired with lethal softness.

He would kill her, Kate thought. With the last reserves of air, she croaked, "Brian took it."

The stench of liquor filled her nostrils. *"Brian McCarran?"* Joe demanded.

All she could do was nod, until he lessened the pressure. "It's not Brian's fault—"

"No," he spat. "It's always *my* fault, isn't it?"

Suddenly he stood. Lying on the bed, Kate felt violated. Her throat was raw and tender.

Turning, Joe headed for the door. Afraid, she asked, "Where are you going?"

"To get back what's mine. It's time that this fucking family remembers whose wife you are."

He stalked from the room. Weak with fear, Kate heard the front door close behind him.

She made herself stand. Dazed, she could not remember Brian's phone number. Then she started dialing, the numbers coming back to her.

His phone kept ringing, and then she heard a click. In the hollow tone of a recording, he answered, "This is Brian McCarran—"

Interrupting Kate's narrative, Terry turned to Meg, "I need to see him. Now."

Meg still looked crestfallen. "Brian's at work," she answered slowly. "I'll go get him. We could be here around five."

He sat on the couch in his crisp khaki uniform, Meg beside him. His cool blue-gray eyes regarded Terry without defensiveness or anger. Then he gave a fatalistic shrug. "Game's up, I guess."

"That's a way of putting it," Terry said tersely. "Another is that you fucked with me."

"Sorry," Brian answered mildly. "But I know Meg feels worse."

Meg looked down. "Yeah," Terry said. "Lying to Meg must have been tough on you."

"Know what's tough about this?" Brian countered softly. "Kate's kids."

"That's why you lied?"

"Kate's all they've got, Captain. I remember how that is. I didn't want them to feel ashamed of her. I still don't."

Terry wondered if, like Meg, Brian suspected that Tony McCarran and Kate's mother had been lovers before his own mother killed herself. But Meg watched Terry with the same willful impassivity, as if more focused on his emotions than her own. What seemed unmistakable was the sadness in Brian's voice. "That's why I took the gun," he said. "I didn't want those kids to lose their mother."

As with Kate, Terry parsed Brian's story for changes.

KATE OPENED THE DOOR of the town house before he could knock. Her face was frozen, her eyes stunned.

Pushing past her, Brian looked swiftly from side to side. "Where is he?"

"At the Officers' Club," Kate said quickly. "He's already been drinking."

Crossing the living room, Brian searched the hallway. "And the kids?"

"With my mom."

He joined her in the living room, his tone softer but still urgent. "Did he hit you again?"

She sat on the couch, awkwardly and abruptly, as though the adrenaline that propelled her had evanesced. "He threatened me with a gun. I can't go on like this."

"Then stop him." Brian sat down beside her, covering Kate's hand with his. "Get help, Kate. You have to go to his battalion commander."

Kate slowly shook her head, a gesture of despair. "*You* know why I can't."

"What if he kills you? Where would the kids be then?" Brian made himself speak slowly and firmly. "We don't have a choice. No matter what comes out."

She put her hands to her face, saying in a muffled voice, "Can you imagine what would happen? I can't do that, Brian."

"Then I'll talk to Joe myself." He paused, then asked in the same insistent tone, "Where's the gun?"

With seeming effort, Kate stood, walking toward the bedroom like an automaton. Following, Brian saw her open the drawer of the nightstand, drawing back from what she saw. Brian withdrew the gun, then snapped it open to scrutinize the magazine. "This is loaded, Kate."

Pale, she sat on the edge of the bed. Brian found the box of cartridges on the top shelf of the closet, next to the cap of Joe's dress uniform. He stuffed the box in his pocket and the gun in his waistband. "What are you doing?" Kate asked.

"Taking it with me."

"Please, Brian—ever since he followed me, he's been on the edge. If he loses control, he'll kill you."

Brian kissed her forehead. "Get help," he repeated softly. "No one matters more than you—"

"BUT SHE DIDN'T GET help," Brian told Terry now. "Because of the affair, she felt as if she couldn't. So Joe came looking for me."

BRIAN HEARD THE SHRILL bleat from the building's outside door, the signal to admit a caller. Getting off the phone with Kate, he removed the handgun from his dresser drawer and walked to the living room. Quickly, he concealed the gun beneath the pillow on his overstuffed chair. Then he buzzed Joe in, opening the door to his apartment.

Thudding footsteps echoed in the stairwell; then Joe D'Abruzzo filled the door frame. His face was flushed, his forehead shiny with sweat, his eyes darting and unfocused. The living room felt claustrophobic. Hand outstretched, Joe said, "I've had enough, you fucking weasel. Give me the gun."

To Brian's ear, his own reply sounded faint. "You threatened Kate—"

"So you had *rights*?" Joe's broad face was a mask of anger, his dark eyes wild with unreason. "I can shatter your windpipe or gouge your fucking eyes out."

He took another step forward. Without thinking, Brian reached for the gun.

It was aimed at Joe before he knew it. "Straighten yourself out," Brian said quickly. "Or I'll protect her any way I can. No matter what."

In a split second, Joe spun sideways, hands raised to attack. Brian's finger twitched, the gun jumping in his hand.

The next thing he knew, Joe was lying against the wall in a pool of blood.

AFTER BRIAN LEFT, TERRY drifted to his window, watching his client walk away from the apartment building, a solitary figure with the tread of an automaton. Terry felt Meg behind him.

"Never believe anyone," he said. "Especially someone facing a charge of murder. I did believe him, though. He's a pretty good liar—or was. I wonder what else one or both of them are lying about."

"That's not fair." Meg's voice was tight and anxious. "He was protecting Kate and her children."

When Terry turned, her eyes were sad but watchful. "Maybe so," he answered. "But now Flynn has his motive. Not only was Brian screwing D'Abruzzo's wife, but Joe could have ruined Brian's career. On the brighter side, the affair gave D'Abruzzo a motive to tear your brother limb from limb. Either way, Brian's future in the army is looking pretty grim."

Dully, Meg said, "I guess you're going back to Flynn."

Watching her, Terry forced himself to recall that, like him, she was also Brian's lawyer and that they had a job to do. Slowly, he nodded. "Even if I wanted to, there's no way I can mislead him. We'll have to see whether he really thinks that lying about sex is tantamount to murder."

6

Two HOURS BEFORE meeting Mike Flynn, Paul Terry drank coffee at his kitchen table, conjuring visions of a long ago sunrise in Mexico.

He had been in college at Ohio Wesleyan. Some friends with resources had taken a house in Cabo San Lucas over winter break and invited him for the price of airfare, earned in a summer of working construction. He had never before traveled outside the United States. Accustomed to rising early, Paul would drink coffee on the porch while his friends slept, watching fishing boats ply the Pacific as spreading dawn turned gray waters to a deepening blue. Letting his subconscious glide from thought to thought, Paul pondered his future without, for once, trying to form a plan.

It was before seven; Paul knew he would not see his friends, slumberous from beer and tequila, for several hours. Without begrudging them their good fortune, Paul accepted that he was different; the rare luxury of feeling time slip through his fingers was worth awakening for. On the beach, a two-minute walk downhill, two slender girls appeared between the palms that lined the sand, heedless of the white fishing boats that sliced the water in their wake. Paul had never seen a place so beautiful.

Someday, he promised himself, he would do this any-time life permitted.

It would not be soon. He had years of work ahead,

divided into days and weeks, exams and quarters, the dogged steps through which he maintained his current scholarship in order to secure the next one. He went to class and to work, wasting no time in between, driven by his own desire to excel—or, when that flagged, his fear of failing like his father, his hope of pleasing the mother for whom he signified that her life still had meaning. When next he returned here, it would not be as someone's guest.

He thought all of this without trying to think at all. On the surface of his mind, he merely watched the fishing boats. By the end of his final cup of coffee, he had chosen a career in law.

He had never watched the fishing boats again. But often he imagined them, letting his subconscious summon what it would. After an hour of this, he was prepared to confront Flynn.

SITTING BEHIND HIS DESK, Flynn seemed to have been waiting there for hours. In the manner of someone driving their preset agenda, he said, "I assume you met with your client."

That Terry chose not to answer was answer enough. "Let's stay with your suspicion about Kate and Brian," he said instead. "Whose motive does that buy you? If D'Abruzzo was a human hand grenade, Brian had good reason to fear for his own life."

Flynn placed both elbows on the desk, inspecting Terry with the chill look of a priest confronting a sinner. "You're awfully blithe about one officer sleeping with another's wife. Especially when it provides so many reasons for Brian to kill D'Abruzzo—covering up an affair; freeing Kate from an inconvenient marriage; and smearing the victim as a misogynistic brute."

Terry smiled without humor. "And look at how well that

worked," he retorted. "You assume too much. Supposition isn't evidence, and adultery isn't murder. It still comes down to what happened in that room, and Brian's the only witness—"

"The sole survivor," Flynn amended caustically. "Thanks to your client, D'Abruzzo can't contradict him."

Unfazed, Terry responded, "Which doesn't erase the fact that D'Abruzzo was drunk, and capable of killing Brian without a weapon. And the physical evidence proves nothing either way." Terry kept his tone reasonable and respectful. "This isn't a case you can win, Major. It's only a case you can prosecute. That would hurt everyone else involved—the McCarran family, Kate's mother and children, Joe D'Abruzzo's parents. And for what? The army loses, and so does everyone else."

"I don't care if *I* lose," Flynn said in a cutting tone. "I don't pick my cases to ensure a perfect record."

At this clear implication that his own success as a prosecutor stemmed from ducking challenges, Terry gazed out a window at the lawn, reining in his anger.

"As to the army," Flynn continued, "it loses only when its integrity is tarnished by its members. That's what McCarran did."

Terry faced him again. "Morality," he said softly, "is not evidence. The reason I never lost a case as a prosecutor is that I've never confused my own antipathies with facts."

Flynn placed both hands on his desk, allowing seconds to pass while he chose his manner of response. "I *have* lost cases, Captain Terry. But they were always ones that needed to be brought on principle."

"So were the cases I *didn't* bring," Terry replied, "I wasn't afraid of losing, Major. I was afraid of winning. I didn't want to prove my talent by convicting an innocent man."

"The defense lawyer's job is to prevent that," Flynn

answered coolly. "We both agree you're adequate to the task. I think we can also agree that your client and his lover lied to the CID." Abruptly, his tone became level and dispassionate. "Here's what I firmly believe happened. Your client and Mrs. D'Abruzzo resolved to kill her husband before he told anyone about their affair—not knowing what D'Abruzzo had let slip to Captain Pace. So McCarran took his gun, then invited D'Abruzzo to his apartment, confident that D'Abruzzo was too proud to resist. The virtual execution that followed included a bullet in the back.

"To cover that, Kate and Brian fabricated the story of spousal abuse, then falsely claimed that Joe had gone to Brian's apartment on his own initiative. Brian justified the murder with yet another lie—that Joe attacked him. Because he feared to concoct a story that the physical evidence might contradict, he feigned amnesia as to the rest. And to ensure that he played his part effectively, he called his sister for advice."

"Which he didn't take," Terry retorted. "She told him not to answer questions."

Flynn shrugged. "He had to. What else would an 'innocent' man do? And how do you know the sister isn't lying to you, too?"

Terry had considered this. "So Meg's also a conspirator? Why not throw in General McCarran—"

"Oh," Flynn interrupted, "he plays a role here, too. Not in the sense that he's culpable, but because his son believed that their surname would help save him."

Terry shook his head, miming wonder. "I'll pass over the idea of familial enablers. You're making Brian and Kate into the Macbeths, coolheaded assassins who plotted murder in advance."

Flynn smiled a little. "That's hardly confined to Shakespeare. It's clear that both of them lied to you as well as to the CID—for the most sympathetic of reasons, I'm sure McCarran told you. But no doubt only after you beat a confession out of him by predicting what I'd do to them both if they testified in an Article 32 hearing. Coupled with adultery, their deliberate lies cast doubt on everything else they've told you.

"There's no way you can keep their affair out of evidence. Especially when I prefer charges for adultery—"

"Doesn't that strike you as overkill?" Terry interrupted. "Personally, I've never seen a prosecution for adultery unless the conduct was flagrant, and persisted despite a warning to the accused. That's not this case."

Flynn's eyes narrowed slightly. "Maybe you think that adultery with D'Abruzzo's wife is a momentary lapse, excused by a lifetime of closeness. If so, you've learned everything from your service save that which is most essential." Flynn stopped himself, then continued with quiet passion: "The army is also a family. By sleeping with Kate D'Abruzzo, Brian McCarran tore the fabric of both families. He ignored his obligation to two children who thought of him as an uncle. He flouted the good order and discipline necessary to military cohesion. He committed the most basic crime within any family, a figurative act of incest that wounded all its members and led, inexorably, to the death of one.

"By all accounts," Flynn concluded softly, "Anthony McCarran is one of the most honorable men we have. Were he here, I firmly believe that he—like I—would tell you that honor is the moral glue that binds us to each other. His son chose to abandon honor. He exemplifies why military justice exists."

This was hopeless, Terry realized. What drove Flynn was more profound than ego or fanaticism: a well of principle—as deep as it was narrow—that meant he could only be a prosecutor, and made him every bit as effective as his reputation held. Calmly, Terry asked, "Then what do you propose?"

Flynn raised his eyebrows long enough to underscore Terry's concession. "Are you asking if I've considered a pretrial agreement?"

"My client hasn't considered one. But there's no point in asking him unless you're willing."

Flynn's gaze lowered in thought. "For the sake of argument, what might he accept?"

"I only know what I'd recommend. Adultery doesn't make D'Abruzzo's death prosecutable as murder. But I recognize that adultery in itself is punishable under the UCMJ." Terry paused. "I appreciate how you feel about an affair. But Brian and Kate *were* close, and two other sources suggest that Joe was abusing her. The one you know about, Nathaniel Pace, says that D'Abruzzo talked about killing his wife. The second, General McCarran, confirms that Kate told him that she was afraid. As you concede, the general may be Brian's father, but there's no question about his honor.

"Under those circumstances, I don't think a general court-martial would dismiss Brian from the army. But I'm willing to discuss that. Terminating the career of General McCarran's son, I'd suggest, would vindicate your concerns in a very public way."

Flynn curtly shook his head. "The affair caused D'Abruzzo's death. Now you're using McCarran's transgression as a 'get out of jail free' card, even though he chose to lie about it." He sat back, palms pressed together. "I grant you that a court-martial for murder carries risks on both sides. But I believe an Article 32 hearing would make my case stronger, and yours weaker. Before I seek one, I'm willing to consider a plea of manslaughter with significant prison time."

Terry felt his resistance growing—armed with too much certainty and a subjective sense of justice, a skilled prosecutor with too little opposition could go too far. "With respect," he said evenly, "I think that's excessive. All I can promise is to inform Lieutenant McCarran of your offer."

"Then tell him this," Flynn answered. "To let him walk away would violate the army's obligations to Joe D'Abruzzo. Brian McCarran has already violated *his* obligation to both. If there's anything left of his father in him, he'll accept the consequences."

7

In EARLY EVENING, Terry and Meg met with Brian on his sailboat.

With his sister beside him, Brian sat on the fantail. Dressed in shorts and a T-shirt, he seemed even younger than usual, his only sign of tension the alert, expectant expression in his eyes, the look of a sentinel. Meg had arrived separately; like Brian, she did not know what Flynn had said. Sitting across from them, Terry again felt like an outsider.

"I got nowhere," he told them. "Because of the affair, Flynn has inverted your story into an edifice of lies constructed to conceal premeditated murder. It all fits: Joe's spousal abuse, the reason you took the gun, Kate's phone call, and the shooting itself."

Besides the slightest narrowing of Brian's eyes, the only sign of emotion was a silent inhalation of breath. Softly, he asked, "Why did I do it?"

"To cover up your affair, save your career, or get Kate all to yourself. Take your pick."

Brian tilted his head, as though considering the choices. "I must have shot him to preserve the family name," he concluded gravely. "If I'd wanted Kate, a mere divorce would have done the trick. I'd have suggested that before I shot her husband. I'm less Catholic than my father."

The gallows humor unsettled Terry further. "The one explanation Flynn hasn't considered," he retorted, "is that you simply hated D'Abruzzo's guts."

"Think so?"

"Definitely. Maybe because of Kate; maybe because of something that happened in Iraq. I wouldn't mind knowing what."

Though her face was etched with worry, Meg still said nothing, her gaze focused on Terry alone. Quietly, Brian said, "A war happened in Iraq. Joe believed in it; I stopped. But I'm not sure I really hated him until he started hitting Kate."

This laconic admission immersed Terry in Brian's complexity: Terry could not tell whether it was a simple statement of truth, or proffered to conceal something deeper. In his silence, Meg argued, "Everyone lies about sex, especially when they're ashamed. And everyone but Flynn knows that's different than covering up a murder."

Brian shrugged. "Either I'm a murderer," he offered coolly, "or I'm not. But Kate *was* afraid. Joe *did* hit her. If Flynn thinks she's going to turn on me, his fantasies are spinning out of control.

"So what does that leave him? A confrontation where one guy winds up dead and the other guy can't remember much. But I do know why I shot him. D'Abruzzo would have killed me."

"It also leaves two alternatives," Terry answered. "Flynn's is that you're lying. Mine is that you reacted based on post-traumatic stress disorder. Most people would remember the last three shots—unless their mind was literally elsewhere."

Though Brian smiled a little, his gaze was cold. "Forget Iraq, Captain. I certainly intend to. As far as I'm concerned, there's no place like home."

With this, Meg looked more fearful than before. Facing Terry, she said, "Flynn's talking to you because he wants something. What is it?"

Terry kept his eyes on Brian. "A guilty plea to manslaughter with 'significant' prison time."

Brian blanched. Softly, he answered, "I can't let them lock me up."

All irony had vanished from his voice. "Because you're innocent?" Terry asked.

Brian closed his eyes. "Because I'd kill myself first."

His dread of confinement was so palpable that, for once, Terry could not doubt him. The look Meg gave Terry bespoke a horror he now understood too well. "Then you'll have to face a trial," Terry said matter-of-factly. "And win. When your next lawyer comes along, you might choose to be more helpful."

Brian turned, gazing at the dusky waters of the Potomac in early evening. "If *you* were trying this case," he asked Terry, "could you win it?"

"Define winning, Brian. Could I get you acquitted of premeditated murder? Based on what I know today, probably. Assuming no more surprises."

"What about the manslaughter charge?"

Terry waited for Brian to look at him. "You're asking if I could do better than Flynn's offer. But all you've given me is a claim of self-defense and a victim with a bullet in his back." Terry's tone became clipped. "How afraid are you of prison, Brian? More afraid than of mounting a defense based on the damage I'm pretty sure was done to you in Iraq? Or would you rather risk a guilty verdict than 'dishonor' the McCarran name still more?" Terry glanced at Meg. "You don't have to answer now. But you *will* have to answer. Flynn is giving you no choice."

Brian leaned forward, chin resting on folded hands, staring into the distance. He could have been weighing his choices or envisioning how a court-martial might unfold. For an instant, Terry imagined him as an infantry lieutenant in Iraq, considering the fate of other men who, Dr. Carson surmised, he had cared about more than himself. "Whatever else," Brian said at last, "I'm not the guy Flynn thinks I am. Tell him I've never committed murder in Virginia. Then tell him no."

AFTER THAT, THERE WAS little else to say. Terry left them there.

Alone in his apartment, he drank a scotch on ice, so absorbed in Brian McCarran that his future in New York seemed far away. Brian was still concealing something, he sensed, but whether this was from guilt or shame, he could not guess. Nor could he decipher Brian's evasiveness. The young officer had given him little except a lie; yet Terry's instinct was that Brian's sense of honor, while different from Mike Flynn's, governed decisions he chose not to explain. Terry knew a loner when he met one.

He was finishing his scotch when the buzzer rang. Pressing the intercom, he asked. "Who is it?"

"Meg."

Terry froze, surprised. Without answering, he buzzed her in.

He waited in the doorway. When Meg appeared, she stood in front of him. "I needed to come here," she said simply. "I was afraid I'd fall apart in front of him, and I couldn't stand to be alone."

Touched by her admission, Terry motioned her inside. "You can fall apart here, Meg. I won't mind."

He closed the door behind them. Inside, the last sunlight cast dim shadows. Looking around her, Meg said softly, "So strange to think the shooting happened in a room like this. Brian felt trapped, I'm sure. Just like he is now."

"Maybe so. For my money, he's also trapped within himself. But I don't know why."

Meg did not answer. Without facing him, she spoke in the same soft, stunned voice, "Is there any chance an Article 32 proceeding won't result in a court-martial?"

"Not much. None unless Brian puts on a defense, and little if he does. All Flynn needs for a court-martial is probable cause, and he can already prove that Brian is a liar and an adulterer. I doubt that Brian's lawyer will think it smart to preview his defense."

Meg sat on the couch. After a moment, she confessed tiredly, "I have trouble sleeping now. When I finally do, I wake up and for a minute none of this has happened to him. Then I realize I'm not at home, or even in my life, and it all comes flooding back." She shook her head. "Some mornings I feel sick. I've never felt that way, even before the hardest trial."

"Go home to San Francisco," Terry said gently. "You can come back for the hearing."

"This isn't Brian's fault, Paul. I can't let him be alone. And you know why."

She said this with such conviction that Terry could not respond. At length he asked, "Can I get you something?"

Slowly, Meg nodded. "A drink."

Terry poured her a scotch and refilled his own, sitting down beside her. After sipping her drink, Meg said, "There's another reason I came. I've wanted to thank you for all you tried to do."

"It isn't much, I'm afraid."

She faced him. "It is, though. You're even patient with me. Believe it or not, I've needed that. I know we're not easy."

Terry tried to smile. "Families seldom are. Why should yours be different?"

He said this lightly. But Meg's defenses seemed to have vanished. "Remember when I kissed you?" she asked.

Her voice trembled slightly. Terry's skin tingled with surprise. "Of course. I assumed it was a passing impulse."

Meg inhaled. "No, Paul. It wasn't."

Putting down her drink, she looked into his face, as though seeking a response. Then she reached behind his neck and guided his mouth to hers.

Her lips were soft and warm. As the kiss lingered, Terry had the stray thought that lawyers should not sleep with their co-counsel. Then he recalled that his role as Brian's lawyer was about to end. At the end of the kiss, leisurely and deep, Meg rested her forehead against his face. Terry could smell the freshness of her hair.

The deepest part of him had begun to want this, he realized. But misgivings tugged at him: surely she had come here less from desire than to escape.

As though to quell his doubts, she rose, standing in front of him. Eyes never leaving his, she slowly took off her blouse.

Seconds passed in silence, a kind of trance.

Meg was round and full-breasted, even more beautiful than Terry had imagined. Her panties slid to the floor. Mustering an uncertain smile, she asked, "Do you need my help undressing?"

Terry slowly shook his head.

In his bedroom, they slid between cool sheets, skin against skin. His mouth found her lips again, then her nipples. As they grazed her stomach, Meg murmured her encouragement. After a time, her murmurs became cries that ended in a shudder.

Terry slid inside her. Her eyes, still open, gazed up into his. He began to move gently, the way he sensed she needed. She thrust against him, demanding more, until her rhythm became a frenzied search for release. She found it seconds before he did.

Afterward, Terry touched her face. "Are you okay with this?"

Meg smiled a little. "*You* were more than okay. If that's what you meant."

"It wasn't, actually."

Her expression took on a fleeting sadness. "I'm always okay, Paul. That's my role."

But she was far from okay, Terry knew. After a time, she dressed, and went to be with Brian.

8

ROSE GALLAGHER'S OFFICE at Fort Bolton School looked out at the playground, where, this morning, kids in a summer program played volleyball and kickball. As she watched them for a moment, perhaps thinking of her grandchildren, Terry noticed the same wedding photo she kept at her apartment, a smiling Joe D'Abruzzo amid Gallaghers and McCarrans.

Turning from the window, she noted this. "I should put it somewhere, I know. But it's so hard to accept what's become of us."

Sitting across from her, Terry reflected that he still kept an old picture in a drawer: his mother and father on either side of him, beaming after Paul's first communion, no one but his father aware of what might come. "I understand," he said. "Sometimes putting away pictures feels like letting go of a dream. You wish you were still in it."

Rose tilted her head, giving Terry a slightly quizzical smile. "That's almost poetic, Captain."

"Everyone has dreams, Mrs. Gallagher. Or illusions."

"Including us." Rose turned to the photograph. "Now Joe's dead; Kate's a widow; Brian's a shell; and Meg's still looking after him. Only Tony has prospered, and not without a price—his wife's suicide, his son's tragedy." Shaking her head, she added softly, "And, it seems, Kate and Brian were having an affair. God help us all."

In a skeptical tone, Terry asked, "That really surprised you?"

Rose gave him a look of characteristic directness. "More than surprised. Shocked. About Brian more than Kate—his code of honor may be his own, but I've always been certain that he has one. Now I can only wonder what will happen to them both."

"For Brian, nothing good. I've bought a few days from the prosecutor. But unless something changes, he'll begin the process for court-martialing Brian on murder charges." Seeing the shadow cross Rose's face, he said, "As to Kate, the military can't touch her. And whatever Flynn's suspicions, I don't think he can mount a case that she helped Brian plan a murder. The price she'll pay, however painful, is more likely to be personal."

Rose looked down. "Not just Kate—the children. I gather her admission tipped the balance."

"The moral balance, certainly. That Brian was sleeping with Joe's wife offends Flynn's deepest beliefs about morality—military and familial. In Flynn's mind, General McCarran would be the first to agree."

Rose was quiet, her expression far away. "Poor Tony. He'll soldier on—literally. That's what a general does. But when I spoke to him after hearing about Kate and Brian, he never sounded so lost. Not even when Mary killed herself."

Once again, Terry found himself wondering, as Meg did, about the history between her father and Rose Gallagher. In a neutral tone, he said, "It must help him that you've always been so close."

As soon as she looked at him, the directness of her gaze disconcerting now, Terry grasped anew how acute this woman was. "Is that quite what you meant to say, Captain? For whatever reason, you've clearly spent some time reading our familial tea leaves. And not just with me."

Cornered, Terry nodded. "True. But it's hardly gratuit-ous, Mrs. Gallagher. I have a very troubled client whose psychology eludes me."

"As well as a complicated co-counsel," Rose amended. "I suspect Meg figures into this pursuit."

The delphic remark did not quite ask whether Meg was a source of Terry's understanding, or a reason why he wished for more. Mildly, he answered, "All of you do."

"I can imagine," Rose answered bluntly. "Meg always believed I wanted her father for myself."

They were edging close, Terry realized, to the ambiguity surrounding Mary's suicide. "Why do you think that?"

Rose clasped her hands. "Because I did," she said at length. "Long before Jack died, when Tony was a cadet at West Point, I fell in love with him. But Tony was drawn by Mary's incandescence. So I married Jack Gallagher instead." Her handsome face held sadness and a trace of wonder. "Our greatest delusion, I think, is to believe that we're deluding others."

Terry had a sudden startling thought—that Rose had resisted imagining her daughter's affair with Brian because Kate was also Tony McCarran's daughter. But that required a lapse of piety and principle—on behalf of both Rose Gallagher and the general—not easy to square with how their families perceived them. Cautiously, Terry inquired, "May I ask you something, Mrs. Gallagher?"

Rose smiled faintly. "You already have. But go ahead, Captain. I can always refuse to answer."

"After Mary's death, why didn't you and the general marry?"

Rose gave him a long, considering look. "How should I respond, I wonder. Perhaps it's better to leave us as two middle-aged victims of repression. But why would you assume that Tony would have wanted that?"

Terry hesitated, uncertain of how far to probe. "Perhaps because Mary thought he did."

The smile that played on Rose's lips did not diminish the keenness of her gaze. "This *is* about Meg, isn't it. And Mary's note."

Terry felt another jolt of surprise. "You saw it?"

"Are you saying Meg still doesn't know that? My God, our silences are breathtaking." Rose's voice softened. "Of course Tony showed it to me—for both Meg's sake and mine, he had to. I was speechless. How many times, I wondered, had I wished her dead. And now she *was* dead, leaving a note that exposed the darker crannies of my soul— and, I knew, her husband's. Perhaps we deserved that. But not when Mary's intended victims included her twelve-year-old daughter."

Silent, Terry absorbed the way Mary McCarran had made her death into a tragedy, still resonant among the living. "It was a deliberate act of cruelty," Rose went on, "designed by a woman who was selfish to her bitter end. She planned for Meg to find her in that bloody bathtub, but not before she found the note. Just as she knew that her poisoned chalice would pass from Meg to Tony to me. The only one she missed was Brian, and he still suffers from the aftershock." For a moment, Rose's voice roughened with anger. "She was the most toxic kind of parent, so consumed with her inner drama that she saw Meg as one more prop. She left it to the living to care if her daughter survived. Or if any of us survived.

"We barely did. Tony was tormented by guilt. So was I. There were times, God help me, when I wished that Meg had flushed that note down the toilet and never told a soul. There must be times she wishes that, too. Whatever else she feels, she surely wonders what would have happened if she had."

Softly, Terry said, "But she was only twelve."

"How well I know it. That's not a choice an adolescent girl should ever have to make, or a burden she should bear alone." Rose fell quiet, and then continued in a calmer tone: "You asked why Tony and I never married. He wanted to. And despite everything, I hoped that, over time, I could help Meg heal. But I couldn't be a surrogate mother to Meg and a wife to her father. It would have confirmed what Mary wanted her to believe—that I had plotted to supplant her mother, and that her father and I had driven Mary to suicide.

"She had left me with a choice, as well. And choosing Tony, I was certain, would cost him a daughter and, in the end, tear us all apart. No matter how I felt for him, or how badly it hurt us both, that had to be my answer. We both lived with that as best we could. All we ever were—all we ever could be—was friends."

Watching her face, Terry felt the depth of this woman's sorrow and resolve. "I can't imagine, Mrs. Gallagher, how hard that must have been."

"Perhaps not. But try remembering yourself at twelve. The adults in your life owed you protection, not the other way around." Rose's tone was quiet but unflinching. "Guilt was also useful. I loved Tony when I married Jack, and I continued to love him through his marriage to Mary. Now Jack and Mary were both dead. In a terrible way, I felt as though I'd willed that. I may have learned something about psychology, but I've been Catholic all my life."

Terry fell quiet. What struck him forcibly was the breadth of needs unspoken or denied, connections missed or misperceived, reverberating through this family in ways both subtle and profound. Yet each mischance, it seemed, bound its members to one another. Terry considered the woman across from him, who had wanted a man too soon, been loved by him too late, and who—because Mary McCarran had not been entirely wrong about her—had forsaken her desires for the sake of children from whom, even as adults, she tried to conceal the depth of her sacrifice. "Were there other men in your life?" Terry inquired at length.

Rose considered a question that, for once, concerned no one but her. "There were," she finally answered. "But there was always Tony and our children. I was raised in the military, and I thought I knew what everyone needed after Mary's death. Perhaps I salved my guilt by making their needs my own." Rose paused, then finished with quiet dispassion, as though pronouncing judgment on her life. "In Tony's case, I succeeded where I could, and failed where I felt I had to. My failure with the children was far more comprehensive. As we're now seeing."

Though Terry could follow the threads of her sadness, her ultimate meaning eluded him still. "I don't quite understand, Mrs. Gallagher. In every case, it seems you left the people in your life better off than you found them."

Rose smiled a little. "That's kind of you to say, Captain. Certainly I helped Tony realize his ambitions. In the army, single men rarely succeed; no single father I've ever known has risen as high as Tony McCarran. When Tony's trajectory took him to Korea, Germany, and Iraq, I looked after Meg and Brian—sometimes with help from Kate—and tended to the unspoken aspects of an officer's career."

Terry nodded. "The politics, you mean."

Rose smiled faintly. "I prefer to think of it as human resources work. Had Mary lived, and been more sane, her job would have been to make new friends among the wives, concerning herself with those aspects of army life that help a family succeed. I did that for Tony." Her face became somber. "When his brigade took casualties in Iraq, I helped families where the soldier had been wounded or killed. I listened to people's problems. As clearly and truthfully as I could, I helped Tony comprehend the lives of those for whom he bore responsibility. And Tony became known as the wise and compassionate man he very much wanted to be, though didn't always know how.

"He remained hurt that I wouldn't—or couldn't—marry him. But he was grateful for what I was able to give him. We both knew that I'd helped him become General McCarran, as Mary never could have."

"So how is that a failure?"

"I failed him in the way I failed myself," Rose answered with resignation. "Tony McCarran is a profoundly lonely man. More and more, the McCarran heritage came to define him. Never having had a father, he never learned to be one. Vietnam not only cauterized him, but cost him his closest friend—my husband. All that you know. But the result after Mary died was that he couldn't truly nurture his own children. And he knows that. He lives in fear of Meg's judgment and, in different ways, of Brian's.

"Aside from me, who can Tony turn to? Within the army he's a hero, an almost legendary figure. And the higher an officer with Tony's ambitions goes, the lonelier he gets, the more afraid of displaying some fatal weakness. Instead he keeps his own counsel, cautious of anyone or anything that could derail him." She shook her head. "Now Tony is chief of staff of the army, and he can't even help his own son, except to find Brian the best lawyer at Fort Bolton. And you're leaving in a couple of weeks."

With this, Terry thought of Meg. "As you say, Mrs. Gallagher, I'm just an interloper. But I can't see how you failed either Meg or Brian."

Though skeptical, Rose's expression was not unkind. "Oh, I think you can, Captain. You strike me as a student of others, even a bit of an anthropologist. Had I been Tony's wife—a day-to-day presence—I might have softened Tony's influence on both children without diminishing their love for him. Brian might never have entered the academy, or become an officer at all. Who among us wouldn't wish that now?" She looked at Terry keenly. "Then there's Meg. In whom, I've begun to think, you take a considerable interest."

Rose Gallagher, Terry thought again, was a very perceptive woman. "Let's say I've begun to detect nuances in her character."

"In other words," Rose amended tartly, "you no longer think she's devoid of human feeling."

Terry smiled. "No. But I'm still working out exactly who she is."

Rose studied him. "And that matters to you?"

Terry considered how to answer. "It's begun to, yes. She's complicated. But beneath the scar tissue, I think Meg has a far more complex emotional life than she allows herself to show. Perhaps even the capacity to trust."

"You won't find out in a week or two," Rose admonished. "No doubt you appreciate the impact of the traumatic suicide of a mother who—aside from being an alcoholic—was the gold standard for maternal unreliability. Meg's defense was to build a wall of self-reliance and self-protection, focusing on the needs of her family rather than her own. Which also impairs her relationships outside the McCarrans, especially with men.

"By now you can tick off the characteristics as well as I can. She can be wary and controlling, with a deep sense of responsibility for her brother and even her father, and an inability to trust anyone else to care for them—let alone for her. She's living with a wellspring of hurt she can never acknowledge." Rose's voice held deep compassion.

"At bottom, Captain Terry, she's deeply afraid. And what frightens Meg more than anything is to face her own need. So she's sublimated that in an intense attachment to her work. For her to face that squarely might be to fall apart."

Terry thought of the night before. "I'm not sure," he answered. "I've begun to think she sees herself more clearly than one might think."

Rose gave him a curious look. "To what degree, I wonder? Brian may be a soldier, but Meg's the one who's made herself as tough as nails. Whether or not she knows it, Meg's first and foremost a McCarran. She may have moved to California, but family is so engrained in her she never truly got away." Her tone was quiet but emphatic. "That's another of my regrets, Captain. I didn't really change the lives of Tony's children. I simply helped them become the best McCarrans they could be. Though that's not the part that makes me saddest. There's Kate."

Terry had begun to understand this woman, and the reckoning she had come to with Joe D'Abruzzo's death. "You say Meg takes too much on herself," he said with gentle irony. "If so, she must have come to you for lessons."

The glint of recognition in Rose's eyes did not change her look of sadness. "Sometimes one simply sees the truth. Kate perceived me as a self-appointed plaster saint, so concerned with the McCarrans that I denied myself and, less forgivably, forgot that I was the only parent she'd ever had. So when her marriage became troubled, she didn't turn to me. Instead, she reached out for the solace I refused myself: an affair with a man she'd always loved—Tony's son." Bowing her head, Rose finished softly: "Kate was the catalyst for the terrible things that followed. Because, like Meg, she couldn't bear the thought of becoming her own mother."

Feeling the weight of Rose's grief, Terry perceived its ultimate cause—the belief that all she had done, or tried to do, had ended in a tragedy. And now, through her grandchildren, the damage would go on.

He sat with her awhile, neither speaking, before he thanked her for her time.

9

THAT NIGHT TERRY slept fitfully, thinking of little but the McCarrans and the Gallaghers, the threads of entwinement that helped define them all and into which, seemingly without much comprehension, Joe D'Abruzzo had been drawn. A death had resulted. Now the law would reduce this psychic web to one brutally simple question: Had Brian McCarran committed murder?

By now Terry had learned that a trial was less than a distillation of truth. He did not know why Brian had killed Joe D'Abruzzo; perhaps Brian did not know. But those assigned to judge him would know less: constrained by the rules of evidence, they would never learn the history Terry had only begun to grasp. Flynn would give them Brian as a calculating murderer; Brian's lawyer would evoke a frightened man acting in self-defense. His peers would pick one version or another, and the actual Brian McCarran—still unknown to them—would go to prison or go free.

It was this that robbed Terry of sleep.

At two A.M., as he watched the red illuminated numbers of his alarm clock, his cell phone rang.

He sat bolt upright. A terrible thought pierced the barrier of his subconscious—that Brian had killed himself. Quickly, he snatched at the phone.

"Paul?" Meg said in a subdued tone. "I'm already sorry I did this."

"Is Brian okay?"

For a moment, she was silent. "I was going to say, 'Of course not.' But I understand what you mean now. Do you worry about that, too?"

Terry inhaled, staring about him at the darkness. "I guess I do. Anyhow, I wasn't sleeping."

"Neither was I." Meg paused again. "It's like I'm watching a train heading straight toward Brian—he can't move, and I can't help him."

Perhaps for Meg, as for Terry, helplessness fed a sense of dread that deepened in the night—when the world slept, time passed too slowly, and nothing could be done. It did not seem strange that they were talking.

"Do you want to come over?" Terry asked. "Maybe we can play backgammon."

Meg laughed softly. "Is that what you do when you can't sleep?" She paused again, then said in a lower voice, "I'm sick of this hotel room. It's become a halfway house between the life I left and all that I'm afraid is coming."

Instinct told Terry to just listen.

"I've been lying here thinking," she ventured. "This is your last weekend at Fort Bolton. Would you like to go somewhere?"

Terry's mood lightened at the surprise of feeling less alone. "Where?"

"Maybe Virginia Beach. A guy Dad served with rents out a cottage there." She hesitated. "If we split the cost, it wouldn't be that much."

Terry smiled in the dark. "My treat," he told her. "I still have a job."

THE HOUSE WAS ON the Atlantic side of Sandbridge Beach, away from the boardwalk on a quiet stretch of white sand and tranquil waters. Their two-hour drive from Bolton had been quiet but companionable, both content with their own thoughts. On arriving, Meg settled a lingering question by following Terry to a bedroom and putting her suitcase next to his.

"Who'd have thought," Terry remarked.

She gave him a wry sideways look and opened the window to admit an ocean breeze.

They had each brought novels—Terry's was by Ward Just, Meg's by Geraldine Brooks. Both choices surprised the other person. But then they were barely acquainted except as lawyers and, to a lesser extent, in bed.

That evening, as they watched the ocean from the deck with a bottle of sauvignon blanc between them, Terry said as much to her. "Not true," she said. "I feel like you've strip-mined my entire life. But I know next to nothing about yours."

She found this unsettling, he knew. "Mine is utterly irrelevant," he answered. "Whereas representing Brian required some appreciation of your family."

Meg turned to him, her deep blue eyes lit by curiosity. "Even now?" she asked with a touch of humor. "You've got a whole weekend to keep me amused, and some of it's going to be spent outdoors. It's time for your oral history."

"Too boring," Terry objected. "No heroes, no medals. A tale of middle-class life in Lake City, Ohio, somewhere in the twilight zone between suburb and small town. Shortly after I was born, a teenage girl named Alison Taylor got murdered. They're still theorizing about it at the supermarket. In Lake City, you never outrun what people choose to believe, or the boredom that makes them care."

Meg looked at him askance. "Did you face this void alone? Or were there brothers and sisters?"

"None." Terry sipped his wine, and decided to go along with her for a while. "My mother struggled just to have me. I'm the first and only of my species."

"What about your folks?"

"My dad's no longer living. He kept the books for a small insurance company, and Mom worked as a secretary at my parochial school. Every day she drove me back and forth; every evening the car pool dropped Dad off at the door. Their lives seemed predictable, and very safe."

"But they were good parents, right?"

Terry felt the old familiar sadness. "*Being* parents pretty much defined them. Early on, the mother superior advised them that I could grow up to accomplish something special. I think they felt as though God had granted them a sacred trust. Suddenly they wanted to give me a life they'd never imagined for themselves."

"You *were* special," Meg rejoined. "Look at what you've done."

"I was different, I suppose. Where both Dad and Mom were shy, other kids saw me as a leader. I started aiming for straight A's—school came easily enough, and my parents always seemed so pleased." He turned to her. "Your brother had a tradition to live up to. In my parents' eyes, I had their mediocrity to transcend. I wish they'd thought better of themselves."

Meg gave him a puzzled look. "Maybe they thought well of *you*. Isn't that how parents want to feel?"

Terry felt a brief irritation at her confidence in speaking for two people she had never known. Then he realized that, compared to Meg's mother, his parents must sound benign. "The problem," he told her, "is that my success became a source of pressure. If I kept doing well, my folks felt they needed to gin up the money for schools they'd barely heard of—like Groton or Yale—where the eastern elite they saw in magazines sent kids less deserving than I. The one caveat was that I'd remain devout."

"Were you?"

Terry laughed. "Lord, no. I liked church best when no one else was there—nothing but light and shadow and stained glass and maybe the hollow footsteps of some other solitary soul. Then I could feel the presence of God. But at Mass the words got in the way, and the parishioners reminded me of Dad waiting for the car pool—dutiful and resigned." Terry sat back, gazing at the ocean. "I might have felt more if they hadn't junked the Latin Mass—comprehension erased the sense of mystery, a timeless connection of past and future. I feel closer to God in a place like this."

"Do you ever miss it?"

Terry pondered how much to say. "Now and then. But as I understand people like your father, religion provides a cosmic reason for the unreasonable. Not for me." Still he did not look at her. "When my father died, I wanted to box with God. Eventually I realized that God is only an idea.

"Some people have it; others don't. I take no position—to fight over the unknowable strikes me as a waste of time. All that matters is what we do on earth, and therefore whether the believers' God is compassionate or a bigot. *That* part's very real."

At the corner of his vision, he saw Meg gazing at the blue-gray waters. "In your heart," she asked, "what do you think happens when you die? Or choose to die."

For an instant, Terry thought of his father. "Ever see a dead squirrel in the road? I don't envision transcendence. It's pretty much the same thing for us, I suspect. No matter how you go."

For a moment, Meg shut her eyes. "That's pretty grim, Paul."

"But useful," he responded. "It reminds us that life is precious, and it places a premium on how we use the years we're got. At the end, I hope, I'll have kids and grandkids who feel good enough about me to say a few nice things."

Turning, she looked at him in mild surprise. "You plan on having a family?"

Terry smiled at this. "I do, actually. So far I've been too busy getting to New York. But I've begun to wonder what I have to show for that besides a destination. In the fullness of time, albeit on my schedule, I want to be some kid's dad."

For a time, Meg studied him. "When did *your* dad die, Paul?"

"Years ago. When I was thirteen."

Terry could read her thoughts—he had been barely older than Meg when her mother committed suicide. Quietly, she said, "I'm sure that was hard."

"Financially, it was ruinous. Dad didn't leave us with anything." Facing Meg, he said baldly, "My character wasn't defined by abstractions, like military honor or the family name. It was defined by money—the money I didn't have, or the money I needed to pay for school.

"Scarcity taught me well. Time was a precious commodity I reserved for part-time jobs, or to stay at the top of my class. I became hyperorganized, a planner who left nothing to chance. The biggest sin, I concluded, was to be surprised by your own life."

Meg gave him a rueful smile. "You sound like me. Even without a watch, I always know what time it is."

Briefly, Terry laughed at this. "Remember the woman I told you about?"

Meg raised her eyebrows. "The undefined relationship with undefined complexities? I probably remember her as well as you do."

"Not true. I'm actually very fond of her. But even though I was off that weekend, I'd lay out my clothes for the next day, and put my keys and wallet beside them." Terry winced in mock embarrassment. "It was habit—in law school, the next day was like a grid in my head. I still can't shake it."

Meg gave him a once-over. "You look carefree enough. At least at the moment."

Terry grinned. "Oh, that's because I planned it."

Meg smiled at this. "Then what have we planned for dinner?" she asked.

NEITHER, IT TURNED OUT, had planned anything at all.

They wound up taking a picnic to the beach, sitting at the water's edge as the setting sun turned the white-capped blue to indigo. Finishing the first bottle of wine, they cracked open some chardonnay. "It's strange," she mused. "Before this happened to Brian, I couldn't envision ever being a defense lawyer."

"Why not?"

Her brow knit. "Maybe I've constructed a black-and-white world. But to me, protecting moms and their kids is a cause. I can't see only caring about whether I win or lose."

Terry felt the glow of wine eroding his caution. Bluntly, he asked, "And you think that's all I care about?"

She was quiet for a moment. "What I'm certain of," she said gently, "is that you want to get ahead, and that no one's going to stop you."

Terry met her eyes. "Then I've left something out," he told her. "My world comes in shades of gray. Moral judgments can be too simple and too harsh; legal judgments can, too. I still don't know why Brian shot D'Abruzzo. He's given me little to go on, and less reason to trust him. But he's said one thing I believe: that he's not the guy Flynn thinks he is.

"The world of people like Flynn is a simple place to live. But I don't believe that the worth of a human being can be defined by the worst moment in his life, or sliced and diced into which facts are admissible and which are not, or captured by some tidy narrative that masquerades as 'truth.'" His voice gained passion. "Granted, I don't see the men you prosecute as very attractive clients. But they were kids once, too—how else did they get that way? When it comes to someone like your brother, there's a whole lot Flynn is missing. Maybe it's not his job to care. But it sure as hell is mine."

Meg turned away for a moment. "I've never met Flynn," she said at last, "but I know him. Joe D'Abruzzo is his client, like those battered women are mine. When it comes to the trial, he won't be driven by emotion, and he won't leave anything to chance. Because, like me, he owes the victims the best lawyer he can be."

"Those people need you," Terry answered. "I'm sorry you had to leave."

For a long time, Meg watched the ocean, pensive. "Once Brian's charged," she said at last, "I'll have to resign my job for good. It's like I've lost a piece of myself. Too big a piece, I think. But there's no help for that now."

Watching her profile, Terry grasped how adrift she was, how completely she had sacrificed her own identity for Brian and her father. Silent, Terry took her hand.

They said little more. Returning to the house, she caught his eye, then angled her head toward the bedroom. This time, their lovemaking was sweeter, slower. She let him hold her until she drifted off to sleep.

10

IN THE MORNING, Meg prepared two credible omelets. After breakfast they walked toward the old stone lighthouse at Cape Henry—Terry in swim trunks, Meg in a bikini. Soft ripples lapped at their feet, and the ocean was pleasantly cool. Unable to resist its lure, Meg ran through an oncoming wave and dived into the calmer sea beyond, swimming parallel to Terry with strong, steady strokes. After a few minutes she returned, grinning like a kid, wet red-auburn hair clinging to her face and shoulders. Grabbing his hand, she said, "Come on."

They waded into the surf until the water was chest-high, glistening with mica tints of reflected sunlight. "When I was a kid," she said, "I always thought of this place as carefree. So was I."

"What did you think you'd become?" Terry asked.

Pausing, she gazed out at the Atlantic, a half smile on her face, perhaps thinking of herself before Mary's problems had enveloped them all. "An aviator—Amelia Earhart without the plane crash. I imagined flying above the world where no one could catch me." She gave her head a shake, shedding droplets of water. "My mother saw herself as a glorified camp follower, captive to other people. I knew I needed something of my own."

For Terry, this brought back something Rose had said. "You remember thinking that?" he asked.

Meg headed for the shore with brisk, determined strides.

"I'm not sure when. Memory is funny—you have these images of a childhood that you constantly reinterpret. But I remember very clearly the first day I felt responsible for her." She shot him a sideways look. "Does any of this really interest you? I feel like I'm being sorry for myself out loud."

They resumed walking along the shoreline. "Self-pity isn't your deal," Terry said. "And yes, I'm interested."

Her gaze refocused on the white spumes of surf. "When I was nine," she told him, "I found her passed out on the bed. For a moment I thought she was dead. Even when I felt her breathing, all I could think of was to call my dad.

"He came home right away. The first thing he did was throw out all the liquor in the house—and I never saw him drink another drop. Then he explained that Mom had a type of sickness some people were unkind about. If anything like this happened again, and he was away, I shouldn't go to anyone but Aunt Rose." She paused, sifting through her memories. "I heard him saying something more: that she was an embarrassment to him—and worse. So when she missed a teacher conference or broke a lunch date, I knew to cover up. I became the misguided adult's idea of what a child should be—so responsible, so caring. When all I wanted was a mother."

Meg still held his hand. "Were you angry at her?" Terry asked.

"I must have been. But I was leading a secret life, even from myself." She seemed to look inward, as though passing judgment on her childhood. "Then she killed herself and left the note—the biggest secret of all. I promised myself never to be like her."

"Then who did you model yourself after?"

She gave him a sardonic smile. "I guess I'm my own creation," she said, then added softly, "I know I should admire Rose. But I saw her as a saner version of my mother, still in orbit around Dad. And now both of them are alone."

"Why didn't they marry, do you think?"

To his surprise, Meg looked pained by the question. "Because I showed Dad the note. After that, he couldn't marry Rose. For my sake."

A shaft of sadness struck Terry—for Rose Gallagher and for the girl she had tried to help, tangled in her own misperceptions about the nature of Rose's sacrifice. But it was not his place to tell Meg the truth. Instead, he inquired, "Did that affect your relationship with Rose?"

In profile, Meg appeared thoughtful. "Whatever happened with Dad, Rose was always good to me. He could take Brian hunting or fishing or to a ball game—the stuff guys do instead of talking. But he knew zero about adolescent girls. So Rose and Kate advised me about boys, and helped me buy a prom dress. They were all I had."

It surprised Terry that Meg was willing to say this much. But perhaps, from her perspective, he was an ideal listener: he had unearthed enough to understand her, and yet would vanish in a week. "So you were also close to Kate?" he asked.

"Yes and no." Meg kept gazing ahead, as though not facing him made it easier to talk. "Dad never had enough for me. Yet I still had to share him with Kate. I'm sure part of that was his debt to Rose—whatever *that* involved. But I remember him giving Kate away when she married Joe, how proud he looked when the two of them danced together." She sounded both angry and abashed. "I know Kate never had a father of her own. But I imagined that she, not me, was the daughter he'd really wanted."

Terry had a vision of three women—Rose, Kate, and Meg—competing for a man with too little to give. "And Brian and Kate?" he asked.

Meg's face closed. "If Kate weren't so damned needy," she said, "this wouldn't have happened to us. As you know, I'm finding that hard to live with." She turned to him, saying in a softer voice, "Enough, Paul. We were getting away, remember?"

THEY SPENT THE DAY pedaling along the bike path, and twilight strolling on the boardwalk, watching families and inventing imaginary lives for the couples they passed. Activity allowed Meg to escape herself, Terry saw, and perhaps forget that she had said so much. He was content to go along.

They ate dinner at a Turkish restaurant, incongruously named the Mayflower Café, which offered generous shanks of lamb and savory home-cooked vegetables. Over their second bottle of wine, they fell back into talk of religion. "If I'm an agnostic," Terry asked, "what are you?"

Meg cocked her head, as though considering the question. "Dad dismisses me as a 'cafeteria Catholic.' I take the bits I like, such as a concern for social justice, and skip the rest. If two guys are happier married, why is that a problem for me? I just worry that they're headed for disappointment."

"You're against straight marriage?" Terry joked.

"That's where *I'm* agnostic." She took a sip of cabernet. "I'm sure my parents married in a fog of mutual incomprehension. But people as 'enlightened' as we are can end up just as lost."

Terry heard something beneath the words. "Have you come close to marrying?"

"Once, when I got pregnant. I chose abortion instead." Spoken aloud, the memory seemed to embarrass her. "God knows why I'm confessing over dinner."

"Maybe because—whatever else—we're becoming friends."

That seemed to give her pause. "Whatever else, Paul, I was too afraid of marriage. When I ended the pregnancy, it ended the relationship." She looked up, her eyes meeting Terry's. "Chris said I was selfish. I couldn't really argue with him. On my more lucid days, I'm not a complete mystery to myself."

Terry sat back. "Really?" he said in mock exasperation. "Just when I think we're actually getting somewhere, you say something completely Martian." He stopped there, then spoke evenly and kindly. "Self-protection is different than being selfish. In some ways, you're the least selfish person I know. But you gave up way too much, too soon, to the idea of the McCarrans. And now you're doing it again."

For an instant she looked defensive, then summoned a belated smile. "Meg the Martian," she said. "You're quick to catch it so soon."

"That's not hard," he said. "But sometimes, when you let go, you're also lovely."

Her eyes widened in a pantomime of bewilderment. " 'Lovely'?"

"It's a compliment," Terry assured her with a smile. "Not that I'd believe for one moment that you're not hell in court."

Meg's smile became more genuine. " 'Lovely,' " she repeated. "I wonder if I could ever live with that."

THAT NIGHT, NEITHER NEEDED to signal their desire to make love.

Lying across him, Meg felt warm, her breasts full and womanly. The smell of her skin, familiar now, enhanced Terry's desire. Kissing his neck, and then his stomach, Meg made him wait. Only when she was done did he slip inside her, his guide her whispered words.

Afterward, as Meg slept, Terry sat on the deck with a glass of wine. The breeze smelled faintly of salt; the moon cast a thin light on the gently stirring sea grass. Terry thought about everything and nothing.

He heard footsteps on the wooden planks, then felt Meg's chin resting atop his head. "Penny for your thoughts," she said. "Is that still the going rate?"

"Certainly for mine." Leaning back, Terry studied the moon. "I was thinking that we're almost like actors on a movie set—our relationship is defined, and confined, by Brian's troubles. For which I'm sorry."

She drew back slightly. "You mean that it's finite."

"Your word, not mine. I was just wondering how we'd be without the case to worry about. Or, for that matter, Mike Flynn."

Meg sat next to him. After a while, she said quietly, "Then tell me about your father. I keep wondering how he died, and why you never say."

Terry felt the familiar ache, a tightening in his chest that made it hard to speak. In a monotone, he said at last, "One evening he bought a gun, went to the police station, and blew his brains out in the parking lot. He didn't want us to find him. In that way, Dad was considerate to the end."

She grasped his hand. "My God, Paul—"

"He was depressed, my mother explained. I was still grieving when she told me we had no money. Two years later I found some papers hidden in his desk and pressed her for the truth." Terry's voice became weary. "He'd been caught embezzling cash, a little at a time, to put in a college savings account Mom knew nothing about. Dad returned the proceeds. But that wasn't enough for Evan Corns, the president of Corns Insurance. 'Mr. Corns,' as

Dad still called him after twenty years, insisted to the county prosecutor that only a prison sentence would keep his other employees honest. Dad couldn't face prison or us. Instead he took the gun and went Mr. Corns one better."

Meg studied Terry in the moonlight. "What was he like?"

"Sweet, with a gentle sense of humor. One night I asked him to take me to a hockey game. Dad seemed too pre-occupied. To impress him, I explained that the visiting team had Guido Fasciani. 'Maybe if they take penicillin,' Dad suggested with mock solemnity, 'it'll go away.' When I didn't see the humor, he relented and took me to the game. He shot himself two weeks later." Terry faced her. "I didn't need Yale, Meg. I just needed my father. What did I ever do, I wonder, to make him think he wasn't enough? But all I can do now is provide for my mother."

"Why did you never tell me?" Meg asked.

He twitched his shoulders. "It didn't seem germane."

"Not even to *my* story? Come off it, Paul." Her voice softened. "You said that a person shouldn't be defined by his worst moment. You were talking about your father, weren't you?"

"And Mr. Corns," he said tersely. "Mike Flynn's spiritual father. So now you know all about me."

"Hardly all." Pausing, Meg touched his face. "We don't have very much time, I know. But I still care about learning more."

Suddenly Terry felt the tears in his eyes, the ones left over from the nights he spent not crying as his mother slept the drugged sleep of prescription pills. "Maybe I should have said something, Meg. But it wasn't you, or even that we're co-counsel. There was no redeeming my father's death, and I couldn't be defined by it. All I could control was this day and the next, working toward a future where I finally outran the misery I felt." His voice lowered. "It's not that I don't know myself; I know myself too well. For the last eighteen years I've believed that every second I lived in the past blocked my hope of transcendence. That's what I see in you. But it hasn't quite worked, has it? For either one of us."

Meg took both of his hands in hers. "Do you know what I sensed when we first met? That we're alike." She gave a gentle, rueful laugh. "Too bad for us, I guess. I wonder if we can ever unlearn what we've taught ourselves."

Terry pulled her close, held her for a time. "Too bad I'm leaving," he said softly.

On Sunday morning, they sat on the deck, drinking coffee and reading the *New York Times*. Terry appreciated the distraction—perhaps, like Meg, he felt exposed.

Her cell phone rang. Glancing at the caller ID, she stood and walked to a corner of the deck. She seemed to listen for a while, then returned with an air of resignation. "That was my dad."

Terry summoned a smile. "Checking up on you?"

"Actually, he wanted your cell phone number. I told him we were together." She paused a moment. "He'd like to see you."

"When?"

Meg seemed to wince. "This afternoon, if possible. In Washington."

Their chance for intimacy, Terry realized, was coming to an end. To Meg, he said simply, "Tell the general I'll make time."

11

Approaching the Vietnam memorial, Terry searched for Anthony McCarran among the visitors standing quietly before the granite wall, shadowed in the late afternoon. At length Terry spotted him. Wearing civilian clothes and sunglasses, General McCarran went unnoticed—an anonymous if distinguished visitor among the many hundreds who would visit on this day. Only Terry would know that his closest friend's name was engraved where the general stood or that, however busy, McCarran came here every Sunday. The ritual was, in Meg's telling, as sacred to him as Mass.

Silent, Terry stood beside the general, gazing at Jack Gallagher's name and the date of his death: June 4, 1972. Only a slight shift in McCarran's posture suggested that he was aware of Terry's presence. Without turning, McCarran said, "Thank you for coming, Captain."

Terry said nothing. Turning, McCarran left the wall and walked, hands in his pockets, toward the bronze statue of three soldiers cast for visitors who found the black granite wall too somber, even for the dead. Stopping by the statue, the general turned again. In a tone somewhere between pointed and apologetic, McCarran said, "I gather when I called Meg you were at Virginia Beach."

"Yes." Terry permitted himself a faint sardonic edge. "It was convenient, I suppose."

McCarran gave him a wintry smile. "I hope you didn't

interpret this as a summons. I know very well that you don't report to me—personally or professionally. But I *am* a worried father."

Terry nodded. "I understand, sir."

"I've spoken to Meg, of course. But you're the expert, Captain. What will happen to Brian now?"

Briefly, Terry considered how to answer. "Procedurally, it's pretty straightforward. The Article 32 hearing will happen quickly. Four months from now, Brian could be facing a general court-martial on charges of murder and adultery."

McCarran removed his sunglasses. "Is that inevitable?"

"I think so. Under Article 32, all Major Flynn has to show to justify a court-martial is probable cause. He can also use hearsay." Terry paused, adding quietly, "Which includes Joe D'Abruzzo's statement that Kate was 'fucking McCarran.'"

The narrowing of McCarran's eyes carried a hint of pain. "You really think that's enough."

"I do. In several other ways, Brian hasn't helped himself. Lying about his affair is only part of that. There are gaps in his story—including a supposed gap in memory. What detail he offers about the shooting doesn't square very well with the physical evidence. And Brian can't—or won't—talk about his combat experience in Iraq."

McCarran scrutinized Terry. "I gather that you suggested invoking post-traumatic stress disorder."

Beneath McCarran's neutral tone Terry heard distaste, or perhaps discomfort. "I did," Terry said flatly. "I think you know far better than I do, General, that PTSD is real. And you know for sure that Brian came back damaged."

For a moment, McCarran studied the haunted faces of the three bronze soldiers. "How would that help him now?"

"It could help explain Brian's memory lapse, or even why he killed D'Abruzzo." Pausing, Terry waited for McCarran to face him. "Maybe," he continued coolly, "Brian's a murderer, and an extremely gifted liar. But it's also very possible that he's a screwed-up guy who slept with somebody else's wife, and is facing life in prison for something he didn't do. At the moment, that's how I read him.

"Flynn, however, is a truly moral man. In his mind, Brian's affair with Kate exposes a pervasive character deficit and provides a motive for murder. Amorality, in Flynn's eyes, is seamless."

McCarran's gaze turned bleak. "I once served as a juror in a case involving an affair between a married colonel and a female officer in his command. We dismissed him from the service. Civilians don't understand that. But I know all too well that adultery is a breach of military honour."

"This case is worse," Tony said bluntly. "Among other things, Flynn imagines that Brian killed D'Abruzzo to avoid what you're talking about—the shame of a ruined career."

McCarran absorbed this, still gazing at the statue. Then he said softly, "Every day that Brian was in Iraq, I would scan the reports of the dead, afraid that I'd see his name. Now, like Meg, I worry that he'll kill himself, or spend his life in prison. But unlike Meg, I have myself to blame— my own pride and self-involvement. Too often I saw Brian as a McCarran, instead of Brian, my son." Facing Terry, McCarran stood straighter. "Perhaps I have no right to ask you. But Meg thinks very well of you, as does anyone who's seen you in court. For Brian's sake, and hers, I wish you'd stay."

Terry hesitated, examining his own emotions. "All I can promise," he answered, "is that I won't leave without meeting with Brian again. If only to recommend the best military lawyer I know to help them both."

McCarran nodded, accepting the tacit rebuff with a look very close to misery. "All right, Captain. I'll wait to hear from Meg."

DRIVING BACK TO FORT BOLTON, Terry called his future litigation partner at home. "Sorry to bother you on a Sunday," he said. "But something's come up. It looks like the army means to court-martial Brian McCarran."

"Too bad," Frank Morrissey said in a neutral voice. "I'm sure you did all you could to prevent that."

"I did. It wasn't enough." For a moment, Terry hesitated. "It'll be a challenging trial, Frank—not to mention well publicized. That might be good for all of us. I was wondering if the firm could give me six months' grace time."

"Wish we could," Morrissey said crisply. "But your month in Europe was a hard enough sell." His tone became practical. "One of our investment banking clients, Ray Fazio, is about to be indicted for insider trading. Looks like the feds have a case, but Ray means to fight it tooth and nail. We're weak in criminal defense— without you, or someone like you, Ray may take his business down the street. We picked you over a hotshot from the U.S. Attorney's Office. I'm sorry, Paul, but if you don't show up on schedule, we'll have to hire the hotshot instead."

Terry felt the vise of his own conflicting desires. It was not easy to imagine giving up this opportunity, or explaining to his mother that the house he had promised her would have to wait. All he could say to Morrissey was "I understand, Frank. Thanks for your candor."

"No problem, Paul," Morrissey said warmly. "See you in a month."

Another door had closed, narrowing Terry's choices.

As TWILIGHT APPROACHED, TERRY found Brian McCarran on his boat, folding its canvas sails. Glancing over his shoulder, Brian said, "You must think I live here."

"I just think you'd like to." Terry kept his tone level. "When you're finished, there's a conversation we need to have."

Brian's smile was a mere show of teeth. "The one where you wish me 'good luck'?"

"No. The one where I explain that you're going down unless you get a grip."

As Brian's mouth formed a silent whistle, his blue-gray eyes watched Terry's face. "I'm listening."

Terry sat across from him. "If you're a liar, Brian, it's not working. And if you're trying to be a stoic, you're also a complete fool. With me so far?"

This time the smile did not diminish Brian's look of vigilance. "That wasn't hard to follow, Captain."

"Okay. Let's assume for the moment you're a stoic." Terry paused for emphasis. "I don't care what you did in Iraq or how much pain it causes you. You need to work with Dr. Carson to uncover why you can't remember what happened that night.

"That's for openers. Once the Article 32 investigation concludes, your lawyer can ask for his own investigator from CID. Unless you're completely self-destructive, you'll give that guy the name of every soldier in your command who saw whatever you went through. Not just to establish a PTSD defense but as witness to your character as a combat leader. When those jurors look at you, they need to see an officer who watched out for his men, not a guy who screwed his murdered CO's wife."

Brian's eyes glinted. "And where will *you* be, sir? In Europe? Or New York?"

Terry leaned forward, hands clasped in front of him. Softly, he said, "I'm not sure yet."

Brian sat straighter. With mild astonishment, he said, "You're thinking about staying."

"I'm considering it."

"Why exactly?"

"Maybe I think you're a liar but not a murderer. Or maybe I just don't want to leave Meg in the lurch. Call me sentimental. But whether I stay is up to you."

"Does that mean I have to ask?"

"More than that, Brian. You'll have to do exactly as I say."

Brian gave him a wary look. "Work with Carson, you mean."

"Yes. But not for the sake of the Article 32 hearing." Terry's voice became crisp. "Other than to cross-examine Flynn's witnesses, we won't offer a defense. If I can manage it, Kate D'Abruzzo won't say a thing at the hearing. And I know damned well that *you* will—"

Brian held up his hand. "No way. Crooks and gangsters take the Fifth—"

"So do officers who dislike prison." Terry slowed his speech for emphasis. "Your story needs work. You should only tell it once, and only when you're ready. Otherwise Flynn will tear you to little pieces. I won't let you serve as his enabler out of some medieval sense of honor—military or familial.

"All I care about is keeping you out of jail. You said you'd rather kill yourself than go to prison. So what do *you* care about most—your life and freedom, or your father and those dead ancestors on his wall?" Terry paused again. "Do what I say at the Article 32 hearing, and you're guaranteed to face a court-martial. But at least you'll have a prayer of winning."

Brian stared at the lacquered floor of his boat. "So you're willing to defend me," he said slowly. "All I have to do is spill my guts, look like a weasel at the hearing, and tee up a court-martial for Major Flynn."

"That's just the start. I also know you're sitting on something. You don't have to tell me what it is. But whatever you *do* tell me had better be true. One more lie, and I walk out." Terry lowered his voice. "Then there's your sister. If I agree to represent you at the court-martial, you'll damn well stay alive for her. One suicide in Meg's life is enough."

Brian stared at him. Softly, he said, "So I'd lose my freedom of choice?"

"Yup. But there's one other thing, Brian. You'll have to start calling me Paul."

Brian's bark of laughter was followed by a grin that, to Terry's surprise, seemed genuine. "Free at last—Paul and Brian's excellent adventure." The smile vanished abruptly. "This won't be easy. Not for me, or you. Or Meg."

Terry nodded. "I know that."

For a moment, Brian shut his eyes. Quietly, he said, "Okay, Paul. You're on."

PART THREE

THE PROSECUTION

NOVEMBER 2005

1

THE DAY BEFORE jury selection in *United States versus Lieutenant Brian McCarran*, Major Michael Flynn, trial counsel for the army, and Captain Paul Terry, counsel for the accused, met to argue Flynn's motion to preclude the defense from contending that Brian suffered from post-traumatic stress disorder.

Meg sat beside Terry at the defense table. During the past four months, she had been coming to Terry's apartment several times a week, at times as his co-counsel, at other times as his lover. He thought of her as different people: the driven lawyer; the troubled woman who felt unmoored from her own life; the passionate lover; the sister who wished to escape her fears for Brian. The starkest divide was between the lawyer who observed him so clinically and the refugee who, outside the confines of the case, could be tender and even light of spirit. Terry's best hope of reconciling these personae—and sorting out his own feelings of attachment to her—lay on the far side of the trial.

Her expression today was as somber as the courtroom. Stained wood composed the walls, the judge's bench, and the box where the members of the court—military jurors—would sit. Heavy gold drapes were drawn across tall windows, the sole illumination falling from bowls suspended from a high ceiling, lending the courtroom a sepia tone. The solemnity was completed by the presence of

Colonel Carter Hollis, a magisterial African-American, who, as senior judge in the circuit that included Fort Bolton, had assigned himself to the trial of Brian McCarran.

For Hollis, this case might become the high point of a notable career. Known as a superb judge, Hollis had served as prosecution and defense counsel and, after ascending the bench, had presided over a hundred courts-martial, including a challenging trial stemming from the death of Iraqi civilians. While the colonel ran a taut courtroom, by reputation he had an open mind. Particularly hopeful, from Terry's perspective, was that Hollis held a master's degree in criminal law from Harvard, lectured extensively at the army JAG school, and had a sophisticated grasp of the nuances of law, including cutting-edge issues subject to sharp debate. This had led to Terry's first tactical decision: hoping that Hollis would preside, Terry had waived the right—available in such an incendiary case—to request a judge from another branch of the military. Today would tell him much about the wisdom of that gamble.

Until this moment, Terry had never seen Hollis in court. The judge exuded a calm authority; he was accustomed to respect and knew that he would receive it. Tall and lean at fifty, Hollis had smooth features, salt-and-pepper hair, and probing dark eyes that, Terry had heard, hinted at emotions—interest, skepticism, impatience, or amusement—otherwise absent from his scrupulously impassive face.

The high mahogany bench from which Hollis surveyed the courtroom was flanked by the flags of the United States and its army. Behind him stood his bailiff, a sergeant. In the well of the courtroom, the court reporter, a corporal, was stationed near one corner of the bench. To the left Major Flynn, tense and alert, sat with his second chair, Captain Rod Pulaski, dubbed the "Angel of Death" for his deceptively innocent face. To the right were Paul Terry and

Meg McCarran. The gallery at the rear was jammed with reporters and spectators drawn by the facts of the case—a compound of adultery and death—and the identity of the accused. Brian himself was, on Terry's instructions, scrupulously impassive. But through Meg, Terry could feel his tension, and that of their father. Her expression was taut; she knew, as did their opponents, that the outcome of the trial might depend on how Hollis ruled today.

The judge looked from Terry to Flynn. "This hearing," he intoned in a baritone voice, "is to consider the army's motion to preclude any defense based on post-traumatic stress disorder. You may proceed, Major."

Flynn rose, striding to the podium so briskly that Terry thought of a greyhound. "Thank you, Your Honor," he said hurriedly. "The arguments of the accused are without precedent or merit. First, the law. No military court, anywhere, has allowed PTSD to reduce murder to manslaughter—"

"What about the *Rezaq* case?" Hollis cut in sharply.

"That was a federal case," Flynn parried, "not binding on this court. And *Rezaq* merely suggests that PTSD *may* be considered."

Hollis leaned forward. "Then why shouldn't *this* court at least hear evidence regarding Lieutenant McCarran?"

Flynn stood straighter. "Because experience in combat—however harsh—has never nullified the intent to commit murder—"

"Let's stick to *Rezaq*," Hollis interjected. "The defendant was a terrorist who highjacked an Air Egypt flight. His claim was that he suffered from PTSD after witnessing the slaughter of Palestinian refugees many years before. Isn't that a bigger stretch than for Lieutenant McCarran to assert that, in a moment of danger, his reaction was conditioned by traumatic combat experience?"

"Good," Terry murmured to Meg. But doubt was graven on her face.

"It's *all* a stretch," Flynn answered. "The *Rezaq* court imagines that a terrorist who highjacked a plane, endangering innocent lives, could claim that he was gripped by a slow-motion trauma. By that standard, any witness to an atrocity is entitled to commit one—"

"We're talking about Lieutenant McCarran," Hollis snapped, "not Mohamed Atta. Let's stick to the effects of a war from which he returned six months before the shooting."

"What effects?" Flynn said with mild disdain. "We don't know *what* trauma the accused supposedly suffered in Iraq. We do know that he was in combat. No one knows what it means to kill someone better than a combat veteran."

Hollis frowned. "You assume, Major, that combat is like shooting skeet. But doesn't combat also produce reflexive reactions in a matter of split seconds?"

Flynn seemed to riffle the file cards in his head. "In *United States versus Martin*," he replied, "the court ruled that a defendant's delusional belief that his conduct was justified could *only* be considered in mitigation of sentencing—"

"But isn't the real problem," Hollis countered, "that the accused often can't relate the factual origins of combat stress to the violent act in question?"

Terry felt Meg tense, as did he. "Precisely," Flynn said smoothly. "That's also Lieutenant McCarran's problem here—"

"That's a different point," Hollis interrupted. "What you're really saying is that it doesn't matter if the accused *can* relate his combat experience to his crime. Think *that's* how the law should be?"

Terry repressed a smile. Decisively Flynn answered, "Yes,

Your Honor. Captain Terry's argument opens the flood-gates to abuse. There's no way to verify that combat stress—even if proven—means that an accused did not *intend* to do what soldiers are *trained* to do: deliberately kill another human being."

To Terry's discomfort, Hollis remained silent, regarding Flynn with a look of renewed interest. "The second problem," Flynn continued, "is the gap in the affidavit of Dr. Carson, submitted by counsel. Dr. Carson opines that Brian McCarran suffers from PTSD. But he offers nothing that would link his service in Iraq to putting four bullets into his lover's husband—including one in the back. This absence of detail—fatal in itself—confirms the abuses inherent in this defense."

"Captain Terry," Hollis pointed out, "asserts that the investigation of his client's combat experiences is ongoing."

Flynn's eyes glinted. "Hasn't he asked the accused? Perhaps Lieutenant McCarran has also forgotten his time in Iraq."

Hollis placed a finger to his lips, his silence deepening Terry's unease. Firmly, Flynn asserted, "This unsupported claim would confuse the members of the court without illuminating the facts of Captain D'Abruzzo's death. The army respectfully asks this court to preclude all testimony from Dr. Carson, or from any other witness called to establish post-traumatic stress disorder."

Hollis nodded briskly. "Thank you, counsel. I'll hear from Captain Terry."

Rising, Terry was aware of Meg's tension, and that this was the first time she had witnessed him in court. As Terry walked slowly to the podium, Hollis said, "Your papers suggest that you're reluctant to bring Dr. Carson before the court, preventing Major Flynn from cross-examining him. Wouldn't that help clear things up?"

Terry placed his hands on the podium. "It's too soon," he said simply. "We're still tracking down the men who served with Lieutenant McCarran. Some have suffered traumatic brain injury; others are in Iraq and Afghanistan. Still others—particularly those involved in combat operations with Lieutenant McCarran—are dead. Until we locate all the witnesses, Dr. Carson cannot form an opinion. It's as premature to cross-examine him today as it would be to preclude his testimony at trial."

"And what if his testimony is based on vapor?" Hollis asked. "That could create the confusion Major Flynn implores us to avoid."

Terry was prepared for this. "When a man's freedom is at stake, what's the greater risk—confusion or an unjust verdict? I'm certain that this court can instruct the jury to ignore testimony it deems irrelevant."

Hollis raised his head, telegraphing skepticism. "Why risk a sloppy trial, where the members lose track of what testimony is irrelevant when they've already heard it. You may think too highly of this court's ability to cram your genie back into Major Flynn's bottle—although perhaps you don't much care." Having unloosed this barb, Hollis continued, "But let's move on to your next suggestion— that PTSD can support a verdict of not guilty by reason of insanity. Why should this court so boldly go where no courts have gone before?"

The casual reference to *Star Trek* caused Terry, however worried, to smile. "If the law didn't evolve," he answered, "courts would still be applying the 'wild beast test,' where an accused's insanity was measured by his propensity to make the growling sound of predatory animals. With all due respect, Major Flynn would lead us boldly toward the Middle Ages."

The light in Colonel Hollis's eyes might have been

amusement. "According to the major, he's intent on protecting the law from your factitious claim."

"The law," Terry answered, "needs no protection. The legal test for insanity is very clear: At the moment he shot Captain D'Abruzzo, did Brian McCarran have a 'mental disease or defect' that prevented him from knowing that his action was wrong?

"If, as we claim, Lieutenant McCarran acted in self-defense, that question never arises—one can legally take a life if he reasonably believes his own life is in danger. But suppose that, based on PTSD, Brian shot D'Abruzzo in the mistaken but honest belief that he was acting in self-defense?" Terry paused for emphasis. "If that is the case, then Lieutenant McCarran did *not* know that shooting D'Abruzzo was wrong. By definition, he is not guilty by reason of insanity."

Hollis raised his eyebrows. "I'll grant you points for creativity. But is PTSD a recognized 'mental disease or defect'?"

"Absolutely. Hundreds of years of military history confirm that combat is traumatic to those engaged in war. First they called it 'soldier's heart'; then it became 'shell shock.' Since Vietnam we've known it as post-traumatic stress disorder. But the symptoms are the same: hyperarousal, nightmares, reflexive violence, substance abuse, and, in the case of one of Lieutenant McCarran's men, suicide. We know that many veterans evince these things. PTSD is the cause." Terry paused, then added, "It is also possible that Captain D'Abruzzo suffered from PTSD. Specifically, that the same impulses that caused him to hit his wife, hold a gun to her head, and drink himself senseless also drove him to threaten Brian McCarran—"

"What about adultery?" Hollis inquired mildly. "Think that played a role?"

Terry feigned a calm he did not feel. "Adultery is not an excuse for murder. Nor does it mitigate the effects of combat." He paused again. "There is time enough for Major Flynn and me to contest the role—if any—played by the lifelong closeness between my client and Kate D'Abruzzo. But the question now is whether the officers who will determine the fate of the accused are capable, with this court's guidance, of sorting out the facts. We say yes; Major Flynn says no. The future of too many returning veterans may depend on this court's answer."

"Thank you," Hollis said at length, then turned to Flynn. "Any response, Major?"

Flynn stood at once. "Yes, Your Honor," he said in a stern voice. "Captain Terry's plea comes down to this: let's figure out what the law is after we've ignored it by admitting evidence that is *contrary* to law. His real purpose is to create sympathy for the accused, instead of the officer he murdered—"

"Killed," Hollis corrected. "It's for the jury to determine whether this is murder." He folded his hands, addressing Terry. "For now, I'm denying the government's motion. But the court will allow testimony on PTSD if—and only if—you come up with a written proffer of evidence that relates Lieutenant McCarran's combat experience to the facts of Captain D'Abruzzo's death. And if the testimony fails to meet that standard, I will instruct the members of the court to ignore it." The quiet of Hollis's tone underscored the force of his admonition. "You surely know that this would not redound to your client's benefit. Before you invoke this defense, please consider it with the utmost care."

With that, the judge brusquely nodded to his bailiff. *"All rise,"* the sergeant called out, and Hollis left the bench, vanishing through the door to his chambers.

As the press stood behind them, chairs scraping and voices murmuring, Flynn stared at the floor. Daunted but relieved, Terry turned to see Meg's brief, uncertain smile. Brian remained expressionless, as though he had removed himself from the courtroom.

A HALF HOUR LATER, using the speakerphone in Terry's office, they reached their CID investigator, Sergeant Ben Flournoy. He had worked with Terry and Meg for the last four months, looking for soldiers who had served with Brian from his arrival in Iraq. Today the connection was not good; Flournoy had just landed in Afghanistan.

"I found the chaplain," he reported, "the one who knew Lieutenant McCarran in Sadr City. But it seems like the other guy I'm looking for—Johnny Whalen—is the only soldier who went all the way through with *our* guy."

Terry glanced at Meg. "What about the ones you found in Iraq?"

"Not much good, sir. They rotated in later, when the worst was over. I don't like saying this. But if Whalen can't help us, I'm feeling like we're done."

"Keep trying," Meg urged.

"What about Lieutenant McCarran?" Flournoy asked. "How's he doing with Dr. Carson?"

"It's still a struggle," Terry admitted. "Carson's trying to unlock him. He thinks Brian's afraid of something. It would be great if you found out why."

After the call was over, Meg slumped in her chair. Because they were alone, Terry took her hand.

"Let's go home," he said.

2

THE FOLLOWING MORNING, counsel and the accused returned to court.

With the others, Terry stood. In the next minutes, Flynn would recite the charges, then the judge would inform the accused of his right to counsel and proceed to the selection of the members of the court. Despite his steady gaze, Brian McCarran looked apprehensive. But then he knew that Flynn and Terry were poised to select the strangers whose votes would determine the course of his life.

TWO WEEKS BEFORE, TERRY had explained the process to Meg.

She had come to his apartment for the night. Terry was scanning the questionnaires filled out by the potential members of the court, placed neatly on his kitchen table like chess pieces on a board. As military law required, all were officers superior in rank to Brian; among them, Terry hoped, were veterans of Afghanistan or Iraq. It was based on this hope, in part, that Terry had advised Brian to demand a jury drawn from these men and women, rather than a trial where Hollis would render both the verdict and the sentence. Another reason—Terry's belief that he could outwit Flynn in the complex art of picking the members of the court—might prove either prescient or, perhaps, fatally foolish.

The responsibilities placed on those members were far

more weighty and complex than those given to civilian jurors. In the findings phase, they would determine guilt or innocence; though Flynn would charge Brian with murder and adultery, the members could find him guilty of a lesser offense. Unless Brian was acquitted, the sentencing phase would follow, in which Flynn and Terry would again present evidence as to the appropriate punishment. Even if the members adjudged Brian guilty of the gravest crime, they could impose a lesser sentence than Flynn requested—or no punishment at all. Here lay Terry's final hope: that non-lawyers, especially veterans of combat, might prove more lenient than a judge.

Meg stood behind him, kneading his shoulders with capable hands. "What do you see?"

"A math puzzle—a peculiar feature of military law. When you pick a jury in San Francisco, you have to come up with twelve. Brian's jury *could* number twelve, or as few as five." He glanced up at her. "Another quirk is that, to get a conviction, all Flynn needs to do is persuade two-thirds of the members that Brian is guilty."

Meg's eyes darkened. "Then why did you tell Brian to demand a jury—"

"Because under military law there's no hung jury. If Flynn can't get his two-thirds, Brian walks. That's where the math comes in. What's two-thirds of six?"

"Four," Meg said impatiently. "I'd grasped that by third grade."

Terry laughed. "Okay. Suppose I knocked the number of jurors down to five. How many guilty votes does Flynn need then?"

Meg thought swiftly. "Four. You can't divide jurors into thirds."

"Exactly. So with five jurors, if I persuade just two, Brian still walks. No retrial—ever." Terry waved at the questionnaires. "I don't have to pick twelve winners. I just need to cut this pool down to size, and find a minority of sympathetic souls tough-minded enough to stand up to the rest. Of course, Flynn knows that, too."

Meg sat beside him. "So play this out for me."

"All right. In a twelve-person jury, if I carry four votes, Flynn prevails: eight votes for conviction gives him the two-thirds he needs. But if the jury is only eleven and I still get my four, we can all go home."

"So," Meg interjected, "if Flynn gets a nine-member jury, and you persuade only three, Brian loses. But in an eight-person jury, three votes means acquittal."

"And so on down the line. If Flynn wants six jurors, I want five. Then the challenge becomes finding the two jurors who will vote to acquit Brian."

"How do you get to the right number?"

"It's like a chess game. Flynn and I get only one peremptory challenge; our sole chance of booting a potential juror without offering any reason. The remaining challenges must be for cause: one side can argue to dismiss a juror, the other to keep him, and then the judge decides." Terry pointed at the questionnaires. "*This* is where I need your help. Flynn and I will be bluffing each other, holding back the challenges we think are strongest, in hope that we end up with our number. So if we get down to six members, for example, pray that I'm sitting on a challenge that Hollis will grant—giving us five. The problem is that Hollis understands the game better than anyone."

Meg gave him the intent, practical look that had become so familiar. "So you want me to look at these questionnaires and help find Brian some winners."

"For openers, yes. You'll see the usual data: education, career, family, combat experience, prior service on a court-martial, whether they've been the victim of a crime. At the level of sheer guesswork, I'd want a divorced psychiatrist; Flynn, a fundamentalist Christian with six kids."

Meg nodded. "Pretty routine. I do this all the time."

"I'm sure. But we can also use this stuff to do some informal digging. You've got over a half million people in San Francisco—it's not easy to investigate a jury pool. But Fort Bolton is smaller, a place where people you know may know the folks on this table. A phone call here, a cup of coffee there, and pretty soon we learn who may be sleeping with the neighbor's wife, or knows someone who suffers from PTSD. A little inside knowledge can mean the difference between keeping a juror and knocking him off. But it's delicate. That's why I'm doing it myself instead of using our investigator."

Meg looked dubious. "Okay," she said after a moment. "I assume you want me to design questions for potential jurors—were they stationed in Iraq, have they lost family or friends in combat, et cetera, et cetera."

"Exactly. Sometimes the judge will ask them for us. But we also get to question them individually. That's when you and I decide who to keep and who to challenge." Terry nodded at the questionnaires. "Out of all those people, we'll end up with our members and an opinion on how we did. But we won't really know until they vote."

Meg reached for a questionnaire and began reading it intently.

THE NEXT TWO DAYS were a battle of wits and nerve.

Judge Hollis cleared the courtroom of spectators. Then he convened the fifteen potential members of the court, all with the rank of captain or above. Within three hours, questioning by the judge and lawyers had winnowed them to eleven, a number more satisfactory to Terry than to Flynn.

"Trial counsel would like to question Colonel Luke-hart," Flynn announced. The chess match had begun in earnest.

LIEUTENANT COLONEL JACK LUKEHART was a slender man with prematurely white hair and the serious mien of an officer who left no detail to chance. "What's Flynn's problem with *this* guy?" Meg whispered.

Terry glanced at Brian, who, from his faint smile, seemed to have guessed. Under his breath, Terry said, "Six to one he knows your father."

"Prior to your current posting," Flynn asked Lukehart, "did you serve in the Pentagon?"

"I did, Major Flynn. As an aide to General Carstairs."

Flynn nodded. "What were your duties, sir?"

"Several. But my principal duty was to help General Carstairs review and revise training procedures for the infantry."

"And to whom did the general report?"

Briefly, Lukehart glanced at Brian before turning back to Flynn with self-conscious attentiveness. "General Anthony McCarran."

"During this time, did you form an impression of General McCarran?"

Lukehart hesitated, then answered firmly: "Like others who served with the general, I thought him to be a model senior officer—intelligent, incisive, inclusive, as skilled at listening as he was at asking questions. He seemed to have no ego. One of his outstanding traits was to give everyone a fair hearing."

"Did he give *your* views a fair hearing?"

"Always. On several occasions, in spite of some initial misgivings, he adopted General Carstairs's suggestion for significant changes. When he disagreed, his reasons were sound and clearly stated." Lukehart nodded in self-affirmation. "One of the many reasons why General McCarran commands respect is the respect he grants to others."

This endorsement caused Flynn to cock his head, scrutinizing Lukehart closely. "Did you also form an opinion of General McCarran's integrity?"

Lukehart pondered the question. "Before I met General McCarran, I knew by reputation that his integrity was beyond question. What I learned was that General McCarran spoke with total candor. He never kept us in the dark about what he knew or thought. In all of our dealings, he was a completely honorable man."

"And," Brian murmured wryly, "overdue for canonization."

"That's the problem," Terry scribbled on his notepad.

"In your observation," Flynn asked, "can integrity be passed from father to son?"

Once again, Lukehart gave Brian a swift, surreptitious glance. "I think so. Yes."

"On what basis?"

"My own father. He, too, was a colonel, and believed in our code of honor. For him, there was no sin worse than dishonesty. I may not have always lived up to that, but he set a powerful example."

"The man's a goner," Brian wrote. But whether he meant mired in hero worship, or gone from the jury, Terry could not tell.

"That's all I have," Flynn told Hollis.

Terry stood, appraising Lukehart with an air of puzzlement. "From your questionnaire, I gather you've never met Brian McCarran?"

Lukehart nodded, touching the bristles at the side of his head. "I have not."

"Outside this case, do you know anything about his reputation?"

"Nothing at all."

"Do you feel that you can judge him without bias?"

"Absolutely."

Terry paused for a moment, considering how to attack the problem of Brian and Kate D'Abruzzo. "Despite your father's example, sir, have you ever lied to anyone?"

Lukehart blinked. "Yes. I have."

"On more than one occasion?"

"Yes."

"I assume you had your reasons."

Lukehart paused. "It never feels right. But, yes, I had my reasons."

"Despite this, do you consider yourself to be an honorable man?"

"I try to be," Lukehart answered softly. "Most days I succeed."

Turning to Hollis, Terry said, "I have nothing more for Colonel Lukehart."

"You're excused," Hollis told Lukehart. "Please join the others."

"What's your guess?" Meg scribbled as Terry sat down. In answer, Terry wrote, "I'm okay with this guy. But Flynn will try to dump him."

When Lukehart was gone, Flynn whispered briefly to Pulaski, then stood to address the judge. "We challenge Colonel Lukehart for cause."

Hollis cupped his chin in one palm. "On what grounds?"

"His deep admiration for General McCarran. It might be difficult for him to find the general's son guilty of a serious crime. More generally," Flynn continued, "if Colonel Lukehart knew the accused, he would be automatically disqualified. Given the reputation of the McCarran family with the army, this court should exclude anyone connected to the general *or* his son."

Briefly, Hollis considered this. "Any argument, Captain Terry?"

"Absolutely, Your Honor." Quickly, Terry stood. "Major Flynn's argument seeks to repeal human nature. How many colonels are going to say in public that the army's chief of staff is less than an admirable figure? This *is* the military, sir." With an edge of humor, Terry added, "Both Major Flynn and I have the highest respect for this court. But even if we did not, we'd be well advised to lie."

A hint of amusement flickered in Hollis's eyes. "I take your point, Captain. It's a comfort that your respect for the court doesn't seem to have crippled you." He sat back, surveying the courtroom. "Nonetheless, I'm granting trial counsel's challenge. Personally, I have no doubt of Colonel Lukehart's impartiality. But this court-martial should be free of bias not only in fact, but in appearance. Particularly when, as Major Flynn points out, the prominence of General McCarran is a fact we all must live with."

When Terry returned to the table, Brian had scribbled, "No kidding."

THE NEXT VOIR DIRE belonged to the accused. Checking their list, Meg inclined her head toward Terry. "I'd go after Clair," she murmured. "Let's try to get rid of him for cause."

Standing, Terry told Hollis, "We request voir dire on Colonel Robert Clair."

The officer who appeared had curly gray hair, a gaunt face, and a closed expression that lent him an air of certainty. Hands in his pockets, Terry asked, "Are you familiar with the condition known as post-traumatic stress disorder?"

Clair pursed his lips. "I've heard the term," he said in a dubious tone.

"What does it mean to you?"

Briefly, Clair considered the question. "A soldier claims that he can no longer function, especially in combat. Essentially, that his nerves are shot."

"Do you know anyone who has been diagnosed with PTSD?"

"I do not."

"Are you familiar with the symptoms associated with PTSD?"

"Not specifically, no."

"Nor have you served in Iraq."

Clair frowned. "Not at this time."

Terry gave him a curious look. "Do you believe that PTSD is a genuine condition?"

As Clair paused again, Terry sensed him choosing a politic answer. "I have an open mind, Captain. I'll listen to the evidence before deciding if this is real."

Though Terry doubted that, he decided to switch subjects. "You currently serve as the commanding officer of a battalion, is that correct?"

"It is."

"In that capacity, have you ever referred any soldier in your command for criminal charges?"

"I have."

Knowing the answer, Terry asked, "How many times?"

Clair's eyes narrowed, as though trying to remember. "Three. The charges were assault, theft, and insubordination."

"Were those three soldiers subsequently court-martialed?"

"Yes," Clair responded with a touch of satisfaction. "And convicted."

"Did you believe those verdicts were appropriate?"

Annoyance briefly surfaced in Clair's eyes. "I did," he said firmly. "Otherwise I wouldn't have referred them."

"In this case, the charges were referred by General Heston, commander of Fort Bolton. What do you conclude from that?"

Clair looked to the side, seeming to parse the implication of the question. At length, he said, "That General Heston believes that the evidence justifies a court-martial."

Terry gave him a probing look. "In light of your own experience, Colonel, what does that say to you about the guilt or innocence of the accused?"

"That there are significant grounds to believe a crime has been committed." Clair seemed to play back the answer in his mind, then added, "After that, our job is to exercise independent judgment."

"In your mind, does that require you to presume that Lieutenant McCarran is innocent unless proven otherwise?"

"Of course," Clair said curtly. "That's the law."

"All right, Colonel." Terry moved closer to the jury box, standing a few feet from Clair. "In your role as commanding officer, do you write fitness reports for any member of the court?"

From his nettled look, Clair knew where the question led. "I do. For Lieutenant Colonel Alex MacDonald."

"Suppose that during your deliberations, Colonel MacDonald vigorously disagreed with your conclusions as to the innocence or guilt of Lieutenant McCarran. Would that affect his fitness report?"

"Absolutely not," Clair said in an offended tone. "I'd completely erase that from my mind."

"But is it possible that the colonel might fear otherwise?"

"No. It's *not* possible."

Terry smiled faintly. "So your reputation for fairness precedes you?"

"Yes," Clair said firmly. "Based on my willingness to encourage dissenting voices. Including, on at least two occasions, Colonel MacDonald's."

Terry knew better. By reputation, Clair did not brook disagreement, and those who challenged him paid the price. But there was no way he could call witnesses to discredit this man's self-concept. Mildly, he said to Hollis, "With thanks to Colonel Clair, that's all I have."

Returning to the defense table, he saw Flynn shoot him a knowing smile. "Does trial counsel have anything?" Hollis asked.

"Just one question." Without standing, Flynn asked Clair, "Knowing the charges and the identity of the accused, could you judge this case impartially?"

Clair nodded briskly. "Absolutely. That's what makes our system of military justice work the way it should."

Terry caught Meg's brief shake of the head. On his notepad, Brian wrote, "Sure wouldn't want him for *my* CO."

Terry touched his arm, a signal not to worry. As soon as Clair left the courtroom, he stood. "Your Honor, we challenge Colonel Clair for cause."

"On what grounds?"

"Several. He's preferred charges three times and, in his view, was right each time. That suggests a belief that a referral of charges equals guilt—"

"Does it, counsel? All this tells me is that three separate courts agreed with him. I might be more worried if they hadn't."

Terry paused, frustrated that he could not reveal his intelligence on Clair. "Beyond that, Your Honor, his responses on PTSD are troubling. He's never been in combat—to him, PTSD is just a rumor. In fact, he came perilously close to equating it with malingering.

"Finally, the colonel may *think* that a subordinate officer could feel free to challenge him—in fact, his refusal to entertain any other possibility is unnerving in itself. But the possibility exists with respect to Lieutenant Colonel MacDonald, and it could taint these proceedings. In fairness to the accused, Colonel Clair should go."

Hollis looked inscrutable. "Major Flynn."

After standing, Flynn said evenly, "As the court suggests, three courts-martial have confirmed the soundness of Colonel Clair's judgment. As to PTSD, the man says he has an open mind. It's not like he professed neutrality on some matter of proven fact—like that the earth orbits around the sun. As for Colonel MacDonald, counsel can always ask him if he's intimidated by Colonel Clair. But in my judgment, Colonel Clair is the kind of juror the accused should want."

Glancing at Meg, Terry saw her mouth the word "Bullshit." Swiftly, he stood again—in his gut, he knew that Clair was a prosecution juror and sensed that Hollis must know this, too. "That may be Major Flynn's belief, Your Honor. But we represent the accused, and the Uniform Code of Military Justice provides that challenges for cause should be liberally granted. With respect, nothing in his responses suggests that Colonel Clair has ever felt doubt about anything—reasonable or otherwise."

Hollis frowned. "That may be your *suspicion,* counsel. It may also be unfair. With respect to Colonel Clair, absent something more, it's you who's failed to raise a reasonable doubt. Do you have anything else?"

Nothing I can reveal, Terry thought. In the lightest tone he could manage, he answered, "Only that I'm right, Your Honor."

"I'll just have to live with that," Hollis answered dryly. "Challenge denied."

At the corner of his eye, Terry caught Meg's troubled gaze. Terry felt equally worried. He had expected to get rid of Clair, and this failure skewed his calculations. There were still ten jurors—a number better for Flynn than Brian. Worse, as matters stood, Clair, as senior officer, would be president of the court. The question now was what Flynn—who, like Terry, had not yet used his peremptory challenge—would choose to do. Terry imagined Flynn's own calculation: no doubt Terry would use further challenges to reach a number better for Brian. And the number created by the next successful challenge, nine, was still to Flynn's advantage.

Pulaski whispered something in Flynn's ear. Briefly nodding, Flynn announced, "We request voir dire on Lieutenant Colonel Boyer."

BOYER WAS BLOCKY, CREW-CUT, and clearly battling a problem with his weight. From the moment he sat in the jury box, he looked unhappy to be there.

Quickly, Flynn established why. "This case includes a specification of adultery. Do you have any experience in the army relevant to that charge?"

"Yes, sir." Boyer looked up at him, abashed. "Six years ago, I was briefly involved with the wife of an enlisted man."

"Please elaborate, Colonel."

Boyer seemed to steel himself. "I was his company commander. She came to me for help with their marital troubles, hoping I could counsel him. Instead, I took advantage. Eventually she confessed our involvement to her husband."

Brian, Terry noticed, frowned at this. "What was the result?" Flynn asked.

"I lost my command, and was admonished by the battalion commander." Boyer paused, then said defensively, "There was no repetition of the conduct. My life got back on track."

"Thank you, Colonel. That's all I have."

Terry stood, saying in a sympathetic tone, "This was obviously a painful experience, Colonel. Will it affect your ability to judge the accused fairly?"

Boyer seemed to search his conscience. "No," he said softly. "Every situation is different. And Lieutenant McCarran is innocent until proven guilty."

Terry liked the answer. But what he could not say, and could not escape, was that—with respect to adultery—Brian was guilty as charged. "Thank you," he said, and sat down, uncertain of whether he should challenge this man.

Flynn had no such doubts. When Boyer was gone, he stood. "Challenge for cause, Your Honor. Colonel Boyer's experience is too close to the facts of this case. We can't expect him to sort that out."

Flynn, Terry saw, feared that Boyer would sympathize with Brian. But there was no way to argue Flynn's point. When Hollis granted his challenge, the jury pool stood at nine.

At Terry's request, the judge called a fifteen-minute break.

HASTILY, MEG AND TERRY huddled with a chart that listed the pool, the possible grounds for further exclusions, and the peremptory challenges that remained. Brian ignored them, his spectral gaze directed at the judge's empty bench.

"You'll have to use up an easy challenge," Meg urged. "Get the pool down to eight, then see what Flynn does next. He's still sitting on his peremptory."

This move seemed sensible, Terry concluded, likely

forcing Flynn to expose more of his strategy. When the judge returned, Terry asked for voir dire on Major Tom Mazzili.

As he readily acknowledged, Mazzili had served on a jury that voted to find Corporal Carlos Maldonado guilty of adultery. But what clinched Terry's challenge was the severity of the sentence leveled during the guilt phase—six months in prison followed by a dishonorable discharge—and Mazzili's insistence that this result was, if anything, lenient. Within ten minutes, the jury pool numbered eight.

As Terry expected, Flynn's next challenge for cause was also a likely winner: a major who admitted hearing that Brian McCarran was a superb platoon leader in Iraq. Terry barely had time to wonder how Flynn had known that when Hollis excused the major, trimming the pool to seven.

Hollis glanced at his watch. "It's now four o'clock, counsel. Is our work done here or is there more to do? Major Flynn?"

Briefly, Flynn conferred with Pulaski. Turning, he said to Hollis, "We respectfully request a brief recess, to review our options."

"Captain Terry?"

Terry smiled agreeably. "I'm with Major Flynn, Your Honor. Except that we'd prefer breaking for the night."

"Done," Hollis responded with the barest hint of amusement. "I'm sensing that this process hasn't quite played out. You might want to sleep on that."

MEG AND TERRY DINED on pizza at his kitchen table. For hours, they studied the chart and questionnaires, refining voir dire questions for each remaining pool member, imagining Flynn's next move, designing counterstrategies, and, at length, picking their ideal five-person jury. The complexities were many: both sides had their one peremptory left; both wanted a different number of jurors. Flynn's number, six, would require one successful challenge, whether peremptory or for cause. Terry's preferred jury, the minimum of five, required two. This meant that Terry must force Flynn to challenge a juror for cause, or to use up a peremptory. This would not be easy, given that Terry felt certain that Flynn had guessed how they would use Brian's peremptory.

Approaching midnight, Meg said, "You'll have to dangle Captain Leeds in front of Flynn. Leeds is the only Iraq War veteran left."

Slowly, Terry nodded. "I think that's right. The problem is that I'm not sure we want him, either."

They went to bed. But neither slept well. At around two A.M., the bedroom still dark, they began rehearsing the voir dire questions for Captain David Leeds.

3

WHEN THE COURT reconvened the next morning, Terry requested voir dire on Captain Leeds.

Sitting in the jury box, Leeds fit the stereotype of the evangelical Christian Terry knew him to be. His gaze through unfashionable flesh-colored glasses was serious and sincere, his sandy hair was cut short, and his pale, line-less face—more suited to a seminary student than a soldier—looked untouched by sin or even impure thoughts. But Leeds *was* a soldier and, by all accounts, a brave and resourceful combat leader. That he had proven this in Sadr City had implications for both the prosecution and the accused.

Terry got to this at once. "In 2004," he said, "you served as the executive officer of a company based near Sadr City."

Leeds folded his hands. "Yes, Captain. I did."

"How would you describe the conditions encountered by your soldiers?"

Leeds hesitated, then answered simply, "I'd say it was hard duty."

"In what respects?"

To judge from his expression, Leeds was reluctant to imply criticism of his superiors, or the war itself. The struggle to be honest was written on his face. "The mission was extremely dangerous," he said at last. "The population was hostile, and we didn't have enough troops to control the area. In the first six months, our platoon took a lot of casualties from snipers and rocket-propelled grenades and IEDs." Speaking more quietly, he added, "A lot of dead, a lot of wounded. Several were maimed for life. It's something you don't forget."

At the corner of his vision, Terry saw Brian's body tense. He seemed to take a deep breath and then, quite visibly, detach from his surroundings. "Were there other difficulties?" Terry asked.

Leeds slowly nodded. "Among the civilians, we couldn't tell our friends from enemy combatants. The Iraqi soldiers were undertrained and unreliable, and the police were infiltrated with Muqtada al-Sadr's people. We were pretty much on our own."

Encouraged, Terry asked, "How was the morale of your men?"

Again, Leeds weighed the question. "Their performance was excellent," he said in a quiet, firm voice. "But as time went on, morale gradually declined. The feeling grew that we were taking heavy losses without achieving much. After a while they started calling it 'Mission Improbable.'"

"During this experience, did you form any opinion regarding what is commonly known as post-traumatic stress disorder?"

Leeds's expression grew more troubled. "I did."

"What was that opinion?"

"That PTSD is very real. Some men who managed to function well in combat couldn't seem to leave Iraq behind."

Brian, Terry noted, looked away. "How did this manifest itself?" Terry asked.

"A number of ways: marital discord, excessive use of drugs or alcohol, bar fights that—near as I could tell—weren't about anything. A lot of my guys seemed depressed." Leeds compressed his lips. "I'm praying for these men. I'm no psychologist, but I don't think we've seen the worst."

Terry saw Flynn making notes, his expression nettled: uncertain of whether he could eliminate PTSD from the trial, he was forced to factor it into his choice of jurors. "Is it fair to say," Terry inquired of Leeds, "that you believe that PTSD can contribute to violent behavior outside of combat?"

Leeds frowned. "I don't know. But some of my guys have a hair trigger I didn't see in them before."

Terry moved closer. "Are you willing to consider the possibility that, at the moment of the shooting, PTSD could have caused Lieutenant McCarran to relive his combat experiences in Iraq?"

Eyeing Brian, Leeds waggled his head, miming doubt. "Put that way," he said slowly, "it seems kind of far-fetched. But like I said, we saw some bad things, and you can't just make them go away."

Even Hollis looked intrigued by Leeds's responses: through this witness, Terry had managed to further plant the subject of PTSD in the judge's mind. Satisfied, he decided to explore another delicate subject. "You mentioned praying for your soldiers. Do you think of yourself as a religious man?"

A look of calm came over Leeds's face, perhaps relief at returning to safer emotional ground. "I do," he said firmly. "Since I was seventeen, I've placed Jesus Christ at the center of my life."

"Does that commitment help shape your personal morality?"

"Without question."

"Including on the subject of marital fidelity?"

For an instant, Leeds looked defensive. "You're wondering whether I can be fair to the accused on account of my beliefs."

"I respect your beliefs," Terry said easily, "just as I respect your candor. So let's discuss this a little more. As one example, how do you feel about divorce?"

Leeds steepled his fingers. "I believe that it's a great moral failing, all the more so when children are involved. My wife and I believe that we have a covenant with each other, and with our son and daughter."

"Given that, how do you view adultery?"

"As a sin," Leeds said with certainty. "For me, that infidelity violates military law is the least of it. Adultery flouts God's law, and the compact two people make when they enter into marriage." Leeds paused to consider his own answer. "In extreme conditions, like where the husband becomes a danger to his wife or children, divorce may prevent an even greater tragedy. But adultery is not a substitute for divorce. There is never a good excuse for that, and only harm can come from it."

Brian, Terry noticed, had a smile so faint and enigmatic that it was almost undetectable. Terry focused on Leeds, hoping to achieve an unspoken compact with this man. "Lieutenant McCarran is charged with murder and adultery. Do you believe that you can judge him fairly on each charge?"

Leeds met Terry's gaze. Without hesitating, he answered, "Yes. I do."

"Specifically, given your feelings about adultery, can you separate your judgment on that charge from your judgment on the charge of murder?"

"Yes." Leeds smiled a little. "There's only one God, Captain Terry, and one Judgment Day. In this court-martial, I will do my duty as an officer. That includes trying to be as fair as any fallible human can."

"Thank you, Captain," Terry said. Nodding to Flynn, he sat down. When Meg slid her notepad across the desk, Terry read the words "Keep him." Leaning closer, Brian whispered to Terry, "The man has been there. Be nice if *someone* in this trial knows what it's like."

Flynn was already up. "With respect to so-called PTSD, Captain, are you claiming that it caused the behaviors you described—drinking, volatility, depression, and the like?"

Leeds shook his head. "All I'm saying is that several of my men behaved very differently after serving in Iraq. See enough of that, and you've got to think there's some cause and effect going on." His voice softened. "Put it this way, Major. None of my guys are better off on account of going to war."

Brian's smile seemed bitter now. Perhaps, Terry thought, he was remembering the soldier who had hanged himself. Flynn moved closer to the jury box, asking, "Do you believe that *you're* different because you served in Iraq?"

For the first time, Leeds appeared distressed. He inhaled visibly before responding, "I'm not myself. I'm less patient and less forbearing. But we'll get through. My wife *is* patient and forbearing, and we pray together on it every night."

For a moment, Flynn was quiet, taken aback by Leeds's apparent anguish. "Thank you, Captain. That's all I have."

"You're free to rejoin the others," Hollis said to Leeds. Leaving, Leeds appeared more unsettled than the jurors who'd preceded him.

"Captain Terry?" Hollis asked.

Terry paused for a few seconds, studying Flynn as he quelled his remaining doubts. Then he said, "Captain Leeds is acceptable to the accused."

"Major Flynn?"

Flynn was deep in thought he did not bother to conceal. Terry could read his calculations. If he failed to challenge Leeds and Terry exercised his peremptory, the number of jurors—six—would be favorable to the prosecution. The questions were how David Leeds would affect the chemistry of the jury; whether his status as a combat veteran would enhance his influence; and whether, conversely, his moral beliefs might be helpful to Flynn's chances. Flynn turned to Pulaski, who silently shook his head.

Standing, Flynn said, "Challenge Captain Leeds for cause, Your Honor."

"On what grounds?"

"His predisposal to accept a PTSD defense without sufficient skepticism." Flynn's tone took on the faintest edge. "Given that we don't know what testimony the accused will come up with, or whether it will be part of the trial, we have to consider that in assessing a juror's fairness. Captain Leeds's responses suggest a belief that service in Iraq—at the same time and place as Lieutenant McCarran—is ipso facto traumatic. That is prejudicial to the government."

Promptly, Terry stood. "What is prejudicial, Your Honor, is impaneling a jury without any combat veterans, and therefore anyone with experience relevant to Lieutenant McCarran's service. And nothing in Captain Leeds's responses suggests that he will be anything but fair, or that he would fail to heed the instructions of the court."

Hollis gave Terry a keen look. Plainly he knew the gamble Terry was taking and its implications for the jury. He also might be pondering, Terry guessed, whether he owed Brian a make-good for denying the challenge to Colonel Robert Clair.

At length, Hollis turned to Flynn. "The court denies your challenge, Major Flynn. I agree with Captain Terry that combat experience is a qualification. Nor have you shown that Captain Leeds's perception of that experience will prevent him from following the law. The only question remaining is whether you wish to exercise your peremptory challenge."

A split second of annoyance flashed through Flynn's eyes, followed by a complex mix of unhappiness, calculation, and, in the end, resignation. He stood, saying simply, "We exercise our peremptory challenge to excuse Major Leeds."

Turning to Terry, Hollis asked, "Do you question the legality of the challenge, Captain Terry?"

"We do not."

The jury stood at six, Flynn's number. "Does the accused have a peremptory challenge?" Hollis asked Terry.

"We do," Terry said with a casual air. "The accused wishes to excuse Colonel Robert Clair."

The glint in Hollis's eyes suggested his appreciation of the tactical war that Terry had now concluded. "Do you question the legality of the challenge, Major Flynn?"

"No, Your Honor," Flynn answered.

"Then we have our members, gentlemen."

Flynn smiled sourly at Terry. Flynn had a jury free of Iraq War veterans. But Terry had reduced the jury to a number—five—from which he needed only two votes for acquittal.

Hollis instructed the bailiff to return with the members of the court who would render judgment on Brian McCarran. As they filed back inside, Terry considered them.

By virtue of Clair's exclusion, his subordinate, Lieutenant Colonel Alex MacDonald, was now president of the court. A stocky, placid-appearing man with bright red hair, MacDonald had a service record devoid of combat. Next to him sat Major Randi Wertheimer, an attractive woman with dark attentive eyes, who served as an internist at Fort Bolton Hospital. Partly because of Meg's intuition, Wertheimer was one of two jurors Terry would target. The other was Major Bobby Wade, a soft-spoken African-American with gold-rimmed glasses, recently divorced, who had stated his willingness to consider the effects of combat experience on a soldier's reflexes and perceptions. The last two jurors were both captains: Doug Young—slender, serious, and hard to read, the commander of a company in training for a tour in Iraq; and Adam Chase, of the supply corps, a southerner with an air of laconic good humor. All had one thing in common: as survivors of the selection process, they had not given either party a concrete reason to doubt their objectivity. But Terry knew that Flynn's spadework and guesswork, like his own, suggested that these five jurors were persuadable. The difference was that Flynn now needed four of them.

As Hollis explained their duties, Brian regarded the five officers with open curiosity. Terry could imagine his thoughts—which of them, driven by unfathomable sympathies and motives, might tip the delicate balance between a life of freedom and, perhaps, a lifetime in prison. Terry felt his own ambivalence about Brian overcome by sympathy and deep worries of his own. It was harder, he had learned, to defend the brother of the woman he had come to care for more than he had thought possible.

"The court will adjourn until Monday morning," Hollis announced. "At that time counsel will give their opening statements."

"*All rise,*" the bailiff called, and jury selection was done.

Across the courtroom, Flynn gave Terry an ironic salute. Seeing this, Brian murmured, "I'm glad you stayed, Paul. Like my sister, I know you gave up a job you really wanted."

Terry turned to him. "There are other jobs," he answered. "Are you doing okay?"

Brian gave a wry smile. "As okay as 'the accused' can be. But right now I'm going sailing. Storing up memories, as our Aunt Rose used to say."

He kissed his sister on the forehead and was out the door. For a moment Terry wondered if Brian would have gone to Kate had he not forbidden him to see her.

TERRY AND MEG SPENT the next few hours in bed, a release from tension that made their coming together even more abandoned and intense. When, for the second time, they had satisfied each other, Terry looked into her face, softened by lovemaking, and brushed a damp strand of hair from her forehead.

"You know," he said, "I've never seen eyes this big and this blue. At the risk of sounding flowery, it feels like I could swim in them."

Meg grinned. "And I'm feeling like I could swim in you," she answered. "Sometimes it's hard to set aside how I feel about you, even for Brian's sake. Nonetheless, I'm grateful."

"For what?"

"That you're also good in court. Again with my help, of course." She laughed softly. "We kept Flynn from blocking a PTSD defense. And we picked Brian the right jury, I think."

Terry smiled. "Actually, I'm hoping it may be a little better than Flynn knows."

"In what way?"

"Colonel MacDonald, our new president, is up before the promotion board. He'll hear sometime during the trial. For him, it's either up—to full colonel—or out."

Meg looked puzzled. "And so?"

"I got a call from a friend this morning. Nothing certain, but the rumor is that our friend Colonel Clair has shafted the poor guy." Terry's tone mingled sympathy with satisfaction. "Bad for MacDonald, good for Brian. A juror who's angry at the army is one we want."

"That was part of your calculation?"

"All along."

To Terry's surprise, Meg looked more disturbed than pleased. "It's so hard to believe that Brian's entire life may turn on quirks like this. What if MacDonald gets promoted?"

As to this, Terry had nothing to say.

4

AT NINE A.M. on Monday, the court-martial commenced.

In that last pregnant moment before Hollis took the bench, Paul Terry sat at the defense table with Brian and Meg. Across the courtroom, Flynn glanced at Brian and whispered something to Pulaski. The bailiff stood ramrod straight; the court reporter sat poised at his machine. MPs were stationed at the rear of the courtroom, prepared to quell any disruption among the reporters and spectators who had filled all the available seats. In the first row were Joe D'Abruzzo's parents—a large, rough-hewn man with iron-gray hair and dark, wounded eyes; his wife, small but plump, staring fixedly downward into what, Terry thought, must be a bottomless well of grief and anger. General Anthony McCarran was absent—even were he not a potential witness, Terry had warned that others might perceive his presence as a calculated reminder of his influence. Beneath the table, Terry saw Meg touch her brother's hand. His blue-gray eyes troubled, Brian acknowledged this with the glimmer of a smile.

An odd silence fell. Even without a signal, Terry reflected, the participants in a court-martial always sensed its imminence. The door to Hollis's chambers opened, and the judge walked briskly to the bench.

"All rise," the sergeant called out. "The court is called to order in the case of *United States versus Lieutenant Brian McCarran.*"

Though Terry had experienced this over a hundred times before, the moment still instilled a sense of awe. "Major Flynn," Hollis said. "You may commence your opening statement."

Flynn approached the members of the court with renewed resolve, appearing rested and relaxed. Crisply, he outlined the physical evidence against Brian McCarran, then moved to the essence of his case. "The accused," he said with measured passion, "told the CID a tale of self-defense that, as you will learn, did not conform to the evidence." Turning, he faced Brian, his tone accusatory. "Then this officer in the United States Army lied about the most crucial fact of all: that he and the victim's wife were involved in an adulterous affair. A *lie* made possible only because Lieutenant McCarran had just shot an unarmed man four times, causing him to bleed to death. A *death* made possible because, for the next twelve minutes, the only call Brian McCarran made was *not* to the paramedics but to the woman sitting next to him: his sister, Meg."

As Flynn intended, for an instant Brian and Meg looked defensive. Turning from them with an expression of disdain, Flynn told the members, "When you listen to the witnesses, ask yourself these questions: If the accused acted in self-defense, why does the physical evidence contradict him? And why did he choose to violate the army's code of honor by lying about his affair?

"The answer is inescapable: he lied about the affair for the same reason he shot Joe D'Abruzzo—to cover up his adultery and take Kate D'Abruzzo for himself. Far from 'forgetting' how Captain D'Abruzzo ended up with a bullet in his back, Brian McCarran is trying to conceal his guilt. And, in the end, you will know this."

As Flynn sat, Colonel MacDonald and Major

Wertheimer regarded Brian with dubious expressions, the doctor's dark, probing eyes lingering on Brian's face. Standing, Terry rested his hand on his client's shoulder until he had drawn the jury's attention. "Major Flynn," he said with casual dismissiveness, "has just told you a story. That's really all it is—a smattering of the evidence he believes will be presented, selectively plucked from a mass of less convenient facts, then neatly arranged in a narrative that casts his accusations in the most favorable light. But the undisputed evidence will present a very different story.

"That Captain D'Abruzzo repeatedly hit his wife.

"That Captain D'Abruzzo held the gun in question to Kate D'Abruzzo's head.

"That Kate D'Abruzzo called Brian McCarran, her close friend since childhood, out of fear for her own life.

"That Brian took D'Abruzzo's gun to protect her.

"That on the night of his death, Captain D'Abruzzo choked his wife until, fearing for her life yet again, she confessed to him that Brian had taken the gun.

"That Joe D'Abruzzo went to Brian's apartment in an alcoholic rage.

"That Joe D'Abruzzo, a black belt in martial arts, could have killed Brian McCarran with his bare hands.

"And that, when Joe D'Abruzzo spun to attack him, Brian shot him in self-defense."

Terry looked into the face of each juror, pausing to focus on Randi Wertheimer. "When this court-martial is done, I believe that you will conclude you would have chosen as Brian McCarran chose in the split seconds Captain D'Abruzzo allowed him—to survive. But the ultimate question is simply this: Has the prosecution, as required by the Uniform Code of Military Justice, proven beyond a reasonable doubt that Brian McCarran did *not* act in self-defense? I am confident that Major Flynn's story, however artfully he presents it, will not satisfy this burden."

Walking back to the defense table, Terry was aware of Meg's look of gratitude, Brian's troubling opacity, the stricken look of Joe D'Abruzzo's mother.

WHEN FLYNN CALLED HIS opening witness, the lead investigator from CID, Terry's first thought was how likable the man seemed.

Sergeant Gordon Frank had an amiable, observant face and, though he was not yet forty, the avuncular air of an older man. His frame, bulky without being fat, lent an impression of solidity, and the blue eyes beneath carefully combed gray-brown hair were sharp yet kind, suggesting he had seen a lot without becoming disenchanted. In Terry's estimate, he was a jury-friendly witness.

Methodically, Flynn laid out Frank's qualifications—extensive training; nineteen years at CID; sixteen homicide investigations. Then Flynn positioned himself so that the witness could speak directly to the members of the court. "When did you first learn, Sergeant, of the shooting at Lieutenant McCarran's apartment?"

"The MPs called to say that Lieutenant McCarran had reported shooting Captain D'Abruzzo. The time of his call was seven forty-one P.M. on Friday, June 17."

Walking to the defense table, Flynn picked up a digital recorder and gave it to Frank. "I hand you a tape recording of the lieutenant's call, premarked as Prosecution Exhibit One. Would you please play it for the court?"

Brian studied the lacquered table, while Meg drained her face of expression. Behind them, Terry felt the stillness of anticipation.

Placing the cassette on the arm of the witness chair, Frank pressed a button. At the edge of Terry's vision, Brian blinked, as though startled by his own voice echoing in the courtroom, his tone so unemotional that he could have been ordering pizza. *This is Lieutenant Brian McCarran. I just shot Captain Joe D'Abruzzo in my quarters. Send the EMTs to 240 Meade Drive, apartment four.*

At once, Terry realized that this might be the studied calm of a platoon leader reporting casualties on the radio. But the contrast with Frank's soft but nuanced southern baritone made Brian's voice sound even less human. "When you arrived at the scene," Flynn asked the witness, "what did you find?"

"Lieutenant McCarran was sitting in a chair. Captain D'Abruzzo lay on his side near the opposite wall." Frank paused. "There was a gun beside the lieutenant's chair. The victim was lying in a pool of blood, and there was a blood-stain on his back where his sweatshirt had been perforated."

With the discipline of a trial lawyer, Meg maintained a studied blankness that suggested that nothing she heard was troubling or remarkable. In the same brisk manner, Flynn asked, "What was the distance between Lieutenant McCarran and Captain D'Abruzzo's body?"

"Fifteen feet."

"Was there any sign of a struggle?"

"Not that we could see."

"What did you do then?"

Brian, Terry noticed, had begun to watch and listen carefully, trying to recall the image. In a phlegmatic tone, the witness answered, "Sergeant Palko and I led Lieutenant McCarran to the bedroom and asked him what had happened. The lieutenant told us that the victim's wife had called him three days before, and said that her husband had threatened her with the gun. He claimed that he'd taken it to protect her."

"Did he explain why Mrs. D'Abruzzo had called him?"

"Yes, sir. The lieutenant told us that he'd known Mrs. D'Abruzzo all his life, and that they were extremely close."

"Did he offer any further explanation of their relationship?"

"He did not."

In the jury box, Bobby Wade put a curled finger to his lips, appraising Brian closely. "How was the lieutenant's demeanor?" Flynn asked.

Frank seemed to weigh his answer. "Very unemotional, almost detached. You wouldn't have known that Captain D'Abruzzo was lying dead in the next room—"

Terry stood at once. "Move to strike, Your Honor. The witness is disparaging Lieutenant McCarran for trying to be steady and responsive in a difficult time." With a hint of sarcasm, Terry added, "To clear this up for Sergeant Frank, that's what leaders in combat learn to do. He should skip second-guessing a man in shock."

"Your Honor," Flynn shot back, "in the guise of an objection, Captain Terry has just indulged in what he rebuked the witness for—gratuitous interpretation of the lieutenant's mental state. At least Sergeant Frank was *there*."

This was true enough, Terry knew—and exactly what he'd meant to do. Addressing both Flynn and Terry, Hollis said sternly, "You invited the answer, Major Flynn, and created the opportunity for Captain Terry to turn his objection into testimony. I warn you both that I won't let this court-martial become a food fight." He turned to the witness. "Confine yourself to facts or your observation of facts. The members of the court don't require your services as a mind reader."

With that, Terry had accomplished everything he could. Erasing his brief look of annoyance, Flynn asked the witness, "Did you ask the accused what led to the shooting?"

Frank settled in the witness chair, preparing for the heart

of his account. "The lieutenant said that he'd been in the shower and heard the phone in his bedroom ringing. When he got out, and listened to the message, it was Mrs. D'Abruzzo saying that her husband was coming to confront him.

"According to Lieutenant McCarran, he called her back. She said that her husband was drunk and angry, and that he'd forced her to tell him that the lieutenant had taken the gun. He claimed that she warned him not to let her husband in."

"Are there telephone records of those two calls?"

"Only the second."

Flynn cocked his head. "Why is that, Sergeant Frank?"

"Both the accused and Mrs. D'Abruzzo stated that she'd made the first call on her landline, leaving a message on the lieutenant's landline. Unfortunately, the telephone company doesn't keep records of local calls on landlines."

"Were you able to replay Mrs. D'Abruzzo's message?"

"No. Lieutenant McCarran claimed that he'd erased it."

Flynn raised his eyebrows. "In light of Mrs. D'Abruzzo's urgent warning, did you ask why he'd taken the time to do that?"

"We did. He said it was just a reflex."

Terry caught Randi Wertheimer's flicker of doubt. "But there *is* a record," Flynn prodded, "of the lieutenant's call to the D'Abruzzo home?"

"At seven-fifteen. The lieutenant used his cell phone, and Sprint keeps records of every call."

"Why didn't he call from the landline on which he'd supposedly erased the message?"

"The lieutenant said he couldn't remember the D'Abruzzos' home phone number, but that it was on the speed dial of his cell phone."

"Other than what Lieutenant McCarran and Mrs.

D'Abruzzo told you, is there any independent evidence of a call to the accused?"

"No, sir."

Flynn skipped a beat. "Or of who in the D'Abruzzo household answered the lieutenant's call?"

"There is not."

As Terry interpreted his keen expression, Colonel MacDonald grasped Flynn's point—that Brian McCarran's call could have been to Joe D'Abruzzo. Pressing his advantage, Flynn asked, "You say the call was at seven-fifteen. Did Lieutenant McCarran say when D'Abruzzo arrived?"

"He said he couldn't remember."

"Have you timed the drive between the D'Abruzzos' town house and Lieutenant McCarran's apartment?"

"Yes, sir. Driving at normal speeds, it takes approximately nine minutes."

"Subject to proof, is there evidence as to when the shooting occurred?"

Meg's glance at Terry was a silent plea for an objection. Almost imperceptibly, Terry shook his head—objecting would only underscore Brian's problem. Gazing at the members, Frank said, "According to the next-door neighbor, Major Dahl, she was watching *Jeopardy* between seven and seven-thirty. As the closing credits appeared, she heard popping sounds through the wall between her apartment and Lieutenant McCarran's. The TV station in Washington places that time at seven twenty-nine."

Flynn nodded his satisfaction. "For the record," he told Hollis, "we intend to call Major Dahl, and the defense has stipulated to the time of the closing titles."

Noting her sideways glance at Brian, Terry suspected that Major Wertheimer had caught Flynn's further implication: that there was sufficient time between the phone call and the shooting for D'Abruzzo to have answered the telephone and responded to Brian's invitation—which, if true, suggested that Kate and Brian were partners in a premeditated murder. "Did the accused," Flynn asked, "explain how Captain D'Abruzzo got inside his apartment?"

"Yes. The lieutenant let him in."

"How do visitors enter the building?"

"They press an intercom and dial the number of the apartment they're visiting. The occupant of the apartment has to buzz them in."

"So Lieutenant McCarran could have kept Captain D'Abruzzo from entering?"

"Yes."

"Did you ask why he admitted this supposedly angry and inebriated man?"

"We did. According to Lieutenant McCarran, Kate D'Abruzzo had also confided that her husband had hit her repeatedly since returning from Iraq. The lieutenant said he wanted to talk with Captain D'Abruzzo about how he treated his wife." Frank sat back, his tone suggesting skepticism. "But before letting Captain D'Abruzzo in, the lieutenant told us he retrieved the gun and hid it beneath the pillow on his chair."

"Did Lieutenant McCarran explain why he did this?"

"He said the victim held a black belt in martial arts. He wanted to be sure D'Abruzzo couldn't attack him."

Flynn held up a hand. "So, to summarize Lieutenant McCarran's account, the victim's wife called to warn the accused that her husband was on his way, and that he was drunk and angry; the lieutenant knew that D'Abruzzo possessed lethal skills in martial arts; the lieutenant was so fearful that he hid the victim's gun before answering the buzzer; and, in spite of all this, he not only let him into the building but opened the door to his apartment."

Frank's lips became a thin line. "That's what the lieutenant told us, yes."

In the jury box, Bobby Wade stared at Brian in apparent puzzlement. Hands on hips, Flynn asked, "Did the lieutenant describe the events that led to the shooting?"

"Yes. He said D'Abruzzo was irrational and enraged—that he demanded the gun and told the defendant that he could shatter his windpipe and gouge out his eyes. The lieutenant responded by taking out the gun. Then—in his telling—he warned Captain D'Abruzzo to straighten himself out, or that he'd protect his wife any way he could."

"Did you ask how long this heated conversation took?"

"The accused claimed to have no idea." Frank paused. Adding softly, "Specifically, he said that he'd forgotten to keep time."

Eyes narrowing, Brian seemed unamused by his own dark joke. With an edge in his voice, Flynn asked, "Did he say why he shot Captain D'Abruzzo?"

"He said D'Abruzzo whirled to attack him. Before he could strike, the lieutenant fired."

"According to the accused, how close was Captain D'Abruzzo?"

"Very close, he said. Maybe three feet."

"And where was the lieutenant standing?"

"Beside the chair."

Flynn paused to telegraph his disbelief. "And yet you found Captain D'Abruzzo lying on his side, face to the wall, fifteen feet from that same chair."

"Yes."

"Did Lieutenant McCarran explain how he got there?"

"He did not." Frank paused, then told the members in a flat tone, "The lieutenant claimed he couldn't remember anything between the first shot and seeing D'Abruzzo where we found him."

"In other words," Flynn said in an astonished tone, "he offered no account whatever of how D'Abruzzo got there, how many shots he fired, or why there was a gunshot wound in the victim's back?"

"No, sir. None of that."

Flynn was doing serious damage, Terry saw—the members of the court were as still as figures in a frieze. "According to Major Dahl," Flynn prodded, "she heard shots as *Jeopardy* ended—which we've put at seven twenty-nine. Yet Lieutenant McCarran did not report the shooting until seven forty-one. Did he explain this twelve-minute gap?"

"He claims to have been in shock. But he remembered calling his sister." Frank inclined his head toward Meg. "That's Meg McCarran, who now serves as Captain Terry's co-counsel."

Flynn gave a faint, grim smile. "How long did the call last?"

"According to the phone records, five minutes and twenty-nine seconds."

"What did the lieutenant say they talked about?"

Frank shrugged, a heavy movement of his shoulders. "Just that his sister told him to call the MPs. Beyond that, he said he couldn't recall."

"During this twelve-minute period, did Lieutenant McCarran check Captain D'Abruzzo's condition?"

"No." Frank glanced at Brian. "He said he knew D'Abruzzo was dead."

"How did he determine this?"

"From observation, the lieutenant said."

Gazing down, Brian looked pale. "So the lieutenant didn't take his pulse," Flynn said.

"No."

Flynn moved closer to the witness. "During the questioning, what was Lieutenant McCarran's demeanor?"

This time Frank glanced at Terry. Carefully, he said, "Except for one occasion, his manner was very calm."

"What was that occasion, Sergeant Frank?"

"When I asked him if he was romantically involved with Mrs. D'Abruzzo." Frank paused, then spoke more quietly. "At that point, he raised his voice, almost spitting out his words. He said Kate D'Abruzzo was like his sister, and normal men don't sleep with members of their family."

Listening, Meg blanched. Flynn let a moment pass. "Later that evening, did you visit Mrs. D'Abruzzo?"

"We did." Frank's tone became apologetic. "We knew it wasn't a good time, but we needed to get what information we could before she and Lieutenant McCarran talked to each other. So we went to the D'Abruzzo town house."

"Did you tell her the captain was dead?"

"Not at first, no. We wanted the best account of what happened."

"Did she describe the events preceding the shooting?"

Frank nodded. "Her story was essentially the same as Lieutenant McCarran's—that her husband hit her; that he threatened her with a gun; that the lieutenant took the gun to his apartment; that she admitted this to her husband; that she called to warn Lieutenant McCarran he was coming; that the lieutenant called back; and that they were on the phone when he told her Captain D'Abruzzo was buzzing him."

Flynn moved closer to the witness, drawing the attention of the members. "Did you also ask Mrs. D'Abruzzo about her relationship with the defendant?"

"Yes, sir." Frank faced the members of the court, speaking to them directly. "Mrs. D'Abruzzo denied any romantic involvement. In a more controlled way, she seemed almost as offended as Lieutenant McCarran."

Flynn paused another moment, letting the members absorb this. "Thank you," he responded in a sober tone. "No further questions."

5

STANDING, TERRY KNEW that he must rearrange Flynn's carefully wrought narrative, causing the members of the court to question its central premise: that the apparent implausibilities in Brian's statement were lies calculated to conceal a premeditated murder. Challenging in itself, the task was made more difficult by Frank's likability. As he walked toward the witness, his manner casual, Terry made a swift decision about his opening thrust.

"How long did you interrogate Mrs. D'Abruzzo, Sergeant Frank?"

"A little over an hour."

"When did you mention that Captain D'Abruzzo was dead?"

Frank hesitated. In a muted tone, he answered, "At the end."

Terry gave him a considering look. "So for over an hour, you chose to conceal from Mrs. D'Abruzzo that she had lost her husband."

The impulse to explain surfaced in Frank's eyes. Instead he answered tersely, "Yes."

"Did she ask what had happened at Lieutenant McCarran's apartment?"

"Yes. She asked if anyone had been hurt."

Terry kept his face calm, almost conversational. "What was her manner?"

Frank watched him carefully, the speed of his responses slowing with each question. "I'd say she seemed anxious."

"And what did you tell this anxious woman?"

"That there'd been an altercation, and MPs had been called to the scene."

"So, quite deliberately, you deceived Mrs. D'Abruzzo." Frank opened his palms. "It was a strategic decision, Captain Terry."

"Would you also call it a lie?"

On the bench, Hollis looked from Terry to Frank. In a defensive tone, Frank answered, "We withheld information in the interests of law enforcement."

"In other words, Sergeant, you had a good reason to conceal the critical fact that Mrs. D'Abruzzo was now a widow."

"I believe we did, yes."

"But that doesn't make you a liar."

Frank crossed his arms. "Not the way I look at things."

"Did it occur to you, Sergeant Frank, that the accused and Kate D'Abruzzo might have had 'good reason' for their answers regarding their relationship? For example, shame, or concern for children or family, or even the trauma of the moment?"

Frank paused. "I can't speculate."

"In fact, you don't know why they answered as they did, do you?"

Frank frowned. In a lower voice, he answered, "No, I don't."

"All right. Your stated reason for questioning Mrs. D'Abruzzo so quickly was to keep her from comparing notes with Lieutenant McCarran. Was it possible for them to do so?"

The witness shook his head. "No. We had MPs watching the lieutenant."

"So he couldn't have told Mrs. D'Abruzzo what he'd said to you."

"No."

"And yet," Terry said, pausing for the jurors, "her account of the events leading up to Captain D'Abruzzo's death was consistent with Lieutenant McCarran's."

"Yes. It was."

Terry cocked his head. In the same mild tone, he added, "Did you entertain the possibility that they were telling the truth?"

"Of course."

"In fact, for both of them to be lying would have required them to make up a story, embellish it with considerable detail, and then commit it to memory?"

Briefly, Frank grimaced. "You'd think that. Yes."

Glancing toward the jury box, Terry saw that Major Wertheimer watched attentively, her expression curious and open. "Among other things," Terry continued, "Mrs. D'Abruzzo told you that when her husband left, he was inebriated and extremely angry."

"Yes. She did."

"Did the medical report on Captain D'Abruzzo address whether he was intoxicated?"

"It did." Frank hesitated, then added, "His blood alcohol concentration was double the legal limit in Virginia."

Terry nodded. "Might that have affected the time it took Captain D'Abruzzo to drive to the lieutenant's apartment?"

Frank seemed surprised by the question. "I can't really say."

"All right. Did you confirm that the captain held a black belt in karate?"

"Yes. He did."

"In short, he had the capacity to kill Lieutenant Mc-Carran with his bare hands."

"Yes."

Terry paused, giving the members time to absorb his counternarrative. "On direct examination, Major Flynn stressed Lieutenant McCarran's inability to recall the events immediately after the initial shot. You also described him as composed. What possible explanations did you consider for his behavior?"

Frank gave him a look of veiled suspicion. "How do you mean?"

"What did *you* mean, Sergeant? Did you mean to imply to this court-martial that Lieutenant McCarran's gap in memory was a calculated lie?"

Frank pursed his lips, his look of openness vanishing altogether. "It's certainly a possibility."

"You're not trained in psychology, correct?"

"I'm not."

"So you have no opinion as to whether the lieutenant could have been suffering from shock?"

"I can't say."

Terry paused. "Or," he said slowly, "from post-traumatic stress disorder based on harsh combat experience in Iraq."

As Terry had anticipated, Randi Wertheimer, a doctor, was watching Frank with a critical eye. "No," he answered.

"Did you, personally, ever consult an expert concerning potential causes for the lieutenant's demeanor or gap in memory?"

"I did not."

Terry gave him a thoughtful look. "You also emphasized that Lieutenant McCarran called his sister. But you only knew that because he told you, right?"

"That's true."

"When you interrogated him, did he ask for a lawyer?"

"No."

"Did you tell him that he was entitled to one?"

"We did, yes."

"How did he respond?"

"That he didn't need a lawyer."

"Did he answer all of your questions?"

Frank hesitated. "He couldn't remember crucial details, he said."

"But he never refused to answer any of your questions?"

"No."

"All right. On the night of Captain D'Abruzzo's death, did you search Lieutenant McCarran's apartment for weapons?"

"Yes. We found none."

"Is there any evidence that Lieutenant McCarran owned a gun at any time since returning to Fort Bolton?"

"No."

Terry gave Frank a puzzled look. "In other words, until Lieutenant McCarran removed the Luger from the captain's home, he had no weapon with which to shoot anyone."

"As far as we can tell, no."

"So for the lieutenant to 'plan' to shoot Captain D'Abruzzo, he would also have had to 'plan' taking the captain's own gun."

The witness frowned. "I can't say that."

"Is there any evidence to contradict the lieutenant's statement that the gun he took was already loaded?"

"No."

"The crime lab didn't find his fingerprints on any of the bullet casings?"

"No."

Terry cocked his head. "By the way, Sergeant, where were you when the MPs called to report the shooting?"

"In my office."

"What phone did you answer?"

"The one on my desk."

"And the sergeant who took the call from Lieutenant McCarran called you from *his* office?"

"Yes."

Terry smiled a little. "Is there any record of that call?"

Catching Terry's point, Frank gave him a grim smile of his own. "I don't think so, no."

"Why not?"

"Because both phones are on landlines."

Innocently, Terry asked, "Then how do we know the call ever happened?"

On the bench, Hollis seemed to repress the impulse to smile. Slowly, Frank said, "You could confirm that with the desk sergeant."

"In other words," Terry said, "we know *that* call happened because you and the desk sergeant say so."

Caught, Frank hesitated, then said, "Added proof is that I went to the lieutenant's apartment."

"By that logic, Sergeant, isn't the 'proof' that Mrs. D'Abruzzo left a message for Lieutenant McCarran the fact that he called her back on his cell phone?"

Frank shook his head. "All I know is that he placed the call."

"And all *we* know is that you drove to his apartment. So let me ask you this: Aside from the tape you played, is there evidence of Lieutenant McCarran's call to the MPs?"

"Yes." Again Frank hesitated. "There's a record of the call."

Terry smiled again. "Why is that, Sergeant?"

Frank shrugged his concession. "Because he called on his cell phone."

Judging from the members' faces, uniform in their attention and doubt, Terry had done enough. "Thank you, Sergeant," he said amiably. "I have nothing more."

THE DAY'S REMAINING WITNESS, Karen Dahl, was Brian McCarran's neighbor. A major in the supply corps with short hair and an efficient manner, Dahl made an obvious effort to be precise. Just as *Jeopardy* ended, Dahl confirmed, she had heard a series of percussive pops through the common wall of the two apartments.

"I take it," Flynn said, "that the wall is pretty thin."

"It certainly is."

"Did you ever hear voices coming from the lieutenant's apartment?"

Dahl glanced at Brian, seemingly unhappy with her position as prosecution witness. "I could often hear his television. That's how I can tell you that Brian watches CNN and the History Channel."

Flynn nodded. "Prior to these popping sounds, did you hear any voices?"

"Not that I recall."

"Or men shouting, or threatening each other?"

Dahl shook her head. "Nothing like that."

"So you heard nothing prior to the popping sounds to suggest an altercation."

"No."

Flynn nodded his satisfaction. "No further questions, Your Honor."

Standing, Terry was aware that the members eyed him with anticipation. "Let's talk about those popping sounds, Major. Did they occur in rapid succession?"

Dahl's eyes narrowed in thought. "I'd say yes. Except maybe for the last."

"So you remember a delay before the last pop?"

"Yes."

It was the answer Terry wanted, though he could not make that clear through this witness. Instead, he asked, "Have you ever been inside Brian's apartment?"

"Yes. Sometimes we borrowed things from each other. We'd also collect each other's mail if one of us was gone."

"Did you happen to notice where his television was?"

"Yes. It was mounted on the wall between our apartments."

"So it must have been easier for you to hear."

She smiled. "That's how I know the channels Brian liked."

"Back to those popping sounds, Major Dahl—was *your* TV on when you heard them?"

Dahl shook her head. "No. I hit the remote when the credits started. Seconds later I heard the pops."

Noting the members' attentiveness, Terry asked, "Given the thin walls, could you hear the buzzer in Brian's apartment when someone came to visit?"

"If I was in the living room."

"That night, did you hear the sound of his buzzer?"

Dahl paused. "I don't think so. In fact, I'm sure I didn't."

"Any idea why?"

"Yes. My television was on."

"So you might not have heard voices, either."

"Objection," Flynn called out. "Calls for speculation."

Terry faced Hollis. "Major Flynn made a point that the witness heard no voices. I'm merely suggesting a possible reason."

Hollis nodded. "Objection overruled."

"That could have been a reason," Dahl affirmed. "I was going back and forth from the kitchen, so I had the volume on loud."

Terry placed a finger to his lips. "When *your* television is on, can you hear Brian's TV through the wall?"

"No. I can't."

"Even though, when it's off, you can hear the voices of anchors on CNN?"

"Yes."

"So it stands to reason, doesn't it, that you might not hear the raised voice of a visitor who wasn't standing near the wall."

Flynn, Terry saw, regarded the witness with an expression of veiled displeasure. But he had not learned, as Terry had, how much Karen Dahl liked Brian McCarran. "When my television was on," she answered firmly, "I never heard anything in Brian's apartment."

In a throwaway tone, Terry said, "No further questions, Your Honor."

When Terry walked back to the defense table, Meg hinted at a smile with her eyes, the only emotion she dared show. As Terry sat, he saw that his client had written in bold letters "KILLER," then scribbled, "Only a metaphor, Paul."

THAT NIGHT, SPENT, MEG soaked in the tub. Terry sat on the edge, sharing a modest portion of scotch on ice. Meg had forgotten to remove her eyeliner, and it had begun to run in the steam and dampness.

"Great body," Terry told her. "But you look like a raccoon."

"I don't care," she said, then added seriously, "You were really good today."

Terry squeezed her hand. "Thanks. But every day is opening day. We're going to have some hard ones."

"I know," Meg answered softly. "But every day we're keeping Brian alive."

6

As Meg slept, Terry rose before dawn and sat at the kitchen table, sipping a steaming cup of black coffee as a chill November rain spattered the windows of his apartment.

Bleak weather depressed him; surely the enveloping signs of winter deepened his dark mood. But at moments of quiet, he faced doubts he did not share with Meg. One involved Brian, whose depths—for all his spurts of candor and even charm—remained disturbingly elusive. Another was that the gaps in Brian's story were forcing Terry, day after day, to find new shafts of doubt to plant amid Flynn's narrative. Then there was Terry's interrupted life; since turning down his job on Wall Street, he had no clear vision of the future, no time to form one, no deadline by which he could count on being free. The world of this trial—the world of the McCarrans—had become his own.

At times he wondered why. The only explanation he could find was that the congruence of their lives had brought Terry and Meg, prone to solitude and self-protection, together in an effort to save her brother while hoping to find a future in each other. He had no idea how this would end, only what he wished for.

Enough, he told himself. In less than three hours, he must reenter the courtroom a picture of confidence, impervious to the reporters, the gawkers, the bitter presence of the dead man's parents, their loss graven on sagging, pallid faces. He made a note to call his mother, and reviewed his notes for the cross-examination of Dr. Henry Goode.

THE COUNTY MEDICAL EXAMINER, Henry Goode, was a short, soft-looking man with a southern drawl, thinning light brown hair, and small features—pursed mouth, snub nose, the heavy-lidded eyes of a turtle—that seemed to disappear in a large, fleshy face framed by a wide double chin. In a joking mood Terry might have cast him as the result of too much inbreeding, the dim-witted progeny of a Scots-Irish gene pool turned in upon itself. But the alertness in his pale blue eyes, and the precision of his answers, established him as a cautious but thorough professional.

Flynn and Goode had worked on their choreography. Within ten minutes, Flynn had placed Goode at the crime scene and moved on to the autopsy, drawing the rapt attention of the members and, though his expression was more guarded, Brian McCarran. To gauge Goode's impact, Terry kept watching Major Randi Wertheimer—it was here that she, a doctor, could most likely influence the others. As she leaned forward to listen more closely, Flynn asked Goode, "Could you describe the bullet wounds suffered by Captain D'Abruzzo?"

"There were four," the pathologist answered promptly. "In the left upper arm, the palm of his right hand, the chest, and the back."

"The back," Flynn repeated.

"Yes."

"In your opinion, which would have caused Captain D'Abruzzo's death?"

"The chest wound."

"Why is that?"

"The bullet punctured the pulmonary artery running from the heart to the lungs." Turning, Goode spoke to the members in the helpful manner of a lecturer in class. "Absent medical attention, such a wound is certain to be fatal. As it was for Captain D'Abruzzo."

As Terry watched her, Major Wertheimer seemed to quickly grasp Flynn's implication—her expression was both grave and alert, as though framing questions of her own. Moving closer to the witness, Flynn asked, "If the accused had shot D'Abruzzo in the leg, would that have caused his death?"

Though surprised, Terry stood at once. "Objection," he interjected. "The question calls for speculation."

"The question," Flynn rejoined, "properly solicits a medical opinion. As an expert witness, Dr. Goode is entitled to latitude in testifying."

"Objection overruled," Hollis said in clipped tones that suggested that he, too, wished to hear the doctor's response. "Please answer, Dr. Goode."

Hollis folded his hands. "Unless the bullet struck an artery," he answered, "a leg wound would be unlikely to cause death."

Silent, Terry resigned himself to watching Randi Wertheimer's face reflect the damage to Brian McCarran. "Could such a wound," Flynn prodded, "have prevented Captain D'Abruzzo from posing a threat to the accused?"

Narrowing in thought, the witness's small eyes became slits. "It very well could have," he answered carefully.

"Even though Captain D'Abruzzo was skilled in karate?"

This time the witness's lips formed a thoughtful O. "I can't give you a definitive answer, Major Flynn. But karate depends on leverage and swiftness of movement. That requires a working pair of legs." He paused, then added, "Most leg wounds would have seriously impaired Captain D'Abruzzo's abilities. A bullet in the kneecap would have put him on the ground."

"In other words, a well-placed shot could have severely diminished his ability to kill or injure Lieutenant McCarran."

"Without a doubt."

Frowning, Major Wertheimer seemed both riveted and restless, like someone who wanted to take notes but lacked a pen or paper. Flynn pressed forward. "You mentioned a wound in the palm of Captain D'Abruzzo's right hand. Do you have an opinion on how he could have received such a wound?"

Forming his answer, Goode settled in his chair, causing his chin to overlap his shirt collar. "Again, I can't be absolutely confident. But from the angle of the bullet, a distinct possibility is that he raised his hand in a reflexive effort at self-protection."

"What can you conclude from the fact that there were wounds in four separate parts of the captain's body?"

When less certain, Terry noticed, Goode addressed Flynn rather than the members. "One obvious conclusion," he said after a moment, "is that D'Abruzzo was moving. There's really no other way to explain wounds in the left arm and right palm. Not to mention a wound to the back."

Flynn paused, miming curiosity. "When you say that the captain was moving, Dr. Goode, could he have been coming forward *toward* Lieutenant McCarran?"

"During all four shots?" Goode briefly shook his head. "That's hard to imagine, Major Flynn. The shot in the captain's left arm was direct, clearly suggesting that D'Abruzzo was turned sideways, rather than facing the accused. More obviously, it's almost inconceivable that the decedent was backing *toward* the lieutenant when he took a bullet between his shoulder blades."

Glancing at Meg, Terry noticed that she had taken

refuge in scribbling notes. Colonel Alex MacDonald had crossed his arms, his expression grim. "Were you able," Flynn inquired with a trace of satisfaction, "to conclude anything else from the wound in D'Abruzzo's back?"

"Yes," Goode said incisively. "When he received it, Captain D'Abruzzo was pressed chest-first against the wall, directly above where his body fell to the floor."

"How did you conclude that?"

"There was a smear of D'Abruzzo's blood on the wall at chest level. Even more telling, the bullet that entered his back was shored." As he faced the members, Goode's manner became tutorial. " 'Shored' means that the bullet did not completely exit the body. The explanation—confirmed by an indentation in the wall—is that the wall helped stop the bullet from going through."

Either Brian was a superb actor, Terry thought, or his expression of confusion was real. But the members were focused on Goode. "The accused"—Flynn spoke the word with a trace of scorn—"claims to have fired to prevent Captain D'Abruzzo from killing him with his hands. Beyond the shot in his back, did you reach any conclusions that discredit this assertion?"

"Several. The wound in the decedent's left arm would have rendered it largely useless. This is also true of his right palm." He paused, then said with quiet emphasis, "There's also the matter of how close Captain D'Abruzzo was to the accused, and therefore the degree of threat posed.

"One measure of proximity is gunshot residue, GSR—the amount of powder on the victim's clothing surrounding a particular wound." Goode's speech slowed, lending his words an added import. "When expelled from the barrel, GSR travels a short distance before it dissipates. Up to perhaps four feet, we can use the size and density of the pattern GSR makes around the wound to determine the distance between the gun and the victim. The closer the gun, the tighter the pattern. At four feet or a little less, the GSR stops leaving a pattern at all. Distance becomes anyone's guess."

He stopped there, allowing Flynn to ask, "Did you find gunshot residue around any of Captain D'Abruzzo's wounds?"

"None. Therefore, we can conclude with certainty that all four shots occurred when Captain D'Abruzzo and the accused were—at a minimum—more than three feet apart. For any given shot it could have been four feet, or fifteen feet, or anything in between—the only limit being the size of Lieutenant McCarran's living room. But we know for sure that none of these shots came from within three feet."

Behind them, Terry heard a spectator's stifled cough, underscoring the silence in the courtroom. Turning sideways to watch both the witness and the members, Flynn asked, "Did your examination of the body yield any evidence that supports Lieutenant McCarran's claim of self-defense?"

"Affirmatively supports?" Goode responded with raised eyebrows. "No. In fact, quite the opposite—the absence of GSR and the wounds to the arm, palm, and back all suggest a threat that was not immediate and diminished with each shot."

Pausing, Flynn stood very still, drawing attention to his next question. "Is it possible that the accused could have shot Captain D'Abruzzo as soon as he closed the door behind him?"

"That's very possible. The mark for the shored bullet was two feet from the door frame. That's where the captain's body fell."

In the jury box, Bobby Wade adjusted his glasses, peering at Brian more closely. "When I asked you for the cause of death," Flynn said to Goode, "you identified the first wound inflicted by Lieutenant McCarran. On what did you base that opinion?"

"As I said, the bullet nicked an artery. In essence, Captain D'Abruzzo bled to death. Which accounts for the pool of blood found beneath his body."

Watching the members of the court, Terry felt the vise around Brian closing, the pressure to somehow discredit this witness building. "Tell me," Flynn continued, "can you estimate how long it took for Captain D'Abruzzo to die?"

Goode frowned, his expression betraying distaste and disapproval. "It's impossible to be precise, Major Flynn. But my best estimate would be that Captain D'Abruzzo lived for roughly ten minutes."

"In other words, Dr. Goode, you believe it likely that the victim died sometime between Lieutenant McCarran's phone call to his sister and the arrival of the EMTs."

Brian closed his eyes. "Yes," Goode answered. "I think that's highly possible."

In the jury box, Doug Young leaned closer to Adam Chase, briefly whispering before Chase nodded, his expression of disapproval similar to Dr. Goode's. Glancing at the members, Flynn asked, "Is it also possible, Doctor, that Captain D'Abruzzo would have lived had the accused called the EMTs instead of Ms. McCarran?"

As Meg turned to him, silently beseeching, Terry stood to object. "The question solicits an answer that, by its nature, is inflammatory and wildly speculative. Latitude doesn't mean license."

Hollis turned to Flynn. "To the contrary," Flynn responded. "The question follows logically from Dr. Goode's estimate of the time that Captain D'Abruzzo remained alive. That the implications may be unpleasant doesn't make them prejudicial."

Hollis paused, openly reflective. In a flat voice, he said, "I'll allow the witness to answer."

Turning, the judge watched Goode closely, reflecting the reaction of the members. "That's hard to pinpoint," the pathologist answered slowly. "Captain D'Abruzzo would have required immediate surgical attention and a considerable infusion of blood. But survival would not be out of the question." He paused, then finished: "What I can say for sure is that Lieutenant McCarran's delay in calling ended the captain's chances."

Behind him, Terry heard a muffled sob from Joe D'Abruzzo's mother.

7

FOR A MOMENT, Terry remained at his table, fixing Goode with a look meant to signify puzzlement and disbelief. Then he stood quickly and walked toward the witness. "How drunk was Captain D'Abruzzo when he arrived at the lieutenant's apartment?"

The unexpected question seemed to startle Goode. Carefully, he answered, "According to the toxicology report, his blood alcohol concentration was at one-point-five, almost twice the legal limit for intoxication."

"That was based on a blood sample you drew during the autopsy, correct?"

"Yes."

"When you drew that sample, how long had the captain been dead?"

Goode hesitated. "Roughly four hours, I'd say."

"Even after death, Doctor, doesn't the blood alcohol content lower every hour?"

"It does."

"So that at the time of the shooting, D'Abruzzo's level of intoxication would have been about *three* times the legal limit?"

Goode nodded, watching Terry with a guarded look. "That seems accurate."

Terry paused, then asked his next question with mild incredulity: "Couldn't that have made D'Abruzzo more likely to be violent and irrational?"

"Objection," Flynn swiftly interposed. "Calls for speculation."

Terry did not turn. "It's hardly speculative," he told Judge Hollis, "to suggest that inebriates lack judgment."

"Nor is it controversial," Hollis told Flynn. "The witness may answer."

Goode sat back, folded hands resting on his ample belly. "Alcohol," he said slowly, "operates as a disinhibitor. It adversely affects judgment and self-control."

"Then it might well have intensified D'Abruzzo's anger."

"Yes."

"And, given that, made him much more threatening in his words and actions."

"It could have, yes."

"So that the lieutenant's description of D'Abruzzo as aggressive, bellicose, and threatening is consistent with his extreme intoxication."

Goode's eyes narrowed, as though he was tempted to debate the premise. Then he said simply, "It's true that those behaviors are often fueled by alcohol."

"Thank you, Doctor," Terry said dryly. "Let's move on to the gunshot wounds. Are you absolutely certain of their sequence?"

Goode shook his head. "Except for the back shot, no. It's pretty clear that that one came at the end."

"Is there any way of determining how rapidly Lieutenant McCarran fired?"

"No."

"So you have no reason to dispute Major Dahl's testimony that the first three popping sounds she heard occurred within split seconds."

"I don't."

Terry put his hands on his hips. "For the record, you're

not suggesting that firing three quick shots to stop an angry man with lethal skills is overkill, are you?"

"Objection," Flynn called out. "The question is argumentative and addresses an implication the witness never made."

"That's simply not true," Terry told Hollis with a trace of anger. "The thrust of the witness's direct testimony was to cast this shooting as tantamount to execution. If Brian McCarran had been resisting a home invasion, no one would quarrel with the number of shots, or the location of the wounds. What I'm addressing is the extremely unsubtle premise underlying Dr. Goode's responses to Major Flynn."

Hollis frowned, pensive. Turning, he asked the witness, "For the record, Dr. Goode, does anything in the medical evidence allow you to determine Lieutenant McCarran's motive or state of mind at the moment he fired those shots?"

Terry tried to conceal his surprise and satisfaction. Perfectly posed, the question undermined the influence Flynn had constructed with such care: that D'Abruzzo's wounds suggested the calculated murder of a defenseless man. Glumly but respectfully Goode answered, "No. Nothing."

Hollis nodded to Terry. "You may continue, Captain."

"Thank you, Your Honor." Facing the witness, Terry said, "Let's turn to the impact of the gunshots. Do people who get shot always fall down?"

A brief look of irritation crossed Goode's face. "Of course not."

"The captain was tall, well-muscled, and very strong. Is it likely that his wounds in the arm or palm would cause Captain D'Abruzzo to collapse?"

"No. Fairly obviously, they didn't."

"Nor, given that the captain was still standing when wounded in the back, did the chest wound bring him down."

"True."

"Could a man with wounds in the arm and palm continue to move forward?"

"Yes."

Terry paused. "Even with a chest wound, could D'Abruzzo keep on coming toward Lieutenant McCarran?"

A corner of Goode's small mouth turned downward. "He could have, yes."

"Is it also true that a man with gunshot wounds can appear to be moving deliberately when he's actually having involuntary muscle spasms?"

"Yes."

"Could such spasmodic movements appear violent and aggressive?"

"They could," Goode conceded grudgingly.

"Is it also possible for a man with fatal gunshot wounds to continue attacking his opponent?"

Goode puffed his cheeks. "Yes."

"Perhaps you could give us an example from your own experience."

As Goode studied him, Terry saw a new awareness creep into his eyes. With mild asperity, he answered, "As you seem to know, Captain, we had an incident last year after an armed robbery. In the ensuing gunfight with police, the perpetrator took five bullets—one in the mouth—and continued firing for another minute. Just before the robber collapsed, he killed an officer."

Glancing at the members, Terry saw Dr. Wertheimer nod to herself. Satisfied, Terry said, "Let's talk about the location of Captain D'Abruzzo's wounds. Are you familiar with the attack positions used in martial arts?"

Goode waggled his head, as though searching for an appropriate answer. "To a limited degree." He smiled faintly. "Obviously, I'm not a martial artist."

"So you don't know whether some attack postures begin with a sideways movement?"

"I have no real insight into that."

"But if Lieutenant McCarran claims that D'Abruzzo whirled with his hands raised, preparing to attack, you're not aware of any medical evidence that refutes that?"

Goode paused. "No," he answered. "I'm not."

"In contrast, you suggested that the wound to the captain's palm may have resulted from a defensive reflex—in which he raised a hand to protect himself."

"Yes. I did."

"You certainly did," Terry said coldly. "But isn't it also possible that the wound occurred when D'Abruzzo was lunging for the gun?"

In truth, Terry had no idea—Brian had fired this shot after his purported loss of memory. "What about the absence of GSR?" Goode parried.

"We'll get to that. Please answer the question as posed."

Goode briefly touched his chin. "The angle of the wound was upward. But depending on where the accused held the gun, your proposition is at least conceivable."

"Not just conceivable," Terry shot back. "Isn't my 'proposition' as likely as yours?"

"I can't quote odds," Goode said with faint resentment. "Both are possible."

"With respect to the chest wound, you already conceded that D'Abruzzo might have been moving forward. Is that consistent with the angle of the bullet?"

"It could be, yes."

"So let's take up gunshot residue. By your own testimony, the wounds we're discussing could have been inflicted from three to four feet without leaving GSR. Is that right?"

"Right?" Goode repeated. "All I can say is that it's theoretically possible."

"So for all you know, less than four feet separated Captain D'Abruzzo from the lieutenant."

Goode shrugged. "That's possible, yes."

Terry stood straighter. "If you were facing a karate expert with lethal skills, would three to four feet feel safe enough to you?"

"Objection." Rising, Flynn said, "There's no foundation for the question. Dr. Goode has already stated his unfamiliarity with martial arts."

"Which is all too apparent," Terry answered. "But that didn't stop him from suggesting that Brian McCarran had time to disable Captain D'Abruzzo with a well-considered and perfectly aimed bullet to the kneecap."

A keen look that could have been amusement surfaced in Hollis's eyes. "Then maybe you should ask him about that, Captain Terry."

"Thank you, Your Honor." Facing Goode, Terry asked, "On what basis—if any—do you believe that the lieutenant had time to consider and execute a shot to the leg if D'Abruzzo was attacking him from four feet away?"

For a moment, Goode said nothing. "I simply can't answer that," he allowed.

"All right. Major Flynn also asked if it was possible that Lieutenant McCarran shot the captain as soon as the door closed behind him. So let's consider another scenario." Moving closer, Terry spoke as though he were telling a story. "Drunk and angry, D'Abruzzo told Brian McCarran that he'd gouge out his eyes and shatter his windpipe. He kept moving closer, threatening Brian until he reached for the gun. When he was perhaps six feet away, he whirled sideways, ready to attack.

"Reflexively, Brian fired, hitting his upper left arm. Already in motion, Captain D'Abruzzo reached for the gun, taking a second bullet in the palm. As momentum carried D'Abruzzo forward, a third shot struck him in the chest." Pausing, Terry asked, "Is *that* sequence of events consistent with the captain's wounds?"

Goode slowly nodded. "It's one possibility, yes."

"But what *isn't* conceivable, Doctor, is that the lieutenant's first shot could have hit D'Abruzzo directly in the kneecap."

Goode looked and sounded weary. "If I accept your premise—that D'Abruzzo was turned sideways—such a shot would be unlikely. But we haven't covered the shot in D'Abruzzo's back."

"Which you assume came last. What do you know about the trigger pull on a nine-millimeter Luger?"

"My sense is that it requires little pressure. But I'm not an expert on ballistics."

"Then we'll stick to your expertise," Terry responded amiably. "Earlier this morning, you suggested that Captain D'Abruzzo bled to death in roughly ten minutes. During that time, is it likely that he was moving?"

Goode hesitated. "I suppose not."

"In fact, the carpet contained no smears of blood suggesting movement."

"No."

"Would Captain D'Abruzzo have been talking?"

"No." Goode answered curtly. "While he lived, Captain D'Abruzzo was certainly in shock."

"So if he didn't move and didn't talk, wouldn't it be reasonable for Lieutenant McCarran to believe that he was dead?"

"He might have," Goode retorted. "Unless he'd troubled himself to check D'Abruzzo's pulse."

"'Troubled himself'? What if the *lieutenant* was in shock?"

"I can't answer that."

"And I appreciate your humility. But earlier, you intimated that, even though D'Abruzzo probably died within ten minutes, he might have survived had Brian McCarran promptly called the EMTs. In fact, you virtually implied that Brian McCarran allowed the captain to die. Remember that?"

"What I said," Goode parried, "is that Captain D'Abruzzo might have benefited from rapid medical attention."

Terry moved closer yet, his voice filling with anger and disdain. "Are you serious, Dr. Goode?"

"Objection," Flynn called out.

"I'll rephrase that," Terry said over his shoulder. "Tell me, Dr. Goode, how long did it take the EMTs to respond?"

"Five to six minutes."

"Do they carry blood for transfusions?"

"They do not."

"How long would it have taken them to get D'Abruzzo on a stretcher, out the door, and into the ambulance?"

"Maybe two minutes."

"And to deliver him to the emergency room at Fort Bolton Hospital?"

At the corner of his eye, Terry saw Dr. Wertheimer make her own calculations. "Another five minutes," Goode responded.

"So far I count approximately thirteen minutes. By which time, using your own estimate, Captain D'Abruzzo is dead on arrival. Do you disagree?"

"I can't say. My only point is that a prompt call was preferable."

"But isn't it also true that Captain D'Abruzzo surely would have died before an ER doctor, however skilled, could have commenced surgery?"

Goode's puffy eyelids lowered. "I suppose so."

"Then what in the world," Terry said with real anger, "were you trying to tell the members of this court?"

"*Objection,*" Flynn snapped.

Terry waved a dismissive hand. "No matter," he said scornfully. "I'm through with Dr. Goode." Returning to the defense table, he noticed Dr. Wertheimer whispering to Colonel MacDonald, who nodded.

FLYNN'S REDIRECT WAS CAREFUL, almost laborious. It reprised his central themes: no GSR, a wound in the back, no evidence that exclusively pointed to self-defense. But that was Flynn's problem, and he knew it as clearly as did Meg, who, her face more relaxed, had stopped taking notes: while the medical evidence, as a whole, was unhelpful to Brian, none of it was unequivocal. From the confusion on the faces of the jurors, they understood that well.

On his legal pad, Terry wrote, "I'll buy you dinner," and passed it to his client.

THE ELEGANT DINING ROOM of the Officers' Club was half full, groups of men among husbands and wives or parents and kids out for a special dinner. A few heads turned toward Brian—among Terry's motives was to show this small community an officer who, knowing his innocence, was unafraid to surface in public. His sculpted features serene, his blond hair glinting under the soft light of the chandeliers, Brian was as Terry wanted him to be, the vision of a brave young officer who had been unjustly charged.

Across the table, Terry saw a different picture: haunted eyes; the care Brian took to sit with his back to the wall. In a belated show of companionship, he raised his glass to Terry. "Meg says you're the best cross-examiner she's ever seen. For my part, I can't imagine anyone better."

Carefully, Terry considered his response. "What you saw today is the same magic show you saw yesterday. Day after day, I can try to pull another rabbit out of yet another hat. But come the day of reckoning, I'd better have your help in creating something more substantial."

For an instant, naked fear flashed through Brian's eyes. The blank expression that followed reminded Terry of a curtain falling across a window. In a monotone, Brian said, "I really don't remember, Paul."

"The man took a bullet in the back," Terry pressed him. "Was it a reflex? Did he turn as you were firing? Did the gun go off in your hand?"

"Or maybe," Brian interjected coolly, "I wanted to give the son of a bitch an extra shot for sport."

"That's not what I'm saying," Terry responded flatly.

Almost imperceptibly, Brian's shoulders sagged. "Sorry."

"What happened between you and D'Abruzzo in Iraq?"

Brian looked past him. "Nothing that matters here."

Terry felt his client slipping away. Silent, he took another sip of scotch.

"Well," Brian said in the same quiet voice, "what should we talk about now?"

"I don't know, Brian. How about girls?"

Brian considered him. "How about Meg?"

Surprised, Tony said, "What about her?"

"I think she's in love with you." Emotion returned to Brian's voice. "Not that she'd admit that—especially to you. She's the most frightened strong person I know. But she's also the best and most loving, the biggest reason I survived. She deserves that in return."

Despite the oddity of the conversation, Terry was curious. "What are you asking me?"

An expression of candor entered Brian's eyes, so lacking in irony that Terry almost trusted it. "This court-martial may not turn out too well. No matter how it ends for the rest of us, she needs to leave the past behind. I hope that you can help her."

Terry tried to sort out his feelings—the entwinement of the trial with his relationship to Meg, the strange sense that their future might be governed by how the trial ended, and what might surface before then. "Maybe I will," Terry answered. "But you could help us both by getting acquitted."

8

THE NEXT MORNING the squalid weather had become a slate-gray drizzle.

Terry and Meg hurried to his car, silently preparing for reporters seeking comments, the grim presence of the D'Abruzzos, Flynn's assault on her brother. Meg broke their silence. "Did you see the *Post* this morning?" she asked. "Their guy thinks we're doing well."

"All I know," Terry answered, "is that Flynn has pushed his witnesses one step too far. Which allowed me to cut their legs off." He switched on his windshield wipers. "I'd never make that mistake—if it is one. But Flynn is trying to create an image of Brian that lingers in the jury's mind. All he wants is to make us put on a defense. That's where he thinks he can win."

Meg gave him a look of worry. "What do you think?"

They came to a stop near the courthouse, spotting the clumps of reporters and cameramen awaiting them beneath black umbrellas. Briefly, Terry touched her hand. "Ask me when the case is over," he said.

SERGEANT DAVID MARTINI, THE ballistics expert, was a wiry, dark-haired man of around thirty, with a thoughtful but decisive manner punctuated by constant gestures with his hands. He delivered his answers in a clipped tone that wasted no words.

Flynn's own demeanor was crisp, well-organized, and

uninflected, a deliberate effort, Terry suspected, to avoid any taint of overkill. After establishing Martini's qualifications, Flynn handed him the black handgun that had killed Joe D'Abruzzo. "Can you identify this firearm?" Flynn asked.

"Yes, sir." Cradling it in both hands, Martini seemed to gauge its weight and balance. "This is the nine-millimeter Luger that belonged to Captain D'Abruzzo."

"Can you describe its features?"

Facing the jury, Martini held up the gun. "It's a semi-automatic pistol, fed by a magazine that holds fifteen bullets. Once the first round is fired, the pistol will be ready to fire on the next pull of the trigger, and keep on firing until the magazine is emptied. A trained shooter can squeeze off three to four rounds in a second."

"Is this exhibit the gun you found in Lieutenant McCarran's apartment?"

"Yes. Specifically, on the floor beside his chair."

"After you retrieved this weapon, what steps did you take?"

Placing the gun in his lap, Martini ticked off steps by jabbing the fingers of his left hand. "To begin, we noted the location of the expelled bullets in Lieutenant McCarran's living room. We examined the four bullets for trace materials like blood, bone, fibers, and damage to the bullet itself. We also looked for evidence that would indicate the proximity between the weapon and the victim—seared and blackened skin, powder in the wound tracts, or gunshot residue on skin or clothing.

"Related to that," Martini continued, "we fired this weapon to establish the maximum distance at which it still deposited gunshot residue: four feet, one inch. Equally critical, we used the shell casings at the scene to determine the position from which Lieutenant McCarran fired each shot, and whether he or the victim was moving as he fired."

In the austere manner of a scientist, Flynn asked, "What did you conclude?"

"First, the absence of GSR on the victim shows that Lieutenant McCarran fired each shot from a distance beyond four feet. Second, the fact that one of the bullets was shored by the wall above the defendant's body suggests that this was the lieutenant's final shot." Steepling his fingers, Martini aimed them toward the members. "Most telling was the location of the bullets and, especially, the expended shells. Taken together, they indicate that both Lieutenant McCarran and Captain D'Abruzzo were moving as the lieutenant fired."

Though he'd expected this, Terry felt on edge. Calmly, Flynn inquired, "Could you tell the direction in which these men were moving?"

"I certainly formed an opinion. The pattern of bullets and casings and the location of the body all suggest that Lieutenant McCarran shot Captain D'Abruzzo while he was moving forward. The victim appears to have been moving backward."

As Meg scribbled on her notepad, Terry read, "No instant execution." But her face was tight, a sign of worry. "On what do you base this conclusion?" Flynn asked.

"The expended bullets were a few feet apart, along the wall, suggesting that Lieutenant McCarran fired all four shots from the same direction. But the bullet casings were scattered between the lieutenant's chair and where the body fell." Facing the jury, Martini spread his hands. "It follows that Lieutenant McCarran fired four times while moving forward, firing the last shot when Captain D'Abruzzo was facing the wall."

The expression on Flynn's gaunt face implied dispassionate curiosity. "Isn't the alternative that Captain D'Abruzzo was moving toward the accused?"

Martini briskly shook his head. "That doesn't seem likely, sir. As we know, Captain D'Abruzzo was lying near the wall. Lieutenant McCarran told CID that he fired the first shot—the only shot he claims to remember—from near the chair. Each of the other three bullets is a few feet closer to the body."

"Based on that, Sergeant Martini, what do you conclude about the shooting?"

Martini glanced at Brian before speaking to the members in the same calm but confident voice. "In my opinion, Lieutenant McCarran was the aggressor. He was moving forward as he shot the victim, four times, from a distance that always exceeded four feet. That's hard to square with self-defense."

In the jury box, Major Wertheimer looked down, her eyes narrowed in thought.

STANDING, TERRY ASSUMED A manner that was matter-of-fact, his tone suggesting mild curiosity. "You mentioned divining Lieutenant McCarran's movements from the position of the shell casings. In what direction do casings eject from the gun?"

"Perpendicular and to the right. That's how we can assess the position, or positions, of the shooter."

"Let's talk about the casings themselves. In a fifteen-by-twenty-foot apartment, are there variables that affect where they end up?"

Martini rubbed his palms together. "Yes," he said. "For one thing, they can bounce off walls or furniture."

"What kind of floor did the living room have?"

"Most of the floor was covered with a Persian carpet.

At the border of the carpet was maybe a foot of hard-wood."

"Can casings bounce off a wooden floor?"

"They can."

"Or even Persian rugs?"

"To a lesser degree, yes."

Edgy, Terry paused, uncertain of how far to push this somewhat tendentious point. "So the 'pattern' could reflect bullets bouncing off walls, the chair, the coffee table, the carpet, or the wooden border of the floor."

"For any given shell, yes. Of course you're talking about four separate casings."

"But you can't be certain where Lieutenant McCarran was when he fired any particular shot."

"No."

"You also can't determine which shot came first, correct?"

"That's true."

"You mentioned the position of the expended bullets. If bullets pass through different parts of the body, could that affect their trajectory?"

"It could."

"According to the autopsy report, the bullet that passed through the captain's chest also struck a rib. Wouldn't that deflect a bullet?"

"Probably."

"So, in and of itself, the position of three bullets near the wall might not tell you very much."

Martini clasped his hands together. "We can talk about any one of them. But my opinion is based on three bullets and four casings."

Martini was a facile witness, Terry acknowledged, without seeming unreasonable or resistant. "You say that three bullets were close together, Sergeant Martini. Might not that suggest that, instead of moving forward, Lieutenant McCarran was standing still?"

"It could. Of course, there's also the casings."

"But if the bullets in themselves tell us nothing about movement, aren't the casings the *only* basis for suggesting that the lieutenant was moving forward?"

For the first time, Martini was still. "Yes," he finally answered. "I'd say my opinion relies heavily on the casings."

"Which could have bounced off walls and chairs and floors and coffee tables?"

"Objection," Flynn called out. "Asked and answered."

Turning, Terry read Hollis's puzzled expression—by underscoring the subject, Flynn had made his first misstep of the day. "Your Honor," Terry countered, "it seems that the witness's central point is that Brian McCarran was moving forward. We just learned that his opinion rests entirely on the bullet casings. It's important to underscore the limitations of that thesis."

Hollis gave Flynn a brief but pointed look. "Objection overruled."

Martini spread his hands in a helpless gesture. "As I said, bullet casings can bounce off various surfaces or objects, altering their pattern."

"Thank you, Sergeant. What's the trigger pull on a nine-millimeter Luger?"

"It's very light. Essentially, it's a hair trigger."

"Why is it made that way?"

"The less pressure needed to pull the trigger, the more accurate the shot."

"Can a hair trigger lead to the unintended discharge of a bullet?"

"It can, yes."

"Would you say that such a trigger is particularly hard to control in high-stress situations?"

"Obviously."

"So is it possible, Sergeant Martini, that one or more of the bullets fired by Lieutenant McCarran was discharged accidentally? For example, the bullet in Captain D'Abruzzo's back, the apparent result of the last, delayed gunshot."

Terry saw Flynn start to rise, glance at Hollis, then reconsider. "With a gun like this," Martini answered, "you can't ever rule that out."

Terry gave him a thoughtful look. "When did you enter the army, Sergeant Martini?"

"In 1994."

"As part of your training, were you taught to shoot a handgun at targets meant to represent an enemy?"

"We were."

"What part of the body were you trained to hit?"

"Objection," Flynn said promptly. "The question introduces a subject outside the scope of direct examination. If Captain Terry wants to make some other point, he should call his own expert."

"Your Honor," Terry retorted, "the witness has suggested that Lieutenant McCarran was the aggressor. We believe that there's another explanation. In fairness to the lieutenant, I'd like to bring that out without waiting days or weeks."

Apprehensive, Terry watched Hollis weigh the question. In a somewhat dubious tone, he said, "I'll allow it, Major Flynn."

Terry faced the witness. "We were taught to aim for the chest," Martini answered slowly. "To inflict a killing wound."

"Were you also taught to fire more than one shot?"

Martini folded his hands. "Yes. Until the opponent was neutralized."

Terry glanced at the members. "So that the bullet in Captain D'Abruzzo's chest as well as the multiple gunshots are consistent with how the army trains its soldiers?"

Martini looked thoughtful. "Yes, sir. I would say that's true."

This was the best place to end, Terry decided. "Thank you, Sergeant Martini."

As with the medical examiner, Flynn's redirect emphasized the absence of gunshot residue, or any other evidence helpful to Brian. But this time, Terry feared, the members appeared more receptive to these efforts.

When Martini left the stand, Hollis glanced at his watch before inquiring, "Who's your next witness, Major Flynn?"

Flynn shot Brian a swift, telling look. "Mrs. D'Abruzzo."

"It's nearly two o'clock. I think that the members should hear her testimony all at once. Absent objection, the court will adjourn until nine A.M. tomorrow."

Within minutes, the courtroom had begun to empty. What lingered with Terry was Brian's downcast look, and the bitterness in the eyes of Joe D'Abruzzo's mother.

As soon as his door closed, Meg wanted to make love. Seized by his own disquiet, Terry was slow to respond. But he had learned that the sight of her body and the smell of her skin could arouse him in ways he had never known before. He let that sweep him along.

Afterward, Meg's gaze was soft. "Making love may not solve all our problems," she said. "But I think we've been given something special."

Terry smiled a little. "I know so. But sometime we should find somewhere more worthy of these moments. Maybe the Italian Riviera. I always liked the pictures."

Meg looked pleased. "How about Venice?" she suggested. "Or Costa Brava?"

"Anywhere," Terry said. "I'm not feeling picky."

Kissing him, Meg went off to take a shower.

Afterward, wrapped in a towel, Meg lay back on the pillow. Her expression became wistful. "In the all-too-real world, Paul, what did you think about today?"

"Viewed witness by witness, I poked some holes in another one. But I think the members have started to wonder about the bigger picture. As I said, all Flynn wants right now is to get the prosecution case past a motion to dismiss."

"And if he does?"

Terry paused, reluctant to answer. "Our toughest decision is whether to call Brian. If we don't, it tells the jury that the only witness to the shooting won't testify in his own defense. But what Flynn really wants is to get Brian on the stand. Absent a PTSD defense—or even *with* one—'I can't remember' could be lethal. I wish to God that Blake Carson could get Brian to talk about Iraq, or recall whatever happened in that room. But he can't."

Silent, Meg gazed up at the ceiling. Finally, she said, "I think I should stay with him tonight."

Gently, Terry touched her shoulder. "Is there something specific that's worrying you?"

"Other than what the trial's doing to him? Maybe it's instinct. Or maybe I keep remembering when our mother committed suicide and Brian didn't want to be alone at night." Her voice softened. "He had nightmares then. Now he has them again. I know that life isn't fair, but the way it's been unfair to Brian is hard for me to live with. I refuse to lose him before he's had a chance to heal. If he ever can."

Terry took her hand. "Staying out of prison would be

a start. After Kate's testimony, I'll do my damnedest to get Hollis to dismiss the homicide charge."

Her smile was doubtful. Attempting lightness, she said, "*Then* what would you do?"

"Take you to Costa Brava with me. We can make love in luxury and leisure. After that I might even get a job."

Meg hesitated. "I don't know if you've considered this, Paul. But for talented trial lawyers, there are jobs in San Francisco."

Feeling a rush of pleasure and surprise, Terry was struck by a sudden image of a future where, with time and patience, he and Meg might truly reach each other. Smiling, he said, "San Francisco's expensive. Where would I live?"

Meg touched his face. "Maybe we should think about that. Someday when we have time."

9

TAKING THE STAND, Kate D'Abruzzo squared her shoulders, a show of self-possession which, though intended to conceal her shame, reminded Terry how closely she resembled her elegant mother. Before taking her oath, she flashed Brian a look that, in the split second it lasted, was naked in its affection. She did not look at Meg, or toward her dead husband's parents. Instead, she turned to Flynn, who intended to destroy her credibility. That Terry had prepared her for this did not improve the moment.

Flynn began with the usual preliminaries: name, address, family relationships. Kate's answer to the last—that she had been married to Captain Joseph D'Abruzzo; that he had left behind two children—prompted Major Wertheimer, herself a mother, to glance at Brian with veiled disapproval. The only positive note for Terry was that, for once, Brian seemed completely present.

Turning toward Brian, Flynn asked, "Can you identify the accused?"

"Brian McCarran," Kate answered in a soft, clear voice. "I've known him all his life."

"Prior to your husband's death, what was your relationship with Lieutenant McCarran?"

Turning, Kate looked directly into the prosecutor's eyes. "We were close," she said. "We always have been."

"In the months before the lieutenant killed your husband, what exactly did that 'closeness' include?"

Both Flynn's phrasing and his muted sarcasm scraped Terry's nerves. But that posed no grounds for an objection. Coolly, Kate answered, "We had a relationship. Do I have to say any more?"

"All I need to know, Mrs. D'Abruzzo, is whether you and the accused became intimate."

Despite his decorous phrasing, Flynn's meaning was clear. Briefly, Kate bowed her head. "Yes."

"For how long?"

"Three months."

"Where did you conduct this relationship?"

Kate's voice became muted. "At the Marriott Hotel near Alexandria."

"Who paid for the room?"

"I did." Kate paused again. "I paid with cash he gave me."

Brian, Terry noticed, listened closely and attentively, as though he were hearing about someone else's life. "Prior to his death at the hands of Lieutenant McCarran," Flynn asked, "did your husband learn that you were involved in an affair?"

Kate's intake of breath resembled a shiver. "Yes."

"How did that occur?"

"One day Joe followed me to the hotel. When I came down to the lobby, he was there."

"Was Lieutenant McCarran with you?"

Kate shook her head. "He always left before me, out the side exit."

The sour look on Colonel MacDonald's face served to underscore Flynn's point—that Kate and Brian were practiced in duplicity. "When you entered the lobby," Flynn asked in the same antiseptic tone, "what did your husband do?"

Kate's voice was softer yet. "He confronted me, saying 'I saw him.' Then he called me a vulgar name."

"Did he also demand that you end the affair?"

"Yes."

"Did you inform Lieutenant McCarran of that fact?"

"Yes."

"When was that in relation to your husband's death?"

"Nine days prior."

"Why are you able to be so precise?"

Kate drew herself up. "I always went to the hotel on Wednesday," she said at length. "Joe died on Friday of the following week."

Kate's admissions, Terry thought, were forming a damaging mosaic of Flynn's design. Watching her, Meg was utterly still; though she held a pen, she had written nothing down. In a more pointed tone, Flynn asked, "Did the accused later remove your husband's gun from the bedroom of your home?"

"Yes."

"Who let him in?"

"I did." Kate's voice rose. "I was very frightened, Major Flynn. My husband had gotten drunk and held it to my head."

"So you told Sergeant Frank," Flynn said coldly. "He questioned you after the shooting, correct?"

Kate clasped her hands together, holding her arms close to her body. "Yes."

"Did he tell you that your husband was dead?"

"No," Kate said with a trace of anger. "Not until the end."

"Did he ask if you were romantically involved with Brian McCarran?"

"Yes."

"What did you tell him?"

Kate shifted slightly. "I denied it," she said flatly.

"That was a lie, of course."

"It was a deception," Kate retorted. "I didn't want our families to know."

Glancing at Flora D'Abruzzo, Terry saw her look away in loathing and disgust. But the five members of the court, eyes fixed on Kate, were motionless. Pressing forward, Flynn inquired, "Did Sergeant Frank also ask how your husband had come to be in Lieutenant McCarran's apartment?"

"Yes," Kate answered harshly. "I told him the truth—that my husband was drunk, irrational, and furious that his gun was missing. That he'd choked me until I nearly passed out. That I'd told Joe that Brian took the gun because I thought he'd kill me. That's why all this happened."

This burst of emotion caused Judge Hollis to study the witness closely. With quiet scorn, Flynn said, "You also told the sergeant that you'd called Lieutenant McCarran to warn him."

"Yes." Kate's voice lowered. "I was afraid of what would happen. I was right to be."

"Specifically, Mrs. D'Abruzzo, you claimed to have left a voice-mail message on the lieutenant's home telephone."

"Yes."

"And that you'd used a landline to call."

"Because I did."

The danger in Kate's anger, Terry feared, was that it verged on the imperious. "During the affair," Flynn persisted, "you must have called the accused."

"Of course."

"Did you call his cell phone or his landline?"

"Both. Sometimes I called his cell if I needed to reach him quickly."

Puzzled, Terry made a note—"Brian's cell phone records"—and noticed Meg's swift, sharp glance. "Did *you* always use a landline to place these calls?" Flynn asked.

"Yes." Kate hesitated, then gave the answer she had given Terry two days before. "There was a reason for that, Major Flynn. I didn't want Joe to see the records of my calls. So I used the landline out of habit."

This answer, while adding to the portrait of subterfuge, was plausible enough that it made Flynn pause. "A moment ago, Mrs. D'Abruzzo, you claimed not to have known your husband was dead when Sergeant Frank questioned you. Does that remain your testimony?"

"Of course."

"But your husband knew about the affair, correct?"

"Yes. I've already said that."

"So how did you think you could conceal it?"

Kate gave him a puzzled look. "I don't understand your question."

Coldly, Flynn said, "Didn't you think you could conceal your affair because you *knew* that your husband was dead?"

Kate's hands flew to her face. *"No."*

"In fact, didn't you and Lieutenant McCarran plan to kill him?"

"No," Kate said angrily. "That's not true."

Flynn stared at her in disbelief. "So you thought you could lie to Sergeant Frank and your husband would just go along?"

"I didn't think about that."

"You didn't wonder if your drunk, angry husband—who Sergeant Frank told you had been in an altercation with Brian McCarran—might reveal why he was so upset?"

"No. *I* was upset, too."

Flynn moved closer to the witness, as though determined to extract the truth. "Didn't the accused call you after the shooting—landline to landline—to tell you he'd killed your husband and to prepare for a visit from CID?"

Adrenaline jackknifed Terry from his chair. "Objection,"

he snapped. "There's no foundation for this question. It's a naked accusation from a prosecutor's fantasies."

Flynn shot Terry a look of anger. "Your Honor, the witness has admitted to a pattern of deceptions that depended on the use of landlines. And the specific basis for the question is in the discrepancy between her lie to the CID about this affair and her claim that she believed her husband—who had discovered it—was still alive. That's no fantasy, and it demands exploration."

"Objection overruled," Hollis said coolly. "Please answer the question, Mrs. D'Abruzzo."

Kate turned to Flynn, drawing herself up. "You make me sound calculating," she said. "I was a mess. All I knew was that I couldn't tell a stranger what I hadn't said to my own mother. Imagine the damage to my children, to Brian's life and career, to everyone in our family—"

"Didn't you consider that," Flynn snapped, "when you embarked on an affair with Brian McCarran?"

Kate slowly shook her head. "I was selfish. I didn't think."

Meg, Terry saw, could not repress the chilliness in her gaze at Kate. "Perhaps not," Flynn said. "But once Captain D'Abruzzo found out, wasn't your only hope of preventing all that 'damage'—and your only hope of a life with Brian McCarran—to conspire with your lover to murder your husband?"

"*No,*" Kate insisted in an anguished voice. "That's completely twisted."

"It surely is," Flynn said scornfully. "No further questions, Your Honor."

STANDING, TERRY ADDRESSED THE judge. "If it please the court, the defense will conduct a brief cross-examination of Mrs. D'Abruzzo. We'd like to reserve the right to recall her, if necessary, as part of our defense."

"Very well, Captain Terry. You may proceed."

Approaching Kate, Terry stopped a respectful distance away. "Major Flynn suggests that you concealed your relationship with Brian McCarran in order to cover up a murder. Is that true?"

Eyes glistening, Kate shook her head in dismay. "No," she said huskily. "Our son and daughter are suffering, Joe's parents are suffering, and all our lives will never be the same. I may have been selfish, but it doesn't take experiencing Joe's death to see how tragic the results would be. Whatever Joe did to me, I could never wish him dead. I can't even live with knowing that my weakness led to so much misery."

"Why did you turn to Lieutenant McCarran?"

Kate closed her eyes. "Joe started hitting me—hard, and repeatedly, on the face. He refused to get counseling. I turned to Brian because I was so lonely and afraid." Her voice was suffused with feeling. "I've never had a father or a brother, Captain Terry. For so many years, Brian was like a member of my family."

"During your involvement, you said that you always called him on your landline. Did he return calls only to that landline?"

"Yes. It didn't matter if he used *his* cell phone. But calling mine would leave a record Joe could see."

"So on the evening your husband died, your call to him and his call to you were consistent with a pattern that was second nature to you."

"Yes."

Terry turned sideways, facing Kate and the members of the court. "In short, except for concealing the extent of your relationship with Lieutenant McCarran, everything you've told the CID was true."

Slowly, Kate nodded. "It was."

"And, having corrected that omission, everything you've told the members of this court is also the truth."

Major Wertheimer studied Kate with a look that, while suggesting doubt, was not judgmental or unkind. Briefly, Kate glanced at Brian. "Yes," she said in a soft, firm voice. "It is."

"Thank you, Mrs. D'Abruzzo. I have no further questions."

"Nor do I," Flynn said with a confident air.

Kate remained motionless. Courteously, Hollis prompted her, "You're excused, Mrs. D'Abruzzo."

Leaving the courtroom, Kate seemed to detach herself from her surroundings—except for a final glance at Brian, she gazed straight ahead, as though unaware of the gawkers, the media, the hatred of her husband's parents. Brian watched her, empathy filling his clear blue-gray eyes, softening the cool perfection of his features.

"Major Flynn," Hollis inquired. "Do you have any further witnesses?"

"The prosecution rests, Your Honor."

A brief murmur came from the onlookers, their expression of surprise. Promptly, Terry said, "May counsel address the court?"

"Of course."

Sitting down, Flynn remained tensile and alert. In a low voice, Terry said, "The defense requests that the jury be excused, so that it can make a motion to dismiss."

"Very well," Hollis said gravely. "We'll excuse the members and reconvene in half an hour."

The light in Flynn's eyes carried a hint of challenge. Saying nothing, he returned to the prosecution table. Meg remained where she was, somber and still, her hand touching Brian's beneath the table.

10

AT THE APPOINTED TIME, Judge Hollis assumed his place on the bench. Across the courtroom, Terry and Meg faced Flynn and Pulaski, whose attempts to appear expressionless betrayed the same tension Terry felt. The court reporter watched them, his fingers resting on his machine.

"For the record," Hollis said, "we are convening under Article 39a to hear a motion to dismiss advanced by counsel for the accused. State your grounds, Captain Terry."

Terry stood at once. "At the end of its case, the army must have offered evidence that—taken alone—would support a verdict of guilty on homicide charges. That requires proof beyond a reasonable doubt. Instead, the case advanced by trial counsel *defines* reasonable doubt.

"The physical evidence is equivocal. The testimony of Sergeant Frank, Major Dahl, Dr. Goode, and Sergeant Martini leaves room for multiple interpretations. As for Mrs. D'Abruzzo, the only concrete evidence elicited by Major Flynn is that she and Lieutenant McCarran were having an affair. The fact of an affair—or its concealment—does nothing to prove that the accused is guilty of homicide." Terry paused, then added succinctly, "On the evidence before you, this case should never have been brought. That's all Major Flynn has proven. Accordingly, this court should dismiss the charge of homicide."

"Thank you, Captain Terry." As Flynn began to rise,

Hollis held up his hand for silence, continuing to address Terry. "I admire your skills as a cross-examiner, Captain. You deserve your reputation, and you've served your client well. But, in my view, Major Flynn has offered sufficient evidence to put you to your proof and, at your discretion, to call Lieutenant McCarran in his own defense.

"That's up to the accused, of course—no prejudice will accrue if he chooses to remain silent. But a charge of premeditated murder also includes lesser offenses such as voluntary or involuntary manslaughter." Leaning forward, Hollis continued, "Whatever you achieved on cross-examination, you've offered no physical, medical, or forensic evidence that affirmatively helps the accused. Nor is it helpful that Mrs. D'Abruzzo testified that she and the lieutenant misled the CID about such an important matter.

"The court does not wish to quash a case so serious. Where so much room for interpretation exists, and so much rests on the credibility of witnesses like the victim's widow, I'm more inclined to leave this judgment to the members of the court." Hollis's deep brown eyes met Terry's. "File papers if you like. I'll read them with an open mind. But your time might be better spent impressing the members of the court with that reasonable doubt you seem to rely on."

It was done, Terry knew. Startled by the swiftness of his defeat, he was left with the familiar response of a deflated advocate: "Thank you, Your Honor."

IN LATE AFTERNOON, Terry, Meg, and Brian sat at Brian's kitchen table. "On Monday," Terry said, "we're starting our defense. I'd like to lead with Kate."

Brian watched him fixedly, saying nothing. "Is that wise?" Meg asked. "She comes with a built-in credibility problem."

"Nonetheless," Terry countered, "we need her. She gives us a frightened victim, and Joe as spousal abuser quite possibly afflicted with PTSD. Plus, she reinforces Brian's story about the events leading up to the shooting. Right now," he told Brian pointedly, "that's the only story we've got. Fortunately, Flynn has no story—whatever he thinks happened, he's got no one to prove it. But there is one other witness, Brian. You. I want you to consider testifying on your own behalf."

Brian shook his head. "I've been working with Dr. Carson," he said softly. "You know that. What makes you think that I'm not trying?"

"The results," Terry snapped. "Look, you're a combat veteran with a fine war record—including good reports from D'Abruzzo. It's clear that your experience came at a very steep price. We're looking for at least one guy who served with you to spell that out. And we can also call your father and Meg to say how much you've changed. But only you know why or how it may have affected your reaction when D'Abruzzo came looking for you. And only you can say what happened when he did.

"Without you, you've pretty much seen your defense. I'm not calling our own pathologist or a ballistics expert—we've done as well as we can out of the mouths of Flynn's own witnesses, and we're better off not giving him a second chance. And there's no changing the physical evidence. What do you suppose that leaves?"

Brian stared at the table. "I'm right," Terry told Meg. "And you damned well know it. As of now, Brian's a cipher. We need to give the jury a human being."

Meg faced her brother. "Please try to remember what happened," she asked softly. "Then we can decide."

After a moment, Brian nodded.

PART FOUR

THE DEFENSE

NOVEMBER 2005

1

IN THE MOMENTS BEFORE Paul Terry opened the defense by recalling Kate D'Abruzzo, her mother entered the crowded courtroom.

With considerable grace, Rose Gallagher navigated the emotional crosscurrents stemming from her son-in-law's death. Terry watched as she approached the D'Abruzzos, bending closer to kiss Flora's pallid cheek, eliciting from her a wan smile as Joe senior watched them, uncertain of what to do or say. Having called Brian the night before, she confined herself to a glance in his direction, its warmth apparent in her eyes. She followed this with a look toward Meg that somehow conveyed empathy for her burden. Then Rose sat alone near the front of the courtroom, her expression neither apprehensive nor falsely serene, supporting through her presence the daughter whose adultery, by her own admission, had led to Brian's fatal confrontation with Joe D'Abruzzo. Terry had seldom been so struck by quiet dignity.

Her daughter had by far the harder role. "What we're doing," Meg had told her with brutal candor, "is prosecuting a domestic violence case against a dangerous man. Joe's dead; Brian's alive. Your sole purpose is to save him. You can't do that by sparing your in-laws' feelings, or airbrushing a spousal abuser for the sake of the kids. The only debt you owe on Monday is to Brian."

Kate's eyes had flashed with resentment. Then she'd

simply nodded, composed again. No doubt she knew that worse awaited her.

Now, retaking the witness stand, Kate carefully arranged her simple dress, gave Brian a brief half smile, then watched expectantly as Terry rose to commence tarnishing Joe D'Abruzzo's reputation. "Before your husband went to Iraq," Terry began, "how would you describe your marriage?"

Kate folded her hands. "I would have said that we were happy. The two of us were different—Joe was fun and confident and full of energy; I'm quieter by nature, more of a reader. Joe wasn't one to examine himself, while I may do too much of that. But we appreciated each other. So it worked."

Her tone was perfect, Terry thought—without being maudlin, it was laden with regret about what the two of them had lost. "You mentioned that you and Captain D'Abruzzo have children. What are their names and ages?"

"Mathew is nine; Kristen is seven." Kate smiled a little. "Mathew's like his dad—always ready to go, with no sport he doesn't like. Kristen's our thinker."

The members of the court listened gravely; by humanizing Joe D'Abruzzo, Terry was also humanizing Kate, preparing them to empathize with her shock at confronting a different man. "How was your husband as a father?" Terry asked.

"Joe was a good dad," Kate answered. "Of course, he was intent on advancing his career. But he was attentive when he had time, especially to Mathew. He was a great one for doing things—picnics, sightseeing in Washington, baseball games or movies or just going to a playground." Her voice became rueful. "I got the parts that weren't so much fun: toilet training, carpooling, and checking homework. Sometimes I felt a little like wallpaper. But my own father died in Vietnam before I was born—I was grateful my kids were so happy. That's the whole point, isn't it?"

Major Wertheimer listened with apparent sympathy, as though recognizing pieces of her own life. "After he returned from Iraq," Terry asked, "did your husband's behavior change?"

The split-second shift in Kate's expression—misery erasing nostalgia—was as effective as her answer. "Joe changed totally. It was like some frightening stranger had taken control of his body."

"Could you explain that?"

"It started in Iraq. His phone calls became less frequent, and his tone was flat and distant. He stopped asking about the kids, or asking me to put them on the phone." Kate shook her head. "I told myself it was the war—that we'd make things okay again. But when he returned, the man I knew was gone.

"He'd sit alone, drinking. He couldn't say what was bothering him. When I tried to push him, he'd flare up at me. The simplest conversations would suddenly go off the rails, Joe shouting without me even knowing why. Then he started calling me names he'd never used before." Kate averted her eyes. "First it was 'bitch,'" she finished softly. "Then it was 'cunt.' That one stuck."

In the jury box, Major Bobby Wade—soft-spoken and religious—winced. Noting this, Terry asked, "How did Captain D'Abruzzo treat your children?"

"He withdrew." She paused, her voice filling with puzzlement. "He acted like he'd been trapped in an out-of-control day-care center with someone else's obnoxious kids. The only time he acknowledged them was to bark in irritation. Matt started getting into fights; Kristen's schoolwork slipped. But the most painful part was watching them learn to fear their own father."

"Did you ask him to seek counseling?"

"I begged him, over and over." Kate's voice lowered. "One night, after he snapped at Kristen and then me, I told him he was losing his family. That was the first time he hit me."

"Hit you where, Mrs. D'Abruzzo?"

Kate touched her cheek with her fingertips, as though feeling for a bruise. "Across the face, with an open palm. But hard. My ears rang, and my legs got wobbly. My lip was bleeding." She paused, remembering the moment. "Joe's eyes got big, like he'd surprised himself. Then he just walked out."

Terry inclined his head, a gesture of inquiry. "Why do you think he changed?"

"It had to be Iraq, Captain Terry. The year he spent in Sadr City."

"Did you ever talk about what happened there?"

"I tried. He never talked about specific incidents, or even said anything very coherent. But it was clear that he was angry." Her voice became hesitant. "He called Muqtada al-Sadr's people 'sand niggers'—he'd never used that word before. He seethed with feelings that had nowhere to go. That was why it scared me when he started keeping a loaded gun in his nightstand. Who was going to threaten us at Fort Bolton?"

Judging from the faces of the members, they were absorbed in Kate's description of a volatile and unstable man. It was time, Terry judged, to start tying this more closely to Brian's defense. "With respect to Iraq, did your husband ever mention Brian McCarran?"

"Very little. When Joe was still in Iraq, I began to think they'd had a falling out—even though our families were close, Joe stopped mentioning Brian altogether. When I'd ask about Brian, he would change the subject."

"Did Joe ever say anything specific about their experience in Iraq?"

Kate's eyes were grave. "Only once, before any of this happened. When Brian was in Sadr City, he was nearly decapitated by an IED—that's why there's a scar on his neck. I never knew about it until after they got home. When I asked why no one had told me, all Joe said was 'I'd have been better off if those monkeys had taken off his head.'"

For an instant, Terry hesitated; over the weekend Kate had told this story for the first time. But Joe D'Abruzzo was dead—no one but his widow, Brian's lover, knew if it was true. "After the time he split your lip," Terry asked, "did your husband continue to hit you?"

"Yes," Kate answered in a monotone. "Eight more times, always on the face. I remember every one of them."

"Was he sexually abusive?"

"No." Kate looked down. "He had no interest in sex at all. I told myself to be patient. But he seemed incapable of showing affection."

Terry paused. "Was that why you became involved with Brian McCarran?"

"Not at all," Kate said with a rush of feeling. "I went to him because I was frightened and sad and very alone. And we were always part of each other's family: Tony—General McCarran—Meg and Brian; my mother and me." She turned to Brian, speaking in a quiet tone. "Brian was always gentle, empathetic, and completely present. When you talk with Brian, you know that he's listening, and that you matter to him."

"How did your affair start, Mrs. D'Abruzzo?"

Kate bowed her head. "After Joe started hitting me, I didn't know where to turn. If I went to his commanding officer, it might end his career. If I told my mother, she'd be angry at Joe and frightened for me. But I desperately needed to tell someone." She drew a breath. "At first he just listened. When I was done, he held me for a very long time. I'd been so lonely, and so was he. We felt it at exactly the same moment, like this had been waiting to happen, but neither of us knew it. Suddenly we both did."

As her voice trailed off, Kate seemed unable to look at anyone. Gently, Terry asked, "Did you and Brian talk about how to stop your husband from hitting you?"

"Brian wanted me to go to Joe's battalion commander. I asked for time, hoping that somehow I'd get through to him." She paused again. "Once Joe found out, it was like mutual assured destruction. Joe could ruin Brian's career, and I could ruin Joe's. I didn't know what to do. That was when this terrible thing happened."

Hands in his pockets, Terry paused, allowing the members to absorb Kate's regret, the contrasts between Brian and her husband, the poisonous entwinement of these three people that had ended in a death. Then he asked, "Did you ever consider leaving your husband for Lieutenant McCarran?"

Kate shook her head. "It would ruin his career, tear our families apart, and traumatize our children. How could I ask them to substitute a family friend for their own father? When I was truthful with myself, I knew it had no future." She spoke more softly. "But in a very real sense, I'd loved him all my life. In those three months, he gave me the moments of peace and safety that made me feel more human."

"When your husband found out, did you break off the affair?"

"Yes." Her voice became brittle. "But Joe couldn't let it go. He kept asking what kinds of things we'd done in that hotel. The language he used was graphic and disgusting.

Before, he couldn't talk about our relationship. Now he couldn't stop talking about my relationship with someone else."

On the bench, Judge Hollis watched her closely, his clinical gaze revealing neither sympathy nor disapproval. Evenly, Terry said, "You described the incident where Brian took your husband's pistol. What led up to that?"

"Joe held the loaded gun to my temple and threatened to fire. He was drunk. He said that he could kill me anytime he wanted to. And that he wanted to kill me every time he imagined me 'spreading my legs for McCarran.'" Kate briefly lowered her eyes. "I was certain that he would. Instead he went to the Officers' Club. All I could think to do was to call Brian."

"How did he respond?"

"He came right over. He found out that the kids were at my mother's and told me I should go there right away. When I said I couldn't, Brian took the gun."

"On the night of the shooting, what happened between you and Captain D'Abruzzo?"

Kate sat back, composing herself. "Joe was drunk again. When he found out the gun was missing, his face became so rigid he almost looked insane—it was like someone had thrown a switch in his brain." Her speech became rapid, almost jittery. "He threw me on the bed, hands around my neck, fingers digging into my windpipe. He was staring into my eyes, and then his face went dark. I turned my head, gasping for air, and managed to rasp, 'Brian has it—'" Kate stopped abruptly. "He was going to kill me, I swear it. Instead he went after Brian."

The courtroom was silent—watching Kate, Flynn could have been a waxwork figure. After a moment, Terry asked, "When Brian came back from Iraq, did you also notice a change in *him*?"

"Yes. Sometimes he'll get very quiet, like something's hurting him too deeply to express. In that way he was like Joe. But there's no meanness in Brian, none."

"Did Brian ever talk about it?"

"Only once, when I told him that Joe was suffering from his time in Iraq. Brian gave me a funny look. Then he said, 'Does he mention the guys who died there?' Pausing, Kate looked troubled. "I said no. The look that crept into Brian's eyes was somewhere between bitterness and despair. 'You know that one of them named his kid after me?' he told me in a quiet voice. 'Imagine that.' Then he went completely silent."

"During your relationship, did you ever spend the night with him?"

"No. I couldn't."

"So you didn't know whether Brian suffered from broken sleep or nightmares?"

"No. But I wondered. He always looked so tired and drawn."

"Did Brian express any fear of Captain D'Abruzzo?"

"Not in words. But he knew Joe hit me. He knew that Joe had threatened to shoot me, because of him. And he knew that—with or without the gun—Joe could kill someone if he completely lost control." Her voice thickened, and dampness surfaced in her eyes. "The night he went to Brian's apartment, Joe was out of control, and Brian knew it. Because I called to warn him."

"Liar."

The shrill cry of rage and anguish made Terry flinch before he turned instinctively toward Flora D'Abruzzo. *"Liar,"* she repeated, pressing against the rail of the court as she pointed to Kate. "You helped him murder my son."

For an instant, Terry had a jumble of images: Kate's stricken gaze, Meg's pallid face, the naked horror in Brian's eyes, Joseph D'Abruzzo's desperation as he clutched his wife around the waist, Flora struggling until, all at once, her body sagged and tears ran down her papery cheeks. Terry felt sick.

The gavel cracked behind him, cutting through the cacophony in the courtroom. "Ma'am," Hollis said in his deep baritone, "the court knows you're under stress. But if you can't control your emotions, you can't be here. I am asking the military police to remove you for the day."

With this, the two MPs who had reached Flora's side steered her toward the exit. She went with them passively, her husband trailing behind, drawing the sympathy of those who watched, even as she drained the impact of Kate D'Abruzzo's words.

2

WHEN JOE D'ABRUZZO'S parents were gone and the press and spectators had quieted again, Flynn commenced cross-examination of his widow. But the ugly moment left a residue—Meg looked unsettled, and the life had vanished from Brian's eyes. Awaiting Flynn's assault, Kate appeared stunned, as though she had just realized that her husband was dead.

Flynn stopped in front of her, his voice and posture again hinting at his dislike. "We've agreed, as I recall, that you lied to Sergeant Frank about your affair with Lieutenant McCarran."

For an instant, Kate seemed to bridle. Then, as if too dispirited to quarrel with Flynn's phrasing, she answered: "Yes."

"And you've further told us that you habitually called Lieutenant McCarran on a landline in order to conceal that affair."

"Yes."

"Other than your purported disclosures to Lieutenant McCarran, did you tell anyone that your husband hit you?"

"No." Abruptly, Kate seemed to awaken from her trance. "I didn't want to hurt Joe's career, or our marriage."

"You didn't think sleeping with his subordinate might damage your marriage?"

Kate looked away. "I didn't plan that."

Flynn stared at her in astonishment. "Did you at least tell someone other than the accused that your husband had held a loaded gun to your temple?"

"No. Brian took the gun away that night."

"Before Lieutenant McCarran killed your husband, did you tell anyone about *why* he had taken the gun?"

"No."

"Even though you worried that your husband could be dangerous—with or without a weapon."

"Yes."

"And even though he posed a specific threat to Lieutenant McCarran, a man you claim to care for."

Kate inhaled. "I didn't know what to do. If all of this came out—"

Her voice trailed off abruptly. In a tone of disbelief, Flynn asked, "Do you think Brian McCarran loves you?"

Kate seemed to inhale. "Yes," she said firmly. "We've loved each other for years, as friends."

"Yet as far as you know, the accused never reported to anyone that your husband—this volatile and dangerous man—hit you repeatedly?"

"Not that I know about."

"Or held a gun to your head?"

"No." Her voice rose. "I asked Brian not to turn Joe in."

Flynn stared at her. "So for the sake of your marriage, you asked your lover not to stop your husband from hitting you or threatening you with a gun?"

Terry stood, breaking Flynn's rhythm. "Asked and answered," he said. "In how many different ways can counsel ask the same question?"

"Sustained," Hollis said promptly. "Please move on, Major."

Intent on Kate, Flynn did not change his expression. "You're also the only witness to these incidents, correct?"

"Yes."

"Your children never saw your husband hit you?"

"No."

"Or hold a gun to your head."

"No." Again Kate's voice rose. "That night Matt and Kristen were with my mother."

"So your husband—this violent man—was considerate enough not to strike or threaten you in the presence of your children."

Kate looked ashen. "I don't know what was going through Joe's head," she said tiredly. "I'm just grateful Matt and Kristen don't have that to remember."

"I thought your husband would get drunk and lose his self-control."

"He did."

"Didn't your husband always start drinking before he hit you?"

"Yes."

"And yet this drunken, violent, and volatile man maintained sufficient self-control that he never once struck you in front of your son or daughter?"

At this, Terry decided to buy Kate time. "Objection," Terry called out. "Once again, trial counsel repackages his previous question. But this time he asks the witness to speculate on motives she can't know about and that, quite possibly, Captain D'Abruzzo never had."

Hollis gave the witness a thoughtful look. Then he said, "I'll allow this one, Captain Terry. Mrs. D'Abruzzo can respond based on what her husband might have said or whatever she was able to observe."

Facing Flynn, Kate drew herself up straighter. "Joe felt a lot of rage, Major Flynn. But he also felt deep shame. Most people try not to shame themselves in front of others—their children most of all. That's why I concealed my relationship, and why Joe didn't hit me, or threaten me, or call me a 'cunt' when anyone else was around. Joe was also desperate not to damage his career. He still wanted to feel pride in himself, even when he no longer did."

Terry watched Flynn search for another question, then fall back on the only line of attack he had left. "Isn't it true," he said coldly, "that your husband never hit you at all? Or threatened you with the gun Lieutenant McCarran used to kill him?"

"No," Kate said tersely. "That's not true—"

"In fact, didn't you invent these incidents to smear Captain D'Abruzzo's reputation and conceal Lieutenant McCarran's plan to murder him?"

"No." Kate's voice was quiet but firm. "Joe came back from Iraq a man I didn't know. That man did things to me I could never have imagined. The only person being smeared in this courtroom is Brian McCarran, who's being prosecuted for responding to *my* weakness and *my* need. And the only thing that could make this tragedy worse is for *you* to send him to prison."

Stymied, Flynn chose to fix her with a look of disbelief. But the members of the court appeared less judgmental than perplexed. Glancing up at Kate, Brian gave her an ambiguous smile. Only Meg's face was devoid of all expression.

"No further questions," Flynn said coldly.

Terry had no desire to extend Kate's time in court. Within a minute, she had left the witness stand, pausing only to touch her mother's shoulder before leaving, as before, with a bearing so unbowed by her ordeal that it evoked her mother's example. It struck Terry once again that he did not know this woman at all.

When the court adjourned, he approached Rose Gallagher as she gathered her coat and purse to leave. "Can I buy you a cup of coffee?"

Sadness and uncertainty lingered in her eyes. "No," she said. "But you can buy me a drink, Captain Terry. I'm sure this trial taxes your resources. But you'd have to be Kate's mother to know how hard today was."

ON THIS DAY, CLOUDY without rain, the choppy surface of the Potomac was slate gray with spumes of white. Through the window of the Officers' Club, Rose considered the river before contemplating her Manhattan. "I haven't had one of these in years," she told Terry. "I first ordered one my senior year in college, when Jack and Tony took Mary and me to the Oak Room at the Plaza in New York. I felt so sophisticated that I forgot how terribly young we were. Of course, there wasn't any way of knowing what awaited us."

Terry could imagine her thoughts: one of the foursome lost in war; another dead by her own hand; the son of one survivor killing the son-in-law of another. "No one could imagine this, Mrs. Gallagher."

"And yet we keep on going—because we must, and because we have other people who depend on us. Especially the children."

Terry nodded in sympathy. "How are they?" he asked.

Her striking face betrayed a melancholy mixed with fatalism. "They miss their father. They'll both be going along, and then one or the other turns very quiet and faraway. We try to shelter them, but they hear things at school—there's too much about this on television and in the newspapers for us to control what both kids hear.

"They know about Kate and Brian, though they never talk of it. Sometimes I can read the judgment in Mathew's eyes when he looks at his mother. But they seem to drift in and out of reality. As I do, I suppose."

Terry nodded. "I know Meg struggles with this, as well. Both the affair and the deception."

Rose put a finger to her lips. "If I might ask, how are the two of you getting along?"

Terry smiled. "As co-counsel, you mean? She's very sharp."

Rose's own wispy smile came with a shake of the head. "That much I know. I was asking whether she trusts you enough to begin letting go."

Terry sipped his scotch, wondering how to answer. "It feels like she does—at least sometimes. But Meg and I live in a schizoid world. She'll stay with me at night, and the next day we're trying to keep Brian out of prison. For hours on end we completely shut our feelings down. Right now there's no future beyond the verdict."

"That must be fairly confusing."

"It's hard having a relationship in fits and starts, with so much on the line that's so immediate and so draining. Sometimes I look at her and see the possibility of contentment, a future I think we both want. But this trial is so consuming that nothing outside it seems quite real. Like you, I think it's hard enough for Meg to believe what's happened."

Rose gave him a candid look. "Perhaps so, Captain Terry. But I was speaking literally, and only for myself. Of course, I may be practicing for old age, deploying the weapon old people use to escape what they can't change—complete denial, the erasure of unpleasant facts. That's the kind of disbelief I experienced today."

Terry felt the stirrings of alarm. "Concerning what?"

"Kate's affair with Brian. I know my daughter better than she imagines. There were times today when I didn't believe a word she was saying." As though distressed, Rose looked away. "It must be true, I know. Unless Brian's a coolheaded murderer—which I don't accept for an instant—why else did this terrible chain of events occur? But when I try to imagine it, I can't."

"What exactly do you mean?"

"Nothing more than what I've said." After a moment, she raised her glass to Terry, her expression neutral again. "I sincerely wish you luck, Captain. With Brian *and* with Meg."

THAT NIGHT, MEG STAYED with Brian.

Terry worked alone at his kitchen table. A little before ten o'clock, he put the outline of tomorrow's examination aside and let his thoughts drift where they would.

They kept returning to Rose Gallagher. She remained beautiful in her late fifties—if he had been the young Anthony McCarran, Terry was certain, Rose would have held far more appeal than Mary. Certainly, this had become true for the general once Mary's verve for living had deteriorated into the erratic behavior of a self-involved drunk. But it might also have been true, at least for a moment, before Tony McCarran and Jack Gallagher left for Vietnam.

Rose was also a wise woman, he believed, and an honest one. But honesty had its limits—with others, and with oneself. The suspicion he had put aside surfaced once again: the possible reason, long concealed, that Rose Gallagher could not accept what Kate and Brian had openly acknowledged.

He went to his desk, removing a file he had not shared with Meg.

The manila folder was labeled "Questions." Inside was a single piece of paper. Beneath the sole previous entry— "Brian's cell phone records"—he wrote, "Is Kate the daughter of Anthony McCarran?"

Terry did not want to believe this. But Kate's resemblance to her mother was so complete that it shed no light on her paternity. To see Kate at thirty-four was to see Rose at that same age, and to imagine her at twenty-two, smiling at Tony McCarran as she sipped her first Manhattan.

Terry closed the file and stuck it back into the drawer.

3

IN THE HOURS BEFORE DAWN, Terry's cell phone rasped.

For a moment, he was confused. Then the sound pierced his consciousness, and a sharp, sudden fear for Brian caused him to snatch at the phone.

The connection was poor. By the time Terry identified his caller—Sergeant Ben Flournoy, his CID investigator—he was alert but calmer.

Flournoy was in Afghanistan. He spat out his message through the static. "I found Johnny Whalen, the lieutenant's platoon sergeant. He's been doing semisecret stuff near the Pakistani border."

"Did he talk about Sadr City?"

Through the cell phone, Terry's voice echoed back to him, causing a delay. "He didn't really want to. But yeah." A brief crackle punctuated Flournoy's words. "I've heard war stories before, Captain. But this is a bad one."

"Give me the worst of it."

Hastily, Flournoy outlined Whalen's account. In those few minutes, Terry's comprehension of Brian McCarran was utterly transformed. Tersely, Terry ordered, "See what kind of arrangements you can make to fly him out ASAP."

Flournoy promised he would, and got off.

For several minutes, surrounded by darkness, Terry did not move. Then he picked up the phone and called Meg.

She was sleeping on Brian's couch. "Sorry to call so early," he said. "Ben found Johnny Whalen."

Anxiety cut through Meg's sleep-shadowed voice. "Can he help us?"

"We'll know better when we talk to him. But we've got some adjustments to make. Can you spend today preparing your father to testify?"

"When?"

"Tomorrow, I hope. Directly after you."

There was a brief pause. In a subdued tone, Meg asked, "What shall I tell Brian?"

"Nothing. I don't want to make him anxious."

"What *did* Ben tell you, Paul?"

Terry considered his answer. "Enough," he told her. "It may explain why Brian's changed. But whether the members of the court will ever hear it depends on Hollis."

Terry hung up, then left an urgent message for the judge.

AT NINE O'CLOCK, JUDGE Hollis sequestered the members, convening the lawyers in the courtroom. As Flynn and Pulaski listened, the judge addressed Terry. "For precisely what purpose," he asked, "are you requesting me to order this man stateside?"

"As far as we can tell," Terry responded, "Whalen is the sole survivor among those who served with Brian McCarran from beginning to end. The incidents he described may illuminate the role of post-traumatic stress disorder in the death of Captain D'Abruzzo. Including the lieutenant's loss of memory and, conceivably, his state of mind at the moment of the shooting."

Flynn rose to speak. Holding up a hand for silence, Hollis prompted Terry, "Can you spell that out for me?"

"To do that, I need more than a secondhand account over a staticky cell phone. All I'm requesting is to interview this man so that I can determine whether to seek permission to call him as a witness. If I do, I'll make sure the court has sufficient information to determine relevance."

Thought furrowed Hollis's forehead and drew down the corners of his mouth. "That's a limited request," he told Flynn. "Unless Captain Terry can tie whatever this man says to the lieutenant's conduct, the members of the court will never hear it."

"That may be so, Your Honor. But PTSD is already creeping into the case without the foundation you just described. Specifically, in Captain Terry's plan to call the sister and father of the accused." Flynn's staccato speech underscored his point. "That is highly prejudicial, Your Honor. The alleged purpose is to show that the accused has changed—based on a condition we don't even know he has, and which defense counsel still hasn't linked to the shooting. That end run around the standards of relevance is bad enough. But the damage will be intensified when it's given the imprimatur of one of the army's most decorated and respected general officers. We can't expect the members not to respond with deference, no matter how little this testimony has to do with the guilt of the accused."

From the gravity of his expression, Hollis was troubled as well. "Captain Terry?"

"If nothing else, Anthony and Meg McCarran are character witnesses—"

"With limited credibility."

"Perhaps. But they know the accused better than anyone, and can describe changes in behavior consistent with PTSD. If we can't show how that relates to Captain D'Abruzzo's death, Major Flynn can make a motion to strike—"

"Which the court will grant," Hollis said crisply. "Subject to that, you can call the two McCarrans. I'll also order the return of Sergeant Whalen from Afghanistan. What happens after that depends on what he has to say. Unless the lieutenant's combat experiences prove relevant, the members of the court will be deciding this case in a matter of days. With or without Lieutenant McCarran's testimony on his own behalf."

"Thank you, Your Honor," Terry said, suspended between gratitude and doubt.

THE NEXT WITNESS FOR the defense, Victor Lee, was a black belt in karate who had been Joe D'Abruzzo's last instructor. Among his other qualifications were that he had once disarmed a gang member who had accosted him with a gun. Wiry and alert, Lee told this story while perched on the edge of the chair, his eyes at once calm and watchful. Even his spiky jet-black hair looked ready for a fight.

"Did you kill this man?" Terry asked.

"No," Lee said matter-of-factly. "But I could have. Instead I kicked him in the groin. He was still retching when the cops showed up."

"Could Captain D'Abruzzo have done the same thing?"

For an instant, Flynn half-rose, then seemed to swallow his objection. "Yes," Lee answered promptly. "Captain D'Abruzzo was fully capable of killing someone with his hands. By the time I taught him, he was a fifth-degree black belt, with thirteen years of training. Constant repetition and practice had turned his movements into reflexes, connecting his body to his brain. He no longer had to think."

The admiration in Lee's voice was unmistakable. "How would you describe Captain D'Abruzzo's physical capabilities?"

"Superb reflexes, superior hand-eye coordination, and decent foot speed." Lee frowned, adding solemnly, "At the time of his death, he was the only student I had who came anywhere close to matching me."

Glancing at the members, Terry saw Randi Wertheimer watching Lee raptly. "Suppose," he asked Lee, "that D'Abruzzo confronted an armed man unskilled in martial arts. Suppose further that they were four to five feet apart. How long would it take the captain to disarm his opponent and strike a fatal blow?"

Lee stroked his chin. "Two seconds, I'd say. Certainly no more than three."

"Do the karate students you encounter have different levels of aggression?"

"Definitely."

"How would you characterize Captain D'Abruzzo?"

Lee steepled his fingers. "There are two types of instinctive reactions to danger—fight or flight. Joe was an attacker. He did not back off."

"How would he react to someone drawing a gun on him from close range?"

"Objection," Flynn called out. "Calls for speculation. Mr. Lee never saw the victim confronted with such a threat."

"Mr. Lee is an expert in martial arts," Terry responded promptly. "He sparred with Captain D'Abruzzo three times a week for over six months. As such, he's qualified to speak to D'Abruzzo's physical *and* mental qualities as a martial artist."

Pensive, Hollis considered this. "Overruled. Please answer, Mr. Lee."

Lee nodded. "Danger instantly releases chemicals in the brain. In all likelihood, Captain D'Abruzzo would react with swift, violent moves—blunt and direct."

"How would that appear to his opponent?"

"Threatening, obviously. With good reason."

Walking back to the defense table, Terry picked up a black handgun, then showed the judge and members that its chambers were empty of bullets. "I'd like to attempt a demonstration," he told Lee. "Please step down from the stand."

Lee faced Terry in the well of the courtroom. Moving to within five feet, Terry aimed the gun at him. "How would you disarm me?"

"I'd turn," the witness answered briskly. "To present the minimum target." He spun sideways, so taut that he resembled a blade of steel. "Like this."

Terry felt the jury members watching. "So that if I shot," he suggested, "I might hit you on the side of the arm."

"Sure. But you'd better do it quick." Without warning, Lee whirled, knocking the gun from Terry's hand with a painful twist of his wrist. It happened so quickly that Terry felt numb. "Now you're disarmed," Lee said.

Terry shook the pain from his wrist. "Unless I shot you in the palm."

"True. Otherwise you're vulnerable to whatever I do next. Pick up the gun."

When Terry did this, Lee backed off to five feet. He spun to the side, whirled to knock the gun from Terry's hand, and thrust two fingers at his eyes, stopping an inch short. "Now you're blind," Lee said, then thrust his right palm at Terry's esophagus.

"And now you're dead," he informed Terry. "The blow to your esophagus just collapsed your windpipe."

Terry's skin tingled. From their silence, those watching felt it too.

"Thank you," Terry said. "No further questions."

FLYNN WALKED TOWARD THE witness, his demeanor calm and unimpressed. "At a distance of four feet, the accused would have two to three seconds to pull the trigger before Captain D'Abruzzo could disarm him. Is that right?"

On the witness stand, Lee leaned forward. "Yes."

"Suppose the captain was ten feet away when Lieutenant McCarran aimed the gun. Could he close that distance and disarm him in a comparable time?"

"That's unlikely."

"What tactics would the captain use to keep from getting shot?"

Lee examined the question with narrowed eyes. "Most probably, he'd move toward the shooter in a rapid zigzag pattern, trying to avoid bullets. Then he'd try to do what I just did to Captain Terry."

"Against a capable marksman, what chance would he have?"

"From ten feet? Not very good."

"What about his chance of being wounded as Captain Terry suggested—in the shoulder and palm?"

"That would be much better, I'd say."

"And in the chest?"

For the first time, Lee glanced at Brian. "As he reached for the gun, Captain D'Abruzzo would be facing the shooter. That's when he'd be most likely to take a bullet in the chest."

"In short, Mr. Lee, the greater the distance between Captain D'Abruzzo and the shooter, the less a chance he had to survive."

"Yes."

In the jury box, Major Bobby Wade nodded to himself. "According to our ballistics expert," Flynn said, "the weapon used to kill Captain D'Abruzzo can fire three to four rounds a second. Even at four to five feet, who would you say had the advantage—the victim, or the shooter?"

"The shooter, obviously. That's six to eight rounds in the two seconds."

"Would a black belt in karate consider that?"

"Of course. Mental self-control is essential to our training." Lee paused, then added, "I mean, Captain D'Abruzzo was shot with his own gun, right? So he knew the weapon's capabilities."

Flynn smiled a little. "Of course, Captain D'Abruzzo was also legally intoxicated. How might that affect his physical capacities?"

"He'd be slower, his strokes heavier. His footwork might be messed up."

"Would he be slow enough to get killed from a distance of four feet?"

"Objection," Terry called out. "The question asks for speculation."

"The question asks for an expert opinion," Flynn rejoined. "Captain Terry has qualified the witness as an expert. The effects of intoxication on martial arts capabilities is well within his expertise."

"Overruled," Hollis said, and turned expectantly toward Lee.

"He'd be easier to kill," Lee answered slowly. "In the moves I demonstrated with Captain Terry, footwork is critical. That's where Captain D'Abruzzo was least strong and where alcohol would have affected him the most."

"Would severe intoxication also skew his judgment?"

"Yes. The last thing a martial artist needs is alcohol— you add the potential for mental errors to increased physical limitations." Lee stopped to parse his words. "If a naturally aggressive man chooses to attack someone with a gun, drunkenness would measurably increase his chance of getting killed."

Flynn glanced sharply at the jury, as though to demand

their strict attention. "In other words, even at five feet—let alone ten—Captain D'Abruzzo was far less of a threat to Lieutenant McCarran than McCarran was to him."

"Yes, sir," Lee responded quietly. "I would say that's right."

"Thank you, Mr. Lee. No further questions."

Terry stood at the defense table. "Even drunk, Mr. Lee, beginning five feet away could Captain D'Abruzzo kill Lieutenant McCarran in three seconds?"

"He could. If the lieutenant didn't shoot him first."

"So if Captain D'Abruzzo had attacked him, the lieutenant would have three seconds to keep himself from getting killed. During which Captain D'Abruzzo would have been making swift and violent movements toward Lieutenant McCarran."

"Yes."

"Does that seem like sufficient time to make a considered judgment about how to incapacitate Captain D'Abruzzo without killing him?"

Lee shook his head. "I can't say that it does. It's all a matter of time and distance. Change the distance, and you change my answer."

That, Terry decided, would have to be enough. When he returned to the table, Brian's cool blue-gray eyes were grave.

THAT NIGHT, MEG WORKED at her father's apartment, helping to prepare his testimony. When she called him, Terry asked, "How is he?"

"Dad?" Meg hesitated. "Stoic. The sense of responsibility is weighing on him. But he won't fail Brian on the stand."

She sounded tired. "We'll go over this in the morning," he said. "I'll see you both at seven."

"Is Brian's platoon sergeant on the way?"

"As we speak. Try to get some sleep, all right?"

Softly, Meg answered, "I miss you, too." She got off before Terry could reply.

THAT NIGHT HE DREAMED again of his father. But instead of offering words of comfort, Frank Terry ordered his son not to open the desk drawer where—Terry now knew—his mother had concealed the papers exposing his father's guilt. What jarred him most was that, in the dream, the desk was Terry's own.

Splashing water on his face, he pondered the dream's mutation. Perhaps it meant nothing. Perhaps he felt misgivings about concealing his inchoate doubts from Meg. Or perhaps it was simply the memory of his long ago disquiet, deepening the shadow of his father's suicide.

For several years, his mother had concealed the truth. But even then Paul had known that something beneath the surface of his father's life had caused the changes in his own. Without knowing the reason, Terry felt that way again.

4

TAKING THE STAND, Meg McCarran looked softer than before. Instead of a suit, she wore a simple dress with pastel colors, and her makeup, carefully applied, accentuated her deep blue eyes. Meg was more aware of her attractiveness than she let on, Terry understood, and had flawlessly chosen a role intended to appeal to the members of the court— Brian's concerned and beautiful older sister. Hands folded, she listened attentively as Hollis addressed the members.

"Ms. McCarran," he explained, "has acted as co-counsel to the accused. But she was also named by the defense as a potential witness. Because she has agreed that this will be the sole capacity in which she speaks on the behalf of Lieutenant McCarran, the court is allowing her to testify."

With a grateful half smile, Meg nodded her agreement, then turned to Terry and the members of the court. After his preliminary questions, Terry asked, "Can you describe your brother prior to his service in Iraq?"

She paused, gazing at Brian with evident affection. "There are so many things I could say, Captain Terry. Brian was—and is—intelligent, sensitive, quiet, and self-contained. But he also had a very keen sense of humor."

"Would you call him nervous?"

"Then? Not at all."

"Or angry?"

"No. At most, when Brian got annoyed he'd become more quiet. But I never once saw him lose his temper."

"Did you know him to have difficulty sleeping?"

"Only for a brief period, when he was nine and I was twelve." Meg's voice softened. "Our mother committed suicide. For the next few weeks, Brian took an air mattress and slept on the floor of my room—or Dad's, if he was home. One night he started sleeping in his own room again."

Brian, Terry was certain, was mortified at this invasion of his privacy. But this was the best opportunity for members to see him as a person. "Did your mother's death change him?" Terry asked.

Meg contemplated this. "Brian was always an observer. But he became a little quieter, more inclined to drift off into his own thoughts."

"After your mother's suicide, did Brian receive psychiatric help?"

"Not formally, no. But Rose Gallagher, Kate D'Abruzzo's mother, helped take care of us—when Dad was gone, we lived with Rose and Kate. Rose has a master's degree in child psychology, and she was always receptive when Brian needed to talk. In many ways, she was like a mother to us both."

"What was Brian's relationship to Kate?"

Meg answered as though the question had no overtones. "Kate was in high school when our mother killed herself. So she helped shuttle us around, Brian especially. Sometimes she'd watch his soccer or baseball games. They were close, and Brian clearly cared for her."

"But not romantically."

"Of course not," Meg answered with a brisk shake of her head. "They were nine years apart. Even after Brian was an adult, they were family friends with a deep connection."

Terry gave her an inquiring look. "Do you consider Brian to be empathetic?"

"I do—especially after our mother's death. As he got older, he sympathized with people who were vulnerable or hurting. Looking out for people became part of Brian's way. Even as a teenager, he had no meanness in him."

"How did he perform in school?"

Meg's fleeting smile hinted at nostalgia. "Brian did well all around. He was a top student, a terrific athlete, and a natural leader—the kind who never looked back to see if he was being followed but whom others saw as an example."

"Did that continue at West Point?"

"Yes. He remained a leader, and finished near the top of his class." She paused, then added wryly, "Almost as high as our father."

With this reference to Anthony McCarran, Terry and Meg slid into the version of family they had so carefully rehearsed. "Do you know why Brian chose the infantry?"

Meg's expression became grave. "For the last four generations, McCarrans have served as officers in the infantry. Our great-grandfather received the Medal of Honor in World War One; our grandfather a Silver Star in Korea. Both of them died in combat. Our father fought in the Gulf War and, before that, received a Bronze Star in Vietnam." She paused, adding softly, "Military service is what the male McCarrans do. I don't think Brian ever considered another life."

Terry let this answer linger for a moment. "When was Brian sent to Iraq?"

"The beginning of 2004. Seven months after graduating from the academy."

"Prior to Iraq, how was his relationship with Captain D'Abruzzo?"

"It was always fine. By the time they both went to Iraq, Joe had been married to Kate for nine years, so he and

Brian had known each other since my brother was thirteen. Even when it became clear how different they were, he and Joe seemed to enjoy each other at family gatherings. I never saw any change in that. Nor any change in Brian's relationship with Kate."

"How would you describe your own relationship with Brian?"

Looking toward Brian, Meg smiled a little. "We've always been close, especially since our mother died. Dad was away a lot—in terms of blood relations, Brian and I often felt like each other's only family." She turned to Terry, adding simply, "I hated it when Brian went to Iraq. I didn't want to lose him."

The image of Brian as a beloved younger brother was precisely what Terry wanted to impart. "Did Brian know how much you worried?"

"I couldn't hide it. For my benefit, he tried to be nonchalant. When I told him to skip trying for any medals, he flashed me that fantastic smile of his, the one I used to see so often. Then he said, 'Don't worry, sis—the McCarrans are on a winning streak. Dad made it back from two different wars.'"

Her answer suggested both fondness and foreboding—that Brian would return alive but deeply changed. Glancing at Major Wertheimer, Terry divined her sympathy and interest. But Flynn's expression held the stoicism of a prosecutor forced to listen as his opponent created a picture of his client. "Based on a lifetime of knowing him," Terry asked, "did Brian strike you as well-suited to be a combat leader?"

Doubt seemed to surface in Meg's large blue eyes. "I'm not a soldier, obviously. My brother is smart and resourceful, with a sense of responsibility and deep concern for other people. But fighting and killing is not a job that rewards sensitivity and introspection. In that way, our father's a tougher man—he can block out painful thoughts for the sake of pushing forward. That's neither good nor bad. I'm just saying that they're different."

By her own description, Terry thought, Meg resembled her father more than she did her brother. "Once Brian was in Iraq, how often did you hear from him?"

Meg tilted her head. "At first, fairly often. I'd say almost once a week."

"In these initial phone calls, what did he tell you?"

"He was in Sadr City when Muqtada al-Sadr declared war on American soldiers. He knew I was scared, so he didn't go into detail. He did say that they didn't have enough soldiers, and couldn't tell their enemies from bystanders. But he also told me the war was even harsher for Iraqi civilians."

"Did he describe his combat experiences?"

"Not specifically. He always tried to sound light about it. But it was clear that he worried for his men." She paused, glancing at Brian. "It was only later that I learned what he wouldn't tell me—that some of them were already dead."

Terry paused for a moment. "Was there a time when Brian seemed to change?"

"About three months in. Brian's voice became flat, he called less often, and he wouldn't talk about the war at all." Meg's face set. "I got so anxious that I tried to push him, find out what was happening. All he said was 'You don't want to know, Meg.' After a while, he stopped calling anyone—not me, or our dad, or Rose."

"How did you react?"

"I tried to learn more from Dad. As chief of staff, he wasn't in the chain of command when it came to executing the war. But he knew a lot." Meg bit her lip, suggesting her reluctance to betray a confidence. "You have to know our father to know how tight-lipped he can be. But finally he admitted how bad it was in Sadr City. Brian was right, he said—there weren't enough troops, and no one had planned for the occupation they were facing. It was one thing to beat a fourth-rate army, Dad told me, and another to control someone else's country." Meg's voice fell. "I could tell that it hurt him to say that—both because of his loyalty to the army, and because his own son was at risk on account of mistakes he couldn't correct. Then we went to Mass together and prayed for Brian to come home unharmed."

At the corner of his vision, Terry saw Brian close his eyes. Quietly, he asked, "After Brian returned, when did you first see him?"

"I flew out two weeks after he arrived at Bolton. At first, I was so overjoyed all I wanted was to hug him. But then I realized how changed he was."

"In what respects?"

She looked down, as though not wishing to answer in front of Brian. "He was way too quiet. He seldom smiled, and his jokes all tended to be dark. He seemed hollowed out, like his soul had left his body. Then I realized he'd left it in Iraq."

Flynn watched her closely now, poised to object. "How did you conclude that?" Terry asked.

"By staying with him. During the day, while he was working at his battalion's headquarters, it seemed like he kept things together. But he was different at night, or out in the world." Meg's speech quickened. "On the highway, he kept looking to the right and left, like he was still at war. Traffic jams enraged him; unexpected sounds made him flinch, like a car backfiring or a waiter dropping dishes. In restaurants, he sat with his back to the wall, constantly scanning the room." She paused. "Brian has a great deal of pride, and he exercises all his willpower to try to keep a lid on behavior people might notice. But that breaks down at night."

"In what way?"

"He can't sleep. When he does, he has terrible nightmares he won't describe." Meg's voice filled with remembered fear. "One night he woke up screaming. When I tried to calm him, his eyes were wild, and he didn't know who I was. He started to choke me, then stopped at the sound of my voice crying out. He just sat there, slumped, his sheets tangled and damp with sweat. He told me I was the only person he'd let be near him when he tried to sleep. Then he just held me and said, 'I'm sorry, sis.'"

"Did you suggest that he get help?"

"Of course. But he said that calling himself a head case would kill his career. He was an officer, he told me—he understood what had happened to him, and he'd get through it. Just like our father got through Vietnam."

The last phrase had a brittle tenor. "Did Brian put a label to his problem?"

"Not in so many words. But one night I found him searching the Internet for articles on post-traumatic stress disorder. So we talked about that a little." She paused again. "He did admit to feeling numb, and to hating enclosed spaces. Even his apartment made him feel trapped. It was like he was looking out for enemies and needed a means of escape."

Once again, Flynn stirred; as Meg had intended, this came close to invoking Brian's state of mind on the evening he had killed D'Abruzzo. Quickly, Terry said, "Did he ever hint at any aspect of his nightmares?"

"Only once." Meg seemed to swallow. "I heard him stirring. When I went to the bedroom, tears were running down his face. 'What is it?' I asked him. 'I can still see them,' he answered. Then, as if it were a separate thought, he said, 'He named his kid after me.' "

Looking at the members, Terry saw Bobby Wade connect this to Kate's description of a similar remark. "Did you ask him what he meant?"

"Yes. He wouldn't say."

"Since he was charged with murder, how would you describe his state of mind?"

"Worse." Now she looked at Brian directly. "I'm very worried for him. I don't think he can see a future anymore."

"On what do you base that?"

She turned her gaze to Terry, her features slackened by sorrow. "When I try to talk to him about the trial, he'll say things like 'What's the point?' And I know he's not talking about the trial at all. I, too, have read up on PTSD. So I discovered that the ultimate symptom is suicide." Her eyes misted, and she gave her brother a pleading look. "One of Brian's men hung himself. I know how it feels to lose someone you love like that. I couldn't stand that happening to Brian."

They had crafted her testimony to affect the jury. But her answer affected Terry as well. For an instant, he saw through the woman on the stand to the determined twelve-year-old with a vulnerable brother, protecting him from what their mother had done to them both.

"No further questions," Terry said.

As he walked to his chair, he saw that Joe D'Abruzzo's parents had returned, perhaps intending by their presence to affect the balance of sympathy. By accident or design, Flora was a portrait in dignity, her face betraying grief without malice. But what struck Terry even more was Brian's expression, so remote that he seemed to be willing himself off the face of the earth. In Brian McCarran, Terry understood, this was what shame looked like.

APPROACHING MEG, FLYNN HAD an air of skepticism and reserve. There was little good to be done here, he surely knew, and every question had an underside of risk.

"According to Lieutenant McCarran's statement to Sergeant Frank, he called you moments after the shooting. Is that true?"

Terry had left this subject open, knowing that Flynn would be forced to pursue it. As they planned, Meg's expression and tone were undefensive. "Yes, it's true."

"Why did Brian call you?"

She shifted her gaze, partially facing the members of the court. "From his voice, he was in shock. It was like he couldn't describe exactly what had happened."

Flynn turned to Hollis. "We move to strike the answer," he said flatly. "The witness's interpretation is unsupported by fact—including any account of the lieutenant's actual words."

The judge turned toward Meg. "I'm going to allow your answer, Ms. McCarran. But please refrain from putting a gloss on the events that may say more about your sympathies than it does about the facts."

"I understand," Meg said respectfully. "I know my brother, and that was why I answered as I did. But I'll try to be more careful."

The brief narrowing of Hollis's eyes, not visible to the members, suggested his awareness that Meg McCarran was a very clever woman. "The judge asks the proper question," Flynn told her coolly. "What *did* your brother say?"

Meg faced him. "I believe his exact words were 'I just killed Joe.' I couldn't make any sense of it. 'Joe who?' I asked. 'Joe D'Abruzzo,' he answered. 'I shot him.'"

"Did you ask him why?"

"He said that Joe was beating Kate, and that he'd come to Brian's apartment." Distractedly, Meg brushed a strand of hair from her cheek. "It sounded so disjointed I thought Brian was having some sort of breakdown. It took me a moment to comprehend that Kate's husband was lying dead on the floor of Brian's apartment."

"Or dying," Flynn retorted. "You don't know that he was dead, do you?"

"No," Meg answered softly. "I'm just saying what Brian thought."

Nettled, Flynn raised his eyebrows in the judge's direction, making his point without words. In a tone of exasperation, he asked Meg, "How did you respond?"

"I told him to call the military police at once." She paused, then added quietly, "I also told him not to answer any questions. He sounded so confused that I was afraid he'd create trouble for himself just by trying to be helpful. Unfortunately, he didn't follow my advice."

Flynn's dilemma was written on his face: in the guise of a worried sister, Meg the lawyer was artfully planting seeds of doubt and sympathy. Her skill at this was a reminder, if Terry needed one, that Meg McCarran was far more subtle than she appeared. At length Flynn found a question calculated to elicit an answer helpful to his case. "Did Brian tell you that he was having an affair with Kate D'Abruzzo?"

Meg looked astonished. "It wasn't that kind of conversation. He called because something terrible had happened, which he didn't seem to comprehend."

"How did you learn about the affair?"

Terry stood. "We object, Your Honor. Within two days of the shooting, the accused had established an attorney-client relationship with Ms. McCarran—"

"Which she waived by testifying," Flynn interrupted.

"That's not true," Terry answered smoothly. "On direct, we were careful to confine ourselves to events prior to the death of Captain D'Abruzzo."

"Objection sustained," Hollis told Flynn. "Frame your questions accordingly."

Facing Meg, Flynn put his hands on his hips. "So despite your extraordinary closeness prior to the shooting, Brian never told you he was sleeping with a woman you'd known your entire life?"

"No. But I wouldn't expect him to. It's Brian's nature to protect people."

Terry suppressed a smile. Beside him, Brian looked closely at his sister, his interest reengaged. Coldly, Flynn asked, "When the accused called you to report that he'd shot Captain D'Abruzzo, did anyone else hear the conversation?"

"They couldn't have. My office door was closed."

"So no one can corroborate any aspect of your conversation with the accused?"

"No," Meg said simply. "There was no one in my office when Brian called."

"So no one can confirm what your brother said to you?"

"No."

"Or what you said to him."

Meg's voice was tighter now. "No."

"Did you report it to anyone?"

"I called my father right away. This affected Brian, and our extended family—Rose, Kate, and Kate's children. Dad needed to know."

"What did you tell him?"

"Only what had happened. The conversation wasn't long—he was too anxious about Brian."

Flynn skipped a beat. Casually, he asked, "Did you also call Kate D'Abruzzo?"

"I did not." Meg allowed a quiet indignation to seep into her voice. "But let me see if I understand you. You've suggested that Kate and Brian are part of a conspiracy to commit murder that included concocting elaborate lies. You're now insinuating, it seems clear, that I became part of that conspiracy. I'm a lawyer, Major Flynn. You may not like my testimony, but I don't tell lies under oath. Not in answer to this question, or any other."

Flynn stared at her with palpable anger. "Your Honor," he told Hollis, "I move to strike every word of that answer except 'I did not.'"

Terry stood. "It seems to me," he responded mildly, "that counsel got the answer he was asking for."

"And then some," Hollis retorted. To Meg, he said sternly, "I've already warned you about answers based on speculation. You can add to that argumentative responses that exceed the scope of the question asked. We'll have no more of either." Facing the members of the court, he instructed, "The jurors will disregard the witness's answer following the words 'I did not.'"

But Terry knew that they would not. Watching her contrite expression, Terry realized that when she cared to be, Meg McCarran was a gifted actress.

THAT NIGHT, OVER DINNER at Terry's apartment, Meg drank more wine than usual. They had barely finished when she led him to the bedroom and slid out of her pastel dress, her eyes intent on his. Her lovemaking was quick, almost fierce, as though she wished to block out everything but the man inside her.

Afterward, they lay in the dark. "Was I all right?" she asked.

Terry kissed her. "When?"

Meg did not smile. "In court."

"You were perfect," Terry assured her. "I already told you that. Do you want to talk about it a little more?"

"No," she replied flatly. After a moment, she said in a quieter voice, "It was the hardest thing I've ever done. At least until I watch my father."

Terry asked nothing more.

5

THE ENTRANCE OF General Anthony McCarran transformed the courtroom.

He walked to the witness stand in his bemedaled green uniform, his clear gray-blue eyes offset by the deepening creases in his face. To Terry, he looked careworn, much older than the man he had met five months before. His charisma remained undeniable. But part of this was a sense of distance, as though a space existed around Anthony McCarran that belonged to him alone. The members of the court watched him with respectful gazes; which, in Major Wertheimer's case, was leavened with an open curiosity. Erect even when sitting, Anthony McCarran might seem like a legend brought to life, the straight line of his service marked by courage, faith, sacrifice, and honor. Even Colonel Hollis, usually opaque, seemed to regard him with regret—his only son, the heir to the McCarran legacy, stood accused of murder and adultery.

From the defense table, Brian regarded his father with what struck Terry as a dispassionate, almost chilly, curiosity. Meg's tension showed in the stillness of her body, the caution and alertness in her eyes. Briefly, the general glanced at his son and then, as though pained, looked past him. Following his gaze, Terry saw that Rose Gallagher had returned, watching the general with an affection and concern absent from the faces of his children. It occurred to

Terry that he knew little about how father, son, and daughter were coping with one another now.

Terry began his questions. With economy, they outlined the general's service, his medals, the hallmarks of a unique career. McCarran answered sparingly, a man who did not wish to dwell on his achievements. But when Terry evoked Brian's successes prior to Iraq, the general responded with more emotion, as though reentering a moment or time filled with hope or, perhaps, the comfort of illusion.

"How did you feel," Terry asked, "when Brian's unit was sent to Iraq?"

As before, McCarran's spine did not touch the back of the chair. "I knew it was inevitable," he replied in his clear, soft voice. "This was the career he had chosen, and I knew his brigade commander, Colonel Northrop, to be a very fine officer." He paused, as though prompting himself to say more. "What I felt, I suppose, was a father's hope and a father's concern. I had learned what war is long ago."

"Brian was a platoon leader, correct?"

"Yes. As I had been in Vietnam."

"And Captain Joe D'Abruzzo was his company commander."

For an instant, McCarran glanced toward D'Abruzzo's parents, his eyes conveying regret. "Yes."

"Did you know him well?"

McCarran nodded. "Because of Kate, his wife, and her mother, Rose. As you know, our families were close."

To Terry's ear, the last phrase had a faint valedictory quality. "Did you have an opinion of D'Abruzzo's abilities as a company commander?" Terry asked.

"I did not." McCarran hesitated. "But my sense was that Joe was aggressive, perhaps somewhat impulsive. It takes combat to show how these attributes work out."

"During the time Brian served in Iraq, did you monitor Brian's company?"

"I did," McCarran answered gravely. "They faced some of the hardest fighting in the war, in one of its most difficult periods. There were thirty men in Brian's platoon. By the end of the year, most of them were wounded or dead."

Terry paused, allowing the members to absorb this. "Did Colonel Northrop specifically comment on Brian?"

"Yes." McCarran glanced toward Brian, his voice becoming warmer. "He told me that Brian was a resourceful officer, undeniably brave, and that his men seemed to love him. That account never changed."

"You must have felt a great deal of pride."

"Less pride than comfort." McCarran's voice was quiet again. "I always wondered if Brian went to the academy because of me. Now I was able to believe that he knew his own nature, which was to be a soldier."

The regret in the words was understated but clear. Evenly, Terry asked, "Did you still feel that way when he returned from Iraq?"

McCarran's gaze flickered. "I still knew he was a brave officer. But I began to wonder what that had cost him."

"Had he changed?"

"Certainly to me. He refused to talk about Sadr City or what had happened to him there. But he made it very clear that he felt the army, and his country, had failed the men he led."

"How did he express this?"

"With a great deal of anger." The grooves in McCarran's face deepened and then, as if knowing that he must, he continued to speak. "His contempt for those who planned this war was profound. Generals don't fight, he told me— I hadn't seen a war in fourteen years, and my Iraq war was nothing like his. He said that he'd seen his men maimed and slaughtered and stripped of any belief in the mission they'd been sent for. And when they came home feeling lost, we abandoned them."

McCarran seemed to repeat the words almost literally, as though Brian's fury had seared them into his memory. "Beyond the anger you mention," Terry asked, "how was Brian different?"

"He had lost his faith," McCarran said reluctantly. "In the army, in our leaders, in the church—even in the existence of God."

"How did you find those conversations?"

McCarran's eyes were bleak. "Difficult," he said softly. "That's not how I came up. A good officer, like a good Catholic, may sometimes be faced with doubt or questions. At times it may be necessary to express them. But then he must go about his mission, and his life, with faith and without complaint. That's the only way an army can function, or a man can transcend his own frailties."

The speech had the sound of a core belief, the fortress against doubt that had enabled McCarran to survive tragedy and war but which now, faced with his son, no longer sustained him. "Did you express those thoughts to Brian?" Terry asked.

"I did." McCarran looked down and then, as though against his will, recited in a monotone the answer Terry had extracted from him three hours before. "He said that I had too many verities: that God exists, that Christ's mother was a virgin, and that the secretary of defense is worthy of respect by virtue of his office. And that these illusions sheltered me from facing the fact that the meaningless death of his men was a mercy compared to the lives that the survivors might lead at home."

The savagery of Brian's response seemed to echo in the

courtroom. Softly, Terry inquired, "Did you react to your son's comments, General McCarran?"

"I'm afraid I became angry, and refused to discuss it further."

"Did there come a time when Meg, your daughter, told you that Brian himself was struggling?"

"Yes."

"How did you reply?"

"That Vietnam was hard, and that what I experienced there affected me for a while." Glancing toward Rose, he added softly, "The loss of my closest friend, Jack Gallagher, is with me still. But I told Meg that I was able to come out the other end, more or less intact. So I thought Brian could, too."

"Did Meg reply to that?"

"Yes." A rasp entered McCarran's voice. "She said that was the illusion that Brian clung to, because of me. But that we were different men, and that it was time to set him free."

When Terry looked toward the members of the court, the fissure within this family was graven on their faces. Even Flynn stared at the table, his eyes hooded. Terry did not attempt to glance at Meg or Brian, or even Rose. "After Meg came to you," Terry asked, "did you try to talk with Brian?"

"Yes. It did not go well."

"Could you describe that conversation?"

McCarran's erect posture seemed more telling now, his last defense against the misery and failure he was forced to recite in public. "I told him that I felt sympathy and that I'd suffered from combat more than I'd let on. But that the only cure was to push forward, keeping up appearances until appearance again became reality. And that if Brian let himself fall to pieces he might never be able to pick them up again."

"How did he react?"

McCarran shook his head, a gesture of dismay that seemed directed at himself. "Brian became very quiet. Then he said, 'Listening to you, I realize that your father and grandfather were the luckiest McCarrans. Dead men feel nothing, and they keep up appearances just fine.'"

Even Terry felt a chill. "Did you discuss post-traumatic stress disorder?"

"Not with respect to Brian himself. But one of his men, a sergeant, was so shattered by a specific combat experience and a divorce that Brian sent him to the VA hospital for immediate psychiatric evaluation. Apparently, they put him on a six-month waiting list. Shortly thereafter, the man hanged himself in his former wife's garage.

"Brian was filled with rage. Maybe he should have brought the sergeant to me, he said—I could have slapped him across the face, as George Patton supposedly did to a shell-shocked soldier. It was irrational, of course. But beneath his anger, I saw that Brian also blamed himself." Though his voice lowered, McCarran's gaze at Terry was unflinching. "A good officer, Brian said, looks after his men. Now I realize that he was telling me that a good father does, as well."

At once Terry understood the psychic space McCarran had chosen to occupy—at whatever cost to himself, he had a mission to fulfill: the salvation of his son. "Do you regret your advice to Brian?" Terry asked.

"Yes. My son was very troubled and deeply changed. Telling him to suck it up—in essence—isolated him still further. As a father, I left him on his own." McCarran glanced at Brian, his eyes holding a silent apology. "After Vietnam, no one talked about how we felt. All I learned was to seal it off. So I sealed off my son from the help he needed, and from his own father."

He stopped abruptly, as though whatever more he could confess was not suited to this moment. "Thank you, General," Terry said respectfully. "I have nothing more."

Returning to the defense table, Terry saw Brian's thousand-yard stare, as though he were gazing through the wall at something in his past. The general and his son could have been in different rooms.

FLYNN STOOD SLOWLY. TERRY was quite certain that he knew better than to attack General Anthony McCarran, the chastened father. Instead he would ask his questions, and later request that Hollis strike the testimony of both McCarrans, arguing that Terry could not connect the change in Brian to the facts of D'Abruzzo's death. Pending his meeting with Johnny Whalen, Terry still liked Flynn's chances.

Flynn stopped a good fifteen feet away, according respect through distance. In a tone of polite reluctance, he asked, "Prior to Captain D'Abruzzo's death, sir, did Brian tell you he was involved with the captain's wife?"

For what seemed a long time, McCarran did not answer. "No," he said softly.

"Did you have any indication that they were romantically involved?"

"None."

"Have you discussed that subject with anyone after your son killed Kate D'Abruzzo's husband?"

McCarran stared at Flynn with wintry eyes. Quietly, he answered, "If you don't mind, Major Flynn, that's personal to me. I consider it a family matter—for the D'Abruzzos, the Gallaghers, and the McCarrans. Joe D'Abruzzo is dead; now the families must heal. There's no good to be found in scraping our wounds any further."

Flynn could have pushed the subject. Terry watched him

consider that and then decide—contrary to what Terry might have done—to finish there. At whatever cost to himself, General Anthony McCarran had prevailed once again. This time he might even have helped his son.

As TERRY AND MEG had planned, the McCarrans left the court together, a tableau of family with Rose at Tony's side, and Meg between her father and Brian. The two men did not speak, or even look at each other. Terry did not envy them the hours that lay ahead.

He went back to his apartment and poured himself a drink, reflecting as he waited for a report on Johnny Whalen's arrival.

Perhaps it was the McCarran way, the military way. Perhaps Terry's wish that McCarran's effort might bring him closer to his son reflected his own sense of loss, the father whom nothing could bring back. But this evoked for Terry the fault lines in the lives of the McCarrans that preexisted Brian's war: the way Mary McCarran's suicide had distanced Meg from Rose and, perhaps sadder, Tony from Rose. Just as Meg and Brian's mother had intended.

An affair between Tony's son and Rose's daughter did not seem driven by this history. Yet it seemed to have had a similar effect, distancing the general from his children, and Meg from Kate. The two who still hewed to each other, as always, were Brian and his sister.

6

TERRY AND MEG spent the entire weekend closeted with Sergeant Johnny Whalen and their expert psychiatrist, Dr. Blake Carson.

The work was intense. Gathered around a conference table at the headquarters of the regional defense counsel, Terry and Meg questioned Whalen about his service as Brian's platoon sergeant in minute detail, taking notes in order to prepare a motion for Judge Hollis. At times Meg and Carson shuttled between Whalen's and Brian McCarran's quarters, checking details and hammering away at Brian to discuss the war. By Sunday evening, Meg in particular looked exhausted by the work and, even more so, the effort to repress her anguish at what she was learning. "Can you connect this to the shooting?" she asked Blake Carson.

Carson, too, looked exhausted. "It's complicated. To me, the psychological parallels seem compelling. But the circumstances aren't the same."

"We have to try," Terry said. "It explains too much about Brian."

By the end of the weekend, they had filed their motion with the judge.

On Monday afternoon, they came before the judge. From his expression, he had read the motion papers carefully, as well as Flynn's response that Brian's year of combat was irrelevant to the case. "I want to hear from this man Whalen," he told Flynn flatly. "Also McCarran's company chaplain. You can move to strike their testimony at the end of Captain Terry's case."

Flynn asked for a recess until Tuesday, in order to prepare. That night Meg stayed with Brian again. Not only was she filled with pity, Terry knew, but she feared what the memories jarred loose by Johnny Whalen might drive her brother to do.

SERGEANT JOHNNY WHALEN WAS Boston Irish, with a teamster's frame and the blunt speech of a blue-collar kid who had seen too much to pull his punches. Except for his eyes, he was the portrait of a tough enlisted man—squat and thick; curly black hair on top; sidewalls of black bristles and pink, sunburned skin; a cleft chin; a square, wide face; and a guarded way of looking around the courtroom as though wary of unfamiliar surroundings or, perhaps, ridicule. But when he focused on Brian, an expression of dogged loyalty stole into his dark brown eyes, transforming his face entirely. He nodded at Brian, a gesture of respect that his lieutenant answered with the briefest of smiles. Then Whalen turned to Terry, ready to do his job.

Terry walked forward, aware of the almost suffocating attention of the members and the onlookers who today jammed the courtroom to overflowing: media, curiosity seekers, and family—the D'Abruzzos, Rose Gallagher, and, for the first time, General Anthony McCarran. Meg was as still as a caught breath.

Terry's first questions were low-key, designed to elicit background information while increasing Whalen's comfort with speaking about hard things in such a public way. Then he moved to the core of his testimony.

"Prior to your deployment in Afghanistan, did you serve in Iraq with Lieutenant Brian McCarran?"

"Yes, sir. Beginning in January 2004, I was platoon sergeant of the third platoon of Charlie Company, First Battalion, Third Infantry Regiment. Lieutenant McCarran was our platoon leader."

"How many men were in your platoon?"

Whalen scowled. "Should have been forty, broken into squads. But we started with thirty and went down from there."

"By 'went down,'" Terry asked, "what do you mean to say?"

"Some got killed. Some got wounded too bad to fight."

"Can you describe the conditions in Sadr City?"

Whalen hunkered down, squinting, as though trying to put pictures into words. "It was the worst part of Baghdad," he said. "The streets were crowded and dirty, filled with people and roadside stands. The big problem was not knowing which Iraqi was harmless and which wanted to blow your head off. We were pretty much surrounded by people who hated our guts."

"Was there a reason for that?"

"Yeah. Muqtada al-Sadr ran the city. His people infiltrated the government and police forces and every group we had to deal with. He had something called the Sadr Bureau that controlled all that—even who got welfare." Whalen glanced at the members. "Al-Sadr put it out that we should die. The same for any Iraqi who helped us or had anything to do with us at all. You'd go up to someone on the street, and they'd flinch like they'd seen a ghost, then start looking over their shoulder.

"Couldn't blame them—second week in, we're moving down an alley, and somebody throws our translator's head off a roof. Ali's just staring up at us from near a pile of dog shit, like maybe we could help him find his body. We all stare back. Then Lieutenant McCarran gets out of his

Humvee, picks up Ali's head, and wraps it in a blanket. He drove around the rest of the day with the head in the back of his Hummer."

Randi Wertheimer turned to gaze at Brian. But Whalen resumed staring fixedly at Terry, as though to block out the image of a severed head. Quietly, Terry asked, "Were there other challenges dealing with Iraqi civilians?"

"Yeah," Whalen answered in the same flat tone. "The way al-Sadr's people used them. Early on, we were told that they'd use women and children to block a road and set up an ambush. If that happened, our orders were to drive right through them, even if it meant mowing down some kid or his mother.

"It made you paranoid. You never knew if a woman was pregnant or had a bomb. One poor guy at a checkpoint shot at a woman who had something concealed under the burka, and ended up killing a mother and her newborn kid. One way or the other, al-Sadr's plan was that every dead Iraqi made them hate us more."

"In Sadr City, what was Charlie Company's assignment?"

"Just about every day we'd have a mission, usually patrolling the streets. The kids in our platoon pretty much lived in constant fear. Before this, none of them had even seen combat, and no one knew anything about these people. So the lieutenant took us through the rules for getting by. 'Don't show the soles of your feet. Don't touch them with your left hand. Don't refuse a cup of tea, but don't accept another one. Don't mention their women, don't look at them, and never touch one. Don't wear sunglasses when you talk to them. Don't wear shoes in their houses.' A lot of stuff about cultural sensitivity." Whalen shrugged. "Problem was that we could make things worse but we couldn't make anything better. We just kept getting killed."

"How?" Terry asked bluntly.

"Mostly by IEDs—improvised explosive devices." Whalen stared down, as though into his own past. "That's what you remember, the thing you were most afraid of. Every turn down some street or alley was a game of Russian roulette. You never knew where they'd hidden the IEDs or which one had your name on it."

"Can you describe how IEDs work?"

"The bad guys would make them from antitank mines, or pack an empty bomb casing with plastique, or wire together daisy chains of explosives by the side of the road." Briefly, Whalen glanced at Brian. "They got real good at hiding them. They'd put them in a rotten log and float it in an open sewer. They'd gut a dog, stuff its carcass, and lay it in the road. Or they'd leave one in a broken-down car, or mold explosives into curbsides. They'd put IEDs in potholes or milk cartons or soda cans or behind anti-American posters which exploded when a soldier tore it down." His voice softened. "Next thing you knew, you were picking up pieces of a dead friend. And if you didn't, they'd stuff one of the pieces with an IED. IEDs were everywhere, every day."

"How did al-Sadr's people detonate them?"

"They'd use some sort of shortwave radio transmitter, like a garage door opener. Later on it was cell phones— they'd be far enough away that you couldn't see them, but where they could see you. All the sudden you'd be staring at a dead soldier, and you knew the guy who killed him is sitting there with a cigarette in one hand and a cell phone in the other, laughing and watching you dredge up the remains."

The steady accretion of details had begun to permeate

the courtroom, Terry sensed, conjuring the world in which Brian and his men had struggled to survive. "Was driving itself a hazard?" Terry asked.

"Like I said, you didn't want to stop even for a second, because you never knew if that'd be the thing that killed you. So you'd bounce over medians, hop curbs, streak through intersections, speed through markets—anything to keep moving." He twitched his shoulders. "It made the Iraqis mad, and you could see why. But there was just too much to worry about—not just IEDs but the drivers all around you. We even looked for pedestrians in clean clothes, because that could be a sign that they were ready to meet Allah. You were always on alert."

As Colonel MacDonald studied Brian, Terry saw him make the connection between Whalen's testimony and Brian's twitchiness on the highway. "As part of your mission," Terry asked, "did you also conduct house-to-house searches?"

"Yes, sir. We'd cordon off an area of Sadr City and go from one house to the next. Sometimes we'd knock at some family's door, interrupt their dinner, and order them outside while we searched for weapons that weren't there. The worst that happens then is that we've made a few more enemies. Other times the bad guys were waiting, and there'd be a firefight. Or maybe some Iraqi would pop out of an alley and shoot one of us in the head." Whalen paused, then said slowly, "Our company commander had this slogan: 'Be the hunter, not the hunted.' At first it was a joke among the guys, seeing how we were like targets in al-Sadr's video game. But too many of our guys got killed for the rest of us to keep laughing."

Terry put his hands in his pockets. "Who was your company commander?"

Whalen kept his eyes on Terry. "Captain Joe D'Abruzzo."

"Did he accompany you on patrols?"

"No, sir. Lieutenant McCarran would be in charge."

"Okay. Say you were on patrol, Sergeant Whalen, going down a dangerous street. Some of you were in Humvees and some on foot, correct?"

"Yes, sir. Some men felt safer on foot than in Humvees. Less of a target."

"Relative to the rest of you, where would Lieutenant McCarran be?"

"Always in the lead vehicle."

"Are you aware of the reason for this?"

"The lieutenant never said. But he started doing it the first week we were on patrol, right after what happened to Corporal Bronsky."

Glancing at Brian, Terry saw that he had touched his eyes, head bent slightly forward. "Could you describe that incident, Sergeant Whalen?"

"Yes, sir." Whalen paused, gathering himself. "The Humvees now are steel-plated, with either a machine gun and or a grenade launcher in a turret. But ours had the weaponry without the protection. So they were vulnerable to IEDs and rocket-propelled grenades.

"We figured that out pretty quick, going down a crowded street with Bronsky driving the lead vehicle, and the lieutenant's Humvee right behind—he's in the front seat, with me in back. It's maybe noon, and this block we've turned down is almost empty. 'Too quiet,' the lieutenant says.

"In the lead vehicle, Bronsky speeds up. All that's in the way is a green plastic bag stuffed with garbage. 'Stop!' I hear the lieutenant shout into his transmitter, and then the bomb goes off." Whalen's speech slowed. "The Humvee's lying on its side. The lieutenant jumps out, telling me to cover him if anybody starts shooting. The other guy with Bronsky, Private Velez, is lying there with a broken leg. Bronsky's on his stomach, bleeding all over but still alive. Then the lieutenant rolls him over, me right behind him.

"Bronsky's eyes are covered with film—the contact lenses he's wearing got melted by the heat of the explosives. You don't have to be a doctor to know he's blind." Whalen shook his head. "Bronsky starts to scream. The lieutenant picks him up and we rush him to an aid station. He never said that much about what happened. But after that, Lieutenant McCarran always made sure he was the guy in the lead vehicle." Whalen glanced at Brian again. "It was the lieutenant's way of saying that he wasn't telling anyone to take risks *he* wouldn't take."

Flynn was listening intently, Terry noticed, his lips pressed tight together. "In your experience, what kind of leader was Lieutenant McCarran?"

Whalen fixed his gaze on Terry again. "He was the best young officer I ever saw. He had guts, and he always kept his cool. He knew when to take advice, when to trust his instincts. And he was just stone smart." Whalen paused, searching for a way to explain himself. "The thing was, you felt he cared about the guys in the platoon. He always took an interest in everybody's lives. When we had a mission, he explained things clearly. He even learned a little Arabic to help him get on with the Iraqis—they'd tell him things they maybe wouldn't have said to someone else. Even with the language barrier, he seemed to have a real good sense of who to believe and who not to believe." Whalen paused, then finished: "You knew that he didn't want any of us to die for no good reason. At least not if he could help it."

"Can you recall any specific instance of that?"

"You could just see it. His driver, Corporal Shores, had a pregnant wife at home—if something risky came up, the lieutenant watched out for him. But he was looking out for all of us when Captain D'Abruzzo got shot at."

Whalen stopped there, as though conscious that any statement involving Brian and D'Abruzzo might be dangerous to his platoon leader. "Could you describe that?" Terry prodded.

Whalen nodded slowly, willing to comply but reluctant to do so. "It was early on," he said at length. "We're on patrol. The captain's voice comes over the radio, saying that he's gotten shot at on a road leading out of town. He wants us to go out and clean up the area. 'By the time we get there,' I hear the lieutenant say, 'they'll have scattered.'

"'Just do it,' D'Abruzzo orders. All of us know it's pointless; all that'll happen is that someone else will be taking potshots at us. So the lieutenant tells him okay, then we just breeze through the area, reporting back that we made no contact. See, he obeyed the order, but he didn't ask us to hang around and get ourselves killed because some guy shot at the captain. We got shot at every day."

The delicacy of this story, Terry realized, was that Brian's compassion could suggest a disregard for his duties, or disdain for a superior officer. He decided to counter this with a question. "During your service with Lieutenant McCarran, did he ever mention that his father was chief of staff?"

"He never talked about himself at all, only asked about the rest of us. Then someone in another unit told Willie Shores who the lieutenant's dad was, and about all the people in his family who'd won combat decorations. So we started calling Lieutenant McCarran 'the natural-born killer.' When the lieutenant found out, he just laughed. It was only a joke until the thing with the Iraqi sniper."

"We'll get to that," Terry said. "You mentioned worrying about al-Sadr's people using civilians to block traffic, or as human shields. Did you ever encounter that?"

"Yes, sir." Whalen hesitated. "Twice."

"In as much detail as you can, could you describe the first such instance?"

Whalen seemed to concentrate. Then, summoning the images Terry had extracted from him, he tried to put the members of the court in the place of Brian McCarran's soldiers.

THEY WERE GOING DOWN a narrow street crowded with roadside stalls selling fruit and meat. The lieutenant's Humvee was in the lead; Whalen was in the one behind. The sun beating down on them felt like a sky full of heat lamps. Then they turned a corner and everything changed.

The street was empty except for a line of school-aged children, from which a sudden fusillade of bullets clattered off the Hummer. Then Whalen saw the militants shooting from behind them. Human shields, he thought. A bullet hit Kenny Sweder in the arm.

The standing order was for the platoon to plow through the line of kids. Instead, the lieutenant's voice crackled over the radio, ordering the platoon to turn around. As Whalen's driver wheeled their Hummer, he saw the lieutenant leap from his vehicle, crouching behind an open door to return the fire coming from behind the kids, to keep the gunmen from advancing. As ordered, Whalen and the convoy retreated the way they had come. Minutes later, when the lieutenant's Hummer joined them, he saw that Brian McCarran had gotten out alive. But he had never seen their platoon leader so shaken.

"WE DIDN'T LOSE ANY of our guys," Whalen finished. "But the lieutenant couldn't make himself run down a line of kids."

"Were there any consequences to Lieutenant McCarran?"

"Rumor had it that Captain D'Abruzzo chewed him out

for not engaging in a firefight with the militia, no matter who else got hurt." Whalen's tone became clipped. "I wasn't there. But after that it seemed like Captain D'Abruzzo assigned our platoon all the worst missions. That was how we got stuck with defending that police station."

Terry nodded. "Could you describe that mission, Sergeant Whalen?"

FROM THE BEGINNING, IT was weird.

D'Abruzzo assigned the platoon to fortify an Iraqi police station against attacks from militants loyal to al-Sadr. The problem was that the police might kill them first.

They were trapped with two hundred or so undertrained Iraqi cops who hadn't been paid for a month. Whoever dreamed this mission up had to know it was odds-on that al-Sadr's people would pay these guys to kill twenty-one Americans before bailing on their duties. Which—besides getting a good vantage point to survey their surroundings— was the other reason Lieutenant McCarran placed his platoon on the roof and forbade them to go below to the station itself.

The mission was to last a month: three days on the roof, three days patrolling the streets, then back to the roof again. The cops were below; snipers were on the rooftops all around the station. The Americans were sitting ducks.

The lieutenant's solution was simple. He told the police to stay off the roof; he told the platoon to kill any Iraqi who disobeyed. The only fraternization occurred when the Americans passed through the squat concrete building to begin another three days on the roof, during which Corporal Shores would pass out cigarettes to the police. "When they come to get us," he explained, "I want them to remember how generous I was. I've got plans to meet my kid after he gets born."

On the roof it was hot as hell, with the one latrine in an old shower stall you might get shot at for using. The guys took turns sleeping at night, or in the shade of the low concrete walls that were their only cover from snipers on the rooftops. They learned to keep their heads down.

But every day got a little worse. One of the squad sergeants, Martinez, was a zombie—he kept reading the letter from his wife that said she was leaving him because her life was better with Martinez in Iraq. Friese got wounded, then Rotner. There weren't enough soldiers out there to clear the streets. So Lieutenant McCarran ordered the cops to erect a barricade to stop some car bomber from blowing the place up and burying them all in a pile of rubble. The biggest question, Whalen began to think, was not whether he'd die a pointless death, but how.

It was not that he and the other guys minded fighting; they were soldiers. But this was the worst kind of mission—dangerous, and stupid. That the battalion commander and Captain D'Abruzzo didn't seem to give a shit only made that worse. The men knew better than to say that in front of Lieutenant McCarran. But they all believed that if it were up to him, none of them would be here. And they sensed that getting them out alive meant more to him than what the colonel or D'Abruzzo thought.

So they stayed there on the roof, talking laconically among themselves, the lieutenant talking with them all. The sun dried them out; instead of cooling them, the wind brought the stench of raw sewage in sickening waves. Bullets pinged off the roof, pinning them down. The smell of diesel fuel wafted from the street, bringing with it the Iraqi crud—a screwup of their respiratory system that caused headaches and postnasal drip. When this was over, the lieutenant said, he was moving to Los Angeles for the air.

All this time they could feel the Iraqi cops beneath them becoming more sullen and restive. Then Saddam showed up.

They nicknamed him out of boredom, a sniper who took up residence behind a chimney on the nearest roof. But Saddam was a professional. The first day he took out Private Barker with a bullet through the eye. For the next two days, they were stuck on the roof with their friend's decomposing body, stiffening and then bloating under a blanket, a reminder of what might happen to them all.

Saddam liked his work. He stayed up there for hours, invisible yet laying down such constant fire that he made it almost impossible for them to look out for whatever gang of militia might be heading for the station or tearing down the barrier.

You could see the lieutenant thinking.

They were sitting on the roof with their backs to the wall, the lieutenant and Whalen, McCarran drinking a warm bottle of Mountain Dew. "Haven't heard anything from Saddam," the lieutenant remarked.

"Yeah. Wonder what he looks like."

Leaning back, Whalen squinted up at the searing noonday sun. Then, cautiously, he stuck his head over the wall, glancing at the street. The bullet creased his skin before he even heard the crack of Saddam's rifle.

Crying out in surprise, Whalen ducked and felt the streak of blood on his forehead. Startled, McCarran asked him, "You okay?"

"Yeah. But the son of a bitch is still there."

"I can see that."

McCarran fell quiet for a moment, like he was resigning himself to something, or maybe just deciding. Then he took off his helmet and handed Whalen the bottle of Mountain Dew. "Hold this for me, will you?"

"What the fuck you doing, Lieutenant?"

"Going to visit our friend. Just keep your head down, Johnny."

At once, Whalen grasped what the lieutenant meant to do. Before he could stop him, the officer was zigzagging near a corner of the roof, his bright blond hair a target that drew bullets zinging all around him. Then he vanished from Whalen's sight line.

Whalen heard two more shots and then, a few seconds later, the last one.

Whalen saw his fears reflected in the eyes of Willie Shores, hunched down on the roof. Then Shores's eyes widened, and his shoulders sagged in relief.

Running bent over a little, the lieutenant reappeared. He slid against the wall and settled back next to Whalen. "What the hell happened?" Whalen asked.

Reaching for the Mountain Dew, the lieutenant took a swallow. "Head shot," he answered laconically. "By the way, Saddam was bald."

His men loved Brian McCarran.

"WHEN HE TOOK OUT that sniper," Whalen said, "he risked his life for us."

Terry nodded. "Could you describe the events that ended your mission at the police station?"

"Our time was almost up," Whalen answered slowly. "One more three-day stint on the roof. The night before, an Iraqi cop comes out to our encampment—Kasseem, one of the guys Shores was always giving packets of cigarettes to. He asks Shores to find Lieutenant McCarran. We take him to the lieutenant. Kasseem looks kind of twitchy, then tells us that al-Sadr's guys—the Mahdi Army—are set to ambush our platoon on the way back to the station."

"How did the lieutenant respond?"

"He asks how Kasseem knew this. Kasseem wouldn't say. But he says even if we made it, the cops would be gone. They'd been given a choice: desert or die.

"Lieutenant McCarran thanks him, and Kasseem gets out of there. I ask if the lieutenant believes him. The lieutenant says he does. He can't see how making up this story buys the Mahdi Army anything. If we don't show up, he reasons, the Mahdi gain nothing—another platoon is already guarding the police station. If we do show up, they'd figure it's likely to be with reinforcements. So he goes off to tell Captain D'Abruzzo."

"What happened then?"

Whalen shrugged in resignation. "An hour or so later, the lieutenant comes back. All he says is 'We're going back tomorrow.' So we did."

THERE WERE EIGHTEEN OF them now—they'd lost three guys on the roof. Four Hummers transported them shortly before dawn; Lieutenant McCarran put squad sergeants in the other three and asked Whalen to stay with him. Shores was driving, with Lieutenant McCarran next to him, Whalen behind them, and Corporal Sava in the gun turret. Entering Sadr City, the lieutenant was looking around in the morning light, even though he was chatting with Shores like they were going on a Sunday drive. Then Shores got kind of shy. "Did I tell you, sir, that our baby is going to be a boy?"

The lieutenant kept watching the road. "Figure out a name yet?"

"Yes, sir." Shores hesitated a minute. "If you don't mind, Emmy and I are naming him Brian McCarran Shores."

The lieutenant laughed. "How did you talk her into that?" he asked. "Don't you want this kid to have a future?"

Shores got real quiet. The lieutenant saw how serious

he was, maybe even hurt. He put a hand on Willie's shoulder, his voice almost gentle. "I'm honored, Willie. When we get back home, I'm coming down to Alabama to visit young Brian." Right then they turned the corner onto a street that dumped into the one to the police station.

Everyone was thinking the same thing. If the Mahdi militiamen were waiting, this would be the place: a narrow street lined with concrete houses and beat-up cars, with alleys on either side, a tangle of phone wires running in all directions from rooftops that were perfect for snipers. And you could tell right away something was off. It was Monday morning, and no people were in the streets. Then a grenade exploded in front of them, rocking the Hummer so hard it shot pain up Whalen's spine into his skull.

"Keep on going," the lieutenant ordered Shores, and gunfire started pinging off the armor like hailstones. The Hummers sped up, sniper fire coming from the rooftops. An Iraqi kid about ten years old sprinted from an alley with a Coke can in his hand, running beside the Hummer. From the turret Sava blasted him in the legs with the machine gun and the kid crumpled on top of a bomb that blew him three feet in the air as his skinny frame came all apart. Shores stomped on the accelerator.

By now the platoon was taking fire from all directions. Thirty yards ahead more Iraqi kids scrambled from an alley, like a gaggle of skittering birds, their eyes wide and their mouths gaping in fear. Then men with AK-47s were running to kneel behind them, yelling "Muqtada" as they opened fire.

"Hit the brakes," the lieutenant shouted. In sickening slow motion a rocket-propelled grenade arced toward their stationary Hummer. Whalen ducked before it exploded, shock waves rocking the vehicle so hard it nearly toppled on its side. When he stuck his head up, there was a gash of blood across Lieutenant McCarran's throat and Shores's head was gone, his blood and brains all over the windshield. Throwing open the door, the lieutenant pushed the headless body into the street and slid behind the wheel.

The Hummer jumped forward. The kids and gunmen were fifteen yards away, then ten. Bullets pinged off the bonded glass; another RPG rocked the truck.

Five yards.

A bearded gunman pushed a boy in front of the Hummer. The lieutenant kept on going. In the last split second the kid's stricken brown eyes were like cat's-eye marbles. With a sickening crunch, the Hummer lifted him into the air, his limbs flapping in rag-doll motions before he hit the pavement and the wheels ran him over with two dull thuds.

Ahead were garbage bags that had no business being there. "Swerve," the lieutenant shouted, and Whalen screamed that over the radio as the lieutenant ran over a bag without the wheels blowing up the IED inside. Behind them Whalen heard an explosion that could mean only one thing.

The other three Hummers had made it to the police station.

Except for the Americans, it was empty. The last of the Iraqis had stolen away shortly before dawn. Lieutenant McCarran radioed the company, then led the platoon back to retrieve the dead and wounded, the lieutenant wearing a bloody rag around his neck. No one talked about Willie Shores, or the Iraqi children, or the son who would be named after Brian McCarran. No one mentioned the fact that they had stopped.

Lieutenant McCarran spent nine more months in Iraq. He still watched out for his men. But he seldom talked except when he had to, and never smiled that Whalen could remember. The thing that stayed with Whalen most was that every night the lieutenant would clean his M-16, whether or not he had used it, as if his life depended on keeping a spotless weapon.

IN THE JURY BOX, Colonel MacDonald and Major Wertheimer were staring at their laps. Terry saw Rose Gallagher's pallor; General McCarran's fixed expression; grief at war with loathing in Flora D'Abruzzo's eyes. Though Meg had moved closer to Brian, he stared ahead in silent dissociation. Terry could imagine him oiling his spotless gun.

"After the mission at the police station, how did your platoon fare?" Terry asked Whalen.

"The same. We always got the worst assignments."

"Who gave you those assignments?"

Whalen stared at him. "Captain D'Abruzzo," he said with quiet bitterness. "It was like he set out to kill us all. By the end, he'd pretty much succeeded."

Terry saw Flynn consider rising to object. "No further questions," he said and walked back to his client, still blank-eyed in a courtroom as quiet as death.

His expression wary, Flynn stood at once. "Do you mean to imply that Captain D'Abruzzo's literal aim was to wipe out your platoon?"

"No, sir," Whalen answered coolly. "I'm talking about cause and effect. Sometimes a mission means that men are gonna die for the country. We got that honor more than the other platoons. I think Captain D'Abruzzo had it out for Lieutenant McCarran, and the rest of us were in the crosshairs."

Flynn stared at him. "Other than speculation, do you have any basis for believing that personal animus played a part in Captain D'Abruzzo's decisions?"

"The fact that the two officers were so different."

"Wasn't it Lieutenant McCarran's duty, as platoon leader, to execute the missions ordered by his company commander?"

"Yes, sir. That's why most of us are dead."

Flynn's eyes narrowed. "You didn't like Captain D'Abruzzo, did you?"

"I didn't know him," Whalen answered. "All I know is that Lieutenant McCarran was right about the ambush."

"Was it your impression that the accused disliked Captain D'Abruzzo?"

Whalen hesitated. "In public, he treated the captain like you would any commanding officer. That's all I can say."

"You admire the lieutenant, don't you?"

Turning, Whalen gazed at Brian. "Yes, sir," he said firmly. "I do."

"And part of what you admire is the way he never lost his self-possession."

"Yes."

"Did that continue after the ambush?"

Whalen gave him a measured look. "Yes."

"Ever see him lose his temper?"

"No."

"Or forget where he was in moments of stress?"

"No."

"Other than that he became less animated, did you see any difference in Lieutenant McCarran over the year you served with him?"

Whalen stared at the floor, as though wrestling with a complicated question. "He just seemed changed inside."

"In what other ways?" Flynn prodded.

Whalen looked up at him. "I don't know," he said softly. "And I don't want to find out. That's why I volunteered for Afghanistan instead of coming home."

WHEN HOLLIS ADJOURNED THE court, his expression dark with thought, the members began filing slowly out of a courtroom that remained too quiet. But Brian seemed to awaken. He went to intercept his platoon sergeant before he left the courtroom. Bracing Whalen's blocky shoulders, for an instant Brian McCarran looked fully present, his eyes intent on Whalen as he murmured a few quiet words. Terry could imagine him as a leader.

But Meg was studying the members of the court as they left, her eyes brimming with worry and confusion. "What if they think Brian hated him enough to steal his wife, then kill him?"

"Too late to wonder," Terry said. "We're in Iraq now, and so is Brian. We have to see this through to the end."

That night, Meg served as sentinel again, protecting Brian from himself.

7

TERRY SPENT THE EVENING preparing Father Michael Byrne to address the aftermath of Brian's mission.

Ben Flournoy had found Byrne well before locating Johnny Whalen. But Whalen's account provided the context for Byrne, making the chaplain's story relevant to a PTSD defense. As with Whalen, Flynn objected to Byrne's testimony in its totality; as with Whalen, Colonel Hollis was allowing it subject to a motion to strike once Terry concluded his defense. But, for now, Terry could complete the story of Brian's service in Iraq. It was, as Father Byrne pointed out, Joe D'Abruzzo's story as well.

MICHAEL BYRNE WAS A slender man in his early forties with a high forehead, a thin, sensitive face, and the thoughtful manner of a man forced to balance his faith with the needs of men fighting and dying in harsh conditions. Watching him take the witness stand, Brian seemed more relaxed. But Terry suspected that listening to his chaplain might be harder than he knew.

After establishing that Father Byrne had served with Charlie Company in Iraq, Terry asked, "How well did you know Captain D'Abruzzo and Lieutenant McCarran?"

Byrne folded his hands. "For that year, quite well. Both were Catholics; both were under stress; both were precluded by their leadership role from intimacy with other soldiers. I was a place for them to go."

"Did the matters each discussed with you include their own relationship?"

"After a time, yes."

On the bench, Hollis took one of his infrequent notes. "How would you characterize that relationship?" Terry asked.

"Even at the beginning, I saw them as very different men. Brian was from a family of military aristocrats, a graduate of West Point. The academy had rejected Joe. He saw himself as more of a blue-collar kid, fighting to get ahead."

"Did service in Iraq intensify these differences?"

"Not at first. Joe's worries in his new command were all-consuming—how would he execute this difficult assignment in Sadr City, how could he get the most out of men who were stretched too thin. He struggled, as Brian did, with believing that we didn't have the troop strength necessary to pacify the area." Thoughtful, Byrne smoothed the black crown of his hair. "Their relationship changed after Brian retreated in the face of the Mahdi Army using kids as human shields."

Terry saw Major Wertheimer's eyes narrowing in thought, as though she was filling in pieces of a human puzzle. "How did you become aware of that?" Terry asked.

"From Captain D'Abruzzo. Knowing that the Mahdi Army used kids as weapons troubled him a great deal. But you didn't get to choose your enemies, he told me, or forget your oath to achieve victory for your country." Byrne paused, glancing at Brian with an apologetic air. "I paraphrase, of course. But the gist was that Brian needed to toughen up."

"Did Captain D'Abruzzo elaborate on that?"

Byrne hesitated, as if reluctant to discuss a delicate subject. "Joe's wife was close to the McCarrans, so he'd known Brian for years. In Joe's view, Brian had eased into the academy, then the infantry. Now his duties included testing Brian's mettle as a leader."

"Did Brian give you *his* viewpoint of this incident?"

Byrne nodded. "When Joe chewed him out for retreating, Brian was deeply disturbed. Running down Iraqi children, he said, would only make the atmosphere in Sadr City more poisonous and deadly. In his mind, the problem wasn't going to be solved by plowing over kids, but by having enough troops to deal with the Mahdi Army, which exploited them." Byrne paused, then added judiciously, "I knew that Joe agreed. But Joe believed making such a judgment wasn't Brian's job as a junior officer. And Joe also suspected, as I did, that Brian had a difficult time accepting that his obligations as a soldier might require him—however reluctantly—to cause the death of innocent kids. Whatever Brian's reasons, that difference led Joe to assign his platoon the mission of protecting a police station filled with restive Iraqis."

"How did Brian react to that assignment?"

"He tried to be fatalistic. He felt the mission was futile, but he couldn't act on that. Then he started losing more soldiers." Byrne's light green eyes reflected his sympathy for Brian's dilemma. "I sensed him beginning to redefine his role. When the mission made no sense, he told me, preserving the lives of your troops is the only moral thing for an officer to do. As their leader, he had to put some distance between himself and his men. But I saw him also starting to distance himself from the people he reported to, including Captain D'Abruzzo. Brian began to occupy a moral no-man's-land."

Brian, Terry noticed, stared at the table with a faint but bitter smile. Turning back to the witness, Terry asked, "Can you give me an example?"

Byrne sat back as he organized his recollections. "One

incident was when General Banks, the brigade commander, visited the battalion to ask Colonel Northrop and his officers if they needed anything. Apparently, Northrop said no. Afterward, Brian said to Captain D'Abruzzo, 'What about more troops?' When Captain D'Abruzzo replied that questioning the plan wouldn't help anyone, Brian said something like 'Except for the guys who'll die carrying it out.' "

Flynn sat up, projecting an air of tolerance stretched thin. "Your Honor," he said, "I've tried not to interfere with this witness's recollections. But they're marbled with hearsay. This witness should confine himself to facts within his personal knowledge."

"He is," Terry responded. "The confidences that Captain D'Abruzzo and Lieutenant McCarran shared with Father Byrne establish their state of mind, the state of their relationship, and the impact of events on their psychological well-being."

Hollis nodded. "We'll allow this," he said briskly. "Proceed, Captain Terry."

"Thank you, Your Honor." Facing Byrne, Terry asked, "Did there come a time, in your view, when Lieutenant McCarran faced a spiritual and moral crisis?"

Byrne's expression became somber. "Yes. I can recall the day and hour."

"Please describe that for the members."

"It was four A.M. Lieutenant McCarran came to my trailer and asked me to hear his confession." Byrne hesitated. "His platoon was heading into an ambush that morning, he told me. An Iraqi informant had warned them, but Captain D'Abruzzo didn't believe what he said— or didn't believe that this was grounds for altering their mission. Brian felt he had no choice but to carry out the captain's orders."

"Did he describe his feelings?"

Byrne gave Brian a look of compassion and regret. "'I expect to die today,' he told me. 'If so, I can accept that. Better that than to remember having led good men into a slaughterhouse for no good reason.' Then I listened to his confession, and he left."

"When was the next time you saw him?"

Byrne steepled his fingers in an attitude resembling prayer. "Early that evening, after he brought his wounded to the aid station."

IT WAS A TERRIBLE day in a terrible war, and not just for Brian's platoon.

Byrne had been at the aid station for hours. Cots were set up outdoors. As dusk settled, the medics relied on the dust-caked headlights of Humvees circled around them, illuminating the trauma of soldiers he did not know—exposed intestines, splintered bones, shrapnel wounds to the head—inflicted in numerous firefights throughout the area. Three times Byrne had performed last rites for men now dead. Looking about, he saw Brian McCarran.

Brian was holding the hand of a dying man, Corporal Francisco Sava. As they recited a prayer, Sava's lips barely moved: *Lord, protect us. Give us angels as you promised and bring peace to this soldier as he goes out.* Then Brian nodded to Byrne, and he gave Sava the last rites of the church. Sava died still gazing at Brian.

Brian kept holding the hand of a dead man as others died around him and choppers evacuated the more fortunate to a hospital. When Byrne's work was done, Brian approached him, his face pale in contrast to the bloody bandage around his throat. "Come with me," he said. Weary, the chaplain hesitated, then followed Brian to the trailer where medics took the bodies of the dead.

The inside was dim and cool. Perhaps twenty dead in body bags lay on gray metal tables. Brian moved among them, reading the tags until he found a name he knew. He paused for a moment, head bowed. Then he unzipped the bag, exposing the calm, lineless face of a black soldier in his platoon.

Brian gazed down at him. In a quiet voice, he said, "I'm sorry, Kevin. I wish that I had saved you. It made no sense, but you did everything I asked of you."

Slowly, Brian zipped up the bag, as though closing the man's life on earth. He found another bag, then two more, performing the same ritual. Only with the fifth bag did he fail to unzip it. "I'm sorry, Willie," he said. "You'd have been a great father. I'll tell him that when he grows up." Byrne saw the tears on Brian's face.

Without looking at the chaplain, Brian asked, "Pray with me for them, Father."

They did that. Then, together, they stepped back out into the darkness.

Hands in his pockets, Brian gazed up at the sliver of a quarter moon. "Back home," he said, "it's still daylight. Their families don't know yet. I hope they enjoy their last few hours of peace."

He stood there for a time, staring at the moon, as though wishing he could make time stand still. Then he said, "Once they're notified, I'll call them. I've learned to speak to people who've lost a husband or a son. But I never know what to say to the families of the wounded. How do you tell somebody's mother, 'Your son's wounds may heal, but I'm sending him home with a broken heart'?"

Byrne put a hand on his shoulder. "What about you, Brian?"

Brian shook his head in a profound hopelessness. "I

killed a kid today, an Iraqi boy not over eight or nine. Even worse, I ran him over when it was too late to save the men we just saw. And maybe the ones who survived."

After a moment, Brian said that he would return to what remained of his platoon.

"Did he mention Captain D'Abruzzo then?" Terry asked.

"No. Not then, or ever. It was like Joe ceased to exist."

"In your observation, how did this ambush affect Lieutenant McCarran?"

"He seemed to withdraw." Pausing, Byrne shook his head. "The best way I can express it is that Brian started living an inch beneath his skin. I tried to talk to him about it. But he had a sickness in his soul. 'Am I guilty of murder?' he asked. 'If so, which murder—of that boy or Willie Shores?' Once he said, 'Is this what God intended for the men I lead? I can't believe that. But all I can do is try to keep a few of them alive.'

"Brian never stopped caring for his men, and nothing I heard suggests that he let them down in combat. And he made sure his men utilized whatever mental health services we had." Byrne's voice lowered. "There was one sergeant, Martinez, whose wife had left him, and who was suffering from the aftershock of Brian's ill-starred mission. Brian was determined to get Martinez home before he put a gun in his mouth. He succeeded in that. But the upshot, I later learned, was that Martinez hanged himself."

The members of the court, Terry sensed, were absorbing that Brian's story seemed to be coming together, combining the strands described by Meg and Anthony McCarran, Johnny Whalen, and now by the only man to whom Brian had spoken about his own scars. But one more strand was missing. Quietly, Terry asked, "Did you ever discuss the ambush with Joe D'Abruzzo?"

Byrne looked troubled. "Yes," he answered. "In contrast to Brian, Joe was quite voluble. He also seemed angry."

"At whom?"

"Perhaps himself, but also at Brian. He was convinced that Brian blamed him for the deaths of his men."

"Did Joe admit the reason?"

"That Brian had warned him about the ambush? No. Instead he said things like 'Brian never says anything about it. But the way he stares right through me is as plain as speech.'" Byrne paused, as though trying to imagine how D'Abruzzo must have felt. "In my mind, Brian McCarran became like the ghost of Hamlet's father, indicting Joe by his very presence. I began to sense that Brian had scraped the cover off Joe's insecurities, exposing a subliminal resentment he had always felt for the McCarrans."

"Did you come to believe that Captain D'Abruzzo wanted Brian dead?"

"Objection," Flynn called out in an angry tone. "Unless the victim said as much, speculation on a matter so incendiary is inherently prejudicial."

Hollis faced the witness. "Did Captain D'Abruzzo ever say such a thing?"

"No, sir," the chaplain answered carefully. "And I can't know what was in his heart."

"Thank you," Hollis said. "Ask your next question, Captain Terry."

"Do you have a basis for believing, Father Byrne, that Captain D'Abruzzo hated Lieutenant McCarran?"

Byrne sat back, hands clasped in front of him. "His feelings seemed quite complex. Captain D'Abruzzo articulated a deep moral belief in carrying out the mission as assigned. If his men didn't risk their lives, he argued, then other soldiers would be forced to come to Iraq and risk theirs, and those who survived might be forced to return a second time, or even a third. As to that, events may prove him right.

"But Joe meant to get ahead by pleasing his superiors in whatever way they asked. In his mind, Brian was accusing him of moral cowardice of the worst kind—needlessly sacrificing the lives of Brian's men to advance his own ambitions. Whether it was Brian who accused him, or simply his own conscience, Joe seemed riven by alternating currents of passion and anger. Like Brian, he seemed more and more shut down." Byrne's voice softened. "To me, it's tragic. I think both men were sincere in their beliefs. As a military matter, Captain D'Abruzzo no doubt had the better of the argument—however difficult, an officer must be prepared to sacrifice his men to carry out whatever mission his commanders have ordered him to execute. But Brian had a sense of himself that was separate from his role.

"Joe never did. They were always fated to be different, and then we sent them to war together. And now we're here."

It seemed, Terry thought, the best place for him to end.

On cross-examination, Flynn made the points he had to. Despite his pain, Brian's outward behavior never changed. He always knew precisely who and where he was. There was no sign that Brian ever lost his prodigious self-control, or failed to grasp the consequences of his actions. He acted like a leader.

Nor did Joe D'Abruzzo, as far as Byrne could tell, lose his grip on his emotions. His frustration with Brian stemmed from the burdens of command, the necessity that his subordinates carry out the orders D'Abruzzo had been given. To their temperamental differences, Flynn forced Byrne to add another: whereas Joe still looked forward to rising in the military, Brian seemed not to care whether he lived or died. By the end, Meg no longer needed to express the lingering concern Terry read in her eyes: a man careless of his own life might be willing to take another's.

THAT NIGHT, BRIAN SEEMED to view his quarters—the confinement of which he usually despised—as a refuge from scrutiny. Tonelessly, he said to Terry and Meg, "The last two days I've felt like some human exhibit on reality TV. Maybe we could call it *Survivor: Iraq*."

"Can the self-pity," Terry responded coolly. "Whalen and Byrne laid it on the line for you. Now it's your turn. You owe them, you owe Meg, and you damned well owe it to yourself."

To his surprise, Brian gave him a crooked smile. "What about you, Paul? You gave up a fancy job on Wall Street."

"You owe me the better job I'll get for getting you acquitted." Terry softened his tone. "Look, I know reliving all this has been difficult."

"Not as difficult as testifying."

Meg rested her hand on Brian's shoulder. "You have to testify, Brian. You can save yourself. And, no, it's not 'too late' for that."

Slowly, Brian nodded in resignation. "You know the problems," he said softly. "But I'll do what I can."

Watching him, Terry was still unsure that he knew what all the problems were.

8

WITH A CALM THAT APPROACHED detachment, Brian McCarran occupied the witness stand, ignoring those who packed the courtroom: members, reporters, gawkers, fellow soldiers, Flynn, the D'Abruzzos, Dr. Blake Carson, even his father and Rose. Terry knew that the narrow focus of his gaze—on Meg or on Terry himself—was his means of self-protection. But the members of the court would see a strikingly handsome young officer whose poise was either admirable or troubling. Terry had both reactions.

Swiftly, Terry went to the heart of Flynn's case. "Before you went to Iraq, Lieutenant McCarran, how long had you known Kate D'Abruzzo?"

As they had practiced, Brian's voice and manner remained even, as though the question had no overtones. "All my life. When I was a kid, she babysat me, drove me to practices, birthday parties, the doctor or the dentist. She even looked over my homework and helped teach me how to drive." He paused, glancing at the members. "That was part of life for me. Our father was gone or busy; our mother was dead. The constants in our lives were Kate and her mom, who we always called Aunt Rose. Together two families with missing parents made one family that worked."

"Did you attend Kate's wedding?"

"We all did. Dad stood in for her father."

Terry paused. "At that time, did you have an opinion of Kate's husband?"

"I liked him," Brian said firmly. "I was a teenager, and what I saw was a friendly guy who made Kate happy. I didn't subject their relationship to deep analysis."

"What about as an adult?"

"That was more complicated," Brian responded at length. "I still thought Joe was a pretty good guy. But I also sensed that he had a chip on his shoulder, a feeling of inadequacy he couldn't quite shake." Brian angled his head, pensive. "He'd say something at a family event, then sneak a look at Dad or me, as though to see how we reacted. I became more conscious of making him feel accepted. As long as he was good for Kate, I never minded that."

Once again, Brian's tone—philosophical yet observant—was at odds with what one would expect of a calculating murderer. "What was your impression of their marriage?"

"I thought it was fine," Brian said cautiously. "As time went on, it seemed built around the kids. I saw them as an old married couple."

"Did you have any romantic feelings for Kate D'Abruzzo?"

"None," Brian answered with a swift shake of his head. "I loved Kate, for sure. But she was like an older sister who'd gotten married. That's how I thought of her."

Satisfied, Terry decided to move on. "When you went to Iraq, Captain Joe D'Abruzzo was your company commander. Did that change things between you?"

"Yes, of necessity. Our relationship became governed by military formality, and the respect and loyalty I owed a commanding officer. As much as I could, I tried to separate that from knowing Joe within our family."

"Did you have an opinion of Captain D'Abruzzo as an officer?"

"I thought he was capable." Brian hesitated. "I also

thought he was still trying to impress people. Especially our battalion commander, Colonel Northrop."

"Did you have a problem with that?"

Brian shrugged. "Personally, I've always thought you succeed by caring about your job, not by looking around to see who notices. But whatever your motivation, the first priority for any officer in combat is to carry out his mission. He can ask questions, but once his orders are set, that's it. My initial problem with Joe, to the extent I had one, was that he asked no questions, and resented it when others questioned him." Brian paused again, as though trying to explain himself precisely. "Aggressiveness is good in a combat leader. Combining that with ambition and insecurity becomes more problematic. Still, as Joe's lieutenant my job remained the same: execute his orders as capably as I could."

So far, Terry thought, he and Brian had presented a careful account of differing personalities. "Did you sense, Lieutenant McCarran, that Captain D'Abruzzo was also affected by the changes in your relationship?"

Brian considered the question. "It wasn't overt," he answered. "But I felt like he was still watching me, worried that I was judging him. Maybe I was. I couldn't help who my father was, and I don't think he could help reacting to that."

"Was there also a difference in your leadership styles?"

Brian frowned at the question. "We had different jobs," he temporized. "I spent a lot more time with my men, and we spent more time fighting al-Sadr's militia. My guys were real to me in a way they weren't to him."

Brian's eyes had clouded. More sharply, Terry asked, "Sergeant Whalen believes that D'Abruzzo singled out your platoon for dangerous assignments. Did he?"

Brian hesitated. In a cool but quiet tone, he answered,

"There were too many dangerous assignments for any one platoon. What I'd say is that, thanks to me, our platoon got special treatment from Captain D'Abruzzo—directly after I pulled my guys back rather than run down some Iraqi schoolkids."

"Did Captain D'Abruzzo confront you about that?" Terry pressed.

"Yes," Brian answered tersely. "As Joe saw it, the Mahdi Army had dictated the rules of engagement. If kids had to die, that was a tragic necessity of war."

"And you disagreed."

Brian still stared fixedly at Terry. "Personally, I wanted to leave Iraq without killing young kids and adding to a legacy of hatred. Professionally, I thought we'd be falling into the Mahdi Army's trap—that one day the survivor of some dead child or another, fueled with hatred, would plant an IED or put a bullet through the head of an American soldier. What I said to Captain D'Abruzzo was that morally repugnant and tactically stupid were a lousy combination." He paused, as though to fortify his self-control. "In fairness, I think the question bothered Joe a lot. I could look into his eyes and see him imagining his own kids. But he also thought that my attitude endangered American lives, and that by retreating I'd emboldened the Mahdi militia." Briefly, Brian closed his eyes before adding softly, "The Mahdi Army did it again, to my platoon. So one could argue that Joe was right the first time. Whatever his reasons, Joe decided to toughen me up. That's why he picked us to guard that police station."

The slight crack in Brian's composure hinted at repressed anguish, deepening the quiet around him even as it increased Terry's watchfulness. In the next few moments, he would learn whether Brian could speak in public about what had damaged him so deeply. Terry hesitated, then asked, "Did there come a time when your relationship with Captain D'Abruzzo ruptured?"

At this, Flynn looked up from his notes, scrutinizing Brian with a jeweler's eye. Brian paused, as if to fight through the difficulty of describing to strangers what he could not tell his family. "Yes," he said in a flat voice. "The night before the ambush."

THEY WERE AT THEIR encampment on the outskirts of Baghdad, resting up at the end of a three-day patrol. Dusk was setting in, and the few scraggly palms were outlined against a blood-red haze of windblown sand and polluted air. Leaning against his trailer, D'Abruzzo asked Brian, "Why believe this Iraqi?"

"Because his story makes sense. We're sitting ducks, sir. The Mahdi know our schedule: we show up every three days, like clockwork, and once we're close to the station there's only one street we can take. It's perfect for an ambush—rooftops all around, alleys coming from the side. They could try to wipe us out anytime they want, and now we know they plan to."

D'Abruzzo frowned. "According to a cop who, by his own account, is planning to bail out. Why would he risk his own head ending up in a pile of garbage?"

"No clue, sir—maybe he likes Willie Shores. But what sense does it make for the Mahdi Army to put him up to this? As far as I can see, none." Urgency quickened Brian's words. "I've got eighteen guys left. If we go back in, we need overwhelming force, not a decimated platoon strung out from a month spent serving as target practice."

"We don't have 'overwhelming force,'" D'Abruzzo answered with strained patience. "Are you asking me to send in the entire company and abandon the other missions Colonel Northrop has ordered us to execute?"

It was a fair question. "Isn't that for the colonel to decide?" Brian responded. "Why not ask him?"

"Based on what?" D'Abruzzo crossed his arms. "That some random Iraqi says you may be ambushed? Consider yourself lucky, Lieutenant—you've been warned. How many soldiers will be shot at tomorrow without the courtesy of advance notice?" D'Abruzzo grimaced, his voice softening. "If we don't clean up Sadr City, who cleans up for us? You want the next bunch of guys to die for you? It's too easy for you to think that the risks your men might take tomorrow are all this is about."

Quietly, Brian answered, "What *is* it about, Joe?"

D'Abruzzo stiffened. In cold, clipped tones, he said, "In the States, we're family. But in Iraq, I'm 'sir.'"

Brian's frustration deepened. "I apologize, sir. But there *is* no doing it right under these conditions—we don't have enough troops for that. By sunrise, I'm convinced, those Iraqi police will be gone—if we're lucky, without having slaughtered the platoon that's already there. But how many of our guys will have already died for nothing? Including the ones who may be fated to die tomorrow."

In the same cold voice, D'Abruzzo said, "Are you questioning the mission?"

"I'm questioning *this* mission, sir. Have you ever asked Colonel Northrop why we're still guarding that police station?"

"We're done here," D'Abruzzo snapped. "Colonel Northrop has issued orders. We're carrying them out. Just like they taught us at West Point and the Citadel."

"And tomorrow," Brian countered, "men will die for an empty police station. But the colonel won't know why, because we won't have told him."

D'Abruzzo stood straighter. "Any more of this, Lieutenant, and I'm going to recommend that Colonel

Northrop relieve you of your command. Tonight, if need be."

Brian was trapped. He could not let his men go without him, certain that some of them would die. "That won't be necessary," he said coldly. "Sir."

ON THE WITNESS STAND, Brian's face was as hard as if he were still confronting Joe D'Abruzzo. "Was Sergeant Whalen's account of the ambush accurate?" Terry asked.

"Yes."

"An Iraqi boy died throwing an IED in a Coke can at your vehicle."

"Yes."

"You then were faced with a line of kids herded by Mahdi gunmen."

Brian's face became a mask. "Yes."

"What happened then?"

"I ordered Corporal Shores to brake." Brian's voice was muted. "Perhaps the militia were counting on me."

"And then?"

Brian drew a breath, his only visible movement. "And then we were sitting ducks, just as I told Captain D'Abruzzo we'd be. But I made that worse by stopping."

"While you were stopped, what happened?"

Brian touched the scar on his throat. "An RPG decapitated Corporal Shores."

"What did you do then?"

"I floored the accelerator, heading for the kids and gunmen." Brian's voice was toneless, as though reporting a minor traffic accident. "One boy couldn't seem to move. He just stood there, eyes begging me to stop. I felt his bones break beneath the wheels."

For a long moment, Terry paused. "Your sister testified

that you have a recurring nightmare. Is it about this Iraqi boy?"

Brian looked away. "And Willie Shores."

"Could you describe it?"

The shake of Brian's head bespoke hopelessness. "It's like a movie of how it happened, playing over and over. I tell Willie to stop, and he dies. I accelerate, and the kid dies. It never changes. Just like I can never change what happened."

"Besides the Iraqi and Corporal Shores, is there anyone else in your dream?"

Brian hesitated. Almost inaudibly, he said, "Captain D'Abruzzo."

Terry quickened his rhythm. "In the dream, what does he do?"

"He orders me to run the boy over. So I do."

Terry felt his flesh tingle. "Other than Father Byrne, did you ever talk to anyone about the ambush?"

"Yes," Brian responded. "Joe D'Abruzzo."

FOR A LAST MOMENT, Brian stood with the chaplain outside the trailer filled with dead men. Then he went to the trailer where Joe D'Abruzzo lived.

He knocked on the door. Within a second, D'Abruzzo opened it, as though he had been waiting for him. He studied Brian in the thin light of the quarter moon.

"Come on in," he said.

"No, thanks. I should be getting back to my platoon."

D'Abruzzo appraised him. "You lost four, is that right?"

"Five. Sava died two hours ago." Conversationally, Brian added, "You heard the police station was deserted, right? So I guess we've completed our mission."

Silent, D'Abruzzo stared at him.

"Don't worry," Brian assured him. "Only two people

know about last night's conversation. Northrop's still where we left him, in the dark. So you and I are the ones who'll be living with your decision. Sir."

IN THE SILENT COURTROOM, Terry said, "According to Father Byrne, Joe never told him about this conversation."

"Would you? Otherwise, Joe told the truth: we never talked about it again."

"Did this conversation have any consequences?"

"Joe would have been the one to ask. All I can know is that he kept assigning us to house-to-house fighting in Sadr City."

"Did that involve getting shot at in confined spaces?"

"Often enough."

Terry paused. "You acknowledged that, in general, Sadr City was a dangerous place. Do you have any way of quantifying the level of danger faced by your platoon?"

"Just numbers. Of the thirty guys I started with, sixteen are dead. Only three of us survived without wounds severe enough to get us sent home. Sergeant Whalen, Sergeant Martinez, and me."

"Are the three of you still alive?"

"Two," Brian said tautly. "As my father mentioned, Martinez hanged himself."

Terry asked for a recess.

IN THE FIFTEEN MINUTES that followed, Terry, Meg, and Blake Carson met with Brian in a windowless room reserved for breaks. Brian slid into his chair, his usual grace diminished by weariness. Only his questioning look at Terry suggested that his mind was in the room.

"Iraq's pretty much done now," Terry told him. "You've given Blake what he needs to testify. Next we move on to the shooting."

Brian's gaze turned inward. "You know what Paul's going to ask," Meg assured him. "Your answers are what they are. And we've prepared you for what Flynn will try to do. You'll be fine."

An ironic smile played on Brian's lips. "I feel like a prizefighter, talking to my corner men. 'Go get 'em, killer. Only ten more rounds to go.' Except you already know that, come the final round, I'm brain-dead."

"That's my problem," Carson reassured him. "You can't invent what isn't there."

Brian shook his head. "But who'll believe me?" he said softly.

Terry wondered.

FOR THE NEXT HOUR, methodically and unemotionally, Terry led Brian through his version of the events that led to Joe D'Abruzzo's death: Kate's account of spousal abuse; their sudden, surprising affair; Kate's reluctance to report her husband; her panicky call after Joe held a gun to her head; Brian's decision to take it from their home; Kate's message on the night of the shooting; Brian's phone call in return. Though the account was familiar, the members of the jury seemed to tense, as though waiting for Joe D'Abruzzo to press the buzzer of Brian's apartment. "When you heard the buzzer," Terry asked Brian, "were you afraid?"

Brian appeared haunted by the memory. "Yes. That's why I took Joe's gun to the living room, and hid it beneath the pillow."

"Wouldn't it have been safer not to let him in?"

"Maybe for me. But not for Kate. I worried that he'd go back home and do God knows what to her." He hesitated. "Joe had lost it, somewhere in Iraq."

Flynn twitched, stifling his instinct to object. Terry knew

his thought process: his turn would come soon enough. In the same dispassionate tone, Terry asked, "What did you think would happen once D'Abruzzo was inside your apartment?"

"Maybe I could reason with him." As if hearing the incongruity, Brian added, "Any anger he released at me might slow him down a little."

"Didn't you think that was dangerous?"

Brian shrugged. "I was used to that. Better me than Kate."

The answer carried echoes of Iraq. "Once you let him in, what happened?"

"He walked right to the middle of the living room, like the space was his own. He was so drunk you could smell it on him. I looked into his eyes and knew right away I couldn't talk him down. Then he ordered me to give him the gun."

"Describe what you mean by 'ordered.'"

"He barked it out like a command. 'Give me my gun, Lieutenant!'" Brian shook his head in wonder. "The weirdest thing was addressing me by rank. It was like the two of us were back in Iraq."

"How did you respond?"

"'You threatened Kate with it,' I said. Joe came toward me. 'So now you have *rights*,' he said. 'I can shatter your windpipe or gouge your fucking eyes out.'"

"How did you react to that?"

"I knew that he could do those things, and in a matter of seconds I'd be dead. That's when I decided to reach for the gun."

"As best you can, describe your thoughts and feelings at that instant."

Brian's eyes narrowed, as though he were transporting himself to another place. "I was trapped. The only chance I had was to freeze him where he was."

"How long did this take?"

"A second, maybe two."

"Had you ever had similar experiences?"

"Yes. House-to-house fighting in Sadr City. You open a door, and someone might be waiting on the other side. You had a split second to react before they killed you." Brian touched the bridge of his nose. "That happened to me twice. Both times I shot a militiaman without thinking, and survived."

"How far apart were you and D'Abruzzo?"

"About the same as you and I are now. Four to five feet."

Turning to the members, Terry allowed them to gauge the distance with their eyes. He could read Alex Mac-Donald's face—"too close for safety." The question was whether the members believed this.

"When you took out the gun," Terry asked, "did you say anything?"

"I told Joe to straighten himself out, or I'd protect Kate any way I could."

"How did he react?"

"He whirled to the side and raised his hands to attack me."

Terry's rhythm quickened. "And then?"

"I felt the gun jump in my hand." Brian shook his head in seeming despair. "That's where it all goes dark."

"Do you remember shooting Captain D'Abruzzo three more times?"

"No," Brian answered dully. "I don't."

"Do you remember where the first bullet hit?"

Brian's eyes became slits. "His arm."

On the bench, Hollis leaned forward, as though watching for any change in Brian's features. "When you fired the first shot," Terry said, "did you know where you were?"

"I didn't think about it. All I saw was Joe D'Abruzzo. Then nothing."

"Had you ever experienced this kind of blackout before?"

"Not exactly. But in the firefights I described, things happened fast. I'd see a dead Iraqi on the floor before I knew I'd shot him. Afterward I couldn't bring back any details." Brian paused. "Maybe I didn't want to. You just move on."

"In the two incidents when you killed a militiaman in house-to-house fighting, how many shots did you fire?"

"I have no idea. You know that you don't always kill someone with a single shot. So you just keep shooting."

"After you shot Captain D'Abruzzo, what's the first thing you remember?"

Briefly, Brian rubbed his temples with the fingers of both hands, as though trying to banish a headache. "Joe was lying near the door in a pool of blood. I remember wondering how he'd gotten there."

"Did you check to see if he was dead?"

"No." Brian hesitated. "There was a lot of blood, and he didn't move."

"When you shot those two militiamen, did you take their pulse?"

"Of course not."

"Then how did you know you killed them?"

"Because they were lying on the floor, riddled with bullets. You didn't stop for a postmortem."

"Is that how you felt when you saw Captain D'Abruzzo on the floor?"

Brian puffed his cheeks. "I can't tell you how I felt. All I can say is that Joe looked the same as those militiamen."

"So what did you do then?"

Brian glanced toward his sister. "I called Meg."

"What do you recall about that conversation?"

"It wasn't a conversation. It felt more like trying to figure out what was real."

"A dead body must have seemed real enough."

"It was. But it seemed like I was in a different world. Staring down at Joe, I went in and out of thinking it was a nightmare." Brian bit his lip. "Then Meg answered her phone, and I knew it was no dream."

"What did she tell you?"

"To call the MPs right away, but not to answer questions without a lawyer."

"Did you take her advice?"

"Only about calling the MPs."

"Why did you talk to CID?"

"Because I'd killed a man. I needed to explain what happened."

"Even though you couldn't remember an important part of it."

"The hole in my memory was part of it, too. So I told them that."

For a long moment, Terry paused. "How did you feel about Joe D'Abruzzo?"

"I'd come to hate him," Brian said softly. "Because of Iraq, and because of Kate."

"Before he came to your apartment, did you want to kill him?"

"No," Brian responded firmly. "I'm not God. And Joe had kids."

"Did you ever discuss killing him with Kate?"

"No," Brian responded evenly. "Mathew and Kristen are her kids, too."

"So you and Kate didn't collaborate on a cover story to conceal a murder?"

"Absolutely not."

"Did you and Kate ever discuss whether she might leave Joe to be with you?"

"Never."

"Did you hope she would?"

"I never thought about it," Brian answered. "The relationship between our two families would have made that impossible. And whatever happened between us, Kate wouldn't have left Joe for another man. Her reason would have been Joe himself."

"So what happened in that room was spontaneous?"

Brian drew himself up. "Joe demanded the gun, then threatened to kill me. When I took out the gun, he whirled to attack." Facing the members of the court, he concluded in a clear voice, "I had no time to think, let alone premeditate. The twitch of my finger was pure reflex."

Scanning the members' faces, Terry saw openness, doubt, confusion, but no hostility. "Thank you," he said to Brian. "That's all I have."

9

TENSILE AND ALERT, Flynn strode toward Brian, his lean profile radiating a caged energy. Brian watched him warily, his attention tightly focused. At that moment, Terry imagined him driving into an ambush he knew was coming, his nerves and sinews taut. Meg was completely still.

"In Iraq," Flynn said harshly, "you learned to hate Captain D'Abruzzo. Correct?"

Brian stared at him. "Joe rejected information. Men died as a result, though I also share the blame. After that, we hated the sight of each other."

"Do you believe an officer has the right to refuse an order from his superior?"

"No. And I didn't."

"So Captain D'Abruzzo had the right to direct you to carry out a mission ordered by Colonel Northrop?"

"I've never suggested otherwise."

"Did it occur to you that Captain D'Abruzzo or Colonel Northrop might have considered factors of which you were unaware?"

"Of course. But I certainly knew something of which Colonel Northrop was unaware. Thanks to Captain D'Abruzzo."

Flynn stopped moving. "So Captain D'Abruzzo deserved to die?"

"Perhaps from a guilty conscience," Brian said coolly. "I confined my revenge to reminding him of that."

"Did you believe he wanted *you* dead?"

"Every time he looked at me. He did his best to find Iraqis to do it for him."

However much they had drilled him, Terry and Meg could not keep Brian from answering Flynn in his own way. Watching the members, Terry hoped that Brian's lacerating candor impressed them more than false displays of emotion. Disdainfully, Flynn asked, "So you believe that Captain D'Abruzzo was also trying to kill your men."

Brian ignored Flynn's sarcasm. "Honestly, Major, I don't think he considered that at all."

"Isn't the real problem, Lieutenant McCarran, that you couldn't accept the necessities of combat, or Captain D'Abruzzo's role as your commander?"

Brian tilted his head, as though to appraise Flynn from a different angle. "Call me soft, if you like. But to me, the 'necessities of combat' means that a soldier's death is necessary. Or, at least, that it's necessary to put his life at risk."

Flynn's aim, Terry understood, was to underscore Brian's hatred of D'Abruzzo while painting him as an arrogant junior officer. "Who gets to decide that?" Flynn prodded. "You?"

"Certainly not. But as an officer I get to have an opinion and express it. Or I'm no good to those above or below me."

"Do you get to decide when a mission—or a war—is necessary?"

"I've already said no to that," Brian said calmly. "But given that you threw in the war, I'm not at all sure it was necessary. And even if it was, the way the occupation was handled was criminally stupid—a waste of American and Iraqi lives that I witnessed at first hand. Including sixteen deaths in my platoon.

"Am I angry about that? You bet. Did I ever disobey an order? Never. Did I shoot Joe D'Abruzzo to avenge my men? Not a chance." Brian's voice lowered. "One could even argue that, long before he died, Joe became a casualty of the conditions under which we were asked to fight. If so, Kate was, too."

"So you took your revenge by sleeping with his wife."

"No," Brian said softly. "That wasn't about revenge. And I cared for Kate long before I ever knew that Joe existed."

With a delphic smile, Flynn asked, "When did you find out that D'Abruzzo knew about his wife's affair?"

For the first time, Brian hesitated. "After he threatened her with the gun."

"Not before? I thought Joe saw you at the Marriott when he confronted Kate. She didn't at least see fit to call you?"

This had always puzzled Terry, as well. But neither Kate nor Brian could give a better answer than the one Brian gave Flynn now: "I don't think Kate knew what to do."

"I assume Mrs. D'Abruzzo knew that an accusation of adultery with a fellow officer's wife could terminate your career."

"I'm sure she did," Brian answered. "But for Joe to have accused Kate would have exposed that he'd abused her, threatening his own career. Perhaps she felt a few days could pass without warning me. Or maybe she was scared."

Meg, Terry noticed, had stopped taking notes. "Before coming to your apartment," Flynn asked, "did Captain D'Abruzzo ever confront you about the affair?"

"No."

"Doesn't that suggest a considerable ability to control his own emotions?"

"It could suggest that, though I didn't see much sign of it when he came looking for the gun. It could also suggest that he felt too vulnerable to charges of spousal abuse to confront me when he was sober."

"Prior to the night you shot him, did you worry that Captain D'Abruzzo might kill or injure you?"

Brian pondered the question. "I'm not sure," he finally answered.

"Well, you must have been worried, Lieutenant. Why else would you take his gun instead of getting rid of it?"

"I'm not sure I thought about it." Brian paused. "I think I reasoned that disposing of the gun would inflame things even more."

"More than shooting him? Why didn't you at least remove the bullets?"

Brian appraised him. "I'm not sure. But had I done that, I'd be dead."

"So you were planning to use the gun?"

Brian shook his head. "I had no plan. I didn't think about the gun as a means of self-defense until Joe came to my apartment."

"When you shot Captain D'Abruzzo, did you know who he was?"

"Of course."

"So you didn't think he was a member of the Mahdi Army?"

For the first time, anger flashed in Brian's eyes. With lethal quiet, he asked, "Have you ever fought in a war, Major Flynn?"

"Answer the question," Flynn snapped.

Brian gave himself a moment. "All right," he said. "In combat, you develop reflexes. That's how soldiers survive. When Captain D'Abruzzo threatened to gouge my eyes out and shatter my windpipe, then wheeled to carry out his threat, my reflexes kicked in. Maybe you'd have stated an objection. I didn't feel like I had time."

Flynn stiffened. "So you shot him."

"Yes. In the arm."

"But you don't remember shooting him in the chest and hand?"

"No."

"Can you explain why the bullet casings were found in different places?"

"No."

"Or why you shot Captain D'Abruzzo in the back?"

Brian looked away. More softly, he said, "I can't."

"Or even how his body ended up against the wall?"

"No."

"And when you awakened from your trance, and saw him in a pool of blood, you never touched him to see if he was still alive?"

"No. As I said, I've seen dead men before. That's what I thought he was."

"So you called your sister."

Brian nodded. "I needed to get a grip."

"Even though you'd seen dead men before. Men you'd killed with a gun."

In the jury box, the members watched this duel intensely, eyes moving between Flynn and Brian. "Yes," Brian answered quietly. "But that was Iraq. This was a man I knew. Kate's husband, Matt and Kristen's dad."

"So after you called your sister, you also called Mrs. D'Abruzzo."

Brian's face froze. "I only called the MPs."

"Then Sergeant Frank showed up and you gave him an account of the shooting, much like you've given today."

"Yes."

"Did Sergeant Frank ask if you were having an affair with Mrs. D'Abruzzo?"

"Yes."

"And you denied it."

"Yes."

"And that was a lie."

"An honorable one, I thought. I was protecting Kate and her family. All our families, really."

From behind him, Terry heard Flora D'Abruzzo's harsh, scornful laugh. Hollis glared at her, inducing a silence more taut than before. Incredulously, Flynn asked, "Weren't you protecting yourself?"

"No."

"Even though you knew that an affair violated military law and the army's code of honor."

"I knew that, yes."

Sitting beside him, Terry saw the muscles in Meg's face tighten. Each new question seemed to impale her. "So in addition to protecting family members," Flynn prodded, "you were protecting your career."

Brian paused again. "Maybe it had that effect. But that's not how I saw this."

"Nevertheless, you recognized that as a benefit of your and Mrs. D'Abruzzo's decision to lie about your affair."

"No," Brian objected. "There was no decision—"

"So your lies were a coincidence?"

"No," Brian answered. "Human nature coincided. That our reactions were predictable doesn't make this a conspiracy."

The answer, brilliant in its simplicity, was of Brian's own design. It made Flynn hesitate. "So if you didn't call Mrs. D'Abruzzo to warn her, why did she think she could get away with lying?"

Terry could have objected. But part of their strategy was to let Brian face Flynn without Terry interceding. "I don't know," Brian answered calmly. "Maybe she thought

Joe would conclude, as we did, that no one would be served by airing something so private. Especially Matt and Kristen—"

"In fact," Flynn interjected harshly, "didn't you kill Captain D'Abruzzo in part to cover up your affair? Didn't you believe your secret would be buried with him? After all, you already hated him enough to sleep with his wife. Once you and Mrs. D'Abruzzo lied, you thought no one could expose you. Isn't *that* why you lied?"

Brian stared at him. "How many questions was that? No, I didn't plan to kill him. No, I didn't kill him to cover up my affair. No, I didn't know what Kate would say. And no, hating someone is different than deciding to murder them. If it weren't, everyone in this courtroom would be in prison." Brian's voice softened. "This was a tragedy, not a murder. I've told the truth about the shooting—"

"Including the shots you can't remember?"

To this, there was little Brian could say. Tiredly, he responded, "I remember the first shot, Major. Whatever else happened followed from that."

Flynn stared at him as though examining a specimen on a slide. "No further questions," he said. Swiftly he turned away, as though he could no longer stand the sight or sound of Brian McCarran.

On Terry's legal pad, Meg had written "Self-defense." Rising quickly, Terry asked, "Why did you shoot Captain D'Abruzzo?"

Brian seemed to reorient himself to Terry, sloughing off Flynn's hostility. "I was afraid he'd kill me."

"Did you intend to kill Captain D'Abruzzo?"

"No. All I wanted was to stop him. If I couldn't, I figured I was done."

"So at the moment you fired the first shot, all you thought about was surviving."

Brian closed his eyes. "At that moment, I wanted to live. That was a reflex, too."

Terry let this linger for a moment. "No further questions, Your Honor."

Returning to the defense table, Terry heard Hollis excuse Brian from the stand and saw Meg's shoulders slump from the exhaustion of watching. "Stay with him," he murmured to her. "We'll have other nights."

Meg thanked him and looked away, seemingly lost in her own thoughts.

TERRY WENT TO THE gym. Alone on the court, he traced the oval his father had created, missing more shots than he made.

Flynn had done well. But so, for the most part, had Brian. The balance lay in the mysterious chemistry through which members of the court determined whether they liked Brian, or at least believed him. Terry could not be sure. Perhaps he would feel more confident if he believed the whole of Brian's story.

Terry kept shooting, allowing his subconscious to do its work, until, at last, he hit seven out of ten, the best he could do for the day. When he emerged from the gym, it was dark, and a light dusting of snow whitened the frozen grass.

Terry went to his apartment and poured himself a tumbler of scotch on ice. He sipped it slowly, moodily, reflecting on the past. Even before he had opened his father's desk drawer, finding the evidence of his crime, the young Paul Terry had known that something was wrong. And something was wrong with Brian's account.

Perhaps it was his supposed loss of memory. Or perhaps it was something just out of Terry's sight, like a fleeting image in the slipstream of a car.

His mother's intentions had been benign, Terry knew—she wished to protect Paul from the secret that had caused his father's suicide. He wondered why the moment when he opened the drawer seemed so piercing now. Pensive, he thought of them all in turn: Anthony and Mary McCarran; Rose Gallagher; Brian and Meg; Joe and Kate—all the ways that, over time, they had acted on one another, and the death that had resulted. Then, against his will, his doubts coalesced around a lingering question.

Picking up the phone, he called Ben Flournoy. "I hear you did good today," the investigator said.

"Brian did. Maybe good enough to get himself acquitted."

"Hope so. Is there anything you need, sir?"

"Just something I'm curious about. Without a lot of fuss, could you get Brian's cell phone records for the last year?"

"I think so. But why not just ask him?"

"I'm not sure he has them anymore." Terry hesitated. "I'd appreciate it, Ben, if you'd keep this strictly between us."

In the silence, Terry imagined Flournoy thinking. Then the investigator asked, "Know the name of Brian's service provider?"

10

Before taking the stand, Dr. Blake Carson had transformed himself: short haircut, sober gray suit, subdued green tie. His expression was grave, his diction precise, and his manner dispassionate—in the service of Brian McCarran, the irreverent and indignant man had morphed into someone ten years older. Terry saw Flynn's co-counsel, Captain Pulaski, making copious notes, no doubt preparing for their motion to strike his testimony and, with it, any defense based on PTSD.

Aware of this, Terry swiftly emphasized Carson's credentials. "Please outline your experience, Dr. Carson, in evaluating post-traumatic stress disorder."

Carson nodded. "In the last twelve years, I've treated over seven hundred veterans who are suffering from PTSD. More recently, I've focused on Afghanistan and Iraq and the factors peculiar to those wars that exacerbate combat stress."

"Can you outline some of these factors?"

Like a teacher, Carson addressed the members. "Among the most important are constant exposure to IEDs and RPGs; the involvement of civilians in combat situations; handling the mutilated bodies of fellow soldiers, particularly close friends; and a feeling of hopelessness or futility regarding the war itself. There are others that bear on Lieutenant McCarran's particular experience."

In the jury box, Major Wertheimer leaned forward,

plainly receptive to a fellow medical professional. "With respect to Lieutenant McCarran," Terry asked, "what preparations have allowed you to assess his psychological condition?"

"I interviewed the lieutenant for over twenty hours, and reviewed the record of his military service. I listened to the testimony of his father, his sister, Chaplain Byrne, and Sergeant Whalen, as well as of Lieutenant McCarran himself. I read the testimony of every other witness, with particular attention to Sergeant Frank, Mrs. D'Abruzzo, and the expert in martial arts, Mr. Lee. Finally, I reviewed the extensive literature on PTSD and compared my observations of Lieutenant McCarran with the symptoms and causes of PTSD in veterans of the wars we're fighting now."

"Based on that, is it your professional opinion that Brian McCarran is suffering from post-traumatic stress disorder?"

Turning, Carson gave Brian a long, sober look, which Brian met with a steady gaze. Then Carson answered simply, "I'm quite certain that he is."

"On what do you base that conclusion?"

"There's a plethora of evidence. The behaviors observed by family members and reluctantly acknowledged by the lieutenant himself: hypervigilance, extreme anxiety in traffic, fear of confinement, inability to communicate his feelings, chronic sleeplessness, and, of course, his recurring nightmares." Facing the members, Carson continued: "These reflect Lieutenant McCarran's experiences of war: his own near death; the continuing deaths of men in his platoon; constant exposure to RPGs, IEDs, and sniper fire; handling the mutilated bodies of his translator, Ali, and his driver Corporal Shores; causing the death of civilians; exposure to lethal house-to-house fighting; inability to distinguish enemies from friends; and a mission that too often seemed both murderous and meaningless. Even for Iraq, his exposure to trauma was severe and unrelenting. And he felt absolutely powerless—unable to change anything, trapped in a cycle of death and violence from which he couldn't protect his men." Carson slowed his speech for emphasis. "Then there's guilt. Guilt over the loss of his soldiers. Guilt over having caused—in his mind—the decapitation of Willie Shores. Guilt about running down the Iraqi child. Brian came home carrying a burden of guilt and trauma few people can imagine. The anguish he feels is close to unbearable."

Brian, Terry saw, again had the determinedly absent look of a man willing himself off the earth. "In your opinion, Doctor, were Lieutenant McCarran's burdens exacerbated by his return from Iraq?"

"Yes," Carson said decisively. "His sister was a help. But the lieutenant felt alienated from his father." Pausing, Carson cast a veiled glance at Anthony McCarran. "To Brian, General McCarran personified two barriers to understanding—institutional and personal. Institutionally, the prevailing ethic in the army is to mask war-related trauma and to see admitting it as a weakness. But his father also represented a family tradition of bravery that felt both oppressive and one-dimensional. No matter how brave Brian proved himself to be, he was overwhelmed by his own feelings.

"He channeled this into concern for his men. In Iraq, he prodded them to seek out mental health support. At Fort Bolton, he sent a survivor from his platoon to the VA, only to see him commit suicide after being put on a six-month waiting list. This tragedy resonated with the suicide of his own mother and deepened his pervasive sense of hopelessness." After pausing, Carson finished succinctly: "At the time he killed Captain D'Abruzzo, the

PTSD suffered by Brian McCarran was six months more profound."

This was the moment, Terry knew, to start linking Brian's symptoms to the shooting. "You mentioned Lieutenant McCarran's hypervigilance. Can you relate that to his experiences in Iraq?"

"Yes. For a year, Brian was bombarded with deadly stimuli. To single out a few, there's the sniper he risked his life to kill—one false move and it's Brian who takes a bullet in the head. Or the ambush: another foot, and that RPG decapitates him instead of Shores. Or the two men he killed in house-to-house fighting who could have killed him instead. He's still alive because he was swift to react—able to move faster, think quicker, and shoot better than highly skilled opponents who could kill him in split seconds."

Terry paused, drawing the members' attention. Quietly, he asked, "Do these experiences have a specific common denominator?"

"Yes. Captain D'Abruzzo."

"Could you explain?"

"Yes. In every case but one, they resulted from Captain D'Abruzzo sending Brian and his platoon on a mission that proved deadly and pointless—guarding the police station. Moreover, the death of Shores and the Iraqi boy followed D'Abruzzo's refusal to heed Brian's warning about an ambush, or even take it to Colonel Northrop. The result was mutual guilt and loathing between Brian and D'Abruzzo. What followed was D'Abruzzo's order that Brian's platoon undertake dangerous house-to-house searches. In Brian's mind, that was a deliberate effort to eliminate the one man—Brian himself—who knew of D'Abruzzo's decision not to go to Northrop."

"What do you conclude from this, Dr. Carson?"

"That Brian came to see D'Abruzzo as the enemy. A man whose orders caused death."

Bobby Wade looked troubled; perhaps he understood, as did Terry, that Carson's opinion could suggest two sides of Brian McCarran: a man who reacted in fear or acted to eliminate an enemy he despised. "That brings us to a critical question," Terry said to Carson. "Based on your analysis, when Lieutenant McCarran shot Captain D'Abruzzo, were his reactions driven by PTSD?"

"Yes," Carson said firmly. "But let me preface that by saying that Brian's actions could have been objectively reasonable in a man *not* affected by PTSD. By that I mean that a reasonable man, confronted by an angry opponent with lethal skills who threatened to kill him in a confined space from which there was no escape, would have been justified in shooting when his adversary whirled to attack at a distance of four to five feet. In such a case, PTSD is superfluous.

"However, what you asked me to consider is not whether Brian's actions were objectively reasonable, but whether Brian *believed* that they were once D'Abruzzo confronted him. For example, let's assume that D'Abruzzo was ten feet away, or even fifteen. Let's further assume that D'Abruzzo whirled and raised his hands out of fear, not to utilize his potentially deadly skills. In those circumstances, a skeptic could argue that Brian was not in mortal danger. Then the question becomes whether PTSD caused Brian to *believe* that he was, causing him to pull the trigger."

"What's your answer?"

"That whether or not the danger was as great as Brian feared, killing D'Abruzzo was a reflex. Because of PTSD, Brian could not stop himself."

Glancing at the members, Terry saw them digest the

nature of Brian's defense: that even if the forensic evidence contradicted Brian's account of an imminent threat, PTSD could have caused him to believe that the threat was imminent. Or, as Flynn had sourly remarked, "Once you have PTSD, the facts no longer matter—all the evidence is locked inside your head." In a dispassionate tenor, Terry asked Carson, "Could you set out the basis for that conclusion?"

"It's implicit in what I've already said," Carson answered. "Brian saw D'Abruzzo as the enemy. He believed that D'Abruzzo wanted to kill him. He experienced following D'Abruzzo's orders as lethal. Those orders included forcing Brian to confront armed opponents in small spaces from which there was no escape. Brian further knew that D'Abruzzo struck his wife repeatedly and had held a gun to her head." Facing the members, Carson spoke succinctly and persuasively. "D'Abruzzo came to Brian's small apartment. He stood in Brian's living room, blocking the exit. He told—ordered—Brian to give him the gun.

"Perhaps D'Abruzzo threatened him, or started moving forward. It doesn't really matter. At that instant, every synapse in Brian McCarran told him he was in mortal danger. To reach for the gun and fire was a reflex—the difference between death and survival. Brian learned that from D'Abruzzo, in Iraq."

From the bench, Hollis considered the psychiatrist gravely, his forehead furrowed in thought. As at other such moments, Terry experienced the courtroom as unusually still. "What about the shots that followed?" Terry asked.

Carson folded his hands, settling them in his lap. "That's entirely consistent with Brian's military training and experience: you keep shooting until you eliminate the enemy and, therefore, any threat to your own life. As to that, the incident you raised with the county medical examiner is relevant: the case where an armed robber, though mortally wounded, kept shooting until he killed a policeman."

Terry nodded. "In that context, Dr. Carson, are shootings of civilians by police relevant to the shooting of Captain D'Abruzzo by Lieutenant McCarran?"

"They can be." Carson faced the members of the court. "As part of my practice, I've done detailed studies of officer-involved shootings in response to a perceived threat, as well as shootings of Iraqi civilians by American soldiers."

"What did you learn from that?"

"First, an officer can fire every quarter of a second. Second, he will keep shooting until he believes the threat is over. Third, even with a fatal wound, the victim won't instantly start falling. Finally, even if the perceived threat ceases, it takes a second for the officer to register that fact—enough time to shoot four more bullets. Therefore, the number of rounds fired can look like overkill when it isn't." Carson paused, glancing at Flynn. "Anyone who's been in combat knows that. But someone who hasn't been can mistake a justified shooting for an execution."

"Can you relate these studies to Lieutenant McCarran's actions?"

"They're certainly instructive. Take the question of where Captain D'Abruzzo was standing when he was shot. We know that bullets don't stop movement—indeed, in a half a second, D'Abruzzo could have taken two steps, moving five feet from where he'd been a split second before. Lieutenant McCarran could have shot him three times at different distances and in different parts of the room."

"What about the bullet in D'Abruzzo's back?"

Carson spread his hands. "The same principles apply. In addition, according to Major Flynn's ballistics expert,

D'Abruzzo's Luger had a hair trigger. Anyone in a state of extreme tension could cause such a gun to fire without thinking."

"Lieutenant McCarran says that he can't remember the last three shots and, therefore, can't explain what happened. Does that surprise you?"

"Not at all. While most shooters in these situations don't suffer total memory deficit, they often experience confusion, distorting their recall of the event. We call this phenomenon inattentional blindness. Essentially, someone whose life is threatened experiences tunnel vision. Human eye movement is not like the panning of a camera, where the lens records a total picture. If you look from right to left—especially quickly—you get isolated images. You can't retrieve a clear and fluid memory of events occurring in split seconds." Once again, Carson faced the members. "Inattentional blindness could distort what memory Brian has. As to his failure to recall the last three shots, that could stem from another symptom of PTSD: dissociative amnesia."

Terry noticed Dr. Wertheimer briefly nodding to herself. "Could you explain dissociative amnesia, Dr. Carson?"

"It's a gap in memory caused by abnormal stress. It can last for seconds or minutes. During this time, the person is in a kind of fugue state." Carson glanced at Brian. "Lieutenant McCarran describes realizing that Captain D'Abruzzo was lying on the floor, then struggling to appreciate the nature of what happened. That's consistent with dissociative amnesia. The aftermath feels like being in shock—which I think he was. Shooting a man who'd been part of his extended family would feel more traumatic than shooting a stranger."

Terry glanced toward Meg and saw her tight, expectant

look. Turning back to Carson, he asked, "How do you explain Brian's call to his sister?"

Carson's own expression was somber. "Given his disorientation, placing that call was logical. That she's a lawyer is irrelevant. Meg was the person who'd tried to help him cope with PTSD. Equally significant, Brian had depended on her since their mother killed herself. In his confusion, reaching out to her was second nature."

"During this period, how would Brian experience the passage of time?"

"His sense of time would be distorted. The period between calling Meg and calling the MPs might not have seemed long at all."

Satisfied, Terry nodded. "A final question. Sergeant Frank stressed Brian's 'detachment.' What do you take from that?"

"That it's part of Brian's identity. Witness after witness has testified to his uncanny self-possession. To me, it's not surprising at all." Carson regarded Brian with compassion. "Deep in his psyche, Brian is an infantry officer, and a McCarran. So he pulled himself together, called the MPs, and did his duty by answering questions as best he could. That's what officers do. That's what McCarrans do."

This was the image Terry wished to leave. "No further questions," he said, confident that Carson had done all he could.

FROM HIS EXPRESSION, FLYNN thought so, too. Brusquely, he said, "The basis for your opinion includes the stories told by the accused and Mrs. D'Abruzzo, correct?"

Carefully, Carson considered the question. "Only to a point. For example, in framing my opinion with respect to PTSD, I assumed that the threat posed by Captain D'Abruzzo to be less than Brian believed."

"That's different than assuming he was lying, correct?"

"True. I was talking about a difference in perception."

"So that if Lieutenant McCarran, in a wholly lucid state, lied about what Captain D'Abruzzo said or did in that apartment, would that affect your opinion?"

"It could, yes. I'd have to know the specifics."

"I'll give you two. Suppose that Captain D'Abruzzo did not ask for the gun, or threaten the life of the accused. Would *that* affect your opinion?"

"Again, it could."

"But, of course, only Lieutenant McCarran knows if he deliberately lied, true?"

"Yes."

"And you're aware of at least one instance, their affair, where the accused and Mrs. D'Abruzzo did lie."

Carson paused, breaking Flynn's rhythm. "Yes," he said slowly. "I'm also aware that that has nothing to do with whether Brian McCarran was suffering from PTSD when he shot Captain D'Abruzzo. My opinion is based on the traumatic nature of Lieutenant McCarran's combat experience, not on whether the lieutenant concealed an affair."

Terry felt himself tense, worried Carson's inherent antipathy toward Flynn would become too visible. "But it's also based," Flynn said sharply, "on what supposedly happened here at Fort Bolton: that Captain D'Abruzzo hit his wife; that he held a gun to her head; that he went to the lieutenant's apartment to claim his gun; and that the accused—despite the terrible stress you describe—decided to let him in. If the accused and Mrs. D'Abruzzo were also lying about all that, would your opinion change?"

"Yes," Carson allowed in a milder tone. "But I'm not aware of testimony that shows any of that to be untrue. If there is some, I'd appreciate your pointing it out."

Flynn's eyes narrowed: despite the seeming innocence

of Carson's response, the psychiatrist was well aware that Flynn's assertion of a cover-up rested on conjecture and circumstantial evidence. "Nonetheless, Dr. Carson, if the accused invited Captain D'Abruzzo to his apartment, would that affect your opinion?"

"It could. But I'd need to review the evidence. Is there any?"

"I'm asking the questions," Flynn snapped. "So even if the accused invited the victim, your opinion might not change?"

"That's a hypothetical, Major Flynn. I can't answer without knowing more facts."

Flynn placed his hands on his hips. "Is PTSD consistent with planning and carrying out a premeditated murder?"

"In an extreme case, it could be—where a man decides to kill another man who he believes is planning to kill him." Carson paused, then added firmly, "But that's not this case. Based on the facts before the court, no one has asked me to answer the hypothetical you just posed."

"Did you consider the fact that the accused was sleeping with the victim's wife?"

"Of course. But one can view that in opposite ways. You can speculate that it's a reason for Brian McCarran to shoot D'Abruzzo. You can also conclude that it helped drive D'Abruzzo into a violent rage." Carson leaned slightly forward. "I haven't been asked to opine on whether D'Abruzzo suffered from PTSD, and I can't. But I do think that alcoholism, spousal abuse, and quickness to anger are also symptomatic. It's possible to posit that these attributes contributed to D'Abruzzo's death."

Flynn stared at him. "Aren't these 'attributes,' as you called them, based entirely on Mrs. D'Abruzzo's testimony?"

Carson raised his eyebrows. "Actually, no. According to the toxicology report, Captain D'Abruzzo was extremely intoxicated when he came to Brian's apartment. That's pretty unhelpful to judgment or self-control."

Terry suppressed a smile. By recalibrating his demeanor, Carson had provoked Flynn's anger, making himself the more likable of the two. As if realizing this, Flynn asked more evenly, "How heavily did you weigh the testimony of the medical examiner, the ballistics expert, and the testimony of the CID?"

Terry had asked Carson the same question, two nights before. As planned, Carson responded in a judicious tone. "I took note of certain facts that aren't in dispute—Captain D'Abruzzo's inebriation, the hair trigger on his Luger. But I'm not an expert in these fields, so I set aside any evidence that was ambiguous or subject to multiple interpretations. I focused much more heavily on Brian McCarran's upbringing, military experience, and behavior before and after Iraq."

"With respect to that, Dr. Carson, the lieutenant admits that he knew he wasn't in Iraq, and that D'Abruzzo wasn't an Iraqi. Did that affect your opinion?"

"In another case, it might have. But it's clear that Brian saw D'Abruzzo as his enemy, and his orders as literally deadly—an intentional effort to kill him. In my view, that triggered his reaction."

Stymied, Flynn decided to change subjects. "Prior to your diagnosis, had anyone else concluded that Brian McCarran suffers from PTSD?"

"No. No one had considered it."

"Despite the debilitating symptoms you mention, had he ever asked for help?"

"No. But part of Brian's ethic is to conceal them."

"But none of his superior officers at Fort Bolton—men

who worked with him closely—ever referred Brian to a mental health professional."

"Not that I know about."

"Are you aware of any prior involvement in acts of violence?"

Carson considered the lawyer. Quietly, he said, "Only in Iraq."

"Prior to the shooting, did his superiors report that the accused had any difficulty in discharging his administrative duties?"

"Not according to his records."

"So the only people reporting changes in behavior are his sister and his father."

"I don't know who else may have noticed them. But my opinion is that General McCarran and Brian's sister reported their observations accurately and in good faith."

This implicit challenge caused Flynn to hesitate. Abruptly, he asked, "How many veterans of Afghanistan and Iraq are stationed at Fort Bolton?"

"I'm not sure. But over a thousand."

"Have any of those combat veterans shot people since returning?"

"Not to my knowledge."

Flynn paused. "So let me reprise, Dr. Carson. Your opinion rests not only on the accused's military service but on the truthfulness of his and Mrs. D'Abruzzo's account of the events leading up to the shooting."

"Yes."

"As well as Lieutenant McCarran's description of the shooting itself."

"As I explained," Carson responded, "not entirely. What I *did* assume is that the lieutenant wasn't planning to shoot Captain D'Abruzzo until he perceived a threat."

For the moment, this was the best Flynn could do. With

an air of satisfaction manufactured for the members of the court, he said, "I have nothing more, Dr. Carson."

Thinking swiftly, Terry decided to press his advantage to the limit. "And I have only one question," he said. "Assume for the moment that Captain D'Abruzzo was not an imminent threat to Brian McCarran's life. But if Brian *believed* that he was acting in self-defense, would he also believe that shooting Captain D'Abruzzo was not 'wrong'?"

"Objection," Flynn said promptly. "Captain Terry has deliberately framed his question to paraphrase the legal test for insanity. In the guise of further advancing his PTSD defense, he asks Dr. Carson to resolve an ultimate question of law and fact reserved for the members of this court: Was the defendant legally insane when he shot Captain D'Abruzzo? Aside from the fact that no court has ever permitted such a defense, asking this witness for a legal conclusion is improper in itself."

Hollis gave a decisive nod. Turning to Terry, he said sternly, "Save it for your argument opposing trial counsel's motion to preclude this defense. We'll reconvene for that purpose tomorrow at nine o'clock."

As Hollis left the bench, the court began to empty. "Nice try," Meg murmured dryly.

Terry shrugged. "Blake was good. We pushed this as far as it can go."

Brian said nothing at all.

11

RISING TO ARGUE his motion to strike, Mike Flynn paused, signaling his awareness that the outcome might determine the verdict rendered by the members of the court.

The members themselves were absent. But the full complement of reporters suggested that they, too, understood how critical this was. Sitting between Brian and Meg, Terry watched Hollis for clues.

They were not long in coming. Before Flynn could speak, Hollis said, "I understand that you want me to preclude any defense based on PTSD. But precisely what testimony are you requesting me to strike?"

Flynn was prompt to answer: "All testimony related to supposed changes in Lieutenant McCarran's behavior, his service in Iraq, or whether he suffered from PTSD at the time he shot Captain D'Abruzzo. That includes the testimony of Dr. Carson, Sergeant Whalen, Father Byrne, General McCarran, Meg McCarran, and substantial portions of the lieutenant's own testimony—"

"So what's left?" Hollis interrupted.

"The testimony of Mrs. D'Abruzzo, Mr. Lee, and the lieutenant's testimony with respect to his relationship with both D'Abruzzos through the day of the shooting."

Hollis rested his chin on the palm of his hand, peering down at Flynn. "Then you've pretty well gutted the defense case."

Equably, Flynn responded, "Captain Terry could have

addressed the facts of the case. Instead, he advanced a theory that this court warned it might not recognize—"

Hollis held up his hand. "The defense gambled, I agree. But you've eliminated any reference to how Lieutenant McCarran's service might have affected him. Are you arguing that PTSD is not a recognized psychological condition?"

"No, Your Honor. What I'm saying is that no military court has ever accepted it as the basis for an acquittal, or even a reduction from murder to manslaughter."

"Why not?" Hollis asked sharply. "The psychiatric profession accepts it as a diagnosis. Shouldn't the law acknowledge its potential to affect behavior?"

"Yes. But only as a mitigating factor in sentencing, should the accused be convicted."

Hollis arched his eyebrows. "How does that work? Suppose he's convicted of intentional murder, in part because I precluded all the testimony to which you object. Do I then tell the members that they should consider the possibility—in sentencing—that Lieutenant McCarran thought Captain D'Abruzzo intended to kill *him*? You can't 'mitigate' a verdict of guilty by deciding after the fact it was a mistake. So let's get back to the law.

"The test for insanity is that a mental disease or defect prevents the accused from knowing that his actions are wrong. Captain Terry's argument is this: Maybe the lieutenant was not in mortal danger. But because his perceptions were distorted by combat stress, he thought that it was necessary to shoot Captain D'Abruzzo in self-defense. Why doesn't that fit the legal standard?"

Flynn's demeanor became rigid. "Because it's wholly subjective. Captain Terry argues that—no matter what the physical evidence—the accused should be acquitted based on what he claims to have thought. If this defense is allowed, it will become the refuge of every veteran who kills someone—"

"You're pushing this too far," Hollis objected. "If the accused had come to D'Abruzzo's home for the purpose of killing him, that would be one thing. But you're asking me to preclude the members from considering the actual facts of *this* case, in order to stave off an imaginary wave of acquittals in cases where the defense would have no basis in fact. I have more respect for juries than that."

"No one respects juries more than I, Your Honor. But lay members of the court need clarity in applying the law." Flynn squared his shoulders. "No doubt the accused had harrowing combat experiences. But that's irrelevant unless they caused a mental condition that negated his intention to commit a crime.

"Who claims that his behavior changed? Only the lieutenant and his family. What's the evidence that it affected his perceptions when he shot Captain D'Abruzzo? None. The lieutenant's own testimony contradicts that. He asserts that he knew that D'Abruzzo was D'Abruzzo, and that they were at Fort Bolton rather than in Sadr City. He asserts that D'Abruzzo was only four to five feet away when he fired the first shot. And he claims not to remember the last three shots—including a shot in the back.

"In sum, there is insufficient evidence that Lieutenant McCarran suffers from PTSD at all, let alone that it governed his reaction to the 'threat' posed by Captain D'Abruzzo." Flynn lowered his voice. "It's not insane to hate someone, Your Honor. Hatred is a motive for murder, not grounds for an insanity plea."

That this argument adduced in Hollis a reflective silence troubled Terry. After a belated nod to Flynn, Hollis said, "You're up, Captain Terry."

Standing, Terry instinctively tossed aside his carefully

wrought legal argument. "After listening to Major Flynn, I believe the central question is this: Will the members judge Brian McCarran as he is or as the stick figure the major asks the court to give them? Trial counsel wants to eliminate everything but the testimony relating to the lieutenant's relationship with Mrs. D'Abruzzo, his removal of the gun, and the shooting itself. But who, then, is Brian McCarran? He has no life—no childhood, no service record, no year in Iraq filled with horror and carnage, no family to observe the changes in his behavior, no trauma whatsoever. In Major Flynn's version, the only thing he ever did was shoot Captain D'Abruzzo after sleeping with his wife—"

"Are you disputing either?" Hollis inquired.

"No, Your Honor. But there's a man sitting next to me, and Major Flynn proposes to erase him. If nothing else, the testimony Major Flynn would discard shows a man who fought honorably and bravely, who looked out for his soldiers, and who—when he had finished doing everything his country asked of him—fought to keep himself together so he could keep on doing his job. The fact that this man also responded, however inappropriately, to the plight of a woman he had always cared for does not define him as a person, or obliterate all that is admirable in his character—"

"Perhaps not," Hollis said pointedly. "But it *does* provide a potential motive for murder. Whereas his honorable service, in itself, seems more relevant to the severity of his sentence. Here I'm inclined to agree with Major Flynn."

Worried, Terry mustered a smile. "And I'm inclined to agree with the court's prior observations. Dr. Carson specified how PTSD could have affected Lieutenant McCarran's state of mind when D'Abruzzo came to his apartment—"

"But the accused, as Major Flynn points out, claims actual self-defense. Specifically, that Captain D'Abruzzo was four to five feet away."

"Regardless of the distance," Terry responded, "D'Abruzzo *felt* like a threat to his life. There are a multiplicity of reasons: Lieutenant McCarran's combat experiences in Sadr City; a history with Captain D'Abruzzo which suggested that D'Abruzzo wanted him dead; D'Abruzzo's violent actions after he returned; and his lethal abilities in martial arts. All of this illuminates the lieutenant's state of mind, and the members of the court should be allowed to weigh it.

"We don't ask this court to change the law. Rather, we ask it to incorporate within the law our current understanding of combat-related stress." Terry paused, then finished in a calm, clear voice: "We send men to war. We know that they may suffer PTSD as a result. But when they come back, all too often we tell them to suck it up, or put them on a waiting list for treatment. In this court-martial, Brian McCarran can't wait around for the army to grasp the damage war has done to him. The law should see him whole."

Solemn, Colonel Hollis checked the papers in front of him. Then he said, "The court is prepared to rule."

Terry heard a stirring, reporters preparing to take notes. "This motion," Hollis continued, "presents difficult questions of law and fact. There is little precedent for reducing a murder charge to manslaughter on the basis of PTSD, and none at all for recognizing an insanity defense. But the law should reflect our knowledge of psychology as it broadens." Hollis paused, then said decisively, "Accordingly, I'm persuaded that the members of the court should consider all the evidence offered by the accused, with appropriate instructions from the court."

The reality of this statement stunned Terry: as Flynn's flicker of astonishment suggested, Hollis had transformed military law in an instant. Aware of this, the judge added wryly, "If my ruling is wrong, I suppose I can live with that. What I can't live with is a system of military justice that is literally blind.

"The motion to strike is denied. Defense counsel may argue that PTSD supports a finding of not guilty by reason of insanity, or a reduction of the charge of murder to manslaughter." Looking from Terry to Flynn, Hollis inquired, "Is there anything else, counsel?"

Poised again, Flynn responded. "Yes, Your Honor. In light of the court's ruling, we would like to call a rebuttal witness: Colonel David Northrop."

Terry was not surprised. "Any objections?" Hollis asked him.

"None, Your Honor."

"In that case, we will reconvene at nine A.M. tomorrow for the purpose of hearing Colonel Northrop's testimony."

"All rise," the bailiff said, and Hollis's disappearance was followed by a hum of voices among the spectators that, to Terry's mind, sounded like an exhalation of breath. Beneath the sound, Brian murmured, "I appreciate what you've done. But I can't tell you how it feels to be crazy."

Terry looked into his client's somber blue-gray eyes. Softly, he said, "Then you need to get over it, Brian. Literally."

Brian smiled a little. "Take my sis to dinner, Paul. I'm okay on my own."

WHEN TERRY AND MEG got in the car, he listened to a message on his cell phone. "It's not Colonel MacDonald's day," he told her. "My friend reports he's being passed over for promotion. That's at least one member of the court who's very unhappy with the army."

Meg turned her head, face resting against the car seat. "Remember the first day we met, when I questioned whether you could handle this?"

Terry smiled. "Not a good day for me. You were tough."

"And now I'm embarrassed," she said gravely. "In fact, I'm deeply ashamed. There must be some way to make it up to you."

"A written retraction?"

"Not good enough. Ever make love in a car?"

Terry looked around them, as though considering the logistics. "Not since high school," he said. "And she didn't look like you. The only drawbacks I can see are that it's eleven-thirty in the morning, I'm in full dress uniform, and we're surrounded by reporters and guys with video cameras. You'd be a smash on YouTube."

Meg's throaty chuckle came with a grin. "How sincere can an apology be if it isn't public?"

Terry gazed at her in pretended shock. "You have a dirty laugh, I just discovered. I've never heard that laugh before."

"You never sold an insanity defense before."

"Certainly not this one." Terry put the key in the ignition. "Think this can wait five minutes?"

"Yeah. But not six." By the time they parked in front of his apartment, Meg had wrapped her panty hose around the stick shift of his car.

AFTERWARD, THEY LAY ON top of his bedcovers, Terry's head on her stomach. Their skin shone with sweat. "What just happened to you?" he asked.

Meg gazed at the ceiling. "I had a vision of a life," she admitted. "It happens now and then. But never as strongly as this morning, when I allowed myself to imagine that my brother will be okay." Her voice fell off. "I shouldn't hope yet, I know—"

"Stay with this for a minute. What kind of life?"

"A normal one. We go to work, and then come home. We take turns cooking, or go out. We make friends we both like. We go to plays and movies, learn something about opera and art, take walks and hikes."

"Where does this life take place?" Terry asked, and began to kiss her stomach.

"Watch that," Meg admonished. "In answer to your question, San Francisco. I checked with my boss. There's an opening—if Brian's acquitted, and I don't have to worry about an appeal, I can get my old job back."

"What will I be doing?"

"You said it yourself. If Brian's acquitted, you write your own ticket."

A shadow of doubt crossed Terry's mind. "Not yet. Too much can still happen."

She gave him an uncertain look. "A girl can dream, can't she?"

Reaching out, Terry touched her face. "I'll make you a deal. If this turns out right, we'll go to Costa Brava. After that I'll visit San Francisco."

Her eyes became very serious. "Do you mean it, Paul?"

"Yes," he said, and realized that he did. Or, at least, that he wanted to.

They made love again, then prepared to cross-examine Colonel Northrop.

12

COLONEL DAVID NORTHROP had short brown hair, watchful brown eyes, and a long face that seemed better suited to dolor than humor. He answered Flynn's questions without inflection or expression, a soldier doing his duty.

Yes, Northrop affirmed, he had been Brian McCarran's commanding officer before, during, and after their service in Iraq. Yes, Captain Joe D'Abruzzo had been one of Northrop's company commanders during the year in Sadr City. And yes, unlike Northrop's contact with D'Abruzzo— who had become an operations officer in another battalion—his interaction with Brian McCarran had continued until the preferral of charges. Watching, Terry awaited Flynn's portrayal of Brian McCarran as a competent and seemingly untroubled man.

"Since his return from Iraq," Flynn asked Northrop, "how would you evaluate Lieutenant McCarran's performance?"

"Outstanding," Northrop said. "Capable, efficient, responsive, and organized."

"Did his level of performance change after he shot Captain D'Abruzzo?"

Northrop sat back, as though pondering the nuance of his answer. "Brian became quieter. That was understandable. But nothing interfered with his work."

In the jury box, Major Wertheimer's puzzled expression

underscored Terry's concern—depending on how you viewed it, Brian's apparent equanimity was either admirable or troubling. In the same methodical manner, Flynn asked, "Since his return from Iraq, how has Lieutenant McCarran related to the officers and men in your battalion?"

"Very well. He was attentive to problems, responsive to concerns, and direct and clear in his communications." After a moment, Northrop added, "Brian didn't try to win you over with personality. Like General McCarran, he drew people by being honest, straightforward, and exceptionally bright. And, like his father, I thought him destined to become a general officer."

"Did you see any difference in his performance during the two years you served as his commanding officer?"

"No. Obviously, serving as a platoon leader is very different from the administrative work he did thereafter. But he did both jobs superbly well."

Flynn gave the colonel a look of exaggerated curiosity. "During these two years, did you see *any* signs of emotional difficulties?"

Northrop twisted his academy ring with the fingers of his right hand, a gesture of distraction that Terry read as reluctance to play his role. At length, Northrop said, "I perceived no difficulties at all. Even with the pressure of combat under harsh conditions, my understanding was that Lieutenant McCarran never lost his judgment or ability to lead. His performance at Fort Bolton was of the same high order."

Flynn inclined his head toward Brian. "Did the accused ever mention that he was suffering from combat-related stress?"

Northrop's glance at Brian mingled puzzlement with regret. "He did not."

"During your tour of duty in Iraq, were you aware of any antagonism between Lieutenant McCarran and Captain D'Abruzzo?"

"Not at all." Northrop's jaw seemed to tighten. "In fact, I understood they had what amounted to a family connection through Captain D'Abruzzo's wife."

"Did Captain D'Abruzzo ever express a negative opinion of the accused on a personal level, or regarding any aspect of his performance in combat?"

Northrop considered Flynn with a faintly gloomy look. "No."

Meg pushed her legal pad closer to Terry, calling his attention to the note she had written: "Murderers don't reveal their methods." It took him a moment to realize that she was referring to D'Abruzzo. "Would you have been aware," Flynn asked Northrop, "if Captain D'Abruzzo had harbored such feelings?"

Northrop looked troubled by the question. "I'm not a mind reader, Major Flynn. The best measure I can give you is that Captain D'Abruzzo evaluated the lieutenant throughout their service in Iraq. His fitness reports gave Brian the highest marks."

Quickly, Flynn introduced as exhibits D'Abruzzo's reports on Brian. Terry had already seen them and knew that they described Lieutenant Brian McCarran as "an exceptional combat leader" who was "unusually resourceful and clearheaded." But to the members, these reports were new, and Flynn gave them ample time to read. Four out of five seemed as struck by D'Abruzzo's praise as Flynn wished them to be; only Colonel MacDonald, perhaps reflecting on his own imminent departure from the army, had a distant, unhappy look.

At length, Flynn asked Northrop, "Based on your observations, do you believe that Captain D'Abruzzo singled out the lieutenant's platoon for the most dangerous assignments?"

Narrow-eyed, Northrop seemed almost to visualize the question, disassembling its component parts and assessing its latent ambiguities. "My answer depends on how I interpret your phrasing. Sadr City was inherently dangerous—it was often hard to predict which mission would be more dangerous than others. Granted, the lieutenant's platoon took more casualties than most. But Captain D'Abruzzo believed that Lieutenant McCarran was his ablest platoon leader, and I had no reason to doubt that." Northrop gave Brian a rueful look. "It's the nature of war that the greatest burdens fall on the best soldiers. Sometimes the price for that is high. But that's what Brian McCarran signed on for, and he never once complained to me."

Flynn's expression was the closest to contentment Terry had seen from him in court. "Thank you, Colonel Northrop. That's all I have for you."

APPROACHING COLONEL NORTHROP, TERRY stopped a respectful distance away. The colonel's expression was neutral; Terry sensed that, while he had once thought highly of Brian, Northrop was determined to answer questions on his own terms—especially in a case where the accused had confessed to adultery with the victim's wife. "Is it fair to say," Terry began, "that because of the nature of the assignments given Lieutenant McCarran, more men in his platoon were killed or wounded?"

Again, Northrop seemed to deconstruct the question. "It's certainly true that Lieutenant McCarran's platoon took more casualties. Whether that could have been predicted from the nature of his missions isn't entirely clear."

"Do you attribute the high casualty rate to failures in his leadership?"

Northrop frowned. "I have no basis for forming that opinion. Certainly not from Captain D'Abruzzo's fitness reports."

"Did Captain D'Abruzzo ever suggest that Brian was insufficiently aggressive, or that he placed the lives of Iraqi civilians above the safety of his men?"

"He did not."

"So isn't it fair to conclude that—whether or not the danger was always predictable—Lieutenant McCarran's platoon drew more inherently dangerous missions than the other three platoons in Captain D'Abruzzo's company?"

Northrop hesitated, then conceded in a flat tone, "You could conclude that, yes."

"Did you ever discuss with Captain D'Abruzzo the casualty rate in Lieutenant McCarran's platoon?"

Northrop gazed at Terry, his expression closing. "Twice," he said tersely.

"When was the first occasion?"

"After the completion of a mission guarding an Iraqi police station. The resulting casualties had left Lieutenant McCarran's platoon more shorthanded than the others. So I suggested to Captain D'Abruzzo that we should consider giving that platoon whatever breaks we could, at least until they got replacements."

"How did Captain D'Abruzzo respond?"

"That Lieutenant McCarran and his platoon were still best suited to handle challenging assignments. At least within reason."

"You expressed a personal opinion that Lieutenant McCarran was an exceptionally able platoon leader. On what did you base that opinion?"

"In part, on my own interaction with Lieutenant McCarran." Northrop paused. "Also on the fitness reports written by Captain D'Abruzzo."

Terry felt his pulse quicken. "Had these reports been less favorable, Colonel Northrop, would you have questioned Captain D'Abruzzo's statement that the lieutenant and his platoon should take more difficult assignments?"

"Of course."

"So as a result of Captain D'Abruzzo's favorable assessments, Brian McCarran's life was at greater risk?"

"Objection," Flynn interjected crisply. "The question calls for speculation."

"Hardly," Terry told Hollis. "It follows from the witness's prior answers."

"Agreed," Hollis said somberly. "Please respond, Colonel Northrop."

"If the reports had been less favorable," Northrop answered slowly, "I'd have been more prone to question the assignments given to Lieutenant McCarran's platoon."

"Let's return to the mission guarding the police station. You considered that to be dangerous, correct?"

"Yes, for two reasons. First, the station was manned by Iraqis with dubious loyalty, some of whom no doubt were tied to the Mahdi Army. Second, it was in a particularly treacherous part of Sadr City, where many residents were followers of Muqtada al-Sadr and which afforded a favorable environment for picking off American soldiers."

"And on the final day of that mission, Brian's platoon took significant casualties inflicted in an ambush."

"That's correct. As I understand it, the militia used children to hem in our platoon. Lieutenant McCarran was forced to drive through them."

Terry waited, hands in his pockets. Mildly, he asked, "Did you ever hear that one of the Iraqi police had warned Lieutenant McCarran that the policemen would desert and that his platoon was walking into an ambush?"

Though clearly unsurprised by the question, Northrop hesitated. "Not at the time."

"So you didn't know Brian had taken this report to D'Abruzzo?"

"I did not."

"Or that Captain D'Abruzzo refused Lieutenant McCarran's request to modify his orders, or to bring this information to your attention?"

Northrop's eyes hardened. "No."

"And that, when Lieutenant McCarran pressed his argument to confer with you, Captain D'Abruzzo threatened to relieve him of his command?"

"No." Northrop seemed genuinely disturbed. "Who said that?"

"Lieutenant McCarran." Terry gave the colonel a long, appraising look. "As battalion commander, shouldn't you have been told about the ambush?"

Northrop propped his elbow on the arm of the witness chair, delivering the answer he had no doubt reached with Flynn. "In the first analysis," he said carefully, "that was Captain D'Abruzzo's call. Several factors come into play, including how he assessed the reliability of the information and whether responding in some other fashion— say, by sending in a second platoon—could have negatively affected other missions where his company was also short of troops. I can't know what went into Captain D'Abruzzo's decision, or what I would have done in his position."

"Or in yours," Terry said sharply, "seeing how you didn't know."

"That's true," Northrop acknowledged.

"Suppose that after the ambush, you'd learned that Lieutenant McCarran had taken this information to

Captain D'Abruzzo, who'd declined to bring it to you. As battalion commander, what might you have done?"

"I'd have questioned Captain D'Abruzzo. Depending on what I learned from him, I might have brought in Lieutenant McCarran."

"Would that have affected your assessment of D'Abruzzo as company commander?"

Northrop folded his hands. "It might or might not have. I simply can't say."

"But you can conceive of circumstances where that assessment could have been unfavorable to Captain D'Abruzzo?"

"Yes."

"Would that information have also raised questions about Captain D'Abruzzo's insistence that Lieutenant McCarran's platoon was best suited to assignments such as house-to-house fighting?"

For a long moment, Northrop weighed the question in silence. "Could you be more specific?"

"Sure. Would you have wondered whether Captain D'Abruzzo felt animosity toward Brian McCarran?"

"It would have crossed my mind."

"Or whether, if only Lieutenant McCarran knew of their argument, Captain D'Abruzzo considered him as a threat to his own advancement?"

Northrop's reluctance to go further showed on his face. "If I understand the implications of your question," he said coldly, "you're asking me to speculate as to whether Captain D'Abruzzo hoped that Lieutenant McCarran would be killed by Iraqi militia. In my dealings with him, Captain D'Abruzzo was honest, responsible, and dedicated to fulfilling our mission. Officers issue orders, and men die as a result. But I won't attribute to this dead officer any other motive than trying to do his duty as he saw it."

But the members might, Terry knew. "Very well, Colonel. You mentioned that Brian McCarran never sought help to deal with post-traumatic stress disorder stemming from his combat experiences in Iraq. Had he done so, might that have adversely affected his career?"

Again, Northrop seemed to search for balance in his answer. "In the past, it could have. But the army is making a concerted effort to encourage soldiers to seek whatever help they need."

"Is that attitude uniformly accepted by all officers?"

"Put that way, no. New policies take a while to catch up with old biases."

"Has any officer in your command sought assistance in dealing with PTSD?"

"Not to my knowledge."

"How many officers in your battalion are veterans of Iraq?"

"Over twenty."

"Yet none of them is suffering adverse affects from combat?"

"Not that they report."

"How about what you observe, Colonel Northrop?"

Northrop gave him a defensive look. "I've seen no behavior in my officers that suggests functioning impaired by post-traumatic stress disorder."

"Which includes, by your account, Brian McCarran. When did you have the opportunity to observe him?"

"During normal working hours, in the discharge of his duties."

"Never outside?"

Northrop seemed to search his memory. "Once," he said at length. "At a cocktail party my wife and I held for the battalion's officers."

"Did Brian bring a date?"

"No," Northrop said after a moment. "I believe he came alone."

"Do you know who Lieutenant McCarran's friends are?"

"No."

"Do you have any idea how well he sleeps at night?"

"No."

"Or whether he has nightmares?"

"No."

"Did you ever drive with Lieutenant McCarran outside of Fort Bolton?"

"No."

"Or see him in any situation after Iraq that might be stressful?"

"No."

"What do you know, if anything, about Brian McCarran's life outside his duties at the battalion?"

Northrop placed a finger to his lips. "Almost nothing. Except that he likes to sail." He paused. "I've since learned about his affair with Kate D'Abruzzo. But I had no idea of that. As I look back at it now, all I really know about Brian McCarran is what I saw on duty. Outside of that, his life remains a mystery to me."

As it was to Terry. "No further questions," he said, and the testimony in the court-martial of Lieutenant Brian McCarran came to an end.

COLONEL HOLLIS SET FINAL arguments for Monday.

Crowded by video cameras, dogged by shouted questions they refused to answer, Brian, Meg, and Terry left the courtroom and made their way to the parking lot, Brian staring straight ahead. Standing beside Brian's car, Meg touched Terry's arm. "Get some sleep, Paul. Think about something else for a night."

Terry wished he could.

Instead, he took his questions home. As nightfall darkened the windows he poured himself a drink.

He could not fault his performance, Terry concluded. He had gotten the jury he wanted, and had expanded his defense to include PTSD. He had exposed the enigmas and assumptions in a prosecution case that, from the outset, had never overwhelmed him. Too many of Flynn's suspicions were based not on his own proof, but on Terry's absence of proof to corroborate the account given by Brian, Kate, and Meg: that Joe D'Abruzzo had ever hit his wife or threatened her with a gun; that Joe had gone to Brian's apartment on his own initiative, rather than in response to a call from Brian; that Brian suffered from sleeplessness and nightmares; that, at the moment of the shooting, Brian had believed himself in danger; and that Brian had not called Kate to warn her that her husband was dead. Flynn's belief that none of this was true did not amount to evidence. The irony was that his case rested on another statement by Brian and Kate—the confession of an affair—the truth of which had been known only to them. Without that, Terry believed, Flynn might not have brought the case at all.

He was finishing his scotch when he saw the manila rectangle someone had slid beneath his door.

The manager, no doubt, delivering an envelope dropped off in his absence. Picking it up, he saw that Ben Flournoy had written "Captain Terry" on the front.

Inside were Brian's cell phone records.

Terry sat down, at first scanning them idly, focused on the months prior to Joe D'Abruzzo's death. Then he reviewed them again, more closely.

Perhaps it was nothing. Certainly the fact that there were so few calls to, or from, Kate D'Abruzzo said nothing in itself. Perhaps their affair, as Kate had suggested, was as regular as clockwork, and required little time and nurturing in between.

I know my daughter better than she imagines, Rose Gallagher had told him. *There were times today when I didn't believe a word she was saying.*

As though in a trance, Terry went to his computer and logged on to the Internet. Within minutes, he found the photograph he wanted and printed it out. Then he went to his car and left Fort Bolton.

PART FIVE

THE SECRET

DECEMBER 2005

1

THE MARRIOTT WAS BUSY, its brightly lit entrance lined with cars and taxis dropping off new arrivals for the evening. When Terry arrived, the bellhop, José Calvo, was shuttling suitcases to the elevator. Waiting in the lobby, Terry positioned himself so that Calvo would see him when he came back down. This took five minutes; from the guarded, unhappy look on the young man's face, he remembered Terry, and preferred to avoid reopening the subject of the lady who came on Wednesdays and her angry, now dead, husband.

But Calvo was polite. When Terry approached him, he stood there, stoic and resigned. "Hello, sir," he said softly.

"Hello, José." Terry angled his head toward a corner of the lobby that held two empty chairs. "Mind if we talk? It won't take long."

José nodded, then followed Terry to the corner. Terry placed the manila envelope on the table between them. "You remember Mrs. D'Abruzzo," Terry said. "You recognized her photograph, but not the one of the man we showed you."

"Yes, sir," Calvo answered cautiously. "I remember."

"I'd like to show you another, and see if you recall the face."

Reaching into the envelope, Terry placed the photo he had printed from the Internet on the table. Staring down, Calvo's eyes widened slightly, fixed on the photograph for a long, silent moment. Softly, he said, "This man I remember."

Terry felt shaken. "You're certain of that?"

"Yes. It is a face you do not forget. Also the way he carries himself."

"You saw him here, then?"

"A couple of different times, one especially. I took my lunch break in the car, eating a sandwich while I listened to a baseball game." Calvo placed a finger on the photograph. "Then I see this man, coming out the side door of the hotel. I remember thinking he acted kind of funny, looking around like someone might see him. Then he walks across the parking lot to the car right next to mine."

"How was he dressed?"

"Normal clothes, nothing special. But when he sees me, he gives me a look—real sharp, like I wasn't supposed to be there. Then he gets in his car and drives away."

Terry nodded. "Is there anything else about that day you remember?"

Frowning, Calvo stroked his mustache. "I finished lunch and came back to the lobby. That was when I saw the lady we talked about, fighting with the dark-haired man I found out was her husband. The man was so angry, and she was so scared. So everything that happened got stuck in my brain."

Terry struggled to absorb this new reality. "Have you told anyone about the other man?"

"No, sir." Calvo opened his palms. "What would I say, exactly? I remembered this man only because of how he looked, and the way he looked at me."

Terry slid the photograph back inside the envelope and gave Calvo twenty dollars for his time.

IT WAS ALMOST NINE o'clock when Terry reached Kate D'Abruzzo's town house, and the light over the front door was off. But a faint glow came through the curtains drawn across the windows of her living room. Terry rapped sharply on the brass door knocker, and then, when no one answered, rapped harder.

The front door cracked open. Through this aperture, Kate D'Abruzzo peered out. Seeing him, she drew back slightly, the light as pale as her face became.

Coldly, Terry said, "May I come in?"

She gave a slight shake of her head, a delayed reaction. "The kids are in bed."

"Good. That'll make it easier to talk."

Her eyes changed as she processed what must have happened, and what might happen now. She backed away from the open door as though Terry held a gun.

They entered the living room. Still watching him, she felt for the couch, sitting as he took the chair across from her. With the ghost of her mother's poise, more remarkable for the trapped look in her eyes, she asked, "Can I get you something?"

"Before the trial, I could have used the truth. Instead, I helped you plant a lie at its heart."

Kate's eyes shut. When they opened, Terry thought of two dark wounds. But she mustered the resolve not to look away. "We didn't mean for it to happen," she said simply.

"The affair? Or lying about it?"

Kate shook her head in dismay. "Both."

THEY MET AT HIS apartment.

Kate had never been there. Though driven here by her own distress, she paused in the doorway, struck by the sparseness of the decor, the sense it conveyed of a transient life lived by a solitary man.

Gently, Anthony McCarran asked, "What is it, Kate? On the phone, you sounded distraught."

She looked into his face, kind yet authoritative and, on

this occasion, puzzled. Then she went to him as she always did at first meeting, hugging, and being hugged, as though he were her own father. As Tony held her, she sensed him trying to imagine what she wanted, and what he could do to help.

After a moment he disengaged, gesturing that she should sit beside him on the couch. He sat several feet away, facing her with a look both attentive and perplexed. Even in her distress, Kate thought fondly that Tony McCarran felt more at ease deploying a brigade than dealing with a woman's fears. Drawing a breath, she began, "Joe's not the same since he came back from Iraq. He drinks all night and won't talk to me about what's happened to him. Now he's begun to hit me—"

"Hit you?"

Kate touched her cheek. "On the face."

She watched him drain the anger from his face. Then he spoke in the level but commanding tone she knew so well. "I need you to tell me everything, Kate."

She did. Each detail—Joe's sudden rages, bursts of violence, the brooding withdrawals, aversion to social life, and even his disinterest in lovemaking—seemed to register in the general's gray-blue eyes.

"What about Matt and Kristen?" he asked.

"They're suffering. They remember how much they loved being with him. Now they're timid around him, even afraid." She shook her head, adding in a thick voice, "I never imagined I'd say that. But in some ways it's worse for them than having no father at all."

The statement resonated with the wound she had suffered before she was born, the death of her father. She saw Tony McCarran mourn, as she did, that Jack Gallagher had not survived his war. "You can't go on like this," Tony said. "None of you can." He paused, then asked, "What does your mother say?"

Kate shook her head. "I just can't tell her. That would ruin her relationship with Joe. And I already know what she'd say: go to his commanding officer."

The corners of Tony's mouth drew down. "Is that such bad advice?"

Kate felt a surge of hopelessness. "Yes," she said vehemently. "It could ruin his career. Without that, Joe would fall apart, and so would our marriage."

"And you still want to save it."

Kate nodded. "Even now."

She watched him absorb this, his concern for her at war with the tenets of his Catholic faith, the deep moral rigor that had caused him to stay with Mary McCarran when their marriage had become an endless well of sadness. Softly, Tony said, "Your mother and you mean the world to me. If it weren't for Rose, I wouldn't be where I am, or know the joy of having you in my life."

Kate felt the constriction in her chest ease. "Talk to Joe," she pleaded. "Not as General McCarran, but as a member of the family. Tell him he has to get help."

After a moment, Tony nodded, clasping her hand in both of his. "If your father were here, he would have done that. So will I."

Kate felt all of her emotions breaking loose inside her: relief, a rush of hope, the certainty that Tony could solve anything, sadness that he and her mother had never married, the sheer aching loneliness of sleeping beside a man who was no longer her lover but her enemy. Then she realized that tears were running down her face. In a trembling voice she explained, "I've felt so alone—"

Impulsively, Tony reached for her. She burrowed close to him, shivering with repressed sobs, her face pressed against his chest. Holding her, he murmured, "I'll make sure you're safe."

There was a different note in his voice, thin and almost choked. Moved, Kate drew back, looking into his face. "I love you, Tony."

For a moment he looked so sad and alone that her heart went out to him. Before she knew what she had done, Kate kissed him gently on the lips.

Tony straightened. "Kate—"

His voice held anguish and confusion. She smiled uncertainly, grasping for a way to reassure Tony that she loved him as before.

But not quite, she realized.

Tony bowed his head. Suddenly she knew that no one but her mother had ever looked out for him, and no one completely.

Gently, Kate placed his hand on her breast.

Gazing into her eyes, he was speechless, as if they were living in a dream. "It's all right," she whispered.

He closed his eyes. When he opened them again, Kate led him to the bedroom.

Afterward, she lay in his arms, feeling the rough surface of his face against her neck, the dampness of his tears on her skin. Only then did she see the picture of Rose beside his bed.

FINISHING, KATE FACED TERRY, looking weary but composed. "I don't need a psychologist to decode this. I married Joe because he felt like a protector. Then I turned to Tony. It was my fault, not his."

The self-discipline it took for Terry to stifle his anger and emotion surprised him. "But he talked to Joe, of course."

"Yes. He told Joe to get help or face the consequences." Her voice lowered. "Joe refused to see a counselor. But he was humiliated in front of Tony McCarran, the man he most admired. So he stopped hitting me, however angry and helpless he felt.

"But Tony and I were helpless, too. We couldn't stop, even though we knew that we could destroy Tony's career, my marriage, and both our families—my children, Joe's parents, my mother, even Meg and Brian. So we had to keep it secret." Kate looked down. "Extramarital affairs, I learned, breed a certain pragmatism. Washington was too far for a mother of two to drive. So we chose a hotel. Each time, Tony gave me cash to pay the bill."

"What about phone calls?"

"He bought me a cell phone I used only to call him, so that Joe would never see the bills." She looked up at him. "It sounds so seedy, I know. But he wanted me, and I wanted to feel safe. When he held me afterward, I did."

"At least until Joe ended it."

"No," Kate said softly. "I did."

THEY LAY TOGETHER IN the chill, sterile room, Kate's breasts against his chest. She could see the fear in Tony's eyes before she spoke.

"We have to stop," she whispered. "You know we do."

The pain on his face gave him a haunted look, as though it was an enemy he had met before. But she could not ask him about this; they no longer spoke of Kate's mother. With a sadness that seemed years deep, Tony asked, "How can we go back?"

The full knowledge of how deeply she had sinned, and against whom, pierced Kate to her core. She felt the weight of her responsibility—she had come to him, and now she must be the strong one. "It will be so hard, I know. But one of the lessons you taught me is that people can bear whatever they have to."

The words left a bleakness in his eyes that Kate would never forget. A few moments later, he left in silence, pausing in the doorway to look at her as she lay naked among the sheets. For a time she wept alone. Then she dressed and left the room.

The husband she dreaded was waiting in the lobby. "I saw him," he told her, and Kate felt her world collapse.

SHE FOLLOWED HIM HOME in a state of numb resignation, not knowing what would happen. When Joe closed the door behind them, the house felt like a prison. The sole mercy was that he had not been drinking.

In a monotone, she said, "I have to pick up the kids at school."

Joe stared at her. "So you remember you're a mother."

Despite her fears, the unfairness of this provoked her. "I try to, Joe. Because you've forgotten you're a father."

His jaw set, and Kate thought she saw the pulse twitch in his throat. Quietly, he said, "On your way to school, call the general on your cell phone. Tell him that if he ever interferes in our life again, I'll bring him down in disgrace. Your mother may have spent her life as Tony McCarran's camp follower. But your 'services' are over, and so are his special privileges. When you come back with our children, you'll be the perfect wife."

A vision of her future filled Kate's mind: days and months and years spent in terrible equipoise, fearful that her slightest mistake—a careless word, an ambiguous glance—might cause him to destroy Anthony McCarran, shattering their families. And it was her doing. By her own act of selfishness and weakness, she had deepened his instability, placing in his hands the linchpin of a potential tragedy whose dimensions she could not lessen by seeking help.

"I have to leave now," she said. "When the children are here, please keep them out of this."

Something close to a smile surfaced in his eyes, disturbing in its anger and contempt.

SHE STOPPED A BLOCK from the school, taking out the cell phone she concealed in her purse. Tony was driving back to the Pentagon. When he answered, his voice was soft and weary, yet filled with concern. "Are you all right?"

No, she thought, *and I may never be again.* Without preface, she said, "Joe followed me to the hotel. He saw you coming out."

In his silence, she imagined a stricken Tony McCarran envisioning his ruin. The quiet stretched as she saw the first kids spilling out of the front door of the school, a poignant reminder of the distance between her daily life and Tony's solitary existence. Then he said, "I won't let him abuse you, Kate. No matter the consequences."

That was Tony, she thought—a stoic fatalism instead of blame or self-pity. "Please, Tony," she said. "Let me deal with this. Not just for our sake, but everyone's."

Surely, she thought, Anthony McCarran could not help but weigh the threat to her against the certain cost of his public disgrace. After a moment, he said, "I won't be blackmailed at the price of putting you at risk."

"Let's wait and see," she said. "Maybe in a year or two, things will be different. Or maybe there'll be an out for me. What I think we need is privacy, time to let this work itself out beneath the surface of our lives."

Through the window, she saw Kristen's dark head and slender form as she searched the street for her mother's car. "Keep the cell phone," she heard him say. "If there's any trouble, call me. I'll know what to do."

"I love you," she said miserably, "and I'm just so sorry."

Kate turned off her phone. When she joined the line of mothers in cars, Kristen spotted her. Skittering to the SUV, she climbed into the passenger seat, pleased to see the parent who had become her only source of security.

Kate kissed the crown of her daughter's chestnut head. "Hi, sweetheart. How was your day?"

"Okay," Kristen said with the pseudomaturity of a child who, however briefly, enjoys pretending to be an equal. "How was your day?"

"Fine," Kate assured her. "Your daddy came home early."

Joe waited until the kids were in bed, then started drinking in the living room, staring silently at his own dark thoughts. Wary, Kate retreated to a warm bath. She was drying her hair in front of the mirror when his face appeared behind her. With ominous quiet, he said, "Turn off the hair dryer."

Kate complied, frozen where she stood. He placed the tumbler of whiskey on the sink, roughly grabbing her shoulders to spin her around. In a low, tight voice, he demanded, "Who knows about you and McCarran?"

Bracing herself, she felt her shame and anger become defiance. "No one. But everyone knows about you. Don't you know how different you are? Are you so far gone you've stopped seeing yourself? If you don't believe me, look in the mirror. Look at *us*."

Joe's eyes flickered toward his reflection. More evenly, Kate said, "I'm ashamed of what I've done, Joe. But together we can face this."

Without speaking, he turned and left.

When he returned, she was in her nightgown, fitfully reading a novel as she struggled to set aside her broken life.

He stood by her bed, staring down at her with an appraising stare almost as frightening as unreason. "Don't worry," he said quietly. "I don't want you. I don't want to smell him on your skin. I just want you to tell me everything you did with him."

Mute, Kate shook her head.

Joe shrugged, a heavy movement of his shoulders. Then he went to the nightstand and withdrew the gun. With an almost companionable manner, he sat next to her on the bed, and then placed the gun to her temple.

"Now you can tell me," he said. A sheen of wetness glistened in Joe's eyes. "Tell me, Kate. Or you'll never know the night I choose to kill you in your sleep."

As Kate closed her eyes, Joe laughed softly. "Maybe tonight," he said. "First I'm going to the club. Wait up for me until I come back."

She did not open her eyes until she heard the click of the front door closing.

THE KNOWLEDGE OF WHAT would follow was graven on Kate's striking but haggard face. Terry felt no pity. "I count another lie," he said coldly. "Either the story you told then or the one you're telling now. Which is it?"

Kate sat straighter, resistant. "Everything I said was true—the fights, the times he hit me, the threats he made. I just changed the time sequence to leave out Tony and our affair."

"With considerable skill," Terry said. But he had no time to dwell on his anger and disbelief. "Tell me the rest."

"I went to the bathroom and threw up." Kate paused, then said slowly, "I was desperate. I couldn't tell anyone what had happened, or why Joe had threatened me with a gun. That left family. Brian was the one safe person I knew."

KATE OPENED THE DOOR of the town house before he could knock. Pushing past her, Brian looked swiftly from side to side. "Where is he?"

"At the Officers' Club," Kate said quickly. "He's already been drinking."

Crossing the living room, Brian searched the hallway. Then he joined her in the living room, his tone softer but still urgent. "What's happening, Kate?"

"He's been hitting me." She sat on the couch, awkwardly and abruptly, feeling the adrenaline that had propelled her evanesce. "Tonight he threatened me with his gun. I can't go on like this."

Brian stared at her in astonishment. Then he sat down beside her, covering Kate's hand with his. "You have to go to his battalion commander."

Kate slowly shook her head, a gesture of despair. "I can't, Brian. It would end our marriage."

"What if he kills you? Where would the kids be then?" Brian spoke slowly and firmly. "You don't have a choice. No matter what comes out."

In response, Kate could only shake her head.

"What is it, Kate?"

She put her hands to her face, saying in a muffled voice, "Joe knows I was having an affair."

She watched Brian take this in. "Whatever you've done, that's not grounds for murder. You need to protect your family."

Kate wished she could look away. But, despite her own shame, she needed to see his face. Quietly, she said, "I've been sleeping with your father."

Brian simply stared at her, the astonishment in his eyes his only visible emotion. Then his shoulders slumped, almost imperceptibly. "You'd better tell me about this."

Haltingly, she did. All she could add was the pitiful

phrase that kept recurring to her: "We didn't mean for it to happen."

For an instant, Brian looked as shaken as she was. "Oh, Katie."

His voice carried such despair that Kate felt the fault line in his soul: the war had upended his beliefs, and now she had shattered his conception of the father who, whatever burdens he imposed, exemplified self-sacrifice and honor. "I'm sorry," she said, words that seemed as hollow as the ones she had spoken before.

Brian did not seem to hear. "All right," he said. "Let's think this through. If Joe exposes my father, the abuse will come out, too. If he doesn't, he can blackmail you into taking more abuse—or worse. Either way, this is too volatile to go on." Suddenly, Brian stood. "I'll find you a way out of this, Kate. In the meanwhile, I'm taking his gun."

With a rush of fear, Kate said, "What happens when Joe finds out it's missing?"

Brian's eyes were cool as ice, as cool as Anthony McCarran's. "Tell him who has it. By then I'll have figured out what to do."

"He surely did," Terry said softly.

"No," Kate insisted. "Please believe me. The phone calls happened almost exactly the way I said."

They were going to dinner. The children were gone, and Joe was drinking.

For once, her affair did not appear to taint his thoughts. He sat on the edge of their bed, watching Kate put her earrings on. "Just the two of us," he said. "Remember how we were before?"

The reference to her transgression, once unthinkable to

her, filled Kate with unspeakable sadness. "Yes," she answered. "I remember how safe I felt."

Something in her tone seemed to transform his thoughts. His face changed, as though a veil had fallen, leaving his eyes distant and suspicious. Then he stood, sliding open the drawer of the nightstand.

She watched him stare at the empty drawer. His voice almost a whisper, he asked, "Where is it?"

He turned slowly, heavily. The rage in his eyes made her dread having to answer. "Brian took it."

Joe pushed her down on the bed, hard, pressing her throat. The stench of liquor filled her nostrils. *"Brian McCarran?"* he demanded.

"It's not Brian's fault—"

"It's never their fault, is it? Always mine."

Turning, Joe headed for the door. Afraid, she asked, "Where are you going?"

"To get back what's mine. It's time to teach the fucking McCarrans whose wife you are."

He stalked from the room. Dazed, Kate could not remember Brian's phone number. When she started dialing, the numbers came back to her.

His phone kept ringing, and then she heard a click. In the hollow tone of a recording, he answered, "This is Brian McCarran—"

"I USED THE CELL phone to call Brian," Kate told Terry. "The one that Tony gave me. That's the reason Flynn found no record of the call."

Silent, Terry absorbed the way in which the truth—if it *was* truth—inverted the narrative of the court-martial. "What happened to the phone?"

Kate looked down. "After Joe was killed, I threw it in

the river. If the CID had found it, they'd have traced the phone to Tony."

"The general again. He's certainly played an honorable role."

"He didn't ask me to," Kate protested. "No one knew how important that call might be—that Flynn would think we planned all this, and that Brian called Joe."

Amid Terry's disbelief, another possibility presented itself more starkly. Perhaps it was true that D'Abruzzo had threatened Brian's life. Or perhaps Brian's solution, whether spontaneous or planned, had been to murder him.

There were things he desperately needed to know, but not from Kate. At once he stood. "I'm going to see Brian," he told her. "If I find out you've called him, I'll blow this whole thing up."

2

DRESSED IN KHAKIS and a polo shirt, Brian McCarran cracked the door of his quarters. Seeing Terry, he spoke without visible reaction: "If you're here for Meg, Paul, she went over to your place."

Terry ignored the door chain between them. "I'm here for the truth," he said. "You can start anytime you want to. We've got until nine o'clock on Monday."

Brian angled his head slightly, appraising his lawyer with an opaque, alert expression. Terry could imagine him on the roof of the Iraqi police station, planning to eliminate a sniper.

"You lied to the court," Terry said with the same cold anger, "and you lied to me. You made me part of a cover-up, a pawn in your twisted family dynamic. Now that's done. The trial isn't. I've got choices, Brian. But first I want the experience of hearing you tell it straight."

Silent, Brian kept watching him. Behind the cool, impervious look, Terry sensed the swiftness of his thoughts. Then Brian unchained the door and stepped aside. "Sorry," he said. "You know how badly I react to angry people showing up unannounced."

Terry entered the living room, hearing the door shut behind him. Brian waved him to a couch. Taking a chair, Brian inquired evenly, "Where do you want to start?"

"The night D'Abruzzo came to see you. If it helps, you can pretend I'm him. But you can skip the bullets, or the bullshit about wanting to reason with him." Terry's voice became hard. "He *owned* you, Brian. Because he owned your father."

To Terry's surprise, a faint, chill smile played on Brian's lips. "So Joe thought."

D'ABRUZZO WAS DRUNK. HE stood there, flushed and angry, heedless that the door to Brian's apartment remained open behind him. Brian stood near the chair. "Close the door," he said. "This is a private conversation."

Turning, Joe kicked the door shut and took two steps toward Brian. Involuntarily, Brian stepped back. Seeing this, D'Abruzzo smiled a little. "Are you afraid of me, Brian?"

"Yes. But not for me. Thanks to you, I stopped caring in Sadr City."

The reference to Iraq caused D'Abruzzo to stop moving, as though immobilized by the shame and fury Brian read in his eyes. "You *are* afraid, Brian—just like you were then. You're a fucking coward."

Brian imagined the gun in his hand, the savage joy of obliterating this man's face until he had emptied the clip. He placed his hand on the arm of his chair, as if to retain his balance. "It takes a brave man," he said softly, "to live with sending good men to the slaughter. I guess it helps to drink yourself senseless or slap around your wife. And when that fails to salve your self-contempt, there's always the thrill of holding a gun to her head.

"Personally, I think the better choice is for you to blow your own brains out. But if you're not brave enough for that, you might consider psychotherapy." He paused, draining his voice of sarcasm. "Let this be, Joe. Get help—for your sake, for Matt and Kristen, and for Kate. You own the biggest piece of what she did. Destroying two families is the coward's way out—"

"You pious little shit. This is all about the Great Man, not any of us lesser fools. Give me the gun or I'll break his marble statue into pieces."

The crazy energy in Joe's voice deepened Brian's fears—caged with this man in his living room, he felt Joe's pathology spinning out of control, with consequences he could not restrain or predict. With the same quiet, he said, "Along with your family, your marriage, and your career? Bringing down my father isn't worth that. And given what you've done to Kate, you haven't earned the right."

"He was fucking her."

Once more, a burst of fury fogged Brian's thoughts. "Maybe *you* should have—"

D'Abruzzo's face turned florid. When he took another step, Brian reached for the gun. It was pointed at D'Abruzzo before he saw D'Abruzzo's eyes widening in surprise. Struggling for self-control, he said in a tight voice, "We're going to talk, Joe. You sit on the couch. I'll sit in this chair. We've got all night for you to sober up. Then we can make sense of this."

Shaking his head, D'Abruzzo took another step, extending his hand palm up. "Give me the gun, Lieutenant. Now."

"No. You'll use it on Kate."

D'Abruzzo took another step forward, as though determined to dominate or die. "Hand it over," he demanded. "Or I'll shatter your windpipe and gouge your fucking eyes out."

Brian shook his head. "Straighten yourself out, Joe. Or I'll protect Kate any way I can."

D'Abruzzo kept moving. Brian felt his gun arm straighten. Flinching, D'Abruzzo whirled as the gun jumped in Brian's hand.

THEY FACED EACH OTHER in the dim light of a standing lamp. "In this version," Terry said coolly, "self-defense seems a little more ambiguous. Was Joe attacking, or afraid of getting shot?"

"Attacking." Brian hesitated. "At least that's what I believed."

Terry watched him closely. "What happened then?" he demanded.

Brian's eyes clouded. "I really don't remember. I don't recall the last three shots at all. The next thing I knew, he was lying against the wall in a pool of blood with a bullet in his back. I sat down in the chair, wondering why I'd shot him." His voice filled with doubt. "Was it to defend myself? Or to protect Kate, or my father? Or because I hated him? Or because I was afraid of taking orders? I didn't know. I *still* don't know."

"So you called Meg."

"Yeah. I was pretty scattered. But I told her everything I could."

"Including about your father?"

Slowly, Brian nodded. "She had to know."

"How did she react?"

"She got very quiet. But when she spoke, she sounded just like always: calm and even cool, someone to rely on. She said I'd be all right until she got to Fort Bolton if I followed her advice: call the MPs but don't talk to CID."

"Why *did* you talk to them?"

"I really don't know."

"Then let *me* guess, Brian. You wanted to cover up for your father. If you didn't give them some kind of story, they might keep digging."

Watching Terry intently, Brian shook his head. "I told the truth as I knew it. You can believe that, or not. All I did was leave my father out." His tone became even.

"Whatever my reason for shooting Joe, he was dead. I wasn't so far gone that I didn't grasp the benefit of that."

The chill pragmatism of the answer made Terry pause. "Did you tell the general what you knew?"

"No." Brian's eyes hardened. "The whole thing made me so sick I could barely look at him. If he hadn't crossed the line, D'Abruzzo would still be alive. Instead he set the shooting in motion by acting contrary to everything he'd told us—told *me*—about honor and integrity. My father was as dead to me as Joe D'Abruzzo. To tell him how I felt was more than he deserved."

"Bullshit, Brian. You lied for him. In fact, you lied yourself into a court-martial for murder."

"That wasn't the plan," Brian retorted. "The plan was just to keep my father out of this. Then you found out that D'Abruzzo had told that army captain that Kate was 'fucking McCarran.' It was obvious that Flynn would keep on digging until he found Kate's lover—"

"So despite your contempt for your father," Terry interjected, "you decided to exchange a charge of adultery against *him* for charges of murder and adultery against *you*, risking your career and a lifetime in prison to save General Anthony McCarran's reputation. Seems a little disproportionate, doesn't it?"

"We're McCarrans," Brian responded with quiet sarcasm. "I had the family honor to consider." His tone changed again, becoming level and practical. "He was a sitting duck for adultery charges. But I didn't know if I was guilty of anything. By the time I had to choose, I understood the basis for our defense—there weren't any witnesses but me. And I'd begun to see how good you were. Consider my decision a vote of confidence—"

"How did you know I wouldn't leave?"

Brian flashed his smile, no less engaging for its irony.

"Let's say I had my hopes. I saw the way you were starting to look at Meg. I'd even begun to imagine you'd want the pleasure of joining our family—"

Terry gave a harsh laugh. "As opposed to the Manson family?"

Brian's smile faded. "Don't blame her, Paul. She had nothing to do with the worst of this. And you should stop to remember who our family includes.

"You think I did this for my father. You're off the mark. If some McCarran had to be Kate's lover, which one of us would be easier for Rose Gallagher to accept? The answer was very clear to me." Brian leaned forward, speaking with a passion and intensity Terry had never heard. "Rose gave us everything. She gave *him* everything. She dedicated the biggest piece of her life to making our lives whole. Maybe Kate resented that. But this was my call, not hers. Rose loves my father. I wasn't going to let Kate turn her mother's sacrifice into a heartless joke. Kate had no standing to object."

Terry stared at him. "Or to deprive you of the unique pleasure of your position."

Brian met his stare, then covered this with a guarded smile. "That's a little deep for me."

"Oh, I think not. I credit your feelings about Rose—if not their primacy. But in the end, I think this *is* about your father." Terry's voice quickened. "For the first time in your life, you felt superior to him in every way. You'd protected Kate from her husband. You'd covered up his moral failure. You, not he, were protecting the family—including Rose. And once he knew that *you* knew, and what you'd done for him, he could never face you again. The fact that no one outside the family would ever know made it all the sweeter.

"That's not all. You'd come to despise the army. But

given the code of the McCarrans, you couldn't find an honorable way out. By admitting to an 'affair' you hadn't conducted, you designed the perfect exit strategy, while standing the McCarran code of honor on its head. Whatever else happened at the court-martial, at its end the army would dismiss you. You could walk out without being seen as a coward."

Brian's face was stone. "I'm glad that's all so clear to you. Speaking for myself, I'm on trial for a shooting I mostly can't recall. I don't know if I'm innocent or guilty—and, if I'm guilty, of what. I get to face how fucked up I am without being able to tell you what that has to do with this. I don't even know why I shot him." A touch of acid crept into his voice. "You think this trial is hard for you to live with? Then you try living with that."

Terry stood. "You've done your damnedest to make me, Brian. But I'm the one who gets to drop out."

Terry turned away. As he headed for the door, Brian repeated softly, "Don't blame her, Paul. Do whatever else you like, but don't blame her."

3

When Terry found Meg waiting for him, her expression filled with resignation, he knew at once that Brian had called her. Looking at him steadily, she said, "So you know."

Terry sat across from her, fighting to tame his hurt and anger and humiliation. "It wasn't hard. Once I realized that you're a gifted liar, relentlessly manipulative, and wholly lacking in conscience, that became the organizing principle for a fresh look at the facts. From that perspective, you're the most impressive woman I've ever met."

Meg's eyes went dead. "Is that all you have to say, Paul?"

"Hardly. I'm not through praising your abilities. Any garden-variety sociopath can take a run at orchestrating a cover-up that includes perjury and obstruction of justice. But few of them are lawyers, and fewer yet have duped their co-counsel into fronting for them. And the speed and spontaneity you brought to the work is a real area of strength." Draining the derision from his voice, Terry spoke in a clipped tone. "Flynn thought Brian called Kate to tell her D'Abruzzo was dead. But it was you, wasn't it?"

Meg held his gaze, as though determined not to look away. "When Brian told me about Kate and our father, I saw what might happen. So I went to an empty office and used someone else's phone." Meg lowered her voice, the only hint of her emotions. "I told Kate that Joe was dead, and to expect to hear from CID. She understood that revealing her affair with our father would only do harm to everyone."

From her manner and expression, Meg could have been discussing legal strategy. "What amazes me," Terry said sardonically, "is your ability to see the central issue. A lesser woman might have stopped to consider that a man was dead. But you went right to what really mattered: covering up your father's affair, while covering your own tracks."

"Don't be that impressed," Meg said quietly. "You'd have seen it, too. If Kate had volunteered that she was sleeping with my father, the CID might have thought that Brian killed Joe to protect his father's reputation. More than that, Dad and Kate's pathetic lapse would have devastated two families, to no purpose." Meg expelled a breath. "All Kate and Brian needed to do was tell the truth about their roles, including that they weren't lovers. And I was certain they wouldn't have to lie about my father. Because CID would never think to ask if Kate and General McCarran were involved."

"Then there's the general himself," Terry said. "I assume that *he* was willing to cooperate."

"Only when I explained his options." Meg folded her hands in front of herself, still watching Terry's eyes. "I took a red-eye that night. The next morning I met Brian, then Kate, and found out what they'd said. After that I went to see my father and told him that I knew about his affair.

"That made him pliable, for once—shame will do that. So I extracted a very thorough accounting of how they'd managed their meetings, and how likely it was that they'd be discovered. He told me about the cash, the secret cell phone, and all the steps they'd taken to avoid being seen together—"

"And you realized that concealment was a McCarran family trait."

"Have it your way, Paul. But I thought there was a pretty fair chance their affair would never surface." Meg's voice became faintly ironic. "As for my father, it was a little late for him to be worried about his tarnished honor. If he chose to fall on his sword in public, others would pay the price—quite likely his son, and certainly Rose. We owed this much to her."

Despite Terry's anger, probing how Meg's mind worked held a certain fascination. "So you volunteered your services to keep the cover-up in place, and monitor Brian's lawyer."

"That's not the reason. I was far more worried about Brian's defense than about my father. I was simply protecting a family secret that would poison lives if it came out. I never imagined what would happen because of that decision."

"Including the grim necessity of fucking me."

Meg gazed at him. In a diminished voice, she said, "I can understand how you might think that—"

"It's not that big a leap. You've been the family caretaker ever since you found your mother in the bathtub. Sleeping with me is nothing compared to risking everything you've worked for." Terry's tone was etched with pity and disdain. "All this cleverness in the service of your own destruction. Being a McCarran has blinded you."

This seemed to deflate her. For the first time, Meg looked away. "Joe was dead," she said dully. "And Kate hadn't told anyone who she'd been sleeping with. I didn't anticipate that Joe would start mumbling the name McCarran at the Officers' Club bar. Once you told me that, everything changed."

"When I told you *that*," Terry amended, "you started sleeping with me. Maybe then it wouldn't occur to me that you went to Brian and Kate without me, serving as the go-between to orchestrate their perjury. Thanks to your efforts, the three of you were always one jump ahead of me. I was the only one left in the dark."

Meg looked up at him. "That's true. But I didn't need to sleep with you to do that. Who would ever believe that Brian would confess to an affair he hadn't had? Especially when that gave Flynn the motive he was looking for." Her voice softened. "Cover-ups and lies are supposed to get a suspect out of trouble, not buy him a court-martial on murder charges. No wonder you and Flynn bought Brian's 'confession.'"

"So why did you help him do it?"

Meg's eyelids lowered, as though she was recalling a fateful moment of decision. "Brian wanted me to stay out of this. If I exposed my father's affair, Brian told me, he'd plead to a murder charge—"

"And you actually believed that?" Terry said in an incredulous tone. "Brian's terrified of prison."

"I know that. But I also know my brother, and what happened to him in Iraq." Meg's voice fell. "Our mother committed suicide. What I believed was that if Brian ended up in prison—either because he pled guilty or because he was convicted—he'd kill himself before sentencing. I made the only choice I could. I never thought Joe's death was about my father's affair—"

"Even Brian knows better," Terry snapped. "This case is all about the McCarrans and the Gallaghers. If your father hadn't slept with Kate, her husband would still be alive. Everything that followed from that put Joe's gun in Brian's hands. You understand better than anyone what a farce this trial has been."

Meg bowed her head. Terry watched the resistance seep from her body, and her features slacken with defeat. "You still don't understand, Paul. Dad showed the suicide note to Rose."

The reference was so removed from the present that at first Terry did not absorb it. Then he asked, "When did you find *that* out?"

"When I confronted my father about the affair. That was when it all came out—his loneliness, his regret, his decision not to marry Rose."

Terry laughed harshly. "The McCarrans have a gift for airbrushing their own history. Rose refused to marry *him*—otherwise, she thought, you'd never accept her love or support. You'd always believe she wanted your real mother dead."

Meg's eyes changed again, surprise replacing sorrow. "Who told you that?"

"The only honest person in your extended family. Or, at a minimum, the least self-deluding."

Meg folded her arms, as if hugging herself. "Whoever made the decision, it really doesn't matter anymore. I drove the two of them apart. Otherwise they'd have married, and Dad would be Kate's stepfather, not her lover—"

"For God's sake, Meg."

Her eyes flashed with emotion. "I hated him for telling me, and I hate myself for showing him my mother's note. But I also saw the whole thing clearly. Kate was my father's last chance to live his dream of Rose." She caught herself, speaking with a controlled intensity. "He was stunted inside. He stayed with my mother out of duty and walled up whatever else he needed in the strictures of honor and religion and military discipline. When Kate came to him, the wall broke. He craved love so desperately that he violated the code he lived by and every boundary within our families. Then Joe's discovery awakened him from his dream.

"The reality of what he'd done was shattering. When I faced him down, there was an almost physical sense of torment. Like with Brian, I didn't know what he might do."

"He's tougher than that," Terry retorted. "He's a general —people sacrifice for him, even his children, his lover, and the widow of his best friend. They've been doing that all his life. That's how he became the presumptive next chairman of the Joint Chiefs of Staff."

"You didn't see how guilty he feels—"

"He'll get over it. Whatever the reason for his ambitions, they've taken over everyone else's life." The visceral sense of her betrayal swept Terry along. "Even now, you don't see yourself. You think you're in control—that's the conceit that drives you. But you're not in charge of anything. Your loyalty to family trumps your loyalty to the law, and any ability you might have to build a life that's your own. Now you're sitting here in the ashes, looking at the man you've forced to ruin your life instead of taking you to Costa Brava."

Meg turned white. Savagely, Terry said, "Disbarment is what happens to lawyers who lie on the witness stand, and solicit lies from others. I owe you nothing, Meg. My debt is to the ethics of our profession, and to my own career." Terry steadied his voice. "As to the McCarrans, only one of you is my client. I could reopen the case, recall you, your father, and Kate as witnesses, and prove that Brian wasn't involved with her. There goes motive."

Meg's lips parted. For moments Terry watched her struggle to master her emotions. Tonelessly she said, "You'd make Brian a liar for the second time, and accomplish nothing. No one would believe he did this for Rose, instead of Dad. Someone who risked his freedom to cover up for his father is capable of murdering the man who could destroy his father's career. So even if Brian allowed you to go ahead, which I don't believe, you wouldn't be doing it to help him—only yourself.

"You've got a perfect right to do that, Paul. But you can save yourself simply by withdrawing from the case." She paused, then added with quiet asperity, "Though that would deprive you of the pleasure of exposing all the rest of us."

"Not entirely," Terry said coldly. "If I ask to withdraw from the case, I'll have to give Hollis a reason. There's only one: a fundamental disagreement with my client. Hollis will know what it is, and so will Flynn: that I found out that Brian has misled the court. After that, Flynn will uncover the truth quickly enough."

From her expression, Meg saw the accuracy of this. At length she said, "You have another choice."

"Which is?"

Her tone expressed a desperate fervor. "You weren't part of the cover-up, Paul—you put on the evidence in good faith. You still can give a closing argument for Brian."

"On what grounds? I can't base my argument on perjured testimony. Otherwise I'd be throwing legal ethics out the window, along with my career." Terry's voice softened. "You'd be astonished how much that means to me, Meg. But then the Terrys aren't the McCarrans, if only because my father's sense of shame actually caused him to kill himself. Maybe that's the difference between a general and an accountant. But I'm not interested in suicide—literally or figuratively—"

"I'm not asking you to do that," Meg cut in urgently. "You don't have to rely on perjured testimony. Your argument is that Brian killed Joe not because of an affair, but as a necessary act of self-defense." She paused. "Brian may be guilty of perjury. But you know why he lied. Do you really think that makes him guilty of murder?"

"I have no idea," Terry said curtly. "I do know that saving Brian means saving all the rest of you. Especially you. Forgive me for wondering if you want me to risk my future to save yours."

Meg's voice was parched. "You don't know me at all, do you? You've accused me of being a better McCarran than a lawyer. Maybe so. But what hurt me even more was misleading you." She leaned forward, looking into his face. "I told you the truth today, every damning detail. I risked our relationship, and my brother and father, rather than lie to you anymore. All I can do now is appeal to your sense of honor."

"'Honor,'" Terry repeated sarcastically. "Knowing all your family did, I should help you in the name of honor."

"Yes," Meg said with quiet intensity. "All Brian did was mislead you. That happens to defense lawyers all the time. Now it's happened to you—probably not for the first time, certainly not for the last, and never for a better reason. Would it make you feel better if he spends his life in prison?"

Terry felt twisted up by misgivings and distrust. Bitterly, he said, "You really are good, Meg. Nothing can stop you from playing me to the end. Speaking personally, my only consolation is that I could never trust you completely. At least now I know that it wasn't just about some deep incapacity in me—that I'd felt so alone for so long that I couldn't give myself to anyone without holding part of me back." He paused, then finished in a flatter tone: "If you want to know what happens to the rest of you, come to court on Monday. Now please get out of my sight."

For a moment her eyes shut. Then she stood, belatedly remembering her purse, and left without speaking or looking at him.

4

TERRY WAS ALONE.

Perhaps he had been alone since the day his father killed himself. As the time crept by, this memory of abandonment struck him with new force. He did not need his dream to feel it again.

Since that day, he had known that he must make it on his own. Now he had reached the brink of the success he craved. All that blocked his way was Brian McCarran.

Sequestered in his apartment, Terry called no one—for this, there was no one to call. Instead, he holed up in his living room, lying motionless on his couch for hours at a time. Until Monday, at least, he was still trapped in the force field of the McCarrans—Tony and Mary; Jack and Rose; Kate and Joe; Brian and Meg. He cursed himself for his blindness.

What had he wanted from her, and she from him?

But another question was far more fateful and immediate. Intermittently, he read discussions of legal ethics on the Internet, scouring the treacherous and murky margins of the law. Like it or not, for now he remained Brian McCarran's lawyer.

Early Saturday evening, the buzzer to his apartment rasped.

Startled, Terry imagined which McCarran it might be: Meg or Brian? Meg, he decided, come to plead her case again. Waiting must be agony for her.

Pressing the button to the intercom, Terry thought of Brian admitting Joe D'Abruzzo. "Who is it?" he demanded.

"Anthony McCarran."

Fresh anger coursed through Terry. He considered not responding, but could not see what he would gain from this. Pressing the button, he opened the door to his apartment.

Unlike D'Abruzzo, McCarran took the elevator. Down the hall, Terry heard it empty its passenger with a sclerotic rumble. A few footfalls later General Anthony McCarran stood in Terry's doorway.

"What do you want?" Terry asked coldly.

McCarran looked somber but composed. "To talk with you. May I come in, Captain?"

This reminder of rank stoked Terry's rage. He paused before curtly nodding McCarran inside.

The general sat on the couch, his angular frame leaning toward Terry in a posture that suggested both entreaty and command. In a quiet voice he asked Terry, "What do you mean to do?"

There was no point in preliminaries, Terry decided. "That's my concern, and none of your business. Of all the people whose fate I control, you're the one I care about least."

A trace of resentment showed in McCarran's eyes. Even now, he was not used to disdain from a junior officer. "I'm not here for myself," he said stiffly, "but as a father."

"I'm touched. But you're way too late." Terry waited for a moment, watching McCarran's eyes. "You asked me a question, General. Given your sense of honor, what would you do?"

McCarran's face hardened. "I'm not here to explain myself, if that's what you want."

"You don't need to," Terry said. "According to Meg,

Kate was your second chance at Rose Gallagher. Or, as I see it, your reprisal against Rose for not marrying you. After all, Rose has done so little for you."

The contempt in Terry's voice surfaced the steel in McCarran's gray-blue eyes. "What interests me more," Terry continued, "is how you rationalized sacrificing your own son to save your reputation and career. Let alone that you expect me to do the same."

"I don't," McCarran responded. "Nor did I ask that of Brian. By the time Meg told me that he and Kate had lied, Flynn believed that it was true. She said that I had put everyone at risk with Kate, and that coming forward now would make matters even worse. That she was taking over—"

"Making Meg the architect, and you her pawn. What narcissistic crap. You *knew* what would happen, General— a trial rife with perjury, a travesty of everything you claim to value. But not as much as you value yourself. The rest of us are bit players, as dispensable as soldiers on a battle-field." Terry paused. "Among other things, you owe me an apology. But I don't respect you enough to want that. I'll get my satisfaction some other way."

McCarran's aquiline face showed nothing. "Then we're alike. You think I sacrificed my children to protect my own ambitions. And now you propose to ruin them to save yours, in the process visiting misery on Rose and Kate and her two children—"

"You selfish bastard," Terry said savagely. "You betrayed every one of them. Now *I* owe them the debts you refused to pay?" He caught himself, lowering his voice. "For years I envied people with a 'real family.' Thank God I'm not part of yours.

"Look at all of you. You're like a cult of the sacred dead. You've become the hero figure, demanding sacrifice from those who follow as you sate your own ambitions by invoking the McCarran tradition. But you're no different than the alcoholic father in a family that covers for him." Leaning forward, Terry stared into McCarran's face. "Denial is the glue that binds you. None of you trusts anyone else with the truth, not even each other. Yet all of you maintain this insane belief that being a 'McCarran' has meaning, when each of you is miserably, achingly, lonely. You're the only one who ever profited, and now it's even caught up with you. If you become chairman of the Joint Chiefs of Staff, you'll still be a hollow man. Worse, you know it. But getting there at the expense of the others is all you've got left."

McCarran regarded Terry in silence. Then he said, "Are you through with me, Captain?"

"Not quite. Everyone professes to worry about how hurt Rose would be to find out you were sleeping with Kate. But only you know how terrible that revelation could really be. So satisfy my curiosity, General. Whose daughter is Kate D'Abruzzo—your best friend's, or yours?"

McCarran stared at him in shock, and then his lips curled in distaste. "My God," he said in a husky voice. "What you must think of me. But Rose deserves more respect and, in this matter, so do I. That Kate is Rose's daughter is painful enough." He paused, then concluded firmly. "I've heard enough from you. I came here to talk about Meg."

Terry shook his head. "There's nothing to say. Meg lied to me. As I think about your family, I can't even take it personally. She'd have lied to anyone."

"Maybe so." McCarran paused, as though drawing on hidden reserves of feeling and resolve. "Nonetheless, my daughter's in love with you. Meg's not the type to beg. But she's devastated at what she's done, and that whatever price she'll pay seems certain to include losing you. Personally, I'd prefer she find someone with less capacity for outrage and self-pity. But the heart wants what it wants, as I found out far too late.

"I can't make you forgive her. But, for the sake of her future, I can ask you to think before you act." Reaching into the breast pocket of his coat, McCarran held out an envelope. "You've got a decision to make, Captain Terry. For Meg's sake, and Brian's, read this before you do."

Terry hesitated, then took the sealed envelope. "That's a copy," McCarran told him. "I kept the original for my own use."

At once McCarran stood, a man with nothing more to say. He looked down at Terry, then left, as quickly as Meg had the last time Terry saw her.

5

IN THE MOMENTS before closing arguments were scheduled to begin, the courtroom had the surface quiet familiar to Terry, tension building as the members of the court waited to hear the last words on which they would determine the fate of the accused.

As before, Terry sat between Brian and Meg. Now no one spoke. Having scanned the courtroom, Terry held in his mind the faces of those who had come here. Sitting with Rose Gallagher, Anthony McCarran held himself tautly, as though prepared for whatever Terry might do. But for the moment, his stoic facade was meant to preserve the fragile balance of his family and, with that, the reputation he prized. On the opposite side of the courtroom, Captain Joe D'Abruzzo's parents huddled together—his father bent by life's blows; his mother vigilant, her suspicious eyes demanding justice from an indifferent world. Only Kate D'Abruzzo was missing.

In the jury box, Bobby Wade whispered to Doug Young and Adam Chase. Colonel Alex MacDonald—as he had since facing the end of his career—seemed occupied with his own private world. But Major Randi Wertheimer watched Brian closely, as if hoping to discover something more. She would find little, Terry thought; like Meg, Brian looked tired and abstracted, and only Terry knew the reasons.

By contrast, Flynn appeared rested, green eyes keen in his angular face. As he listened to some whispered words from Captain Pulaski, he summoned the perfunctory smile of an advocate anxiously awaiting his first moments of action.

Terry had barely slept. Two cups of black coffee had shot through his body, jangling his nerves and making his empty stomach feel scraped raw. His thoughts were jumbled. The contents of McCarran's envelope kept flashing before him. He had not yet petitioned to withdraw; in his mind were the fragments of a closing argument he did not know if he could give. At whatever cost, he was waiting to hear Flynn.

He should have decided, Terry knew. To go further would compromise his sense of self and, quite possibly, place his future in Flynn's hands. To withdraw would provoke a mistrial, signaling a problem so profound that it would point the finger of guilt at Brian McCarran. And to reveal the truth as he now knew it would ruin some lives and damage others, both culpable and blameless, destroying what remained of the McCarrans.

With whom, Terry wondered, did his obligations lie? For once he envied Flynn his moral certainty.

"All rise," the bailiff called, breaking Terry's thoughts.

Colonel Hollis took the bench, surveying the courtroom. Tensing, Meg glanced at Terry; he could almost feel her breathe. Brian's profile remained strikingly handsome but impenetrable, like a sculpture of a soldier's visage. He could have been in Virginia or Iraq.

"The court will hear final arguments," Hollis announced.

FLYNN WALKED SWIFTLY TOWARD the members, stopping a few feet from the jury box. "On June 17," he began, "Lieutenant Brian McCarran killed Captain Joseph D'Abruzzo by shooting him four times—including a bullet in the back. The question you face is why. The answer lies in a despicable breach of the army's code of honor: the accused's affair with his victim's wife."

Briefly, Terry glanced at Anthony McCarran. The general, catching his eye, did not look away. "If revealed," Flynn went on, "this affair would destroy Brian McCarran's reputation and career. Captain D'Abruzzo discovered it. So Brian McCarran murdered him and, with the help of his lover, tried to bury the truth.

"Brian McCarran," Flynn repeated in a scornful voice, "claims that he acted in self-defense. If so, it is the most premeditated self-defense a guilty man could devise.

"Brian McCarran claims that Kate D'Abruzzo called to warn him that her husband was coming to his apartment. If so, why is there no record of this call?

"Brian McCarran claims to have feared his victim's lethal skills. If so, why did he let this dangerous man into his small apartment?

"Brian McCarran claims to have taken the murder weapon only to protect Kate D'Abruzzo. If so, why did he not empty this weapon of bullets?

"Brian McCarran claims that he did not plan to shoot his lover's husband. If so, why did he—by his own account—conceal the weapon to be within his reach once D'Abruzzo shut the door behind him?" Flynn's gaze swept the members, who listened with uniform raptness. "Brian McCarran claims to have killed Joe D'Abruzzo to protect himself from imminent danger. If so, why is there no trace of gunpowder on D'Abruzzo's clothes? And what danger did D'Abruzzo pose with his back to the accused?

"Here, not even Brian McCarran has an answer, however implausible. Rather, implausibly, he claims not to remember his own act of self-defense."

Pausing, Flynn trained his commanding stare at each member of the court. "Brian McCarran," he said in a mocking tone, "claims that he was so shocked to discover Joe D'Abruzzo mortally wounded on his living room floor that he let him bleed to death. If so, why did he have the presence of mind to seek his sister's advice? Why was he able—quite calmly—to call the MPs once his victim was past saving? And how did he muster the presence of mind to lie about his affair?"

Major Bobby Wade seemed riveted by Flynn's words and cadence. The prosecutor slowed his speech, as if pronouncing an indubitable fact. "Innocent people tell the truth because they're innocent. The guilty lie to conceal their guilt. Brian McCarran lied. Because the truth of Joe D'Abruzzo's death is that Brian McCarran executed him.

"But Brian McCarran has a skillful lawyer. To obscure his client's guilt, Captain Terry has picked at the physical evidence—a question here, a quibble there. But he can't erase the cumulative weight of that evidence any more than he can erase a lie." Flynn's voice rose in condemnation. "Nor can he cite a single piece of physical evidence inconsistent with an intentional murder.

"So what is he left with? A desperate effort to distort Captain D'Abruzzo's honorable service in Iraq, and to mock the service of every veteran of that war. How? By claiming that Captain D'Abruzzo's presence in Brian McCarran's living room—to which the accused had admitted him—caused Lieutenant McCarran to relive an ambush in Sadr City. Yet the circumstances of that incident, however terrible, have no resemblance to the circumstances of Joe D'Abruzzo's death. Not even Brian McCarran claims to have confused his former commanding officer—a man he had known for a decade—with an Iraqi insurgent. And as his current commander told you, the lieutenant returned to discharge his duties without any sign of trauma or incapacity."

"So who is it, exactly, who recounts the behavior Captain Terry cites to support the claim of post-traumatic stress disorder?" Flynn turned to Meg, drawing from her a steady gaze that required an effort only Terry could detect. "His sister, and his father. No doubt this is what they wish to believe, and desperately want you to believe. But you must ask yourself why the only evidence of PTSD resides with the McCarrans. Then ask yourself why the only 'evidence' that Joe D'Abruzzo struck his wife—let alone threatened her with a gun—comes from Kate D'Abruzzo, the other person who lied about their affair."

Listening, Major Wertheimer half-closed her eyes, as though attempting to visualize the truth. "Joe D'Abruzzo," Flynn said with quiet anger, "was an honorable man, betrayed by his wife and a fellow officer. That is why he died. The least you can do for him now—and for his parents and children—is to give this brave man justice." Flynn became still as a statue, his gaze beseeching the members to listen and believe. "You know what happened here—a planned killing, tricked out by the defense as the killer's tragedy. I ask you to find Brian McCarran guilty of the crimes he committed: adultery followed by premeditated murder."

Even Hollis, Terry saw, could not help but look impressed.

GLANCING AT BRIAN, TERRY considered his choice for the last time. He could request to withdraw, perhaps dooming his own client; or seek to reopen the case, bringing down this edifice of deceit at whatever cost; or argue Brian's innocence on the record as it stood, attempting to avoid an ethical breach by skirting the falsehood at its core. He felt the complex skein of his emotions—doubt, fatigue, bitterness at having been so badly deceived; a deep anger at those who had created what, for him, had become an existential dilemma. His respect for Flynn's efforts warred with the belief that—despite what Terry knew—the prosecutor's characterization of Brian McCarran was unjust. His face averted, Brian asked him for nothing. But Terry was not Flynn—his world was still a complex place, filled with tangled motives, too often barely understood by people who, at crucial moments, were neither bad nor good. Terry's only certainty was that neither he nor Flynn could ever be certain of the truth.

"Captain Terry?" Hollis prompted.

It was this last reflection that, seconds later, prompted Terry to stand. Walking slowly toward the jury box, he singled out Major Wertheimer—the member whose sensibility, Terry believed, most resembled his own. "Major Flynn," he began, "is so very certain of so many things. But there is only one thing of which *you* can be certain: that you do not know, and will never know, what happened in that living room. Nothing else matters. That uncertainty—that unavoidable and irreducible doubt—requires you to find Lieutenant Brian McCarran not guilty in the shooting of Captain D'Abruzzo."

Judging from Randi Wertheimer's attentive gaze, these words were an apt beginning. "Brian McCarran," Terry continued, "told you that he acted in self-defense. As Major Flynn admitted—and as the court will instruct you—the prosecution must prove beyond a reasonable doubt that Brian did not. So I ask you to imagine yourself in his place.

"Consider, first, what Brian knew beyond a reasonable doubt. That Joe D'Abruzzo was drunk. That D'Abruzzo had loathed him ever since their service in Iraq. That D'Abruzzo could kill him in seconds. And that he faced D'Abruzzo in a room from which he could not escape." Pausing, Terry reminded himself to modulate his tone, a deliberate contrast to Mike Flynn. "Consider, second, the evidence Major Flynn cannot disprove. Kate D'Abruzzo testified that her husband hit her. She told you that Captain D'Abruzzo threatened her with a gun. She stated that Brian took that gun in order to protect her. And she explained that she had called Brian to warn him that Joe was coming for him. Before you dismiss all that—as the prosecution needs you to do—please remember the undeniable essence of their relationship: Brian McCarran has loved Kate D'Abruzzo ever since, as a child, he learned what love felt like."

Feeling stillness all around him, Terry stayed focused on Major Wertheimer. "Consider, third, what the physical evidence cannot tell us. Major Flynn asks you to imagine a coolheaded Brian McCarran executing Captain D'Abruzzo according to plan. But do coolheaded killers, having concocted in advance a bogus claim of self-defense, proceed to shoot their victim in the back? They do not. Far from supporting trial counsel's certainties, the bullet in Captain D'Abruzzo's back undermines them."

Colonel MacDonald, Terry saw, shot a questioning glance at Major Wertheimer. Quietly, Terry told them, "So, again, imagine you're Brian McCarran. A drunken, angry, and deadly opponent has threatened to kill you, and then ordered you to hand him your only weapon of self-defense. You do what any of us would do—you keep it. When D'Abruzzo pivots to attack, you have no time to think. You react. You fire in split seconds: the popping sounds heard by Major Dahl through the wall of Brian's apartment. And then it's over."

Listening, Major Wertheimer closed her eyes again. In the same reasoned manner Terry went on: "That's consistent with the testimony of Dr. Carson regarding studies of police shootings. And nothing in the physical evidence refutes it. The medical examiner can't tell you whether four feet separated Brian McCarran from Captain D'Abruzzo—or six feet, or nine. Major Flynn's ballistics expert can't be sure of where they were standing, or of Captain D'Abruzzo's position when he was shot in the arm and chest and palm. And so the certainty insisted on by the prosecution evaporates.

"Unable to prove his case by the physical evidence, Major Flynn urges you to seize upon another false certainty: that Brian McCarran's state of mind was that of a premeditated murderer. How does he know that? And how does he know that Brian's reactions were unaffected by a year of combat more intense than any one of us has ever experienced? Ridicule is not evidence; testimony is.

"We have proven beyond any doubt what Brian McCarran endured in Sadr City. Ceaseless and brutal combat as deadly as it was hopeless. A fatally flawed mission. An order to lead troops into an ambush he had warned Captain D'Abruzzo would occur. An order Brian knew in his heart would be fatal—if not to himself, to his men. An order Captain D'Abruzzo gave after threatening to relieve Brian of his command should he go to Colonel Northrop." Terry lowered his voice still further. "Death followed. The beheading of Brian's driver. The death of an Iraqi boy when Brian was forced to choose between his men and a line of children. The death of three other men before Brian's platoon could reach an empty police station. And after holding the hand of the fifth man as he died, Brian visited the dead to offer his apologies.

"That day began nine more months of orders where Captain D'Abruzzo singled out Brian's platoon to face one lethal danger after another—fighting door-to-door in spaces no bigger than Brian's living room. D'Abruzzo hated him for knowing the truth about the ambush. And Brian knew that as clearly as did Sergeant Whalen and Father Byrne and, yes, the wife to whom D'Abruzzo expressed that hatred. No wonder Brian McCarran resisted D'Abruzzo's final order: 'Give me the gun.' "

Hands in his pockets, Terry watched the members ponder his last words, then continued with a calm that suggested he had no need for tricks of elocution. "Major Flynn belittles the testimony of Brian's sister and his father, General Anthony McCarran, that Brian suffered from combat experiences other men would find indelible. Who else knows Brian's truth? Does the major suggest they made this up? The fact that Brian discharged his duties at Fort Bolton says much about him. But it does not discredit what his loved ones saw. Brian is a soldier, from a family of soldiers. Day after day, he tried not to let the army down. Then he went home for another night of tortured sleep filled with nightmares he chose to face alone. Perhaps Major Flynn does not recognize these symptoms, but Dr. Carson does. For he has seen them, and will continue to see them, in soldier after soldier.

"Who among us, if exposed to the horrors Brian endured, truly believes they would be unchanged? Which of us, in Brian's place, can say with certainty that they would not have perceived Joe D'Abruzzo—drunk, prone to violence, filled with hatred, and possessed of lethal skills— as a threat to his survival? And who can say that this was not so?"

As Flynn had, Terry looked at each member in turn. "In the end, you are left with Brian's account. When the CID questioned him, he could have—as his sister advised— remained silent. At this trial he could have chosen not to testify. Instead he told you, to the best of his abilities, what happened in that room. There is nothing that impels you to find—beyond a reasonable doubt—that Brian did not act in self-defense. And there is certainly nothing that requires you to conclude—given Brian's experiences in Iraq and with Captain D'Abruzzo—that he did not believe himself in peril.

"One man is dead; the survivor will never be as he once was. And only one thing is clear: what happened in that apartment was a tragedy. You cannot redeem it. Your only power is to compound it by guessing, or to conclude that there's been tragedy enough. I ask you to find Brian McCarran not guilty in the shooting of Captain Joe D'Abruzzo."

Terry stood quiet for a moment, hoping by his steady gaze to seal a compact with the jurors: that they would be fair, that they would allow themselves to live with doubt rather than seek refuge in a certainty beyond their power to reach. This was, after all, the compact Terry had just made with himself.

As Terry sat, Brian turned to him with an expression of quiet gratitude. From the bench, Hollis asked, "Have you a rebuttal, Major Flynn?" Across the courtroom, Flynn listened to Pulaski, then got quickly to his feet.

"Amid all of counsel's eloquence," he asked bluntly, "what's missing? A defense to charges of adultery. Any comment on Lieutenant McCarran's lie. The slightest mention of his affair. Captain Terry treats all that like a dead mouse on the kitchen floor—if he pretends not to notice it, maybe you won't either.

"Brian McCarran lied. Kate D'Abruzzo lied. Their desire for each other—the ruinous secret of their affair—is why the accused killed Joe D'Abruzzo." Flynn paused, then added derisively, "What defense does he offer to the charge of murder? No physical evidence, or any corroboration of his story. All too conveniently, the entirety of his evidence is locked inside his head. Why should you believe his story of self-defense? Because he says so. Why were his actions driven by combat in Iraq? Because he told you. He even asserts that—exclusive of all the soldiers in Captain D'Abruzzo's company—any order resulting in Brian McCarran's exposure to combat was calculated to kill him.

"The defense, in short, offers you nothing but the world according to Brian McCarran. And the only reason he can do that is because he killed the only witness." Standing erect, Flynn concluded sternly, "Do not reward this charade. I implore you to discharge your duty as members of this court: to find Brian McCarran guilty of murder and of the adulterous affair his counsel dares not mention."

Meg, Terry noticed, could not look at him. He wondered how her father was feeling now.

BEFORE INSTRUCTING THE MEMBERS, Judge Hollis called a fifteen-minute recess.

Terry spoke to no one. Motionless, he half-listened to the babble of comments and speculation from the gallery behind him. Then he felt a light touch on his shoulder. "Captain Terry?"

Turning, Terry saw that Rose Gallagher had broken away from Anthony McCarran. Quietly, she said, "There's something wrong, isn't there?"

Looking into her handsome face, Terry was struck again by her perception and, in the end, her kindness. "Why do you think so?"

Briefly, she glanced around them, ensuring that no one could overhear her, and saw that Meg and Brian stood a safe distance apart. "I know there's terrible pressure. But today you barely looked at Meg—neither of them, really."

Terry shook his head. "Belated melancholy," he said.

"I'm left believing that none of this needed to happen. But all I can do is help my client."

Rose looked at him closely. "Who helps you, Captain Terry?"

In lieu of the truth, Terry thought, all he could offer was kindness in return—or, perhaps, the illusion of kindness. Smiling a little, he answered, "I don't need help, Mrs. Gallagher. I'm the one who gets to leave it all behind. But the rest of them will need you, perhaps more than ever."

Rose's own smile did not erase the seriousness in her eyes. "Nonetheless," she said, "I wish you luck." Turning, she walked back to Anthony McCarran, her bearing as composed as before.

CONFIDENT IN HOLLIS'S FAIRNESS, Terry experienced the judge's instructions as a blur: the degrees of murder and manslaughter; self-defense; the standards for insanity. Only at the end did he look up at the bench. "In the specification of charge two," Hollis intoned, "the accused is charged with the offense of adultery.

"To find the accused guilty of this offense, you must be convinced beyond a reasonable doubt of the following elements:

"One, that the accused wrongfully had sexual intercourse with Kate D'Abruzzo;

"Two, that at the time, Kate D'Abruzzo was married to another; and

"Three, that the conduct of the accused prejudiced the good order and discipline of the army or was of a nature as to bring discredit upon it—"

The same cold fury consumed Terry, mingled with guilt at his own complicity. He restrained himself from looking toward Anthony McCarran. Slowly and clearly, Hollis continued: "You may not infer that the accused is guilty of one offense because his guilt may have been proven on another. However, the evidence that Lieutenant Brian McCarran may have had sexual intercourse with Kate D'Abruzzo can be considered for the limited purpose of its tendency, if any, to prove a motive to kill Captain Joe D'Abruzzo—"

Sitting beside Terry, Brian's head was bent in the attitude of prayer. Concluding, Hollis admonished the members as Terry had asked: "Nonetheless, you should not infer from this evidence that the accused is a bad person or has criminal tendencies and, therefore, that he committed the offense of premeditated murder."

Or even, Terry thought, that Brian McCarran had made love to Kate D'Abruzzo.

When it was done, Hollis directed the members to commence deliberations. Terry watched them leave, Randi Wertheimer talking quietly to Alex MacDonald. Leaning closer, Meg spoke to him for the first time. "Thank you, Paul."

Terry looked at her coldly. "I did it for Brian. Not for you, and certainly not for your father." He stood. "I'll be at my apartment. Don't bother to call me until the jury comes back."

He left alone, ignoring Flynn, the crowd, General Anthony McCarran, the reporters who called out questions.

6

FOR THE FIRST TIME in six months, Paul Terry had nothing to do but wait.

As the hours of deliberation crept by, he relived those months in hindsight: the call from Colonel Dawes; his first meetings with Meg, Brian, and Anthony McCarran; his "discovery" of the affair that never was; his weekend with Meg in Virginia Beach; his fateful decision to remain in the army until the end of Brian's trial. All this time he had been standing on quicksand—lies masquerading as truth; truth concealed as a lie. He still could not grasp what was true between Meg and himself.

That evening, after the members had ended their first day of deliberation, Terry turned on the news.

The third story on CNN, a summary of the final arguments in the court-martial of Brian McCarran, was followed by film of General McCarran leaving the courthouse with Rose Gallagher. "In a related development," the reporter's voice-over said, "the Pentagon announced today that General Anthony McCarran has submitted his resignation from the army effective on February 1, citing personal and family considerations. It had been widely believed that the father of Lieutenant Brian McCarran was slated to become chairman of the Joint Chiefs of Staff—"

So it was done. Whether for his children, or to preserve his own reputation, the general had kept his word to Terry. Now his career was over. Terry went to the kitchen and burned his copy of McCarran's letter to the secretary of defense.

But Terry's reckoning with the McCarrans was far from done. If Brian was acquitted of murder, Terry might be able to leave the case behind. But if the members convicted Brian in the death of Joe D'Abruzzo, Terry had no moral choice but to reveal that the motive urged by Flynn did not exist. Neither Flynn, nor the guardians of legal ethics, would be likely to forgive Terry for gambling on the verdict before he revealed the truth.

He had worked so hard for so many years. Now the McCarrans, with his complicity, might write the end to his ambitions.

ON THE AFTERNOON OF the second day, Meg called him. Her voice thick with emotion, she told him, "They're back, Paul."

Distractedly, Terry put on his uniform. The five-minute drive to the courthouse felt interminable.

A crowd of reporters and cameramen had gathered in front. Sweeping past them, Terry entered the courtroom. Abruptly, he was sealed in hermetic silence, the mute anticipation of a judgment in suspension. They were all waiting: Anthony McCarran and Rose Gallagher, Joseph and Flora D'Abruzzo, Brian and Meg, Flynn and Pulaski. All had the same stiffness of affect and tightness around the eyes. Sitting between Meg and Brian, Terry noted that, among the members, only Colonel MacDonald and Major Wertheimer had the serenity of expression that Terry read as satisfaction with the outcome. But he had been wrong before.

"All rise," the bailiff called, and Colonel Hollis ascended the bench.

Those present stood and then sat, remaining focused

on the judge. With the attendant gravity, Hollis said, "The court is called to order. All parties are present, as are the members of the court. Has the court reached findings?"

Colonel MacDonald stood, as president of the court. "We have, Your Honor."

"Are the findings reflected in the worksheet?"

"They are."

Hollis nodded slowly. "Please tender the worksheet to the bailiff so that I can examine it."

In dead quiet the courtroom watched the bailiff take the written findings and hand them to Judge Hollis. Meg bowed her head, as if watching were unbearable. Though he was composed, Brian's face was white. Terry tried to imagine how it felt to have chosen, through a lie, to endure this moment and what might wait beyond it. For once it was not hard—Terry, too, had run the risk of silence, and now would learn the consequences.

Reading the findings, Hollis remained impassive. Then he looked up at the members of the court. "I have reviewed the findings worksheet and it appears to be in the proper form. Bailiff, please return the findings to the president of the court."

Crossing the courtroom, the bailiff placed the verdict in Colonel MacDonald's hand. Turning to the defense table, Hollis said, "Accused and defense counsel, please rise."

Standing, Terry felt numb. "Colonel MacDonald," Hollis directed, "please announce the findings of the court."

MacDonald assumed a martial posture. Facing Brian, he said in a clear voice, "Lieutenant Brian McCarran, this court-martial finds you, of all charges and specifications in the death of Captain Joseph D'Abruzzo, *not* guilty."

A gasp escaped from the gallery, punctuated by a soft

moan from Flora D'Abruzzo. Terry felt himself swallow, then saw Brian's body tremor in relief. From the expression of the members, all but MacDonald and Wertheimer had wanted to convict, perhaps on the charge of manslaughter. But three was not enough.

MacDonald waited for silence to descend. In a flatter tone, he announced, "Brian McCarran, this court finds you, of the charge and specification of adultery, guilty."

Brian's face closed again. "Thank you," Hollis told the members. "The sentencing phase of this court-martial will commence on Thursday at nine A.M."

It was not quite done.

TERRY WAITED FOR HOLLIS to adjourn the findings phase, clearing the courtroom of spectators. When Brian turned to him, Terry snapped, "Wait here." Then he crossed the courtroom to speak with Flynn.

Standing, Flynn extended his hand. Grimly but without visible rancor, he said, "Congratulations, Captain."

"And to you. As you said, it was a hard case."

Flynn shrugged. "Any suggestion on where we go now?"

"One: that we agree on the sentence for adultery. At the beginning of the case, I proposed Lieutenant McCarran's dismissal from the army. The offer stands."

Flynn's smile was no smile at all. "Six months later," he said ironically, "that would at least be *some* satisfaction— if not to the D'Abruzzos. I'm prepared to agree."

In that moment, Terry realized that for Brian, and for himself, the case was finally over. "Thank you, Major," he said, and returned to the defense table.

Brian and Meg watched his face. Ignoring her, Terry said, "We need to talk, Brian. In private."

As they walked to the meeting room, Anthony McCarran caught his eye. McCarran nodded in thanks;

curtly, Terry nodded back, sealing their arrangement. He hoped never to see this man again.

TERRY WATCHED BRIAN ACROSS the conference table. In a soft, astonished voice, Brian said, "Flynn agreed to that?"

Terry nodded. "You've earned a medal of your own devising, and lived not to tell about it. So ends the Mc-Carran legacy. You're free, Brian."

Head bent, Brian covered his face, overcome by emotions that, to him, must feel years deep. When he faced Terry, his eyes were damp with tears he did not bother to conceal. "Thank you, Paul," he said slowly. "But what the hell do I do now?"

"You already know," Terry answered. "Do for yourself what you tried to do for Sergeant Martinez. Deal with what happened, here and in Iraq. Then you can figure out the rest."

Brian exhaled. "What about you?" he inquired at last.

"Thanks to you," Terry answered sardonically, "I'm about to become a howling success. At least as long as I keep your secret. I guess I'll learn to live with that."

Brian studied him. "There's no reason to lie to you now," he said quietly. "So I hope you can believe me. As far as I know, I'm innocent of everything. This much you can be sure of: I never planned to kill him. Maybe that will help."

Terry shrugged. "Give me enough time, and perhaps it will."

"There's also my father," Brian went on. "As best I can read him, he resigned less to save his reputation than to salvage something for Meg and me. He wanted you to help get me acquitted. And he didn't want you resenting Meg every time you saw him in uniform, the ranking military officer in America." When Terry said nothing, Brian added,

"Don't think he got off light, Paul. He has to live with himself. And without that uniform, who is he?"

"I wouldn't know."

"Neither will he." Pausing, Brian added softly, "He's going to be a very lonely man. Next week, Kate moves her family off the base, and Rose is going with her. I don't envy them at Christmas, when Rose in her innocence plans the usual dinner. But for both of them, the alternative is even worse. All they've got left is that Rose doesn't know."

Terry stood, as did Brian. Quiet, they faced each other, two damaged sons who might now shape their own lives. Then Brian said, "There's also Meg."

Terry simply looked at him.

"She wants to talk to you, Paul. I said I'd ask."

Terry regarded him coolly. "Did you now. Remind me to send you a book on codependency."

To Terry's surprise, Brian flashed his incandescent smile. "You don't get it, Paul. I'm trying to get rid of her." Watching Terry's expression, Brian sighed. "Among all of us," he said fervently, "Meg deserves the least blame—nothing she did was for herself, and she's already paying for it. I'm not saying you should feel magnanimous. But, given the outcome, you can afford to be civil."

Nodding, Terry placed a hand on Brian's shoulder. "Be well, Brian."

BEHIND HIM, TERRY HEARD the door open. He did not turn.

"Please, Paul. Look at me."

Terry faced her. With a quiet firmness, Meg said, "There are things I need to say to you. Then I'll leave." Bracing herself, she looked into his eyes. "At first you were a distraction. I was frightened for Brian, and all twisted up with what I was concealing. I'd turned my whole idea of myself inside out. Sleeping with you was a ticket to oblivion—"

"Why not buy a marital aid?"

Meg blanched. "Please—that's not what I meant. You were smart and strong, the things I thought I admired most. But those are my father's virtues." Her voice softened. "Yours are different. You're sensitive, and you see people whole. Your values don't depend on passing judgment, or putting anyone in a neat little box. You always tried to be fair to me. So I began telling you things I'd been afraid to tell anyone, or even admit to myself. I felt like a better person because of you. I started imagining a different life, as you did. And the fact that I was also your adversary began to tear me up inside.

"I told myself we'd get to the other side of this, and then I'd never have to lie to you again. But you *are* smart. By the end, you'd put it all together. But not before I'd fallen in love with you." She shook her head, as if seeing her own folly. "Like my father, I know what I deserve from you. Still, you told me once that no one should be judged by the worst moment of their life. So I'm begging you not to make me your exception.

"No matter what you say, I know how badly I've hurt you, if only because I know how badly I've hurt myself. I don't know what I have to offer you now. But, in time, I hope we'll have the chance to learn. Please don't hate me so much that I can never see you again."

Looking into her stricken face, Terry felt too many emotions to sort through. "Right now, Meg, I don't know if I ever can. That's not said out of malice. Believe me, I'd like to see you whole—even selfishly, it would be far better than the hurt and betrayal I feel. But at this moment I'm not sure I can get past that, however much I might want to. All I can promise is that, weeks or months from now, I'll have more distance. By then, I hope, the habit of caring for you will at least have become caring to find out how you are."

Watching his face, Meg nodded. But she could not seem to turn away. Finally, she said, "Then it's good-bye, Paul. At least for a while."

She turned, squaring her shoulders as she left. Terry felt the pulse of sadness; he had never seen a woman look so alone. The door closed softly behind her.

Terry went home and booked a plane ticket to Cabo San Lucas. He would watch the fishing boats at leisure, reflecting on his past until he saw the future he could claim as his own.

AFTERWORD AND ACKNOWLEDGEMENTS

The debt we owe Americans in uniform has long struck me as a good subject for fiction, as is our system of military justice. But my exposure to the army was limited and long ago. So, as often, I needed help to get things right.

I don't claim for a moment to have provided a fully rounded portrait of military life. But what I set out to do was ambitious enough: to portray the complex life of one military family; to depict how the crucible of the Iraq War changed the lives of two officers; to describe the ways in which post-traumatic stress disorder has affected our soldiers in Iraq and Afghanistan; and to provide an impressionistic, but accurate, portrait of a general court-martial. So I'm very grateful to the far more knowledgeable men and women who helped me take on this challenge.

The essence of army life is opaque to many civilians. My thanks go to those who helped lift the fog a bit: Brigadier General Joe Bass; Lieutenant Colonel David Rabb and his wife, Kim; and Lieutenant Colonel (and Chaplain) Pat Ryan. To help me get a better sense of a military career and the qualities needed in a successful general officer, retired Army General Paul Kern and retired Air Force General Joe Ralston generously contributed their advice.

Our system of military justice differs in significant ways from that which operates in civilian life. The following gave me wonderful advice and assistance: Eugene Fidell; Air Force Lieutenant Colonel Adam Oler; Air Force Major Kate Oler; Lieutenant General Jack Rives, judge advocate general of the air force; and Marine Corps Lieutenant Colonel Sean Sullivan. Dr. Arthur Blank Jr., attorney Gordon Erspamer, and Dr. Chad Peterson helped me better understand post-traumatic stress disorder. Three psychiatrists helped me probe the complicated interactions between the McCarran, Gallagher, and D'Abruzzo families: Dr. Bill Glazer, Dr. Rodney Shapiro, and Dr. Charles Silberstein. And psychologist Philip Trompetter helped me render Brian McCarran's gaps in memory.

Particularly difficult were scenes of combat in Iraq: for civilians other than journalists, firsthand research is impossible. Bill Murphy Jr. was generous in describing his experiences, and I also relied on his wonderful book *In a Time of War*. I'm also deeply indebted to two other riveting accounts of military service in Iraq: *Packing Inferno*, by Tyler Boudreau, and *The Long Road Home*, by Martha Raddatz. Anyone wishing to better grasp what the soldiers and their families have faced would profit from reading these three books. With respect to PTSD, other helpful reading included *Invisible Wounds of War*, a report by the RAND Corporation; several articles by Joshua Kors in the *Nation;* two law review articles, "Post Traumatic Stress Disorder on Trial," by Major Timothy B. Hayes, and "Solving the Mystery of Insanity Law," by Jeremy A. Bell; and documents from the case *Veterans for Common Sense v. Mansfield*. I also drew extensively from the *Manual for Courts-Martial* and the Uniform Code of Military Justice.

Among civilians, I received great advice about the construction, prosecution, and defense of a homicide case from friends old and new: prosecutors Linda Allen and Al Giannini; defense lawyers Jim Collins and Hugh

Levine; pathologist Dr. Terri Haddix; ballistics expert Jaco Swanepoel; and homicide inspector Joe Toomey. As for martial arts, J. T. Collins was patient in helping me imagine Joe D'Abruzzo's lethal skills.

As always, I'm indebted to my literary board of directors: my wonderful agent, Fred Hill; my terrific editor, John Sterling; copy editor Bonnie Thompson; my perspicacious assistant, Alison Thomas; and, of course, my wife, Dr. Nancy Clair.

Finally, there are the people to whom this book is dedicated. Before I ever knew Bill Cohen, I admired him for his novels, his poetry, his nonfiction accounts of Washington life, and, in particular, his courageous service during Watergate and after, first as a congressman and then as a senator from Maine. Since I met Bill thirteen years ago, he has served as secretary of defense and founded his own worldwide consulting firm, the Cohen Group. And his friendship has become one of the great pleasures of my and Nancy's life.

This is all the more true because of Bill's wife, Janet Langhart Cohen, broadcaster, journalist, writer, and playwright. Janet's insight and empathy, along with Bill's, were again evidenced when both of them helped me develop the characters of Senator Corey Grace and actress Lexie Hart, the multiracial couple who were the protagonists of my recent novel of presidential politics, *The Race*.

Through Bill, I met my friend Bob Tyrer, now president of the Cohen Group. In addition to being terrific company, Bob has kindly installed me as perhaps the Cohen Group's most persistent pro bono client. Again and again, on subjects from military life to geopolitics, Bob and his colleagues have given me the same world-class advice and insights their more conventional clients enjoy. In addition to Generals Kern and Ralston, on this fictional trip Jen

Miller and General Maria Owens were unfailingly kind in steering me to great sources. For their friendship and unceasing help, this book is dedicated to Bill, Janet, Bob, and all my friends at the Cohen Group.

extracts reading groups
competitions books new
discounts extracts extracts
competitions extracts reading groups
books new events extracts discounts
events books reading groups
extracts new titles reading groups
interviews events
events extracts discounts
discounts new books events events
events new interviews new books extracts
discounts extracts discounts
www.panmacmillan.com
extracts events reading groups
competitions books extracts new books